# Tangled Strings

# Adam-Troy Castro

# Tangled Strings

**Five Star • Waterville, Maine**

First Edition
First Printing: August 2003

Published in 2003 in conjunction with
Tekno Books and Ed Gorman.

Set in 11 pt. Plantin by Al Chase.

Printed in the United States on permanent paper.

**Library of Congress Cataloging-in-Publication Data**
Castro, Adam-Troy.
    Tangled strings : fiction / by Adam-Troy Castro.—1st ed.
    p. cm.—(Five Star first edition speculative fiction series)
    Contents: The funeral march of the marionettes—The tangled strings of the marionettes—Unseen demons—The magic bullet theory—Sunday night yams at Minnie and Earl's—Afterword.
    ISBN 0-7862-5342-8 (hc : alk. paper)
    1. Fantasy fiction, American. I. Title. II. Series.
PS3603.A89T36 2003
  813´.6—dc21
                                  2003052919

# Dedication

I dedicated another book to you, only a couple of years ago.
I did not suspect, then, how close we would become,
so I suppose I can be forgiven for misspelling
your name for posterity.
Besides, your name's changed, so you deserve a fresh edition.
This one's for my friend, my supporter, and my wife.
I won't misspell your name this time, Judi Castor.

# Table of Contents

# The Funeral March
# of the Marionettes

## 1.

It was in the third year of my indentured servitude that I rescued Isadora from the death-dance of the Marionettes.

This happened on Vlhan, a temperate world of no strategic importance to either the Hom.Sap Confederacy or any of the great offworld republics. An unremarkable place with soft rolling hills, swampy lowlands, and seasons that came and went too gently for anybody to notice the change, it was indistinguishable from a million similar worlds throughout the known universe, and it would have been charted, abandoned, and forgotten were it not for the Vlhani themselves. They were so different from every other sentience in the universe that seven separate republics and confederacies maintained outposts there just to study them. Because the Vlhani had been declared sentient, we called our outposts embassies instead of research stations, and ourselves diplomats instead of scientists, but almost nothing we did involved matters of state; we were so removed from real power that the idea of a genuine diplomatic incident—let alone a war—seemed a universe away.

My name was then Alex Gordon. On Vlhan, I was a twenty-two-year-old exolinguist, born and raised in the wheelworld known as New Kansas; the kind of bookish young man who insists he dreams of visiting the real Kansas someday even after being told how long it's been uninhab-

9

able. Like the three dozen other indentures who made up the
rest of our delegation, I'd bartered five years of service in exchange for a lifetime of free travel throughout the Confederacy, but I'd been so captured by the mysteries of the Vlhani
people that I seriously considered devoting my entire life to
finding the choreographic Rosetta Stone that would finally
make sense of their dance. For it was the Ballet that, once
every sixteen standard lunars, made them the center of attention on a thousand worlds. It was simultaneously tragedy, art
form, suicide, orgasm, biological imperative and mob insanity. The first time I saw it I was shattered; the second time
I wept; the third . . .

But this story's about the third.

The one that belonged to Isadora.

# 2.

It was a warm, sunny day, with almost no breeze. We'd erected a
viewing stand overlooking the great natural amphitheatre, and
installed the usual holo and neurec remotes to record the festivities for future distribution throughout the hytex network. As
was customary, we gathered on the north rim, the assembled
Vlhani spectators on the south. I sat among the mingled humans
and alien diplomats, along with ambassador Hai Dhiju, and my
fellow indentures. Kathy Ng was there, making her usual sar-
donic comments about everything; as was our quartermaster
Rory Metcalf, who talked gossip and politics and literature and
everything but the spectacle unfolding before us; and Dhiju's sy-
cophantic assistant Oskar Levine, who waxed maudlin on his
own personal interpretation of the dance. We were all excited by
the magic we were about to witness, but also bored, in the way
that audiences tend to be in the last few minutes before any
show; and as we murmured among ourselves, catching up on
gossip and politics and the latest news from our respective

worlds, few of us dwelled on the knowledge that all of the one hundred thousand Vlhani in the bowl itself were here to die.

Hurrr'poth did. He was my counterpart from the Riirgaan delegation: a master exolinguist among a reptilian race that prided itself on its exolinguists. He usually liked to sit among the other delegations rather than sequester himself among his own people; and this year he'd chosen to sit beside me, which had a chilling effect on my conversations with anybody else. Like all Riirgaans, he had a blank, inexpressive face, impossible to read (a probable reason why they'd had to develop such uncanny verbal communication skills), and when he said, "We are all criminals," I was uncertain just how to take it.

"Why? Because we sit back and let it happen?"

"Of course not. The Vlhani perform this ritual because they feel they have to; it would be immensely arrogant of us to stop it. We are correct in allowing their orgy of self-destruction. No, we are criminal because we enjoy it; because we find beauty in it; because we openly look forward to the day when they gather here to die. We are not innocent bystanders. We are accomplices."

I indicated the neurecs focused on the amphitheatre, for the benefit of future vicarious spectators. "And pornographers."

Hurrr'poth trilled, in his race's musical equivalent of laughter. "Exactly."

"If you disapprove of it so much, then why do you watch?"

He trilled again. "Because I am as great a criminal as any one of you. Because the Vlhani are masterpieces of form following function, and because I find them magnificent, and because I believe the Ballet to be one of the most beautiful sights in a universe that is already not lacking for beauty. Indeed, I believe that much of the Ballet's seductive power

11

lies in how it indicts us, as spectators . . . and if I must be indicted for the Ballet to be a complete work, then I happily accept my guilt as one of the prices of admission. What about you? Why do you watch?"

I spoke cautiously, as lower-echelon diplomats must whenever posed sufficiently uncomfortable questions. "To understand."

"Ahhhh. And what do you want to understand? Yourself, or the Vlhani?"

"Both," I said—glibly, but accurately—and then hurriedly peered through my rangeviewers as a quick way of escaping the conversation. It wasn't that I disliked Hurrr'poth; it was that his way of cutting to the heart that had always made me uncomfortable. Riirgaans had a way of knowing the people they spoke to better than they knew themselves, which may have been one reason they were so far ahead of us, in decoding the danced language of the Vlhani. We could only ask childlike questions and understand simple answers. The Riirgaans had progressed to discussing intangibles. Even now, much of our research on the Vlhani had to be conducted with Riirgaan aid, and usually only succeeded in uncovering details they'd known for years.

This rankled those of us who liked to be first in everything; me, I just thought we'd accomplish more by cooperating. Maybe the Riirgaans just liked watching others figure things out for themselves. Who knows? If the thriving market in Vlhani Ballet recordings means anything at all, it's that sentient creatures are subject to strange, unpredictable passions . . . and that the Vlhani are plugged into all of them.

A wind whipped up the loose dirt around the periphery of the amphitheatre. The Vlhani spectators on the far rim stirred in anticipation. The one hundred thousand Vlhani in the amphitheatre mingled about, in that seemingly random manner that we knew to be carefully choreographed. Our instruments recorded the movements of each and every Vlhani, to determine the many subtle ways in which tonight's performance differed from last year's; I merely panned my rangeviewer from one end of the amphitheatre to the other, content to be awed by the numbers.

Vlhani have been compared to giant spiders, mostly by people with an earthbound vocabulary, and I suppose that's fair enough, if you want a description that completely robs the Vlhani of everything that renders them unique. Personally, I much prefer to think of them as Marionettes. Imagine a shiny black sphere roughly one meter across, so smooth it looks metallic, so flawless it looks manufactured, its only concession to the messy biological requirements of ingestion, elimination, copulation, and procreation a series of almost-invisible slits cut along one side. That's the Vlhani head. Now imagine anywhere between eight and twenty-four shiny black tentacles attached to various places around that head. Those are Vlhani whips, which can grow up to thirty meters long and which for both dexterity and versatility put humanity's poor opposable thumb to shame. A busy Vlhani can simultaneously: a) stick one whip in the dirt, and render it rigid as a flagpole, to anchor itself while occupied with other things; b) use another four whips to carve itself a shelter out of the local raw materials; c) use another three whips to spear the underbrush for the rodentlike creatures it likes to eat; d) flail the rest of its whips in the air above its head, in the sophisticated wave-form sign language that Vlhani can use to conduct as many as six separate conversations at once. Even a single Vlhani, going about its everyday business, is a beautiful thing; one hundred thousand Vlhani, gathered together to perform the carefully-choreographed Ballet that is both their holiest rite and most revered art form, are too much spectacle for any human mind to properly absorb at one time.

And too much tragedy too. For the one hundred thousand Vlhani gathered in that great amphitheatre would soon dance without rest, without restraint, without nourishment or sleep; they'd dance until their self-control failed, and their whips carved slices from each other's flesh; they'd dance until their hearts burst and the amphitheatre was left filled with bodies. The ritual took place once each revolution of their world around their sun, and no offworlder claimed to understand it, not even the Riirgaans. But we knew it was some kind of art form, and that it possessed a tragic beauty that transcended the bounds of species.

Hurrr'poth said, "They are starting late, this year. I wonder if—"

I took a single, sharp, horrified intake of breath. "Oh, God. No."

"What?"

I zoomed in, saw it again, and shouted: "AMBASSADOR!"

Hai Dhiju, who was seated two rows away, whirled in astonishment; we may have been an informal group on Vlhan, but my shout was still an incredible breach of protocol. He might have taken it a little better if he weren't intoxicated from the mild hallucinogens he took every day—they left him able to function, but always a little slow. As it was, his eyes narrowed for the second it took him to remember my name. "Alex. What's wrong?"

"There's a woman down there! With the Vlhani!"

It wasn't a good idea to yell it in a crowd. Cries of "What?" and "Where?" erupted all around us. The alien reactions ranged from stunned silence, on the part of my friend Hurrr'poth, to high-pitched, ear-piercing hoots, on the part of the high-strung Ialos and K'cenhowten. A few of the aliens actually got up and rushed the transparent barriers, as if inspired by one insane, suicidal terran to join the unknown woman in that bowl where soon nothing would be left alive.

Dhiju demanded, "Where?"

I handed him my rangeviewer. "It's marked."

He followed the blinking arrows on the interior screen to the flagged location. All around us, spectators slaved their own rangeviewers to the same signal. When they spotted her, their gasps were in close concert with his.

I wasn't looking through a rangeviewer at that moment; I didn't see the same thing the others saw. My own glimpse had been of a lithe and beautiful young woman in a black leotard, with short-cropped black hair and unfamiliar striped markings on both cheeks. Her eyes had burned bright with some emotion that I would have mistaken for fear, were it not for the impossibly level grace with which she walked. She couldn't have been older than her early twenties. Just about everybody who saw her the same moment the ambassador did now claims to have noticed more: an odd resonance to the way she moved her arms . . .

Maybe. Neither the ambassador, or anybody else around us, commented on it at the time. Dhiju was just shocked enough to find the core of sobriety somewhere inside him. "Oh, God. Who the hell—Alex, you saw her first, you get to man the skimmer that plucks her the hell out of there. Hurry!"

"But what if—"

"If the Ballet starts, you're to abort immediately and let the universe exact the usual fine for idiocy. Until then—run!"

I could have hesitated, even refused. Instead, I whirled, and began to fight my way through the crowd, an act that was taken by most of those watching as either a testament to my natural courage under fire, or a demonstration of Dhiju's natural ability to command. The more I look back, and re-member my first glimpse of Isadora, the more I think that it might have been her that drew me.

Maybe part of me was in love with her even then.

# 3.

I was free of the crowd and halfway to the skimmer before I no-ticed Hurrr'poth running alongside me, his triple-segmented legs easily keeping up with my less-than-athletic gait. He boarded the vehicle even as I did. He anticipated the inevitable question: "You need me. Take off."

My official answer should have been that this was a human matter and that I was not authorized to take any liberties with his safety. But he was right. He had years' more experience with the Vlhani; he possessed more understanding of their language. If nothing else, he was my best chance for getting out alive myself.

So I just said, "All right," and took off, circling around the rear of the viewing platform and then coming in as low over the amphitheatre as I dared. Once I was over the Vlhani I slaved the skimmer to my rangeviewer and had it home in on the woman. Thousands of shiny spherical black heads rotated to follow our progress; though a few recoiled, many more merely snapped their whips our way, as if attempting to seize us in flight. The average whip-span of a grown Marionette being what it was, they came close.

He peered over the side as we flew. "We don't have much time, Alex; they're all initiating their Primary Ascension."

I was clipping on a Riirgaani-patented whip harness. "I don't know what that means, Hurrr'poth."

"It's what we call one of the earliest parts of the dance, where they gather their energies and synchronize their move-ments. You would probably call it a rehearsal, or a tune-up, but it's apparently as fraught with meaning as anything that follows; unfortunately, it doesn't last very long, and it tends to be marked by sudden, unpredictable activity." After a pause, he said: "Your flyby is causing some interesting . . . I would say clumsy and perhaps even . . . desperate variations."

"Wonderful." The last thing I needed was to be known all my life as the man who disrupted the Vlhani Ballet. "Do you see her yet?"

"I've never lost sight of her," Hurrr'poth said calmly.

A few seconds later I spotted her myself. She was . . . well, the best possible word for her walk is, undulating . . . down the slope on the far side of the amphitheatre, into the deepest concentrations of Vlhani. She was waving both of her long slender arms over her head, in a gesture that initially struck me as an attempt to catch my attention but almost immediately made itself clear as an attempt to duplicate the movements of the Vlhani. She moved like a woman fluent in the language, who not only knew precisely what she was saying but also had the physical equipment she needed to say it: all four limbs were so limber that they could have been Vlhani whips and not human arms and legs. One of the first things I saw her do was loop each of her arms all the way around her other one, not just once but half a dozen times, forming a double helix.

"Jesus," I said, as we descended toward her. "She's been Enhanced."

"At the very least," agreed Hurrr'poth.

Her arms untangled, became jagged cartoon-lightning, then rose over her head again, waggling almost comically as little parentheses-shapes moved from wrist to shoulder in waves. As we came to a hovering stop three meters ahead of her, she scowled, an expression that made the scarlet chevrons tattooed on each cheek move closer to her dark pene-

17

trating eyes. Then she lowered her gaze and retreated.

"Leave her be," said Hurrr'poth.

I stared at him. "She'll die."

"So will all these others. It's why they're here, and why she's here. If you save her, you'll be disturbing the Ballet for no good reason, and demonstrating to the Vlhani that you consider her life more valuable than any of theirs. No: leave her be. She's a pilgrim. It's her privilege to die if she wants."

Hurrr'poth was probably right; being right was his way. But he did not know human beings, or me, anywhere near as well as he knew Vlhani, and could not understand that what he advised was unacceptable. I set the skimmer to land, and hopped out almost a full second before it was strictly safe to jump, hitting the slope ground with an impact that sent jabs of pain through both knees.

The Vlhani loomed above me on all sides: great black spheres wobbling about on liquid flailing whips. One stepped daintily over both me and the skimmer, disappearing without any visible concern into the roiling mob further down the slope; another half-dozen seemed to freeze solid at the sight of me, as if unsure what improvisations I might require of them. None seemed angry or aggressive, which didn't make me feel any better. Vlhani didn't have to be aggressive to be extraordinarily dangerous. Their whips had a tensile strength approaching steel and moved at speeds that had been known to exceed sound. And though we'd all walked among Vlhani without being harmed—we were often picked up and examined by curious ones—those had been calm, peaceful Vlhani, Vlhani at rest, Vlhani who still possessed their race's equivalent of sanity. These were driven pilgrims here to dance themselves into a frenzy until they dropped; they could slash me, the woman, Hurrr'poth, and the skimmer into slices without even being fully aware they were doing it . . .

Fifteen meters away, the woman twisted and arched her back and flailed arms as soft and supple as ribbons. "Go 'way!" she shouted, in an unidentifiably-accented Human-Standard. "Don't dang yeselves! Le' me alone!"

I switched on my harness, activating the pair of artificial whips that immediately rose from my shoulders and snaked above my head, undulating a continuous clumsy approximation of the Vlhani dance for *Friend*. Our delegation had borrowed the technology and much of the basic vocabulary from the Riirgaans; with its built-in vocabulary of fifty basic memes, it was sufficient to allow us clumsy four-limb humanoids to communicate with the Vlhani at the level of level of baby talk. Which by itself wouldn't be enough to get me and the girl out of the amphitheatre alive . . .

. . . broadcasting *Friend* in all directions, I ran to her side, stopping only to evade a huge towering Marionette passing between us. When I got close enough to grab her, she didn't run, or fight me; she didn't even stop dancing. She just said, "Le'me go. Save yeself."

"No," I said. "I can't let you do this."

She twisted her arm in a way wholly inconsistent with human anatomy, and twisted out of my grip without any effort at all. "Ye cannae stop me," she said, flitting away in a pirouette graceful enough to hurt my eyes. I hadn't even succeeded in slowing her down. I turned around, shot a quick Why-the-Hell-Aren't-You-Helping-Me look at the impassive Hurrr'poth, then ran after her again.

I found her dancing beneath, and in perfect sync with, a Marionette five times her height; the eight whips it held aloft all undulating to the same unheard music as her own arms. It had anchored four of its whips in the ground, one on each side of her; turning itself into a enclosed set for her solo performance. The effect was sheltering, almost maternal, which didn't make me feel any safer scurrying past those whips to join her in at the center. Again, she made no attempt to evade me, merely faced straight ahead, looking past me, past the Vlhani, and past the eyes of all the sentients who'd be watching the recordings of this scene for more years than any of us would be alive . . . past everything but the movements her dance required her to make next.

The harness piped a thousand contradictory translations in my ear. *Danger. Life. Night. Cold. Hungry. Storm. Dance.* I had no idea whether it translated her or the Vlhani.

"All right," I said, lamely. "You want to play it like this, go ahead. But tell me why. Give me some idea what you think you're trying to accomplish!"

Her head rotated a perfect three hundred sixty degrees on her long and slender neck, matching a similar revolution performed by the featureless Marionette head directly above us. Her eyes remained focused on mine as long as her face remained in view; then sought me out again, the instant her features came around the other side. Her expression was serious, but unintimidated. "I tryin' to waltz Vlhani. What are ye trying to accomplish? Kill yeself bein' a Gilgamesh?"

"I'd rather not. I just want you to come with me before you get hurt."

"Ye're in a lot hotter stew than I be. Leastin' I ken the steps."

The Vlhani didn't stop dancing; they didn't slow down or speed up or in any visible way react to anything either this woman or I said. If anything, they took no visible notice of us at all. But I was there, in the middle of it, and though my understanding of Vlhani sign language was as minimal as any human's, I did . . . feel . . . something, like a great communal gasp, coming from all sides. And I found myself suddenly, instinctively, thoroughly certain that every Vlhani in the entire amphitheatre was following every nuance of every word that passed between this strange young woman and I. Even if they were not close enough to see or hear us, they were still being informed by those around them, who were in turn breathlessly passing on the news from those farther up the line. We were the center of their attention, the focus of their obsessions. And they wanted me to know it.

It wasn't telepathy, which would have shown up on our instruments. Whatever it was couldn't be measured, didn't translate to the neurecs, wasn't observed by any of the delegations. I personally think I was only making an impossible cognitive leap in the stress of the moment and for just one heartbeat understanding Vlhani dance the way it's meant to be understood. Whatever the reason, I knew at once that this impasse was the single most important thing taking place in the entire valley . . .

*Love,* my harness squeaked. *Safety. Dance. Food. Sad.*

She'd gone pale. "What are ye plannin' to do?"

What I did was either the bravest or most insane or most perceptive thing I've ever done.

Reversing our positions, placing my life in her hands, I simply turned my back on her and walked away . . . not toward Hurrr'poth, the skimmer, and safety, but farther down the slope, into the densest concentrations of Vlhani. It was impossible to see very far into that maze of flailing black whips, but I approached a particularly thick part of the mob, where I might be filleted and sectioned in the time it took to draw a breath, as quickly as I could without actually breaking into a run. It was far easier than it should have been. All I had to do was disengage my terror from the muscles that drove my legs . . .

She cried out: "Hey! HEY!"

Four Vlhani whips stabbed the earth half a meter in front of me. I flinched, but didn't stop walking. The Vlhani moved out of my way with another seven-league step. I stepped over the stab wounds in the earth, continued on my way . . .

. . . and found her circling around in front of me. "Just what the crot do ye ken ye're doin'?"

My first answer was obliterated by stammering: a sign of the terror I was trying so hard not to feel. I swallowed, concentrated on forming the words and speaking them understandably, and said: "Taking a walk. It seems like a nice day for it."

"Ye keep waltzin' this direction, ye won't last two minutes."

"Then you've got yourself a moral decision," I said, with a confidence that was a million kilometers away. "You can bring me back to my skimmer and hold my hand while I pilot us both back to safety. Or you can stay here and dance, and let me die with you. But the only way to avoid putting you on my conscience is to put myself on yours."

*Danger. Dance. Danger.*

Hot wind fanned my back, a razor-sharp whirr following in its wake: the kind of near-miss so close that you feel the pain anyway. I stiffened, held on to my last remaining shreds of self-control, and walked past her.

She muttered a curse in some language I didn't know and wrapped her arms around my chest. I mean that literally. Each arm went serpentine and encircled me twice before joining in a handclasp at my collarbone. They felt like human flesh; they were even warm and moist from exertion. But there was something other than muscle and bone at work beneath that too-flexible skin.

Her heart beat in sync with mine.

"I ought to let ye do it," she breathed. "I ought to let ye

22

waltz in there and get torn to gobs."

I managed to turn my head enough to see her. "That's your decision."

"And ye really think you ken what that's goin' to be, don't you? Ye think ye ken me well enough to guess how much I'm willin' to toss for some mungie catard tryin' to play martyr. You . . . think . . . you . . . ken."

Sometimes, in crisis situations, you find yourself saying things so banal they come back to haunt you. "I'm a good judge of people."

"Ye're a good judge of vacuum. Ye sit on that mungie viewing stand and ye coo at the spectacle and ye shed a brave tear for all the buggies tearin' each other to gobs for yer ball-tinglies. And ye wear those ridiculous things," indicating my artificial whips, "and ye write mungie treatises on how beautiful it all be and ye pretend ye're tryin' to understand it while all the while ye see nothing, you ken nothing, ye understand nothing. Ye don't even appreciate that they been goin' out of their way to avoid gobbing ye. They been concentratin' on ye instead of the show, usin' all the leeway their script gives them, steppin' a little faster here and a little slower there, just for ye, me mungie good judge of people. But if ye keep waltzin' this direction, they won't be able to watch out for ye without turning the whole show to crot, and they gob ye to spatters before yer next gasp!"

If she paused for breath at all during her speech, I didn't notice. There were no hesitations, no false starts, no fleeting "uh's" to indicate blind groping for the phrase she needed; just a swift, impassioned, angry torrent of words, exploding outward like wild animals desperate to be free. Her eyes brimmed with an anguished, pleading desperation, begging me to leave her with the death she had chosen: the look of a woman who knew that what she asked was bigger than any of us, and desperately needed me to believe that.

*Danger. Dance. Birth.*

I almost gave in.

Instead, I spoke softly: "I'm not interested in the moral decisions of the Vlhani. I'm interested in yours. Are you coming with me or not?"

Her grip loosened enough for me to wonder if my bluff had been called. Then she shuddered, and the beginnings of a sob caught in her throat. "Crod it. CROD it! How the hell did ye ken?"

At the time, I didn't know her nearly well enough to understand what she meant.

But already, it was impossible not to hate myself, a little, for defying her.

# 4.

The trip back to the skimmer wasn't nearly as nerve-wracking as the trip out, with her providing us a serpentine but safe path directly through the heart of the Ballet. She told me when to speed up, when to slow down, when to proceed straight ahead, and when to take the long way around a spot that inevitably, seconds later, became a sea of furiously dancing Vlhani. I followed her directions not because I considered her infallible, but because she seemed to believe she knew what she was doing, and I was completely lost.

Before we even got near the spot where I'd left the skimmer, I heard the hum of its drive burning the air directly above us: Hurrr'poth, piloting it to a landing beside us. Which was itself not the least of the day's surprises, since the skimmer was set for a human gene pattern, and Hurrr'poth had no business being able to control it at all. Even as he lowered it to boarding altitude, I called, "What the hell—"

He waved. "Hurry up and get in. I don't know how

much time we have to do this."

She trembled, not with fear, but with the utter heartbreak of a woman being forced to give up that which she wanted above all else. Getting her this far had shattered her; forcing her onto the skimmer would carve wounds that might not ever heal. But at least she'd have a chance to survive them . . . something I couldn't say for her chances dancing among the Vlhani. I said, "You first."

She took Hurrr'poth's outstretched hand, and climbed aboard. I followed her, taking a seat directly beside her in case she decided to try something. Hurrr'poth took off, set the controls for the return flight, then turned around in his seat, so he could gently trill at us. "I hope you don't consider me impolite, Alex."

His manners were the very last thing on my mind. "For what?"

"For taking such liberties with your vehicle. But there were a number of very large Vlhani determined to pass through the spot where we'd landed—and I thought it best for the purposes of our safe escape that I argue with your genetic reader instead. It saw reason a lot faster than I thought it would."

"Think nothing of it."

He turned toward the girl. "My name is Viliissin Hurrr'poth. I am a third-level wave-form linguist for the Riirgaan delegation, and whatever else happens now, I must state my professional opinion that you are an astonishingly talented dancer for one of your species; you did not appear to be at all out of place, among the Vlhani. It is a grand pleasure indeed to make your acquaintance. And you are—"

"Isadora," she said, sullenly. It was a good thing he'd asked; I'd been too preoccupied by matters of survival to get around to it myself.

"Is-a-do-ra," he repeated, slowly, testing each syllable,

committing it to memory. "Interesting. I do not believe I've encountered that one before. Is there an adjunct to that name? A family or clan designation?"

She looked away: the gesture of a woman who no longer had the energy or the inclination to answer questions. "No. Just Isadora."

I saw the silence coming and ached for the wit to come up with the words that would break it. I wanted to come up with a great, stirring speech about the sanctity of life and the inevitability of second chances: about the foolishness of suicide in a universe filled with millions of choices. I wanted to tell her that I was glad that she'd chosen to come with me and live, for I'd sensed something special about her—a strength of will and purity of purpose that would have rendered her special even without the Enhancements that had made flexible whips of her limbs. I wanted to tell her that there were better places to apply those attributes than here, on this planet, in this amphitheatre, among thousands of doomed Vlhani. I wanted to say all of that, and more, for I suddenly needed to understand her even more than I'd ever needed to understand the creatures who danced below. But Hurrr'poth was right: she'd been perfectly at home among the Vlhani, and was just a trembling, devastated young woman beside us.

Below us, the Vlhani writhed: a sea of gleaming black flesh and snapping black whips, their spherical heads all turning to watch us as we passed.

"They look like they're slowing down," noted Hurrr'poth.

I couldn't tell. To me, their Ballet looked every bit as frenetic now as it had five minutes ago. It all seemed perfectly graceful, perfectly fascinating, and perfectly alien: an ocean of fluid, undifferentiated movement, diminished not at all by the deletion of one strange young woman with chevrons on both cheeks. Why not? They'd always danced without her;

they could just go ahead and dance without her again. If anything, they were probably relieved not to have her getting underfoot anymore . . .

I tried very hard to believe that, and failed. Hurrr'poth knew more about their dance than I. Not, it seemed, as much as Isadora—he wouldn't have been able to stride into the middle of the Ballet and expect to keep his skin intact—but enough to read the essence of what he saw. If he said they were slowing down, they were slowing down.

And it could only be because I'd taken away Isadora.

They were as devastated as she was.

Why?

# 5.

We landed the skimmer in the open field behind the viewing stand. Dhiju led a small mob of humans and aliens from their seats to meet us. They all wanted to know who Isadora was, where she'd come from, and why she was here; I don't honestly think anybody actually stayed behind to watch the Ballet. They crowded around us so densely that we didn't even attempt to leave the skimmer: an ironic, unintended parody of the dance we'd all come here to witness.

Dhiju's face was flushed and perspiring heavily—a condition owing as much to his intoxication as his concern—but he retained enough self-control to speak with me first. "Astonishing work, Alex. I'll see to it that you get some time taken off your contract for this."

"Thank you, sir."

He next directed his attention to Hurrr'poth. "And you too, sir—you didn't have to risk yourself for one of ours, but you did anyway, and I want you to express my thanks for that."

Hurrr'poth bowed slightly, a gesture that surprised me a

little, since I would have expected much more than that from a sentient who so prized the sound of his own voice. Maybe he was too impatient for the part that we all knew would have to come next: Dhiju as disciplinarian. And Dhiju complied, with the fiercest, angriest, most forbidding expression he knew how to muster: "And as for you, young lady: do you have any idea just how many laws you've broken? Just what the hell was going through your mind, anyway? Did you really wake up this morning and think it would be a good day for being torn to pieces? Is that what you wanted out of your afternoon today?"

Isadora stared at him. "The buggies invited me."

"To what? Die? Are you really that blind?"

Whereupon Hurrr'poth returned to form: "Forgive me, Mr. Dhiju, but I don't believe you've thought this out adequately."

Dhiju didn't like the interruption, but protocol forced him to be polite. "Why not? What mistake am I making?"

"I daresay it should be obvious. What do we know about this young lady so far? She's obviously had herself altered to approximate Vlhani movement; she's evidently learned more about their dance than either your people or mine have ever been able to learn; she's made her way here from wherever it was she started, apparently without any of your people finding out about her; and she's snuck herself into what may be the most thoroughly studied native ritual in recorded history, without hundreds of observers from seven separate confederacies spotting her until she was in the middle of it. No, Mr. Dhiju, whatever else you might say about her wisdom in trying to join the Vlhani Ballet, I don't think you can fairly accuse her of coming here on a foolish spur-of-the-moment whim. What she's done would have required many years of conscious preparation, a fair amount of cooperation from people with the resources to give her these Enhancements, and a degree of personal dedication that I can only characterize as an obsession."

Dhiju digested that for so long that for a moment I thought the hallucinogens had prevented him from understanding it at all. Then he nodded, regarded Isadora with a new expression that was closer to pity, and met my eyes. He didn't have to actually insult me by giving the orders.

*Find out.*

I nodded. He turned and strode off, not in the direction of the viewing stand, but toward his own skimmer, which was parked with the rest of the embassy vehicles. A half-dozen indentures, including Rory and Kathy and Oskar, scurried along behind him, knowing that they'd be required for the investigation to follow.

I looked at Isadora. "You can save us all a lot of trouble by just telling us everything we need to know now."

She glared at me insolently, the dark alien fires burning behind her eyes: still unwilling to forgive me for saving her life, or herself for saving mine. "Will it get me back to the show?"

"No. I'm sorry. I can't imagine Dhiju ever allowing that."

Her look was as clear as Dhiju's: Then go ahead. Find out what you can. But I'm not going to make things easier for you.

Fair enough. If she could learn to understand the Vlhani, then I could sure learn to understand her. I turned to Hurrr'poth: "Are you coming along?"

He considered it, then bobbed his head no. "Thank you, Alex, but no. I think I can be of better use conducting my own investigation using other avenues. I will, however, be in touch as soon as I have anything relevant to contribute."

"See you, you old criminal," I told him.

It was a personal experiment, to see how he'd react to a joke, and he made me proud: "See you soon . . . pornographer."

# 6.

It may have been the only time in the history of the human presence on Vlhan that the delegation was actually expected to deal with a Major Diplomatic Incident. Oh, we'd had minor crises over the years (uneventful rescue missions to pick up linguists and anthropologists who'd gotten themselves stranded in the field, tiffs and disagreements with the representatives of the other delegations), but never anything of life-and-death import; never anything designed to test us as representatives of the Confederacy, never a dozen separate mysteries all wrapped up in the form of one close-mouthed, steadfastly silent young woman.

And so we worked through the night, accomplishing absolutely nothing.

We took DNA samples, voice-prints, and retinal scans, sending them via hytex to the databases of a thousand planets; nobody admitted to having any idea who she was. We went through our library for records of human cultures with ritual facial tattooing. We found several, but none still extant that would have marked a young woman with chevrons on both cheeks. We seized on the slang phrases she'd used, hoping they'd lead us back to a world where they happened to be in current usage, and found nothing—though that meant little, since language is fluid and slang can go in and out of style at weekly intervals.

She silently cooperated with a medical examination which elaborated upon that which we already knew: that her entire skeleton, most of her musculature, and much of her skin had been replaced by Enhanced substitutes. Her arms alone were a minor miracle of engineering, with over ten thousand flexible joints in just the distance between shoulder and wrist. Her nervous system was also only partially her own, which only made sense, since the human brain isn't set up to work a limb that bends in that many places; she had a complex system of micro-controllers up and down her arms, to translate the nerve impulses on their way to and from the brain. She only had to decide the moves she wanted to make; the micro-controllers let her limbs know how to go about making them. There were also special chemical filters in her lungs, to maximize the efficiency with which she processed oxygen, several major improvements made to her internal connective tissue, and uncounted other changes, only some of which made immediate sense.

There weren't many human agencies capable of this kind of work, and most of them operated at the level of governments and major corporations. We contacted just about all of those, from Transtellar Securities to the Bettelhine Munitions Corporation; they all denied any knowledge of her. Of course, they could have been lying, since some of her Enhancements were illegal; but then they operated in the realm of profit, and there was no possible profit in turning a young woman into a sort of quasi-Vlhani, geared only toward her own self-destruction.

That left nonhuman agencies, some of which could be expected to harbor motives that made no human sense. But we couldn't contact many of them by hytex, and the few we could were a waste of time, since they had a relaxed attitude toward the truth anyway. Kathy Ng, who was in charge of that aspect of the investigation, got fed up enough to grouse, "How am I supposed to know who's telling the truth? None of them have ever been consistent liars!" Everybody sympathized; nobody had any better suggestions.

As for me, I spent four hours at the hytex poring through

31

the passenger manifests of civilian vessels passing anywhere within a twenty light-year distance of Vlhan, finding nobody fitting her general description who couldn't be accounted for. Then I stole a few minutes to check on Isadora, who we'd locked up in our biological containment chamber. It was the closest thing we had to a prison facility, though we'd never expected to use it that way. Hai Dhiju sat in the observation room, glaring at the sullen-faced Isadora through the one-way screen. Oskar Levine sat beside him, alternately gaping at Isadora and feeding Dhiju's ego. When Dhiju noticed me, something flared in his bloodshot, heavy-lidded eyes: something that could have been merely the footprint of the hallucinogens still being flushed from his system, or could have been something worse, like despair. Either way, he didn't yell at me to go back to work, but instead gestured for me to sit down beside him.

I did. And for a long time neither one of us said anything, preferring to watch Isadora. She was exercising (though performing was more like it; since even though the room on her side of the shield was just four soft featureless walls, she had to know that there would be observers lurking behind one of them.) Her form of exercising involved testing the flexibility of her limbs, turning them into spirals, arcs, and jagged lightning-shapes; a thousand changes each instant. It was several different species of beautiful—from its impossible inhuman grace, to the sheer passion that informed every move.

The translation device squeaked out a word every thirty seconds or so. *Death. Vlhani. World. Sad. Dance. Food. Life. Sad. Human.*

None of it meant anything to me. But my eyes burned, just looking at her. I wanted to look at her forever.

Dhiju took a hit of a blue liquid in a crystalline cylinder. "Anything?"

It took me several seconds to realize he'd spoken to me. "No, sir. I don't think she left a trail for us to find."

*Cold.*

"It makes no sense," he said, with a frustration that must have burned him to the marrow. "Everything leaves a trail. In less than one day I could find out what you had for breakfast the day you turned five, check your psych profile, and find out which year if your adolescence featured the most vivid erotic dreams; get a full folio on the past fifteen generations of your family; and still have time to get a full list of the dangerous recessive genes carried by the second cousins of all the children you went to school with. But everybody's drawing a blank with her. I wouldn't be surprised to find out she was some kind of mutant Vlhani."

"It would certainly make her a lot easier to deal with," said Oskar. "Just send her back to the Ballet, and let nature take its course."

I would have snapped at the bastard had Dhiju not beaten me to it. "Not an option."

"Then ship her off-planet," Oskar shrugged. "Or keep her in detention until the Ballet's over."

"I can't. It's become bigger than her." Dhiju looked at me. "In case you haven't heard, the Ballet's off."

I felt no surprise. "They stopped, then?"

"Cold. We weren't really sure until about an hour ago—it took them that long to wind down—but then they just planted their center whips in the dirt and began to wait. They've already sent a message through the Riirgaans that they need her back in order to continue. I've been fending off messages from all the other delegations saying I ought to let her, as the Vlhani have jurisdiction here."

I thought of our superiors back home, who'd no doubt want the Vlhani appeased to preserve future relations. "That kind of pressure's only going to get worse."

He emitted a sound midway between a sob and a laugh. "I don't care how bad it gets. I have a serious problem with suicide. I think anybody foolish enough to choose it as an option is by definition not competent to be trusted with the decision."

*Storm. World.*

I thought of all the Vlhani who made that decision every year—who came, as honored pilgrims, to the place where they were destined to dance until their hearts burst. We'd always found a terrible kind of beauty in that ritual . . . but we'd never thought of them as incompetent, or mad, or too foolish to be trusted with the choice. Was that only because we considered them nothing more than giant spiders, not worth saving?

*Fire. Love. Danger.*

Disturbed, I said, "I was with her, sir. She was one of the most competent people I've ever met."

*Dance.*

"Not on that issue. It's still suicide. And I don't believe in it and I'm not going to let her do it."

I faced the shield, and watched Isadora. She was running in circles now, so swiftly that she blurred. When she suddenly stopped, placed a palm against one wall, and hung her head, I couldn't believe it was fatigue. She wasn't sweating or breathing heavily; she'd just gotten to the point where it made Marionette sense to stop. After a moment, I said, "Has anybody actually tried talking to her directly?"

"That's all I've been doing. I had people in there asking questions until their breath gave out. It's no good. She just keeps telling us to, uh, crod ourselves."

*World. Dance.*

"With all due respect, sir, interrogating her is one thing.

Talking to her is another."

Dhiju came close to reprimanding me, but thought better of it. "Might as well. You're the only one here who's ever demonstrated the slightest clue of how to deal with her. Go ahead."

So I went in.

The containment chamber was equipped with a one-way field, permeable as air from one side but hard as anything in existence on the other. It was invaluable for imprisoning anything too dangerous to be allowed out, which up until now had meant bacteria and small predators. The controls for reversing the polarity were outside the chamber, on a platform within easy reach of Oskar and Dhiju. The second I passed through the silvery sheen at the doorway, I was, effectively, as much as a prisoner as she was. But it didn't feel that way; at the moment, I didn't want to be anywhere else but with her.

She had her back to me, but she knew who I was even as I entered; I could tell that just by the special way she froze at the sound of my step. She turned, saw me, and with a resignation that made my heart break, leaned back against the opposite wall.

I did not go to her. Instead, I found a nice neutral spot on the wall and faced her from across the width of the chamber. "Hello."

Her expression would have been strictly neutral were it not for the anger behind those dark, penetrating eyes. Facing those eyes was like being opened up and examined, piece by piece. It should have been unsettling; against my will, I found I liked it.

"I've got to hand it to you," I said, conversationally. "The Vlhani are on strike, the other delegations are going crazy, nobody here has the slightest clue who you are, and I'm supposed to come in here and get the information that everybody else can't. Who you are. Where you come from, where you got those augmentations, and how you got here."

Impatience. Establishing that she'd already been through this—that she hadn't answered the questions before and wouldn't be answering them now. Wondering just what I thought I was accomplishing by throwing good effort after bad.

And then I folded my arms and said, "The thing is, I really don't care about any of that. Wherever you come from, it's just a place. How you got here is just transportation. And as for who put in those augmentations? That's just a brand name. None of that makes any difference to me at all."

She rolled her eyes incredulously. "What does?"

"Why."

"In twenty-five words or less?"

"Counting those? Sure. You have nineteen left."

She blinked several times, back-counting, then flashed an appreciative smile. "Only if ye ken twenty-five as two words instead of one. Ye shouldn't."

"All right. But that still brings you down to . . . uh . . ."

"Seven," she said, simply. And then: "I'm madly in love with their show."

Damned if she hadn't done it, on the dot. We grinned at each other—both of us understanding that she hadn't told me anything I couldn't have guessed already, but enjoying the little game anyway. I said: "So am I. So's everybody on Vlhan, and half the known universe. That doesn't explain how you came to understand it so well . . . and why you're so determined to risk your life dancing among them."

She waggled a finger at me. "Uh-uh, boyo. It's yer turn. Twenty-five words or less, how can ye say ye love the show when ye don't ken it one bit?"

It didn't come off as rude, the way she asked it—it was a

sincere question, expressing sincere bafflement. I measured my response very carefully, needing to both be truthful and match the precision of her answer. "I suppose . . . that if I only loved things I understood perfectly, I'd be living a pretty loveless existence. Sometimes, love is just . . . needing to understand."

"That's not love, boyo. That's just curiosity. Give ye'reself an extension and riddle me this: what do ye feel when ye watch their show? Do you ken their heart? Their creativity? Their need to do this, even at the edge of dyin'?"

"Maybe," I said. "Some of it."

"And how do ye ken ye're not croddin' the whole thing to bloody gobs? How do you ken ye're not seeing tears when the buggies mean laughs? Or that it's really a big show and not a mungie prayer?"

It was hard to keep my voice level. "Is that what you're saying, Isadora? That it's not an art form?"

She shook her head sadly, and dared me with eyes like miniature starscapes. There was pain, there: entire lifetimes of pain. But there was arrogance, too: the kind that comes from being able to understand what so many others cannot. And both were tempered by the distant, but genuine, hope that maybe I'd get it after all.

After a moment, I said, "All right. How about I tell you what we think we know, and you tell me how and where we're sadly mistaken?"

She shrugged. "Ye're free to toss."

"All right. The Marionette dance isn't a conventional symbolic language, like speech, but a holographic imaging system, like whalesong. The waveforms rippling up those whips aren't transmitting words or concepts, but detailed three-dimensional images. They must be tremendously sophisticated pictures, too, since the amount of information being passed back and forth is huge. And if a Marionette can paint a detailed map of the immediate environment in about ten seconds of strenuous dance, then the Ballet may have enough detail for a complete scale model of this solar system. The problem is, we haven't been able to translate more than a few simple movements—and even then we think they're talking down to us."

Isadora nodded. "Ye're right. That they be."

I had made that part up. Excited now, certain she had the key that the rest of us had missed, I leaned forward and said, "But they weren't talking down to you, were they? They respected you. They made a place for you. How is that? Who are you to them?"

"Someone who kens them."

"And how is it you understand the dance when we can't?"

"Because I ken it's a show, not a mungie code." When I reacted to that with a mere uncomprehending blink, she just shook her head tiredly, appeared to reconsider silence as an option, and said: "Peer this. There's a species out in space, known by a name I can't make me lips say. They're pitifully boring folks . . . born filing-systems, really . . . but they're totally tingled to crot by the idea of the human pun. The idea of ringin' two chimes with one phrase seems as sparkledusty to them as the buggie dance be to us. And their greatest brains been wastin' years of sweat just tryin' to ken. Ye can buy the whole libraries they've penned about it."

I seemed to recall reading or hearing about the race in question, at some point in the distant past. "So?"

"So they crod up the whole sorry mess. They don't ken humor and they don't ken that a pun's supposed to be funny. They think it's Zen-time instead . . . a, how-ye-put-it, ironic human commentary on the interconnectedness of all things. Once upon a time, I peered a pair of the dingheads pickin' apart a old terran comedy about professional athletes with wack names—names that were questions like Who and What and Why. It didn't seem all that laugh-time, to me, but I could ken was supposed to be silly—and they didn't. I vow to ye, Alex, it was like peering a couple of mathematicians dustin' up over an equation. Like ye folks, they peered the mechanism, and missed the context."

Dammit, she did know something. I pushed myself off the wall, and went to her. "So tell me the context. You don't have to give me all of it, if you don't want to, but something. A clue."

And she smiled at me. Smiled, with eyes that knew far more than I ever would. "Will it get me back in the show?"

Against my will, I glanced at the featureless wall that concealed the outer lab; I didn't need to be able to see through it to know what Ambassador Dhiju was doing on the other side. He was leaning forward in his seat, resting his chin on a cradle of locked hands, his eyes narrowing as he waited to see if I'd make any promises he couldn't allow me to keep. He was probably silently urging me to go ahead; like all career diplomats, he'd spent a lifetime sculpting the truth into the shapes that best suited the needs of the moment, and would see nothing wrong with doing the same now. But he hadn't been with her in the amphitheatre, as I'd been; he hadn't bartered his life for hers, and been the beneficiary of the sacrifice she made in return; he couldn't know that it would have been unthinkable for me to even attempt to lie to her. So I came as close to being honest with her as I dared. I said nothing.

She understood, of course. It was inevitable that she would. And though she must have known the answer even before asking the question, it still hit her just as hard; she lowered her face, and looked away, unwilling to let me see what was in her eyes. "Then the deal's bloody gobbed. I don't speak one crot more 'less I get back to the show."

"But—"

"That's final."

After a moment, I understood that it was. It was all she cared about, all she had to negotiate with. Any attempt to pretend otherwise would be an insult. And so I nodded, and went to the door, waiting for Oskar to reverse the field so I could leave.

Except that I was wrong. It wasn't final, after all; there was still business between us, still something she couldn't say goodbye to me without saying.

She said: "Alex?"

I looked at her. "What?"

She didn't meet my eyes: just stared at her feet, as if peering past the floor and past the ground to face a scene now half a day in our past. "Were ye just blowin' dust, back at the show? Were ye . . . really goin' to waltz with the buggies and me . . . if I'd not ridden that skimmer out with ye?"

"Absolutely. I wasn't about to leave there without you."

She nodded to herself, as if confirming the answer to a question that nobody had bothered to ask out loud . . . then shook her head, flashed a dazzling smile, and, in perfectly proper Human-standard, said: "Then you deserve this much. The Ballet doesn't end, each year, just because the last dancer dies. Think . . . the persistence of vision."

# 7.

We didn't find out about it until the post-mortems, but first blood was shed on a swampy peninsula over a thousand kilometers from our embassy: a place equally inhospitable to both Vlhani and Men, with terrain soft enough to swallow wanderers of either race.

Dr. Kevin McDaniel wasn't officially attached to the embassy. In truth, he was an exobotanist, on Vlhan as part of an unrelated commercial project having something to do with a certain smelly reed native to the swamps; it may have been important work, but to the rest of us it was nowhere near as compelling as the mysteries of the Vlhani, which interested him not at all. Usually, we only remembered he was on-planet at all because he was a clumsy oaf, and one of us had to keep him company at all times, lest some absent-minded misstep leave him drowning in the ooze with nobody to pull him out. It was an annoying detail that everybody lower than Dhiju had pulled at least once. We made jokes about it.

Today, McDaniel's babysitter was a plump young kinetic pattern analyst by the name of Li-Hsin Chang, who had entered her servitude one year behind me. Li-Hsin had bitterly complained about the duty rotation that had obliged her, and not anybody else, to miss the spectacle of the Ballet in favor of a week spent trudging through muck in the company of the single most boring sentient on the planet. And the strange developments at the amphitheatre only made matters worse: even as she sat in the skimmer hovering five meters up and watched McDaniel perform his usual arcane measurements among the reeds, she was deeply plugged into the hytex, eagerly absorbing all the latest bulletins about me and Isadora and the Vlhani crisis.

Under the circumstances, Li-Hsin can be forgiven for failing to spot the Vlhani until it was almost upon them.

Vlhani can weigh up to a thousand kilos, but they have a controlled way of running that amounts to keeping most of that weight in the air, and even at full speed they can make significantly less sound than a running man. It's not deliberate stealth, but tremendous inherent grace. And while even they're not quite as quiet splashing through muddy swampland as they are galloping over dry, densely packed earth, they still never stumble, never make a misstep, never release one

41

decibel of sound that they don't absolutely have to. This one's approach was drowned out until the very last minute by the hum of the skimmer's drive and the clumsy splashing-about of Dr. McDaniel. When Li-Hsin heard a particularly violent splash, she peered over the railing, saw that McDaniel had wandered only a few meters from where he was supposed to be, then heard another, louder, splash from the north.

It was a ten-whip mature Vlhani, approaching at top speed. It ran the way Vlhani always run when they push them-selves to their limits—spinning its whips like the spokes of a wheel, with the shiny black head at the center. It ran so fast that the whips blurred together in great gray streaks. It ran so fast that it seemed to be flying. And it was coming their way.

Li-Hsin can also be forgiven for not immediately realizing that it was hostile. In the first place, it wasn't wholly unheard-of for a huge adult Vlhani to be running around in the middle of the swamp. It was unusual, but they did sometimes wander far from their usual habitat. She'd seen a mating pair just the other day. In the second place, Vlhani simply weren't hostile. They may have been too dangerous to approach during their Ballet, but that was a function of the Ballet, not of the Vlhani. In their everyday existence, they were extraordinarily gentle; Li-Hsin had walked among them without protection for two years, and had even developed an easy familiarity with those she saw most frequently. She even considered one or two of them friends—at least, as much as she could when the best our harnesses could do was pipe the meme *Friend* back and forth. That was enough for her. As it was for me. And the rest of us.

So it was that even when she saw that Dr. McDaniel was directly in its path, it still didn't occur to her that it might be deliberately attacking him. She did nothing more drastic than just flip on the amps and cry out: "Mac! Get out of the way!"

McDaniel, who'd been too absorbed in his measurements to see or hear the big Vlhani's approach, glanced up at the skimmer, annoyance creasing his pale, sweaty features. He spotted the Vlhani a second later, stood there dumbfounded, wholly unwilling to believe that this was actually happening to him, then saw that he was about to be run over and leaped to one side, belly-flopping in the middle of a pool of stagnant water. He sank beneath the surface and did not come up for air. Vlhani whips sank deep into the ooze where he had been, with a force that would have pulped him. The Vlhani didn't even slow down. It was ten meters past him before Li-Hsin even had time to yell, "MAC!"

She grabbed the controls and swooped low over the water where McDaniel had disappeared. He came to the surface choking and spitting, but waving that he was all right. She was about to descend further to pick him up when he spotted the Vlhani, fifty meters away and circling around for another go. Unlike Li-Hsin, he was totally ignorant about the Vlhani, and therefore had no preconceptions to shed; he knew immediately that the attack was real, and that the Vlhani would be on him again long before Li-Hsin managed to pick him up. He frantically waved her off: "Go away! It's circling back!"

Li-Hsin looked up, and saw that McDaniel was right. If she still had any doubts about its intentions, the speed of its approach would have banished them: were this an accident, it would have slowed down and returned with exaggerated caution, hanging its head at the angle that we'd all come to recognize as mimed remorse. She glanced at McDaniel and shouted: "STAY DOWN!"

McDaniel yelled back: "DON'T—" But it was too late for Li-Hsin to hear him. In one smooth movement, she'd turned the skimmer around, aimed it toward the approaching Vlhani, and instructed it to accelerate. She did this without thinking, and without hesitation, seized by the kind of desperate inventiveness that takes over only when there are no other options available. A direct collision with a skimmer, moving at those speeds, would splatter even the largest Marionette; Li-Hsin had to know that such a crash would certainly kill her too. She probably hoped it would be intimidated enough to duck and run.

Except that it didn't happen. Just before the moment of collision, the Marionette leaped, and came down on top of the skimmer. Two of its whips were broken at the moment of impact: another one was cleanly amputated by the lift coils. The rest cushioned its landing. The neurec connections, which had so clearly captured all of Li-Hsin's actions and sensations up until now, now documented her helpless astonishment as she suddenly found herself surrounded by a cage of undulating whips. The Marionette's head loomed close behind her for an instant, then disappeared out of frame. A whip slashed across the frame, blurred, and then disappeared, leaving her without a right arm.

The horizon behind them spun like a dial.

Then the skimmer crash-landed into the swamp, and both Li-Hsin and the Marionette were killed instantly.

It took McDaniel four hours to dig out the hytex and call for help. By then, those of us still left alive were way too busy to hear him . . .

# 8.

The only question anybody really managed to answer before everything fell to pieces was the precise manner of Isadora's secret arrival on Vlhan. It was Rory Metcalf who made the connection with a supply transport that, about eight months ago, had entered Vlhan's atmosphere half a world away from its assigned landing position, come within a hair's breadth of a landing before seeming to realize that it was in the wrong place, then risen back to 50,000 meters to travel the rest of the way. This might have seemed suspicious at the time, but the bickering pilots had struck everybody as just a couple of incompetents with no real talent for the work. When Rory looked up their courier license, she found that they'd subsequently been arrested on several charges of carrying unregistered passengers. It was a mildly impressive piece of deduction, which probably solved one minor part of the mystery, but still explained absolutely nothing.

And even if we could put together the parts that mattered, we were running out of time.

We'd placed our embassy on an isolated plateau that was both higher and colder than the Vlhani found comfortable—a location we'd chosen not out of fear for our own safety, but common courtesy and respect for their privacy. After all, we could reach any place on their planet within three hours; we could walk among the Vlhani as frequently as they cared to let us, without obtrusively cluttering up any land they were already using. So, like the Riirgaans and the K'cenhowten and the Cid and all the other embassies, we'd placed our cluster of buildings far outside their normal migration patterns, and normally didn't entertain Vlhani guests more than once or twice a year. Usually, we could stand outside the collection of prefabricated buildings that made up our compound, look down upon the rolling gray hills that surrounded us, and feel completely alone, as if we were the only sentients on the entire planet.

But not today. Today, when a few of us took a break to face the Vlhani sunset, we found a landscape dotted with thousands of spiders. The ones we could see were all approaching from the west; the other embassies reported many more approaching us from every direction, but the herds in the west had been closer, and were first to show up. They didn't approach in formation, like an army, but in randomly spaced groups of one or two or three, like strangers all heading the same way by coincidence. They moved so quickly that every time they crested the top of a hill their momentum sent them flying in great coltish leaps. The sun behind them turned their elongated shadows into surrealistic tangles. The few that had reached the base of the plateau seemed content to mill about there, looking up at us, their trademark flailing whips now reminding me of nothing so much as fists shaken in anger.

Kathy Ng intoned, "The natives are restless."

She gave it the special emphasis she used whenever she lifted a quote from the archaic adventure fiction she enjoyed so much; I'd never heard it before. "Do you think we're going to have to fight them?"

"They certainly look like they're trying to give us the impression, don't they?" She bit her lower lip hard enough to turn it white. "I just hope it's just their ancestral scare-the-shit-out-of-the-bipeds dance, or something."

"Ancestral or not, it's working."

Our chief exopsychologist, Dr. Simmons, tsked paternally. "You're being ethnocentric, people. We can't say they're acting hostile just because, to our eyes, it happens to look that way. Especially since, in all the years we've been here, nobody's ever seen the Vlhani react to any conflict in an aggressive or violent fashion."

"What about the Ballet?"

"That's violent, all right . . . but it's not conflict. It's a highly stylized, intricately planned annual ritual, choreographed down to the very last step. Which means that it's about as relevant to typical Vlhani behavior as your birthday party is to the remaining four-hundred-and-ninety-nine days of the year."

"Which would make me feel a lot better," said Rory Metcalf, "if not for one thing."

"What's that?"

"Today's Ballet Day . . . and it hasn't been typical at all."

That started everybody arguing at once. I missed most of what got said because Oskar Levine chose that moment to scurry out of the main building and summon me to Dhiju's quarters. I hesitated just long enough to spare one more look at the army of Marionettes gathering down below, contemplate just how long we'd be able to hold them off if we had to, and realize that if it came to that, we wouldn't even be able to slow them down. We were a peaceful embassy on a peaceful world; we didn't have anything to fight them with, beyond a few inadequate hand-weapons. We might as well start stockpiling sticks and stones . . . and if it came to that, we were all dead.

I shuddered and went to see Dhiju.

A funny thing. Desks, as practical pieces of office furniture, have been obsolete for over one thousand years. They were helpful enough when most work was done on paper, or on computer screens that needed to be supported at approximately eye-level . . . but since none of that's true anymore, desks no longer serve any function important enough to merit all the space they take up. They're still used only because they're such effective psychological tools. There's something about the distancing effect of that great smooth expanse that inherently magnifies the authority figure seated on the other side. And men like Dhiju know it. When I ran into his office, he was in position behind his, glowering as if from Olympus.

He gestured at the hytex projection floating in the air beside his desk. There were four main images fighting for supremacy there: a panoramic view of the amphitheatre, where the participants in the Vlhani Ballet still stood motionless, patiently waiting for the show to go on; another view of the Vlhani gathering at the base of our plateau; the surveillance image of Isadora, serenely doing multi-jointed leg lifts in the Isolation Lab; and finally, a head shot of Hurrr'poth, looking as grave as his inexpressive Riirgaani face ever allowed him. I was unsure which image I was supposed to look at until Hurrr'poth swelled to fill my entire field of vision. The giant head turned to face me. "Alex," he said. "The pornographer."

"Hurrr'poth," I said. "The criminal."

He trilled, but it struck me as the Riirgaani equivalent of forced laughter: it went on a little too long, and failed to convey any amusement at all. "I thank you for coming, Alex. This is a very important communication, and since you were with Isadora in the Ballet, I felt that you might possess the keen perspective that your Ambassador Dhiju seems to lack. —Have I disturbed you in any way?"

I glanced at Dhiju, saw only anger, and remained mystified. "Uh . . . no. How can I help you?"

"You can listen," said Hurrr'poth. "I was telling your Ambassador, here, that I speak not only as the chosen interpreter of the Vlhani people, but as the elected representative of all the other embassies stationed on Vlhan. The Vlhani have spent the past several hours communicating their wishes on this matter, and we are at their request lodging an official protest against your embassy's continuing interference with the indigenous culture of this planet."

Dhiju made an appalled noise. "This is like something out of Kafka."

"I am unfamiliar with that term, Ambassador, but the Vlhani are trying to be fair about this. They understand that, armed with insufficient information, you and Alex acted to preserve the life of a fellow member of your species. They know that this was only natural, under the circumstances, and they bear you no ill will for doing what seemed to make sense at the time. Indeed, they respect you for it. But they also believe that they've shown you they consider the woman Isadora an integral part of this year's Ballet . . . and that, by irresponsibly prohibiting her return to the amphitheatre, you are inflicting irrevocable damage upon the most sacred ritual of their entire culture. They demand that you surrender her at once, so the Ballet can continue."

"Will she die in the Ballet, like they do?"

"Of course," said Hurrr'poth.

"Then the answer's No," said Dhiju.

"You are interfering with a tradition that has lasted hundreds of generations."

"I am deeply sorry about that, Mr. Hurrr'poth. But Isadora's not a member of Vlhani tradition. She's a human being, and as such part of a tradition that abhors suicide. Nobody authorized her presence here, and I'm not about to authorize her participation in any ceremony that ends with her death. The Vlhani will just have to understand that."

Then Hurrr'poth did trill: but it was a grim, bitter species of amusement . . . one I never would have expected from a sentient I'd imagined a harmless eccentric. "Sir: you are an idiot."

Dhiju's natural impulse to show anger crashed head-on with his professional duty to be totally courteous to all the other members of every alien delegation at all times. "Pray tell. Why?"

"Her presence here is not up to you to authorize. It is up to the Vlhani. It is their law and their judgment that applies on this world, and they have clearly recognized her and welcomed her and honored her with a integral position in their

Ballet. When you behave as if you are the sole arbiter of who
is and who is not supposed to be here, you demonstrate that
you understand even less about this species than you understand about your own—which, if you still think the young
lady doesn't know what she's doing, is saying a lot. If you persist in this course of action, you will only get the Vlhani more
angry at you than they already are. And everything that happens from this moment on will be on your head."

I broke protocol by interrupting: "Are you saying they'll
attack?"

Hurrr'poth faced me directly. "Yes."

We had no way of knowing that the first skirmish had already taken place; neither Dhiju or I even happened to think
of Kevin McDaniel or Li-Hsin Chang, who were half a world
away, and well outside the usual Vlhani habitat. After a
moment, Dhiju just said, "Understood. I'll be back in touch
with you as soon as I confer with my people."

"You are making a terrible mistake! The Vlhan—"

Dhiju thumbed a pad beside him. The hytex projection
folded up, shrank into a mote of blackness the size of a pea,
then faded. Dhiju stuck out his lower lip, made a "t-t-t-t-t"
sound from somewhere deep in his throat, and aside from
that, remained in place, apparently finding volumes of
meaning in the way his hands sat on the smooth desk before
him. Eventually, he just said, "Susan." And a new hytex projection took the place of the one he'd taken away: this one the
static image of a girl in her early teens. She was fresh-faced,
but wan, and she smiled in the patently artificial way that's
been common to all portraits, captured by any recording
media, since the beginning of time.

"My daughter," he said.

I had no idea what to say. So I lied. "She's pretty."

"You think so?—The truth is, I barely even saw her after

she turned nine. Her mother and I became just too much of a bad mistake together, and I found it easier to stay away, on one off-world assignment after another. I got letters and recordings, but saw her in person maybe for a couple of months out of every year. And then, one day, when she was fifteen, a friend at a party introduced her to the latest fashionable import from off-world: a sort of . . . vibrating jewel . . . capable of directly stimulating the pleasure centers of the brain . . ." He shuddered. "It took six months, Alex. Six months of killing herself a little bit more every day. Six months I didn't even get to hear about until I was rotated home and got to find her gone."

He sat there, thinking about that a while, letting Susan's enlarged, joylessly smiling face accuse him at length.

And then he said: "Every once in a while, some poor bastard gets saddled with the kind of impossible decision that destroys his career and makes his name a curse for the next hundred years.—Go tell the others we're evacuating. Deadline one hour. After that we're taking the little gatecrasher with us and leaving everything we haven't packed behind. Then we'll take the transports into orbit and wait there until we can summon a ride home."

My heart pounding past the threshold of pain, I stepped toward him, faced his gray, deceptively watery eyes, and choked out what he already knew: "They'll never let us back. You'll be throwing away all our relations with the Vlhani, and everybody at home will blame you. You know that."

"Yes. I do." He looked past me, past the hytex projection, past the wall, and past the entire worsening crisis, and said: "But at least this time I'll be here to save her."

51

# 9.

The Vlhani were a black horde, covering the hills like flies; and though there were far, far more of them than anybody had ever documented in one place before, it was still impossible to look at them without sensing deliberate choreography at work. Even when threatening war, everything they did was still a dance, albeit a different kind of dance, with nothing graceful or balletic about it. This time, it was more like a march of death, their normally fluid gait reduced to something joyless and rigid, that seemed as forced and unnatural coming from them as a goose-step coming from Man. They were packed most densely in the rocky terrain at the foot of our plateau, more crowded by far than anything I'd seen in the amphitheatre, but never advancing beyond the rocks, even when the competition for space flattened them like creatures being crushed against an invisible wall. If that wall crumbled, the wave of Vlhani swarming up the slope would be upon us in seconds.

There weren't many people visible; everybody was too busy performing the frantic business of a last-minute evacuation. That mostly meant clearing out the food stores, the infirmary, the records, and the tool lab; but everybody was human enough to spend a few precious seconds in their own quarters sweeping them clear of items so personal we couldn't bear to leave them behind. There wasn't much of that, though; indentured diplomats don't get much space for clutter. All I had was a pocket hytex and a length of severed Vlhani whip I'd salvaged from the amphitheatre after last year's Ballet; I irradiated it regularly to discourage decomposition, but time had taken its toll anyway and the chitin that had once been harder than steel was now soft and spongy and cracked at the edges. Only a few days ago, an unworthy part of me had looked forward to the mass carnage at the Ballet so

I could later search the amphitheatre for a new coil to seal in permaglass. I remembered that, shuddered, and left the old one untouched on the shelf beside my bed. It was Vlhani, and if we were truly leaving, it belonged to Vlhan.

With twenty minutes to go, it fell to me, as the closest thing we had to an expert on the Isadora problem, to figure out a way to safely get her onto a transport. After all, her Enhancements made her physically more than a match for any of us; if she decided to resist, she could easily be as formidable as any Vlhani. Drugs were out, since so much of her was artificial that nobody had any idea how to even begin to figure out what dosages would be safe or even effective on those portions of her anatomy that remained; and the embassy didn't stock anything that could restrain her or be legitimately used as a weapon.

In the end, I snagged Oskar Levine—who, as I have said, I'd never liked much, but happened to be the only person not doing anything—and armed him with two tanks of compressed cryofoam from the infirmary, one hose strapped to each arm. We kept the stuff on our skimmers in case of injuries in the field; we hadn't used any at the embassy itself since last year, when Cecilia Lansky came down with a rare form of cancer we couldn't cure on-site and had to be stored on ice until we could send her home for treatment. There was enough in those two tanks to wrap up a single full-grown Vlhani. If Isadora tried to break, Oskar would foam her.

He tried to talk me out of going in. "Use the intercom. Turn off the field, tell her to come out, I'll get her in the doorway. It'll be fast and easy."

"I know. But I still think I can turn this thing around. I want to talk to her first."

He gave me the kind of look most people reserve for unredeemable idiots. "If you walk out together, and I see no reason to trust her, I'll foam both of you."

"That's reasonable enough. Long as you get me on a transport."

"Fine," he said. "Give me more work to do."

"Oskar . . . !"

"It's a joke, jerkoff. Don't worry about it, I'll take care of you either way."

She'd pulled out the folding cot built into the rear wall of the chamber, and curled up to sleep there; a reasonable enough thing to do, given the circumstances, but still one that surprised me no end, as it was the first genuinely human gesture I'd ever seen from her. Somehow, without me ever realizing it, I had come to think of her as far beyond such considerations as any other perfectly designed machine. But she didn't look like a machine now: she didn't even look adult. With her eyes closed, and her knees hugging her belly, and her hands tightly clasped beside her chin, she resembled nothing so much as a little girl dreaming of the magic kingdoms that existed only inside her head. The tattoos on her cheeks could have been make-believe war paint, from a game played by a child . . .

Something stirred in me. A connection, with something. But whatever it was, was too unformed for me to make any sense of it yet.

I knelt down beside her and said, "Isadora."

The illusion of normalcy was broken as both her arms and legs uncoiled, like liquid things that had never been restricted by bones. When her eyes opened they were already focused on me: wholly unsurprised by my presence, wholly unintimidated by anything I might have to say. The shadow of a smile played about her lips, revealing a warmth that surprised me. She did not get up: merely faced me from that position, and said, "Alex."

"I thought you'd like a progress report."

She refused to blink. "That's fuzzy-pink of ye."

"The Vlhani have surrounded us. Dhiju's practically thrown away his career by giving the order to evacuate. We're packing up, getting out, and taking you with us."

She hugged her coiled arms a little closer to her chest. "I don't want to go."

"Like hell," I said softly. "Whatever else you are, Isadora, you're far from stupid. You knew we were watching the Ballet, you knew we would spot you, you knew we'd be honor-bound to try to stop you, and you knew how the Vlhani would react if we succeeded. You could have avoided this whole crisis by explaining everything in advance, or by enhancing yourself so much we couldn't distinguish you from a Vlhani. Instead, you just made a surprise appearance—and got exactly the response you expected."

Her eyes closed. "I didn't ken what ye could do to get me out. Had no idea I'd waltz into a boyo gallant enough to hold himself hostage for me."

Her tone put the word "gallant" in little quotes, defanging it, making it a joke . . . but not a bitter one. Encouraged, I pushed on: "And that's the real reason you're withholding the explanations, isn't it? Even why you're using that ridiculous dialect of yours, when you've already proven you can abandon it when you want to. Not because you're trying to negotiate your way back to the dance. But because you're trying to put off going back. You don't really want to die. You're looking for a way out. Any way out."

"There is no way out."

"Just refuse to participate!"

"I can't do that. It will ruin the show."

"So one year's Ballet gets ruined, and the Vlhani are traumatized. But there's another Ballet next year. So what?

55

What's really at stake here, Isadora? Why are they so determined to get you back?"

"Ye wouldn't ken."

"I . . . ken . . . enough to know when they're angry, and when they're afraid, and when they're so desperate they don't know what to do . . . but most importantly, enough to know when they're holding back. They could have over-run us a couple of hours ago, and they haven't. Because they don't want to hurt us. They don't want to hurt anybody . . . but they're still ready to march all over us to get you back. Why is that, Isadora? What's so special about you that they can't just replace you with one of their own? And what's so special about them that you can't say no?"

In the silence that followed, I could almost hear Oskar fidgeting outside the door . . . maybe even Dhiju himself checking his timetables and demanding to know just where the hell I was . . . but it was worth it. Her eyes glistened, and she faced her delicately tooled fingers. "Alex . . . have you ever dreamed of something so much, for so long, that you had to have it . . . even though you still weren't certain it was what you wanted?"

I just waited.

She still didn't look at me. "If I tell you, will it get me back to the Ballet?"

"Maybe yes and maybe no . . . but either way it might stop a whole lot of good people from getting hurt."

She sat up then—a wholly unremarkable act rendered remarkable by the graceful precision with which she performed it. When a normal person rises from a prone position, their center of gravity shifts. Their muscles come into play, and there's a subliminal moment of danger when they're momentarily off-balance. It's not something you notice in the way normal people move . . . unless you've seen Isadora, simply gliding from one position to the other. She rubbed the bridge of her nose, smiled ruefully, and once again spoke in a voice free of the thick accent she'd used to define herself for me. "Have to hand it to you, Alex . . . you know what strings to pull."

I rose from my kneeling position and sat down beside her. "I better. We're on a planet of Marionettes."

She snorted. "Should I go for twenty-five words or less?"

"Let's not limit ourselves."

"When I was eight years old, I was living in my Uncle's house, as his provisional ward pending . . . well, where I came from, there was a whole legal lexicon for such things, and I don't really have to go into it. The Steinhoff recordings of the '57 Ballet had just come out; I had myself plugged into the neurec, with the feed down low so I could still pay attention to everybody else in the house . . . not full gain, because I always had this need to know everything that's going on around me. And my Uncle and his husband were plugged in too, also low because they were the kind of people who couldn't ever stop talking about everything they saw, and my Uncle recited something straight off the hytex about how dark and mysterious the Vlhani were, and how their minds were so dark and alien that no human would ever understand them.

"It was the sort of platitude-laden gibberish that people learn to repeat so they can imagine themselves clever without ever bothering to think an original thought themselves. And I was eight years old . . . mesmerized by what I was watching . . . and I knew that what my uncle was saying was gibberish. Because it was the third recording I'd seen, over the past few months . . . and I was beginning to have some idea what the Vlhani were getting at."

I swallowed. "How?"

"Crod it, I don't know. Maybe it's just some quirk in me that visualizes things differently, something in my perceptions that's a little more Vlhani than human being . . . and maybe I was just young and impressionable enough to let the message seep through. Maybe it's even a question of talent . . . something that transcended species and gave me the ability to understand when you and Dhiju and my Uncle just saw dancing buggies. But put that aside. What matters is that I saw one tiny aspect of the Ballet *clearer* than the Vlhani. I saw a critical flaw in their performance, something they didn't even see themselves . . . something that made their Ballet a lie, and that only I knew how to correct." She groped for my hand, found it, and gave me a tight squeeze. "I can't describe what it was like, Alex. It was like . . . hearing a single discordant note in the greatest symphony ever written . . . and knowing that only I knew how to correct it. And that night I slipped out the window and ran away from home, determined to make it to Vlhan."

I squeezed her hand right back. It felt human enough: nothing at all like the intricate arrangement of circuitry and plastics I knew it to be. "You were eight years old. How far could you get?"

"As far as I had to. You don't understand: I wasn't really eight years old anymore. The part of me that had been a child was dead. In its place was just this hungry, needful thing, with . . . with a responsibility . . ." She sighed. "I don't want to tell you all the risks I took, all the laws I broke, all the ways I . . . indentured myself . . . to get where I needed to go . . . but I had a primitive version of these Enhancements within two years . . . and I was on Vlhan, communicating with the spiders, within four. They saw I was right, and let me know that when the time came for them to incorporate my ideas, I would have to be the one to dance them. As I always knew."

"But you're not a Vlhani. You can't move like a Vlhani, no matter what crazy modifications you've made to yourself."

Her nose wrinkled. "Maybe so. But don't you see? That doesn't matter. Art isn't just technique, in any culture . . . it's also Content. It's understanding not just How, but also What, to express. And while I may not know everything the Vlhani do . . . the Vlhani still saw that I had something to offer them. Something they hadn't even known they needed. And I've spent all the years since then preparing for that."

"For Death."

"You think I don't have doubts? That I genuinely, honestly want to die? I want to have a life. I want to have all the things other people have. But I have no choice. It's my responsibility. I have to do this."

"No you don't! What if I said that the Vlhani have no right to ask this of you? What if I said that you matter more than the Ballet? What if I said that the Vlhani will just have to muddle along without you, and try again next time?"

"You'd be demonstrating that you understand nothing," she said. "Remember the Persistence of Vision—"

And maybe it was the sheer madness of everything that had happened between us, and maybe it was the memory of that one moment in the amphitheatre when I sensed some small part of how much the Marionettes counted on her, and maybe it was a single moment of perfect telepathy . . . but all of a sudden the bottom dropped out of the universe, and I understood exactly what she'd been getting at. She saw the light dawn, and the most tragic thing happened to her eyes: they filled up with fresh hope she did not necessarily want.

Her hand squeezed mine again, this time with enough pressure to cross the threshold of pain. I didn't particularly mind.

I said, "Maybe—"

And that was really all I had a chance to say.

# 10.

She could have told us we were running out of time. She could have let us know that the Vlhani have a calendar, of sorts—not a written one, since they have no writing, but one they continually calculate themselves, using the passing of the seasons and the movement of the stars across the sky. She could have let us know that they placed an almost astrological importance on such things, especially where the Ballet is concerned; and that while, by their lights, it's all right to put off the Ballet for maybe one or two of their days, everything was lost if they permitted us to delay the festivities much more than that. I'm certain she knew all that: she understood more about the Vlhani than any human being who had ever lived.

Some of the people who later arrived to pick up the pieces said that Isadora as good as murdered everybody who died. They're wrong. Because Isadora also understood about us, and she knew that we wouldn't have listened, any more than we'd listened to Hurrr'poth, who'd advised me to leave her alone in the first place. And I think that even she never expected the attack to come as soon as it did. If she had, she might have tried to warn us harder . . .

In any event, we didn't need to see outside to know that something very bad was happening. The walls and floor shook hard enough to make me think of charging cavalry, trying but failing to keep out the sounds of the invasion in progress outside: shouting, skimmers flying low overhead, wounds being ripped in buildings, and the thunderous drumbeat of thousands upon thousands of heavy metallic whips pounding holes in the ground. I shouted out the stupidest question imaginable: "Oskar! What's going on out there?"

The voice that emerged from the intercom was sweaty and driven by panic. "I don't know—I'm hearing—"

60

I found the wherewithal to ask the question properly. "Oskar! Are the spiders attacking?"

A siren wailed. Our emergency warning system. Installed as a matter of policy, not because anybody had ever expected it to be used. Against that, Oskar's voice was tinny and distant: "Yeah. Yeah, Alex, I think they are."

"Shit," I said, with feeling.

Isadora said, "We have to let them know I'm going back to the Ballet."

"To hell with that," I said. I patched in to Oskar again: "All right, stay close. Let us out in two minutes. And keep your hose ready; you might have to use the foam."

Somewhere not very far away, something metallic—a skimmer, probably—smashed into an infinite number of pieces with enough force to drown out every other sound in the universe. The silence that followed was one of those completely soundless intervals that happen randomly even in the midst of totally uncontrolled destruction—that don't signal the end of the destruction, but merely serve to punctuate it, putting everything that follows in parentheses. By the time Oskar spoke again, the pounding had resumed, and I had to strain to make out his voice. He said: "Take your time. I'm sure as hell not going out there alone."

I turned to Isadora. "You guided us past the Vlhani before. You're going to have to do it again."

She was stunned. "It's two completely different situations, Alex. The Ballet was choreographed. I knew every move, I could predict where the Vlhani were going to be. This is chaos: a thousand individuals rioting in panic. I'm not going to have much more of a clue out there than you do. If I don't let them know you're taking me back to the Ballet—"

"Lie to them."

"Their language can't be lied in. It's . . . like you said, a ho-

61

lographic imaging system, painting a perception of the world. To lie, I'd have to—"

"Then at least get them to back off while we make our way past them."

"I don't know they'll all listen. Some of them have got to be half-insane with grief. Some of them are going to want to drag me back to the Ballet by force, others are going to hate me so much that they'll fall all over themselves trying to kill me. I don't know if—"

I grabbed her by the upper arm. "Isadora. Enough of Can'ts. Can you at least get us to a skimmer and into the air?"

She stared at me, stunned. "Just us?"

"And Oskar. And anybody else we can save. Can you do that?"

For one horrible second there, I thought she was going to offer the condition that I allow her to return to the Ballet. I thought that she truly wouldn't care about all our lives, or for anything beyond going back to this destiny she'd selected for herself; that she would seize upon the opportunity to black-mail us into giving her what she wanted. I expected it. I waited for it.

Her eyes narrowed. And she said: "Yeah. I can try."

I had Oskar reverse the field, and ran for it.

# 11.

Neither Oskar or I had the time to find and don a whip harness, but by the time we got outside, we saw that they would have been superfluous anyway.

The compound had been overrun by Vlhani.

A dozen had attacked the dormitory building. Four were on the roof, punching holes in the building with repeated blows from their long flailing whips. The rest had staked out the windows, and were busily using their whips to probe inside. One gave a sharp tug, and pulled something scarlet and ragged and human out the window.

One of the spiders towered over Foster Simmons and Kathy Ng, rotating in place so quickly that its whips strobed, becoming a transparent gray blur, behind which Foster and Kathy knelt bloody and imprisoned and screaming. The spider didn't seem particularly inclined to tighten its grip and slice them to ribbons—but they must have tried to get past it, because Foster's severed hand lay by itself only a few feet away. His whip harness whined *Hurt Help Hurt Help,* to no avail. I couldn't see enough to tell if Kathy was hurt too.

Rory Metcalf and a bunch of others had gotten to one of the skimmers. They'd managed to take off, but a group of three Vlhani anchored to the ground had reached up and wrapped their whips around the housing. The skimmer strained in mid-air, veering from one side to the other in a vain attempt to break free. Rory pounded at one of the whips with her bare hands. As I watched, the skimmer lurched in a random direction and was promptly reined back in, but not before a burly figure I recognized as Wesley Harris flipped over the side and hit the ground hard.

Ambassador Dhiju staggered through the midst of the carnage, clearly moved by it without ever being touched by it; beyond the fresh bruise on his forehead and a shallow cut on his upper arm, he wasn't hurt at all. He walked blindly, without making any special attempt to avoid the Marionettes striding back and forth across the compound; and though they made no special attempt to avoid him either, their long sinuous whips stabbed the ground to the right and the left and the rear of him without once hitting him. When I got close enough to grab him by the hand I took a close look at his eyes and recognized his secret as the luck of the intoxicated: in trying to dull the pain of what had to be the greatest defeat of his life, he'd pumped himself up with so many recreationals that he simply didn't see anything unusual about the chaos around him. I had to shout his name three times before he recognized it and followed us.

A ten-whip Marionette slashed at me. A cold wave knocked me back; I hit the ground with patches of cryofoam stealing pieces of sensation from my upper arms. The Marionette lay on the ground, four of its whips paralyzed, the others still flailing. Oskar stared, unwilling to believe that he was the one who'd brought it down. I caught a momentary glimpse of the dormitory building collapsing in on itself, saw Isadora frantically signing something in the air above her head, then spotted the silver glint of parked skimmers behind the commissary. There were several Vlhani blocking the way between us and that holy grail, but it was as good a direction as any. I yanked the mumbling Dhiju out of the nearest Marionette's reach, and yelled "There!" We made a run for it.

On our way there, the Marionette tethering Rory's skimmer succeeded in upending it and tossing her out. Half a dozen indentures, some already wounded, fell too far to the ground. I turned, and caught a glimpse of Rory getting batted to one side by a flailing whip. She got up limping and with one hand clutched to her side. The three Vlhani released the now unoccupied skimmer, (which rocketed over the edge of the plateau and plowed at full speed into a fresh assault wave of Vlhani), then converged upon her. I heard her shout as three of the newer indentures, who'd somehow avoided getting hurt or killed or trapped so far, overcame their panic enough to dart in her direction. One went down. I didn't get to see what happened to Rory or the others, because that's when the big bull Vlhani got me.

It wasn't the first time I'd been lifted into the air by a Marionette. They were peaceful, playful people, most of the time, and some of them liked to hoist humans in their whips as a way of saying hello. They'd always indicated their intentions before doing so, and always shown both gentility and a keen understanding of the fragility of human flesh. Not so now. This one looped its whip around me from behind and yanked me into the air with a force that realigned my vertebrae. I didn't know I'd been grabbed until I was already off the ground, being spun around and around with a speed that reduced the compound and the people and the rampaging Marionettes into undifferentiated streaks of color. As its whip tightened around my belly, the air whuffed from my open mouth, and I realized that this was the moment I was going to die.

And then the world stopped spinning and about thirty seconds later my head stopped spinning with it and I stared dazed and confused at a sky dominated by the sun, which abruptly up-ended and was replaced by the ground as the whip holding me circled around and showed me the reason I wasn't dead.

Isadora.

Face flushed, eyes desperate.

Forehead covered with a sheen of fear.

Arms in the air, twisting into impossible wrought-iron loops and curves, circling around each other in ways that hurt the mind to imagine.

The Marionette lowered me gently to the ground, placing me in a standing position, though I was so dizzy that I almost immediately tumbled to my knees. Then it not only stood guard over us, as Oskar and Isadora helped me to my feet; but also silently escorted us, as they helped Dhiju and I stumble drunkenly toward the skimmers.

There were five of the vehicles parked behind the commissary. None were intact. The Vlhani had pounded three into unrecognizable masses of twisted metal and plastic; torn out the hytex and propulsion systems of the fourth; turned the fifth into a collection of dents and broken instrumentation that may have looked like hell, but seemed capable of wobbly flight. The seats had been ripped out, leaving only the metal housings. We got in anyway. The Vlhani protecting us merely looked down at us impassively, flailing its whips in a manner that could have meant anything at all.

I managed to ask Isadora one question, as Oskar lifted off: "Did you tell it you were going back to the Ballet?"

She refused to look at me. "I told you: it's next to impossible to lie to them. I don't know enough of the future to promise that."

"Then . . . what did you tell it?"

"That you were my friend. And that, whatever happened, I wouldn't dance if you died."

Oskar flew low over the embattled compound, looking for other people to save. Everybody we saw was either dead or too tightly surrounded by Vlhani to go after. I saw several indentures running zigzags through the wreckage, clumsily dodging the whips that herded them from one near miss to the next. I saw a few others who through exhaustion or despair had simply given up running; they knelt in the middle of the carnage, hostages to the mercy of the spiders. About half the people I saw were wearing whip harnesses, their little windup cables seeming a pathetic joke in light of all the real whips raining destruction all around them.

The one time Oskar saw an opportunity to save somebody, and tried to go in, about twenty Marionettes went after us, with great springing leaps that drove them thirty meters straight up. We hadn't expected that at all; none of us, with the possible exception of Isadora, even had any idea they could jump. One collided with the skimmer so hard we almost flipped, then grabbed at us in a clumsy attempt to seize hold before falling back down. Oskar took us a hundred meters higher up, circled away from the plateau to put us even further out of their reach, then wiped fresh blood from a gash in his forehead and said: "So? Is there even any place to go?"

Dhiju murmured something incomprehensible. Isadora and I glanced at each other. We held the look a little longer than we had to, exchanging recriminations, apologies, thanks, regrets . . . and more. Neither one of us wanted to break the silence.

In the end, I spared her that much, at least.

I said, "The amphitheatre."

# 12.

We were damaged too badly to make top speed, but the wind-bubble did curl over us when we asked it to, so we were able to go supersonic. At that, it would take us three hours instead of the usual forty minutes to reach the amphitheatre . . . which simultaneously seemed too long and not long enough.

I called the Riirgaans. They patched me through to Hurrr'poth, who was—unsurprisingly—already in the air taking a rescue squad to our plateau. He'd started prepping the mission when I pulled Isadora from the Ballet. He'd suspected what was coming, too; had even tried to warn me, more than once. Even so, I had trouble seeing his help as magnanimous. When he jokingly called me pornographer, I disconnected him.

Less than two hours passed before Oskar and I used up our store of conversation, and Isadora crawled off into the rear screen to stare wordlessly at the landscape racing by down below. Under the circumstances, I was almost grateful when awareness limped back into Dhiju's eyes. He croaked:

"Y-you're not taking her back . . ."

I spoke in a tightly controlled whisper, because I didn't want Isadora to hear. "I'm sorry, sir. But yes, we are."

He tried to muster up enough strength to be indignant. "I . . . specifically ordered . . ."

"I know. And I'm still hoping to work out a way where it doesn't have to happen. But we have to do this. We have no choice."

"They're killers," he said, almost petulantly. "We owe them nothing. Now that they've murdered everybody, they don't even have anything left to threaten us with. We don't have to throw good blood after bad. We can still get her off-world. We can still save her. We can still . . ."

"The persistence of vision," I murmured, hearing not my own voice, but hers.

"What?"

"The persistence of vision." When Dhiju showed no signs of comprehension, I shook my head, as if sheer denial could erase everything I knew. Oskar must have sensed something wrong, just about then, because he left the controls and took a seat between us, looking haggard and grim and desperate to understand. I didn't acknowledge him, or even Dhiju; at the moment, I was too lost in the size of it, too unable to fit other people into a universe which had suddenly changed all shape and form. "You can't even blame them," I said, distantly. "They thought they were going to lose everything. They had to go mad."

"You're not making any sense," crabbed Dhiju.

Isadora didn't turn around even then; but then she didn't have to. I knew she was listening. I shook my head to fight off the shock, and spoke as earnestly as I could, in words meant for all of us. "It's not something I'm comfortable knowing, sir. But with all the things she's said, and all the things that have happened, I've begun to understand, a little. And I've learned . . . that we never had the slightest idea how big this was, for them. We knew their language was holographic. We knew they were drawing pictures for each other. We knew that whatever they were making with the Ballet was more important to them than their lives. And we were right about all that. But we also thought that a new Ballet began and ended every year . . . and in that we were wrong. The picture they paint, sir . . . it's just a single frame. And it blends together, in their minds, with the picture they painted last year . . . and the one they're going to paint one year from now. All arranged in sequence, and merged by the persistence of vision . . ."

"A motion picture," Oskar said hoarsely.

Dhiju's eyes flickered in his direction, then bored in on mine. "So?"

"So that's why she can't quit. For the same reason she surrendered when I threatened my own life. Because she's driven by responsibility. And she knows that if she quit it wouldn't just ruin one Ballet—which would traumatize the whole species but still leave them room to rebuild. No. It would shatter a single evolving work of art that they've been creating for the better part of their history. It would destroy everything they've ever been, everything they've ever dreamed about, and everything they've ever tried to accomplish. It would leave them with nothing to live for. And that's why she can't quit. Because it's either her life . . . or the lives of every Vlhani that ever lived."

Oskar breathed, "Holy," utterly forgetting to specify a Holy What.

Dhiju remained silent. He just looked at me, and then at Oskar, and then at Isadora, who still sat staring out the screen, giving no indication that she heard any one of us. And then he turned back to me, and said, "I'm sorry, Alex. But even if this theory bears any relation to reality, which I doubt, it changes nothing. I'm still ordering you to stop her."

Dammit, he had to understand. "Like I said, sir . . . I intend to try. I don't want her to die any more than you do. But the Vlhani—"

He drowned me out. "The Vlhani are not my problem! It's not my fault they've dedicated themselves to this thing! Their insanity is not my responsibility—and hers is! I won't let her kill herself! And I'm ordering you to turn this crate around and demand asylum at one of the other embassies!"

"I can't. I have to leave our options open . . . in case there's no other way."

Dhiju stared, unwilling to believe that a third-year indenture would risk everything by daring to defy him. He wrested control of his voice, and spoke with the kind of controlled quiet that can be overheard in the middle of an explosion. "Alex. If you don't do what I say within the next five seconds, I'll consider it a gross act of insubordination and extend your contract fifty years."

Oskar said: "Then you'll have to extend mine too."

I glanced at Oskar, astonished. I hadn't expected him to join in my mutiny; I'd been counting on Isadora to help me overcome the two of them. But he faced Dhiju with the stoic intractability of a brick wall, and he gathered up the cryofoam harness, and he held it in his hand, to demonstrate what awaited if Dhiju tried to interfere in any way. It was funny. I'd never liked him, not even the slightest bit; he'd never been anything more to me than just somebody I had to deal with in order to do my job. But right now, I found myself hard-pressed to remember exactly why that was.

As for Dhiju, he nodded, unsurprised, all the strength going out of him all at once. And he reached into the pocket of his tunic and took out one of his vials of blue liquid and swallowed it down in one gulp. He closed his eyes before we got to see them go fuzzy and dilated again, and murmured, "You're both throwing away the rest of your lives."

I began to protest, but Oskar rode me out. "No, Alex . . . that's fair. Get out of the way and I'll foam him, so he doesn't have to watch."

After a moment, I complied. Why not? Had I been in Dhiju's position, I wouldn't have wanted to be conscious either. And the ambient temperature in the skimmer dropped thirty degrees as the liquid bubbling sound filled the air around us.

# 13.

I sat beside Isadora for much of the hour that remained of our flight, not speaking, just making my presence known. Not that she spent all of that remaining hour or so just looking out the screen. All it showed was a nondescript series of hills and valleys and plains and lakes, none of which were by themselves particularly different from the those that puckered the landscape of ten million other worlds. Sometimes we passed over small herds of Vlhani, who were visible only as black dots against brown fields; if they heard the hum of our drive and looked up, to catch a glimpse of the vehicle bearing this year's most honored dancer, it wasn't what she needed to see. And so she spent most of that last hour just quietly sitting with me, not speaking much, not remaining entirely quiet either: just sharing the space, and the wait, for that place which we both knew we'd reach all too soon.

Near the end of that hour, I asked her about the markings on her cheeks, already suspecting what she'd tell me. And I was right: they were merely desperate affectations left over from her first few days on her own—the legacy of an eight-year-old girl struggling to re-invent herself as she finagled her way from one world to another. Both they, and her made-up slang, were remnants of a past she'd created for herself—the

71

kind of past that only could have been created by a frightened child forced to become adult before her time. I thought about the long hours Rory had spent searching her databases for a society that used those ritual markings, and those idioms . . . and wondered whether she'd still be alive to laugh about it when I told her.

Not long after that, I began to spot landmarks—the otherwise nondescript rock formations and dried riverbeds that my previous journeys to this place had taught me to recognize as the vicinity of the amphitheatre. When Oskar pointed out a cratered plain pockmarked by the tracks of the one hundred thousand Vlhani dancers who had passed this way on their journey to the place where they were scheduled to die, my stomach seized up. And when we saw the Ballet . . .

. . . it had always been a magnificent sight. It still was. But today was the first time it filled me with dread.

Seen from a distance, with or without rangeviewers: a sliver cut into the face of the planet, filled with a gleaming black sea that swelled and surged like an intelligent amoeba. With the reflective Vlhani skin glowing red in the light of the rising sun; it looked like a lake of fire. An unworthy part of me wished for plasma cannons so I could make it one.

As we drew closer, we saw that not all of the Vlhani were in the amphitheatre itself—there were several hundred gathered above the northern rim, arranged in two semicircular mobs with single wide pathway between them. The pathway led straight to the heart of the Ballet. An invitation, set out for Isadora.

As for the viewing stand on the opposite rim: it was packed again. Not quite to capacity—since this time, there were no humans and only a few Riirgaans in the seats—but close enough to let me know that all of the alien delegations had returned to their places, eager to see the Ballet resume as scheduled. From this side of the amphitheatre, it was easy to hate them, for their eagerness to see that which I would given anything to stop. Would any of them mourn the Vlhani who died? Would any mourn Isadora?

Oskar told the skimmer to hover, then came over and knelt beside us. His eyes were tearing. "I was . . . going over this in my head. About what we're doing . . . what we're about to let her do. I kept . . . thinking . . . that there had to be some other way. And I think I have one."

Isadora's smile was grateful, but without much hope. "Oh?"

"Participate via hytex."

It hit me like an electric current wired right into the spine. "What?"

"You heard me," said Oskar. He turned to her. "You can dance your part somewhere safe; we'll rig up a micro-remote to hover over the amphitheatre and broadcast your image wherever you have to be. You can do everything you have to do without being anywhere near the Vlhani when they start losing muscle control."

My heart pounded in my chest. "Isadora! Would that work?"

She shook her head sadly. "If the Vlhani were human, maybe. But they don't see on the same wavelengths."

"We can recalibrate! Project something they can see! Even sound, if we need to! Dammit, Isadora, we know so much more than you think! Give us a couple of hours to arrange it, and you'll live!"

"But don't you see what an insult that would be? All those Vlhani dying, and their most honored guest staying alive by remote control? Showing herself above them, by continuing to walk and breathe while everybody who waited for her dies? I can't mock them that way. I won't."

"The spiders killed a lot of good people today," Oskar pleaded. "They can use a little mockery."

"I'm sorry," she said, and leaned forward to kiss him. "But, please. I have to do this. If that means anything to you, please land so I can get it over with."

He lowered his head, shuddered, and went off to the controls.

For me, it was not like we were sinking. It was like the ground was rising to meet us; like the entire planet was a single predator, and the horizons were razor-studded jaws inexorably closing shut. It was hard to remember that neither Oscar nor Dhiju nor I were in the same danger Isadora was: if we just stayed in the skimmer, let her disembark, and then took off, the only person being swallowed whole today was the strange, beautiful, terrified, but unwavering woman who knelt beside me. It didn't make me feel any safer. If she died, it would still be too much like dying myself.

We were still some distance from the ground when I said: "Isadora."

She abandoned the view and looked at me. "Alex."

"Was everything you told the Vlhani true? Back at the compound?"

She smiled sadly. "I told you. It's impossible to lie to them."

"Then please. Listen. You don't have to do this. There are alternatives. You can make them understand—"

She hugged me. "Thank you. But no. I have to do this."

. . . and then she tightened her arms on the edge of the skimmer and lightly jumped to the ground.

We were still about twenty meters up, so both Oskar and I yelped, instinctively certain that she'd just suicidally leaped to her death. But no: when I leaned over the edge I saw her lightly touch ground, wave at me, and start running toward the amphitheatre. She was as fast as one of them; before I even had time to react she had disappeared among the Vlhani.

I wasn't Enhanced. There was no way I'd ever be able to catch her. But catching her was not part of the plan. I'd always known that she had to do what she had to do.

Now it was my turn.

I shouted at Oskar. "For Christ's sake! Land this thing! I have to go out there and talk to them!"

"Talk to—" Oskar started. "Are you out of your mind?"

"Just do it! Now!"

He aimed for a spot fifty meters from the Vlhani spectators. As we landed, I said, "Don't wait for me, I'll be okay! Just get back to the embassy and see if you can help any of the others!"

"B-but . . . what are you talking about, you can't—"

I leaped over the side and hit the ground running.

All my instincts rebelled against the idea of charging creatures who I'd so recently seen on the rampage. But the part of my mind still capable of remaining rational knew that I'd be in no danger from them at all; they no longer had any need to hurt me. They already had Isadora. If I had any fear at all it was that they would be able to recognize me as the one who'd rescued her once before; that for fear of me doing it again they'd bar my way and refuse to allow me into the amphitheatre.

They didn't. The ones on the rim just stood passively by as I ran among them, using the same path they'd cleared for Isadora. Their heads did swivel to watch me as I passed; expressionless globes that could have been registering annoyance, or disgust, or pity, or nothing at all. I like to think that they recognized compulsion when they saw it: that they didn't stop me because they knew stopping me would do no good.

Maybe, in that, I reminded them of Isadora.

I made it over the edge of the bowl and began to half-run, half-fall, down the slope. It was not a gentle grade, like the place where I'd found her the first time, but a dirt slide that with a few more degrees of pitch would have begun to qualify as a cliff. I couldn't remain upright and stay out of the way of the dancing Vlhani at the same time; I allowed myself to fall on my rear end and slide. I caught a glimpse of the viewing stand on the southern rim and wondered if anybody there could see me; if any of them were feeling little twinges of horror at the thought of the great spectacle being delayed yet again. Not that I cared; all I cared about, all I worried about, was Isadora. And she was nowhere in sight.

I came to rest in a sea of slashing whips. There was blood in my mouth and on the backs of my hands. The Vlhani around me were so densely packed that I couldn't see more than twenty yards in any direction. Their whips, waving in the air above their heads, spun so passionately that the whirrs of their passage drowned out everything, even the ragged rasp of my breath.

Isadora wasn't around to lead me out, this time.

That didn't matter. What mattered was being here.

Because though I didn't understand Vlhani dance (and didn't even have the harness that would have physically equipped me to dance it), the language barrier has always been a poor excuse for not making the attempt to communicate.

And as Isadora herself had said: *Art isn't just technique, in any culture . . . it's also Content. It's understanding not just How, but also What, to express.*

So I stood up, and took a deep breath, and appealed to them in the only way I knew how. With words. I spoke to them in sounds they couldn't possibly understand, hoping that the feelings would come through. I painted a word-picture that not only apologized for never truly understanding them before, but also mourned and celebrated the differences between us. It was a picture that flashed upon my friends lying dead or wounded at the embassy, and of just how many light-years they'd traveled to meet such an end; it was a picture that talked about how they'd deserved more, then came back to Isadora and how she deserved more too. It was a picture of a young woman who'd already given up everything—her home, her childhood, her normalcy, and now, probably, her life—for the Vlhani. I let them know that, however they measured such things, it was a sacrifice: and that it was a sacrifice only they were empowered to stop. And finally, I let them know how beautiful she was: as beautiful, in her own way, as their Ballet, and how much it mattered to me that she still be alive when the last dancing Vlhani fell to the trampled earth.

I never spoke at such length, or with such eloquence, in my entire life.

Had they understood the language, I would have broken their hearts.

But even as I poured everything I had into my words, I knew that I was nothing to them but a yapping little creature making noise. They surrounded me without reacting to me, their great spherical heads bobbing like toys.

And when I finally ran down, exhausted, unable to plead any more, unable to think of anything else that I hadn't already said a dozen times, a Vlhani moved toward me, so gracefully that its whips barely seemed to brush the ground. One of its whips came down, gently curled around my waist, and lifted me up to its head. I had the distinct impression of eyes studying me, even though Vlhani don't have eyes; the head merely rotated first one way, then the other, in no way conveying any expression at all. Out of reflex I reached out and placed a palm against its cool, polished surface, thinking of the alien brain that sat pulsing beneath. What did it think of me? Did it think me strange? Ungraceful? Ugly or beautiful?

It passed me to another Vlhani further up the slope. Which passed me to another one, and then to another one after that; until I was handed over to the ones standing up on the northern rim, who gently put me down and encircled me to ensure I wouldn't dash into the amphitheatre again.

They needn't have bothered. I was done.

There was nothing left.

# 14.

Many hours later, the Riirgaan aircruiser flew in from the south, circled above me, and came to a rest on packed dirt a short distance away. The Vlhani who'd come to watch the Ballet milled about all around us, taking special care not to step on me or inconvenience the aircraft in any way. Rory and Oskar were both aboard, looking tearful and exhausted. They gave me weak little waves as Hurrr'poth hopped over the side, approached me, and then, folding his limbs in a manner that must have been painfully uncomfortable for a Riirgaan, knelt by my side. His face was as expressionless as always, but there was a tentative, concerned, uncharacteristically deferential manner to the way he regarded me. I mistook it for simple respect for my grief, and said nothing.

At length he said, "Alex."

I asked him: "How many dead?"

"Vlhani or humans?"

I was in no mood to care about Vlhani. "You know I meant humans!"

"Seventeen. About half your delegation. Foster Simmons,

Li-Hsin Chang, Kathy Ng . . ." When he saw how every name made me wince, he trailed off. "It could have been much worse. Almost half your number survived."

"And Isadora? Did she?"

He placed a reptilian hand on my shoulder. "No."

So I hadn't pulled off the impossible miracle after all. For all these hours, I'd dared to persuade myself that I might have. I thought of her eyes, and the way she moved, and how I'd been the one to deliver her to the moment of her death, and I just knelt there, my shoulders shaking and my mind spinning between the rustle of the wind and the beating of my triphammer heart.

And then, once again, Hurrr'poth said, "Alex."

I refused to look at him. "What."

"I do not know if this will make a difference to you . . . but everybody among the spectators saw what you tried to do for her. What you did do for her. Everybody witnessed it: all the delegations . . . and, soon, thanks to the holos and neurecs, all their worlds."

I closed my eyes more tightly. Yes, that was all I needed. To have the single greatest failure of my life played endlessly throughout the universe. "And?"

"And," he said, "it was not just Isadora and the Vlhani who danced magnificently today."

Whereupon he stood, and returned to the aircruiser, leaving me alone with that.

Neither Hurrr'poth nor Rory nor Oskar came out to hurry me.

Eventually, I got off my knees, and went to them. Not because I'd accepted what he'd had to say. But because the show was done, and it was time for all the performers to go home.

79

# 15.

The Riirgaans offered Oskar and I citizenship and diplomatic immunity. Oskar took the deal, I didn't. Oskar went home, legally nonhuman; I was court-martialed, got twenty years added to my contract, and went to the rancid, half-molten hellhole known as New Pylthothus, where I would be rotting still had I not smuggled myself AWOL two years later. Since then, I've been officially a fugitive. I have no intention of telling you where I am, how I changed my appearance, or what name I use now. I found a world acceptable for spending the rest of my life in hiding; I changed my face and my name and found a life for myself. I have friends, family. It's happiness, of a sort. I'm not complaining.

The Confederacy attempted to suppress the holos and neurecs of that year's Ballet, but when the anger over the violence against our people faded, the recordings still became the biggest thing to hit popular entertainment in centuries. They succeeded in making the long-time interest in the Vlhani an obsession for trillions; even the vast majority who still didn't understand just what the Marionettes were getting at had to agree that, in some indefinable way easier felt than understood, Isadora had just brought their Ballet to an entirely new level. There was some half-hearted talk of reprisals and the "permanent" withdrawal of the installation—but within five standard years the triple-threat combination of a new administration, humanity's notoriously short memory, and the ravenous demand for the new recordings still being made by the other embassies and distributed to human space on the black market, got a new embassy established on the ruins of the old. This one, I understand, is considerably better armed than ours was, though the indentures there haven't yet been forced to prove it.

80

People love to speculate on who Isadora was, and where she came from; a hundred separate worlds have laid claim to being the place where she was born. Most of them don't put forth very persuasive cases for themselves. All I know for sure is that if I ever did find out the name of the place she came from, I wouldn't feel any pressing need to go there. It has nothing to do with her.

Close to three thousand young people have tried to do what Isadora had done. The vast majority of those never made it off their own home-worlds; they were dreamers, yearning to be special and willing to do anything to emulate somebody who was. They either destroyed themselves or found somebody else to imitate. Of those that remained, a few actually succeeded in picking up Enhancements somewhere: usually, pale imitations of Isadora's, that took away their humanity without giving nearly enough in return. A very small number—four women and two men—made it to Vlhan and into the Ballet, where they died. They'd understood little pieces of the show, too. But their names faded. Nobody remembers them, the way they remember her.

I don't know. Whatever the Vlhani are relating with this great fatal Ballet of theirs, I'm told it's beautiful and profound and meaningful and worth dying for. But the other side of the story is that it's not worth seeing the people you care about die . . . and I've personally lost all desire to decode that message for myself.

As a result, I have never seen Isadora's Ballet. I refused to watch it on Vlhan, and I've refused to view the holos or neurecs. I would not be able to stand obsessively watching and re-watching either my own famously doomed appeal or the equally famous, inspirational moment when she fell.

Instead, I live with my memory of that moment at the compound, when she danced to save my life. Unlike the

Ballet, which has been picked to pieces by experts all over the known universe, that performance was not recorded. There are no holos, no neurecs, no hytex analysis breaking it down into the tiniest millisecond fragments. Oskar was half-blind from the blood in his eyes; Dhiju, who lay on his back dazzled and open-jawed, was so much under the influence that no amount of artificial memory Enhancement would ever succeed in separating the real from that which his mind created. As for me, I caught only the last ten seconds.

But I understood it all. Every single nuance.

When she later spoke to me in human words, she did not tell me the full truth about everything that dance had meant.

And what she really told the Vlhani keeps me warm, in a universe that would otherwise now seem dark and empty and cold.

# The Tangled Strings of the Marionettes

## 1.

Travel to a certain plateau in the southern hemisphere of the planet Vlhan. It's a stark windswept place, far from the hives or migration routes of the native Vlhani, and well-hidden from the many offworlders who have come to this world.

That's where you'll find the statue.

Its center is a mirrored black sphere, one meter in diameter, radiating eight long, serpentine cables in a frozen explosion of loops and spirals and helixes. Three of those cables are supports, holding the sphere two meters off the ground. The other five curl about in no obvious pattern, extending twenty meters at their greatest extension. They curl with such elegance that only a blind man would consider their positions random.

You'll no doubt recognize the statue as a realistic life-sized representation of a typical adult Vlhani, waving its prehensile whips in the sophisticated choreography of the all-dance language that distinguishes the species. They were called Vlhani by those who discovered them first, but you might prefer the many competing names other offworlders have given its kind: Spiders. Marionettes. Whipdancers. Even Buggies: Isadora, the first human being to achieve fluency in Vlhani, is said to have called them that.

You might even imagine yourself able to determine the significance of this particular tableau, but that's impossible. The species expresses meaning through movement, not static poses. An isolated instant like this, shorn of context, would be as meaningless to the Vlhani as the ultimate significance of their epic annual Ballet is to those of us who come to this world to watch their hundred thousand Chosen gather and perform and die. No Vlhani could make much of this artifact. Nor would you, unless you knew what it's doing here. You might assume it a monument, but you won't guess which kind.

My name's Paul Royko. I first traveled to Vlhan at the height of the Pre-War Era, a few short years after Isadora became the first human being to join the hundred thousand Vlhani who perform and die in their annual Great Ballet. The holos of her final moments had already been distributed throughout inhabited space, establishing her in the popular imagination as a tragic cult heroine. Thousands of similarly Enhanced youths had already arrived on Vlhan, intent on following her example. But it was early yet. The humans who had not only passed through the various levels of selection, but been chosen for the fatal ceremony, still numbered only four. It was big news throughout human space whenever the Vlhani accepted another Hom.Sap applicant, bigger news when one performed. I came on assignment from a neural linkcaster no longer extant, to interview the latest: a young lady named Shalakan who was reported to be a dancer as brilliant as Isadora herself, and who was scheduled to perform and die in one week's time.

I thought she was the story.

The monument provides vivid testament that I was wrong.

# 2.

Ambassador Walster Croyd didn't want to see me at all; then when the proper strings got pulled, he claimed an emergency and kept me waiting outside his office for ninety minutes past our original appointment time. I spent the time sitting on an uncomfortable chair in an anteroom with a temperature set to raise goosebumps on stone, recording every ache, every distant sound, and every overheard scrap of bureaucratic conversation that kept me company during the wait, letting my future audience know how I was treated, certain that my future audience would infer from all this the desperation of that sad species, the bureaucrat with no other way to demonstrate his own importance.

Then an aide waved me in and I found myself in the presence of Croyd himself. He was a white-haired, gray-eyed functionary, installed behind a desk that served no purpose grander than a place to rest his hands. That, and provide some cover: for Croyd also happened to be stark naked, with a sagging chest the texture of dry riverbeds.

There's always been a certain sad defiance that afflicts those who appreciate their own irrelevance. Even when their conduct is professional and their work is conscientious, even when they began with a passion for the job, the taste of failure remains all around them, rendering everything they do joyless and stale. I'd tasted that flavor in other Dip Corps outposts, when those were places where the natives bore special contempt for human beings. But it was pungent here. Ever since the Dance Pilgrims began to arrive on Vlhan, first in the hundreds and then in the thousands, the Confederate Embassy here had become little more than a shrill voice shouting itself hoarse as it struggled to make itself heard over the voices of thousands of amateurs whose own rapport with the natives was far more intimate than anything the diplomatic professionals could manage. For better or worse, the Dance Pilgrims had become humanity's embassy to Vlhan. The official Dip Corps facility, as represented by Croyd, was only there to maintain symbolic opposition to a thriving civilian movement they possessed no local authority to stop.

I saw at once that Croyd hated the very idea of me. He tapped a wooden implement of some kind against the desktop and said: "You're a vampire, you know that?"

"I'm a neurec slinger. Not the same thing."

"Sure as hell is. You both live off blood."

It was an ancient accusation against the reporters of news. And a facile one. I said nothing.

"People die here," he said.

"People die everywhere," I told him.

"Except that here, it's a good story."

Again I said nothing.

"You don't have the slightest idea," he told me. "You don't live here. You don't work here. Do you even appreciate what it's like for us, to be damned to a place where children line up to commit suicide?"

I considered saying something glib about war. At that point in my career I'd already covered several. But it wasn't exactly appropriate to the present circumstances, so I just stood opposite the naked man, waiting.

"That's what the Ballet is," he said. "You can defend Vlhani culture, you can praise its artistic worth, you can dress it up in any justification you want, but it's still a bloody ritual suicide—and any human beings the spiders allow into the ceremony are just misguided children, destroying themselves in the service of a ritual that for all we know might not even have a bloody point."

The Dip Corps, and the Confederacy behind it, had maintained this position since the first day human beings found a place in the Vlhani Ballet. It failed to impress me. "I can name a hundred respected authorities who feel otherwise."

"Alien authorities. Riirgaans, AIsource, Bursteeni. They have an excuse. They can afford to be generous when it comes to human lives. It gives them more to study." His voice burned with venom now. "But you, Mr. Royko—you're actually here to encourage this madness. Spread its gospel throughout Hom.Sap space. Reward the sickness of these cultists with notoriety, make them heroes to the next misguided children looking for some stupid way to waste their lives."

I could have said that the Dance Pilgrims were notorious already and that I couldn't help it if people were fascinated with them. But that would have only encouraged him to continue the debate, and I had neither the time or the patience for that. So I said: "I'm here to interview a dancer."

"A misguided suicide."

"An artist," I said. "Who wants to give her life for her art."

Croyd was almost purple with frustration. "It's still death."

"That's right," I said.

My easy agreement infuriated Croyd more. His hands clenched and he rose from his seat, revealing more fatty sag than any human being should have to possess in the age of genomod and AIsource Medical. It might have been an affectation all its own, useful for an ambassador desperate to establish a personal style in a service otherwise inhabited by a limited variety of functional types; in that event, the pale blue veins that lined the softer spots struck me as a particularly nice touch. Either way, he lurched across the spongy floor like a man who had never felt such a surface beneath his bare feet before. "I don't know why I even bother arguing with somebody like you. You're not here to have a conscience."

"How do you intend to stop me?"

He emitted a bitter laugh. "Stop you? I can't stop you. This is Vlhan. These aren't my laws to enforce."

"But you're not going to help me find her, either."

He said: "There are other people on-world equipped to do that. The Riirgaans, maybe. No, I just want to provide you a little warning."

A warning. Good. There was little my audience liked more than the whiff of danger. I turned up the gains and concentrated on one particularly ugly pockmark, right below his eye, as he leaned in close, attempting intimidation.

He used his index finger to jab my shoulder at every possible point of emphasis. "I say this to every human being I find trying to do business with the Pilgrim movement. I can't stop you from aiding and abetting this atrocity, but the Confederacy wants to shut down whoever's responsible for bringing these poor souls to Vlhan. We want to know who finds them. Who recruits them. Who installs their Enhancements, and who brings them here." That last was accompanied by an especially sharp jab, intended to hurt. "I warn you. If you ever find out any of this, in the course of producing your recording, you are to bring it to me. If I ever find out that you withheld such information, the authorities will consider you aligned with these crimes against the human species and place you under arrest the second you set foot back inside our jurisdiction. Is that clear, Mr. Royko?"

I seized his finger in mid-jab and held it, motionless, in my clenched fist. "Clear, Mr. Croyd."

He yanked his finger free and blasted me with a faceful of breath so awful that it must have reflected deep inner rot. "Good. And I hope you got that on your precious recording."

# 3.

The Hom.Saps refused to offer any other assistance, so I followed Croyd's suggestion and went to the Riirgaans. Unlike our own officialdom, they actually believed in claims of a deep meaning behind the Vlhani Ballet, and were more than willing to help a lowly slinger intent on spreading the word. They set up the meet and loaded me aboard a remote skimmer bound for Shalakan's desert retreat.

It was dry country, colored in subtle variations of brown dirt. But the air was cool and the breeze was light and the angle of the sun cast a pleasant pink glow over the approaching night. It was the kind of place I might have chosen for a camping trip, had there ever been any chance of me ever taking a camping trip. A lone Marionette grazed on scrub in the distance. Since its big round photoreceptor head was essentially one big three-hundred-sixty-degree eye, I couldn't tell whether it took any particular notice of my arrival. I paid particularly close attention to it anyway, acquiring exotic detail, the chief skill of a good neurec slinger being constant awareness of which sensations needed to be nurtured for the playback.

The only other sign of life in the neighborhood was a sleepcube inflated beside a dry riverbed. It didn't look like a two-man model, designed for long treks into barren country, but a semi-permanent installation, big enough for entertaining visitors. I knew worlds where entire families lived in worse. If that was Shalakan's home, she was well-funded, though I'd have to ask whether that was by patrons or personal savings.

A woman emerged from the cube as my skimmer landed a short walk away. She was lithe and round-faced: the kind of combination that might have tempted me to call her pixie if I'd been willing to get slapped for it. She had the kind of eyebrows that knit together at the bridge of her nose, which might have given her a permanent frown if the metal disk affixed to the center of her forehead hadn't compensated. She wore a Riirgaan caste pendant on a chain over a green jumpsuit.

There was no chance of mistaking her for Shalakan herself, or for any of our own Dip Corps—not in that ensemble. She didn't seem to move like one of Shalakan's fellow Dance Pilgrims either. They had a liquid way about them. She was something else. Graceful, but something else.

Showing off for the pretty lady, I hopped from the skimmer and onto the dirt. Big mistake. My ankles felt like they'd just been riven with spikes. (Probably not a good detail to keep for the playback.) I managed to approach without limping. "Ow. Hello."

She covered her smile with one hand. "Ow yourself. Are you all right?"

"Just temporarily crippled."

"I can see that. Is this your way of establishing rapport with your subjects, Mr. Royko? Major muscle sprains?"

The language was Hom.Sap Mercantile, the accent Riirgaan, complete with their characteristic epic slurred r's. Whoever she was, she'd spent more time with the lizards than with other human beings. An exile?

I slapped the side of the skimmer, sending it back into the sky and from there back to its Riirgaan masters. "Naaah. Sometimes, with the tough ones, I go for compound fractures. And you're . . . ?"

"Deeply amused," she said. Then she relented: "Need any help?"

I took another step and discovered that my leg could take the weight with only a minimal degree of resentment. "No, I can make it. You can call me Paul, if you want."

"My name's Ch'tpok." That was a good accent all right. She managed that central hiccup better than any non-Riirgaan I'd ever heard.

I wasn't nearly as good. I almost choked on it. "Chuppock?"

"Don't worry if you can't get it on the first try," she said, providing an extra-careful pronunciation: "Ch'tpok."
I tried Chitpock, Cheatpock and Chatpock before establishing to our mutual satisfaction that Chuppock was as close as I was likely to get. She didn't take it seriously: I gathered that correct pronunciations from her fellow humans were as rare as generous compliments from the Tchi. By then we'd also established that she was an exolinguist, third grade, trained by the Riirgaans to specialize in Vlhani Dance. She said that she'd been a citizen of the Riirgaan republic since the age of four years Mercantile.
Still working out the limp, I asked: "How did that happen?"
"How else? Crazy idealist parents who thought renouncing their species made some kind of point about an issue long since forgotten." That really was an insistent smile she had, but anybody who grew up among the stony-faced Riirgaans probably had cause to overcompensate. "I'm not bigoted against Hom.Saps, if that's what you're thinking. It was all political, and I never bought into it."
"Parents happy about that?"
"Parents defected again a couple of years later, this time to some kind of sentient spore-colony. Last I heard they were still growing underground somewhere. They were pretty insane, really." She noted this with a friendly wink, establishing, or at least trying to establish, that nothing about these experiences had left her bitter. "Naaah, I recognize my species. I know my biological roots. I just don't use them for legal purposes. I stay Riirgaan because that's where my credentials are."
The phenomenon wasn't unheard-of; I knew of three wealthy Hom.Saps who had aligned themselves with the software intelligences known as the AIsource just to avoid the

Confederacy's ruinous taxes. And the entire Dance Pilgrim movement, here on Vlhan, was about human beings altering themselves to fit into an alien ritual. But it was still discomfiting. Despite being a fine model of her birth species, Ch'tpok's citizenship still rendered her legally not human . . . a status which would have kept her from being recognized as a human being in any Hom.Sap court. Without defecting back to her birth species, she would not be able to own Hom.Sap property, enjoy the protection of Hom.Sap laws, or even enjoy a legal partnership with another human being. I wondered if she'd ever traveled in human space, and just how much inconvenience she must have suffered along the way— questions that rendered her an excellent possible future neurec subject, once I was finished with the story at hand. But right now Shalakan took precedence. I asked, "Did your embassy send you here to meet me?"

"No. Dalmo and Shalakan have been letting me observe her last few months of training."

"Dalmo?"

"Shalakan's husband."

Nobody had mentioned a husband. It disturbed me. Who would get married when their greatest ambition in life was to die violently as soon as possible? "Where are they?"

"Shal's out communing with the Vlhani; she'll be back later. Dalmo's inside. He would greet you himself, but he's not feeling well today."

Ch'tpok lifted the flap of the sleepcube and we went in. The interior was bright, mostly from sunlight filtering through the cloth. It was sparse, too; a couple of hammocks, a food chest, a few instruments likely belonging to Ch'tpok, and one or two other boxes too small to provide much in the way of civilized amenities. The light came from a single hoverglobe. There was soft music playing: not human, as far as I could tell, but something a human being could listen to without retching. Shalakan's ailing husband was not lying in bed, as I'd expected, but standing on one leg. The other leg and everything from the waist up extended parallel to the ground, facing downward, like a body lying on an invisible mattress. Thin, sunken-cheeked, sweaty, and hollow-eyed, he bore the look of a man whose ailments had set in a lot earlier than just today, but he seemed comfortable enough, even if, like me, he belonged to that unfortunate subspecies of sleeper afflicted with terminal drool-mouth. He wore only a thin gray cloth around his waist. His arms, spread out at his sides like wings, each displayed several joints too many; they undulated gently as he slept, the contractions moving from shoulders to fingertips in waves.

My aching bod felt all the more inadequate as I sank into a seated position on the food chest. "That's him, I guess."

"That's Dalmo," Ch'tpok said, adding an unnecessary: "He's a Dance Pilgrim too."

At least that explained how he could bear a suicidal wife; he had the same odd sense of priorities. "How come he's not out with the missus?"

Ch'tpok's smile didn't falter, even as her eyes turned grim. "The Vlhani didn't invite him."

"This party's for Selected only?"

"Uh huh. Last-minute choreography."

I tried to imagine the alien protocols that dictated how Shalakan should move one way, and not another, while dancing herself to death. It knew it made a difference to the spiders; it was the basis of their greatest cultural artifact. But did it make a difference to Shalakan? Did she feel the rightness of these last-minute instructions? Did she change a twitch and say, oh, yes, you're right, that part always bothered me, thanks for helping me finally get it right?

And what about Dalmo? "Doesn't it bother him? Even a little?"

"Not . . . really," said Dalmo. (I attributed his slow speech to his illness, but I soon learned he always spoke like a drunk, or like a man trying to sound drunk. The words left his mouth at irregular intervals, like prisoners escaping in shifts to avoid the attention of guards.) "Mister Royko," he said, and licked his lips. There was an especially long pause as he parsed the rest of the sentence. "My wife has important work to do. Good morning, Chuppi."

It happened to be late afternoon. If Dalmo had gone to sleep the night before, he'd been unconscious for most of a day. But Ch'tpok humored him: "Good morning, Dalmo. Feeling better?"

"Yes." He paused. "Never felt bad. Calculating. Had to work out some variables."

"I figured," Ch'tpok said. "Any luck?"

"Some. Real progress."

"Up to talking about it?"

"Need to dance first." He grimaced and lowered his other leg. His flexible Enhanced arms uncoiling, straightening, assuming fixed joints at elbow-height, he soon became an approximation of any other unEnhanced human—albeit a painfully thin one, with a lip that drooped to the right. I'd grown up in a habitat too poor for an AIsource Medical contract, so I'd seen what unprosthetized stroke victims looked like. It's a rare sight, some other places. Dalmo walked like that, too: no obvious paralysis, but with the slow deliberation of a man for whom every step required careful planning. Ch'tpok hovered close as if she feared he'd fall. I supposed it wasn't hard to see why the Vlhani hadn't cast him in the great honking suicide-show; they needed graceful dancers, and this poor shmo could barely move.

I almost didn't want to follow them outside, for fear he'd mistake my recently-acquired limp as mockery. But I did. No point in alienating the hubby.

Out in the twilight, Dalmo unfolded again, tripling his height, becoming a torso that bobbed like a puppet at the center of four looping and twirling limbs. He showed nothing approaching the grace of a Vlhani, or even of those humans who'd made themselves enough like Vlhani to earn a place in the Ballet, but his performance was still impressive enough, especially the way he made those outstretched arms seem to bubble and twist like vapor buffeted by a strong wind.

"See?" he said, with strain. "I parsed it. I made it work. It's progress."

"I believed you," Ch'tpok said.

"I'll have to show Shal. She should know."

Ch'tpok hesitated a few seconds before answering. "You're right."

Dalmo displayed some more moves, all slow, all impossible for normal human physiology, all well within the peculiar faux-Vlhani anatomy that the pilgrims try so hard to achieve. The performance hurt to watch, but not because of the contortions themselves; I had already seen other Enhanced pilgrims twist themselves into even greater knots. Watching Dalmo hurt more because moving that way clearly cost him more. And it hurt for another reason, too: familiarity. There was something about the hold his art had on his life, that felt like an old friend I'd abandoned a long time ago.

He must have spotted my sympathetic pain. "You like to dance, Mr. Royko?"

I tried to match his flippant tone. "I know a waltz or two."

"Any good at them?"

"Well," I smiled, "Not according to any woman who's ever endured my tries."

His limbs twirled in great jagged jerks. "Nothing Vlhani?"
It was a joke. He had to see I wasn't physically equipped
for it. "Sorry."

"Pity." His limbs retracted, drawing closer to his body. "I
hope you're not one of those people who think we're crazy for
doing this."

"Like Ambassador Croyd?" I said.

"You met him? I'm sorry to hear that. He's exactly the
kind of closed-minded bigot I would have expected the Dip
Corps to send out here. They don't post anybody who
wouldn't like to shut the Ballet down. He won't even keep an
open mind. Just calls us crazy cultists and turns his back
whenever we try to share what we know."

"Sounds like him all right," I said. "If you leave out his
nudity."

Dalmo clucked. "He's still doing that? Ah well. And
what's your opinion, Mr. Royko? Of the dance, not the ambassador's unmentionables."

"I haven't made up my mind yet."

"Sometimes, I don't think I've made up my mind either."
He expanded his limbs again. "This isn't an easy thing to
want to do with your life. It isn't a normal thing to want. It's
especially hard to justify when the people questioning you
don't understand the only language capable of providing answers. But the explanation's in the Ballet. The Vlhani see it.
Isadora saw it. Shal and I see it. I would be overjoyed to make
you see it, too, Mister Roy."

That's as far as he got. He froze in position before fin-
ishing my name, the unspoken ". . . ko" a breath stuck in his
throat.

I waited, but the rest of the sentence did not seem imminent. After a moment, I turned to Ch'tpok and saw tear-
tracks on her cheeks that shone red from the setting Vlhani

sun. Her smile was still there, still as unforced as before, but now informed by a sadness as complicated as the Ballet itself. She said: "Are you beginning to see the nature of his problem?"

# 4.

Back inside the sleepcube, Ch'tpok described Dalmo's ailment as a matter of incompatible software.

The dance that comprises everyday Vlhani language is easy enough for those born to it. The Ballet is no doubt more difficult, but it's just an advanced application of the same basic tools. They have the whips. They have neural pathways capable of manipulating them. They have brains evolved to parse a complex language that expresses multiple-level data streams via the wave-form oscillations of their flexible limbs. They can understand it because it's how they're built. They evolved that way.

We, on the other hand, evolved somewhere else.

The first Dance Pilgrim, Isadora, demonstrated by vivid example that certain human beings were not only capable of understanding the Ballet, but somehow vital to its continuing development as the centerpiece of the Vlhani culture.

This, of course, made no sense. Why would random individuals from a totally different species that evolved three hundred light years away have such a freakish understanding of a ritual that the greatest linguists and behaviorists of a dozen other sentient species were still unable to parse?

It was impossible.

It couldn't be true.

There was no way for it to be true.

But Isadora proved that it was.

And the pilgrims who came after her showed that she wasn't a one-of-a-kind fluke. Most of them were not much more than the children Ambassador Croyd alleged them to be: adolescents, or post-adolescents. But alerted to the Ballet's existence by the holos and neurecs distributed throughout Hom.Sap space, before the Confederacy had a chance to appreciate the forces this would set in motion, all of these people saw something vital in the Ballet, something that had to be preserved—something that only their own participation could fix.

Alas, even those humans who possessed the raw talent couldn't manage the dance without compensating for the limitations of human physiology.

A Vlhani whip is many thousands of times more flexible than the most elastic cord available to humanity, with flexible segments less than a tenth of a millimeter apart, and muscle/joint combinations facilitating an almost unlimited range of movement between them. The average Vlhani possesses a dozen other whips just like it. Creating prosthetics for human use was a serious mechanical problem, but the operating software was a real bitch. Since we've never been wired to manipulate a thicket of limbs that bend in that many places, let alone to move them with such coordinated grace they can function as performance elements in a complex and demanding art form, humans driven to dance Vlhani need AI and bionics to manage it. The unknown agencies responsible for providing the pilgrims with their Enhancements—agencies the Confederacy would have liked to identify and prosecute—dealt with the problem by installing networks of sophisticated micro-controllers, which constantly perform the millions of tiny calculations necessary to translate a human dancer's imagination into a Vlhani dancer's grace.

It's a hideously complicated process that needs direct communication with the nervous systems involved.

According to Ch'tpok, the system still had a long way to go. "The Enhancements work," Ch'tpok said. "Just not very well. Dalmo's nervous system resists the interface."

"Tissue rejection?" AIsource Medical had licked that problem, but human surgeons still encountered it once in a while.

"No," Ch'tpok said. "Software problems."

"Does it happen a lot?"

"Too often," she said. "Dalmo freezes up several times a day. Sometimes for hours. Data traffic while he plots his movements. He has to make millions of calculations just to choreograph a few seconds of Vlhani dance. Even normal human movement isn't easy for him, which is why he has so much trouble walking and talking. It's a fairly common problem among the pilgrims."

"I never heard of it."

"I'm not surprised. Your government may frown on it, but most of human space still glamorizes the Ballet, sees it as something beautiful and even transcendent. Your literature tends to focus on the famous successes like Shalakan or the lost, sainted Isadora." She rolled her eyes in case I didn't get the sarcasm. "But about thirty percent of those who arrive here with Enhancements also suffer some kind of degenerative neurological impairment."

All the pilgrims I'd seen, in the various crèches and settlements I'd visited, had possessed whipdance Enhancements in perfect order. "Where do they keep the disabled ones?"

"Various places around Vlhan. Inside Vlhani hives. They tend not to mix."

"And they can't be fixed? Ever?"

"Hom.Sap medicine can't. Neither can Riirgaan. Even the AIsource Medics say it's impossible. Maybe the folks who originally made the installations could—but they don't provide any of these poor people with the means to contact them for warranty work."

"Because they're afraid of being exposed and shut down," I said.

"You got it," said Ch'tpok.

It made grim sense. Vlhan may have been a sovereign world, unbound by human law, but the Hom.Sap Confederacy still remained dedicated to putting those responsible for facilitating the Dance Pilgrims out of business. Any pilgrim who left the planet could lead our agents right back to them.

Even so, keeping the surgery underground still seemed a cold precaution in the face of somebody whose Enhancements seemed easier to classify as Disabilities. I peered out the window at Dalmo. He had become unfrozen, his limbs spiraling around him in gestures that communicated both exuberance and frustration. "Thirty percent."

"Yes," said Ch'tpok. "Most worse off than him, with nothing to show for it."

I juggled half a dozen possible follow-up questions before settling on the certainty I heard in Ch'tpok's voice. It was the sound of a woman who lived close to this subject, and in her own personal way, considered it Sacred: the sound that had been in her voice all day. I put a few things together and came to a realization I'd been building since my arrival. "And you're not here to study Shalakan, are you? You're not even here to study the Vlhani. You're here for Dalmo."

Her nod was placid. "That's right. I am."

"Why?"

"Because he's the visionary."

The word surprised me. "Visionary?"

"The only kind that means anything on this world. The Vlhani kind." She held my solemn stare, then flashed her insistent smile again. "You'll see."

# 5.

The hours were pleasant but frustrating. Ch'tpok turned out to be the kind of charming conversationalist who specializes in making sure little of value is actually said. I liked her. I had a good time speaking to her. But she provided me with precious little data I didn't already have.

She apologized again for Shalakan's lateness. I told her again that it was okay.

She described the nature of Dalmo's impairments in more detail than my own technophobic education allowed. I pretended to understand.

She made the same grandiose claims about the Ballet's significance that the Dance Pilgrims and her own government's translation project had made a thousand times before. She failed to persuade me.

At one point she quizzed me about my profession. Where had I been? What had I seen? Had I downloaded anything that got distributed in Riirgaan space? I told her about my biggest coup to date, a spectacular close-up view of a bloody political assassination so carefully orchestrated by the opposition party that its scheduled time and location were actually posted in advance via hytex. Then I dove back into my own questions. What I got in return was charm, and very little that differed from the Pilgrim party line.

We heard the first Vlhani three hours after nightfall. People who don't live on planetary deserts can't really appreciate how dark it had become. With the exception of the dim circle of yellow light that surrounded the Dalmo/Shalakan residence, there was nothing, from unseen horizon to unseen horizon, that gave off or reflected any illumination at all. It imparted a terrific sense of isolation, more psychological than sensual, which made it impossible to catch on neurec even

101

with the gains set on full: a lot like being in a locked closet without any doors.

Nor could I gauge the distances of the sounds carried by the cool evening air—the whispering thwuf-thwuf-thwuf made by the pointed ends of many Vlhani whips spearing the earth for traction could have been either meters of kilometers away. I wondered how many there were and if they approached from all directions. Aware that this particular sound hadn't always meant good news for the human beings who heard it (as in the Embassy Massacre of a few years earlier), I even felt a twinge of fear.

But Ch'tpok led me outside, to a spot only meters from the immobile Dalmo. His face, lit on one side by light from the sleepcube, was a pale yellow crescent, glistening where beads of sweat had collected during the day. His eyes had turned toward the desert to follow the thwuf-thwuf-thwuf moving closer with every breath.

"Look," Ch'tpok murmured.

The first Vlhani became visible only as a spot of yellow light: an image of the sleepcube, reflected off the smooth chitin of its great round head. That head, almost an arm's-length across, came into focus a heartbeat later, bobbing along atop four striding whips while three others gestured wave-forms in the open air. It bypassed Dalmo, moved toward us, and undulated its whips at length.

"A greeting," Ch'tpok said. "An acknowledgment. An offer of peace."

"What do we say back?"

"We don't have to say anything. We're not wearing whip-harnesses." That was a Riirgaan invention which, when worn, allowed diplomats to mimic Vlhani movement enough to permit some basic communication. "UnEnhanced people are more or less mute as far as they're concerned, and that it would be silly to expect a response. As long as we do nothing to the contrary, it will assume we got the message."

The Vlhani moved away from us and approached Dalmo. Extending its whips to their full length, lifting its head thirty meters into the air, it stepped over Dalmo and spiked the dirt on all sides of him, imprisoning him in a cage of its own sinuous limbs.

Another yellow reflection popped out of the darkness. Another Vlhani. This one didn't bother to pay its respects to us, probably because its cousin had already taken care of that formality. This one went straight to the living structure that now enclosed Dalmo, and extended a pair of whips inside. They touched Dalmo's cheeks, then withdrew. The newcomer moved aside, not returning to the darkness, but instead waiting as a third and a fourth and a fifth Vlhani also emerged from the desert to caress the altered man's face.

By the time the sixth Vlhani showed up, I knew I was in for a parade that might last a while. "What are they doing?"

"What do they look like they're doing?" Ch'tpok asked.

"I don't have the slightest idea. I don't know Vlhani."

"I don't know it either; this thing," she tapped the silver memory disk on her forehead, "gives me the best working reference my people could compile, but I don't need its help to understand what I'm seeing. Come on, you have eyes. What is this?"

I didn't much like the sensation of being quizzed like a primary-schooler in the prep classes before his first upload. "Are they worshipping him?"

"Good guess. But you're not quite right."

"Where am I off?"

"They're worshipping something."

The Vlhani marching out of the desert all approached Dalmo with clear and unmistakable reverence. But what could be drawing them, if not Dalmo himself?

Ch'tpok moaned with frustration. "Think, Paul. Vlhani don't believe in gods, as far as we can tell, and they're far too smart to worship humans."

"Riirgaans, then?"

She laughed. "Nice try. No, that wasn't species chauvinism. They don't worship us either."

Us, I thought. Another indication of how deeply she identified with her adopted people. "Then what?"

"Come on. It's not hard to figure out. What's their big ritual? The only thing they find sacred?"

"The Ballet?"

"See? It wasn't hard."

"But Dalmo's not in the Ballet."

"That's right. And he won't ever be. He can't process the variables that quickly."

"Then why would they give him such special attention?"

"Because he's still the dance."

I still didn't get it, and I'd run out of time to complain about it. Because the next shape to emerge from the darkness was Shalakan herself.

# 6.

My briefing on Shalakan had included holos taken on the day the Vlhani first selected her.

Like most of the humans chosen, she was barely out of her childhood at the time. She had been a skinny kid not far into her late teens, with eyes too close together and a chin that came to a point; the brief interviews she'd permitted at the time had painted her as a dazed laureate indeed, neither honored nor thrilled but instead overwhelmed that the future she had sought was hers. Back then, her answers to even the simplest questions had been a series of inarticulate sentence fragments isolated by oppressive silences. She'd ultimately chosen to express her feelings the Vlhani way . . . and when she'd danced, following an alien choreography that shouldn't have resonated among humans, she had seemed not only Enhanced but Divine. Her arms and legs, human enough at rest, had elongated and circled her in great, swooping spirals so filled with purpose that it was next to impossible to watch them, even on holo, and not wonder if there was music the average human being was unable to hear.

That had been two years ago.

It was now several surgeries later. None had anything to do with augmenting her fitness for the Vlhani ballet; she'd possessed all that equipment at the moment of choosing. The overwhelming impression given by the newest changes, between the fresh green glow of her eyes and the amoebic tattoos in constant motion beneath the exposed skin of her arms and legs, was shallow exoticism for its own sake. There had been imaginative things done to her breasts, her nose, her hands, her hair, all of which had given her a precious, fussed-over beauty of the sort desired by anybody who courts fame above all things. But as she approached her husband, her flexible arms twisting above her head in the wave-forms of Vlhani dance, the changes seemed less vain than defiant: bids to accentuate her humanity even as she gave herself up to this most alien form of speech.

Then she spotted Ch'tpok and me, patted Dalmo's arm, and moved toward us, her Enhanced legs bearing her upper body with grace so total that she didn't even seem to be walking. She was more like a princess being transported by palanquin.

She nodded Ch'tpok's way, using a Riirgaan honorific: "Hello again, Learned One." Something had been done to her voice too; it had been doubled, trebled, giving every word she spoke the resonance of a Greek chorus.

"Hello," Ch'tpok said. She still smiled, but now there was no warmth behind it; it was just the polite rictus of a woman turning civility into a putdown.

Shalakan turned to me next. "You're the neurec man, right?"

"That's right," I said, calculating how all this body tinkering would play for my mass audience. "Paul Royko."

She shook my hand; though I knew hers to be artificial, there was nothing about its touch that would have alerted me had I not already known. It felt real enough, perhaps even delicate: warmer than the usual touch, but that could be easily explained as leftover heat from a day spent beneath the desert sun. Even so, the moment of contact felt more like a caress: a combination of the added flexibility her Enhancements provided her, and what was probably a deliberate attempt to spike her sex appeal for the neurec. I saw through it at once, and didn't care: it still worked on me. "I'm so sorry I'm late, Mr. Royko. The Ballet is fluid, you know. It always requires adjustments, up to the very moment of performance."

I almost coughed. "So I've been told."

"It will be worth it the day we dance," she said. "You'll see."

The passion in her eyes was that of a woman eager for the moment of her own extinction; it ended my momentary attraction, but only just. She was that good.

I was certain this would be a popular neurec.

"I wasn't told how much you'd changed since your last holos."

She glanced at the recombinant tattoo extending pseudopods along one arm. "It's nonsense, I know. Vanity. The spiders have no use for such things, but I thought it might be useful."

"Why?"

"Because, as a showman like yourself should know, it's precisely the kind of flashy surface detail that fascinates human beings. However long it takes the various recordings of this performance to get past customs—and you know they will, Mr. Royko; the Confederate embargo's a joke—looking like this will ensure them the proper degree of attention in Hom.Sap circles."

"And that's important to you? The fame?"

"No," she said. "But the next generation of human dancers has to come from somewhere."

Her gaze flickered toward Ch'tpok. I saw no warmth in either that look or the look Ch'tpok gave her in return. I got, and recorded, the clear impression that only the respect prevented the unsheathing of claws. Then she addressed me again: "Whatever happens after tonight, Mr. Royko, I hope you take the time to see Dalmo at work. I know it's easy to underestimate him because of his problems. But he's the dance."

"Chuppock said the same thing. But she wouldn't tell me what she meant."

"Maybe she couldn't, Mr. Royko. Hom.Sap Mercantile's such an imprecise language. Maybe the concept would make more sense in Vlhani. But that's still pretty much all there is to it, in words or choreography. Dalmo is the dance."

I struggled to get that. "Are you saying he personifies it?"

"No," she said. "Only that he understands it. That he knows it all the way from the beginning, and all the way to its inevitable end. All its thousands of performances, before and after. And everything that comes after this point won't happen without him."

I tried a retreat to the story I knew about: Shalakan herself. "Can you tell me if you'll—"

Shalakan pressed the tip of her index finger to my lips: it

tasted of equal parts human skin and desert sand, not at all the synthskin compound I knew her flesh to be. "Spend some time with him later. Tell him it was his accomplishment, not mine. Tell him I danced because he can't."

Then she returned to her husband. She wrapped her arms around him: a phrase that would have been a mere hug when performed by most women but was pure literal description when attributed to her. Her arms encircled him once, twice, three times, looping under his arms and over his shoulders and back around his body again. She lashed herself to him so tightly she might have feared being torn away by hurricane winds, and she kissed his lips, his chin, and his shoulders, moving down along the frozen arch of his body with passion that made her malleable spine ripple like a banner. He responded, too: throwing off his paralysis, sinking toward the ground in a moment of absolute surrender, then bracing his limbs against the dirt and lifting both his wife and himself a full three meters from the ground where we stood.

For me, it was like seeing Sleeping Beauty, revived by the touch of her own true love . . . except with the genders reversed and the participants altered into something more Vlhani than human.

It was simultaneously the most repugnant and the most erotic thing I'd ever seen.

"They'll make love now," Ch'tpok said.

And that was the most unneeded explanation. "Looks like it."

I made no other move.

She placed a hand on my shoulder. "They're still human, Paul. They don't particularly mind if the Vlhani watch; they know the Vlhani don't care much one way or the other. But we should show them some privacy."

I'll confess to a moment's hesitation. The temptation to

record this particular coitus for neural playback was so over-whelming it burned. But even a neurec slinger is subject to appeals for decency. The words were resentful, but they did come. "All right."

"They'll probably talk to you tomorrow morning."

Dalmo and Shalakan were all over each other now, thirty meters up: bobbing up and down atop legs like stilts. It looked perverse and grotesque and epic and oddly beautiful. Despite all I would learn and all I would come to understand, it would be the only time in my life I'd ever wish to be En-hanced their way.

After we re-entered the sleepcube, and Ch'tpok activated a white sound generator to block out the noises from outside, I had the thought which banished my envy forever. "That's goodbye for them, isn't it?"

Ch'tpok, who had been getting us some buzzpops from her supplies, nodded. "Yes. She'll be going off with these Vlhani shortly after dawn. They're all headed for . . . you know."

"Damn." I accepted the narcotic but didn't patch any to my flesh. "Won't Dalmo be able to keep her company along the way?"

"In theory, he's allowed to follow along at a respectful dis-tance. Knowing him, he'll freeze up every few kilometers and get left behind. My government will offer him a skimmer ride to the Ballet as a courtesy (that is, if he even wants to watch), but it doesn't really matter either way as far as his relationship with his wife is concerned; once she leaves here, he won't be permitted any communication with her ever again." She flipped the buzzpop and slapped more against her bare skin; certainly more than I'd ever taken myself, even in the long hard times after a download. Her eyes glazed. "I really thought I'd be all right with this; it's all I've been thinking of since I came to live with them . . ."

I patched a buzz just to be companionable, and bit back a grimace at the feedback. Partaking isn't really recommended for a neurec slinger in record mode. "They're your friends."

Another daunting sniff by Ch'tpok. "Dalmo is."

"I noticed you didn't like Shalakan."

Now, a moment's distance. "I don't dislike her. But we're not friends."

"Why not?"

"She's a little too swallowed up by what she intends to do. Everything's about getting ready for her dance. Even her relationship with Dalmo is less about two people supporting each other than it is about providing support for her legend. Until now, I wasn't sure she would have anything left for him even at the end. I was hoping she would, but I didn't think—" She spread her hands, and sat down a little too heavily. "I don't know. Maybe that little display outside is for your benefit, too."

"What do you believe?"

She considered that. "I believe they're geniuses who also happen to be flawed human beings. But it's so hard to watch what it's costing them that I sometimes find myself wishing my people could come up with their own phrase for God Damn It. I get so tired of repeating the Hom.Sap version."

To hell with the feedback. I turned off the recording and patched as much buzzpop as I could stomach. "Yeah. So do I."

She showed enough class to not look surprised. But her eyes were questioning.

I heaved a deep breath. "You know the dumbest cliché about slingers? That we're unfeeling sensation mongers. That we're just sterile conduits, piping sights and sounds to the masses." I took another buzz, shivered, and went on:

"The truth is, most of us stumble into the biz running away from feelings we no longer want."

"Does it work?"

"Not really. We're not just paid to see it; we're paid to feel it. We have to be sensitive to make it real. We sometimes have to feel it so hard it hurts to go on. Otherwise, it's just pointless, sterile crap."

She saw from my eyes that there had to be more. "And?"

"And eventually we see so much we get jaded. We wear grooves in our empathy. And our networks start sending us to bigger and nastier places—catastrophes, civil wars, even assassinations like the one I told you about—just to break through to that part of us which is still capable of being moved." I cast a thumb in the direction of the sleepcube flap. "Like the Ballet. Like watching two people like that destroy themselves in the service of a cause I can't even understand. So yeah. I know what it's like to get tired of saying, 'Oh My God.' "

Ch'tpok chewed on that, then blinked through her tears and switched off the white sound, allowing an occasional gasp or whisper to make its way through the few short meters and thin layer of fabric that separated the two people inside the sleepcube from the two bidding farewell outside.

A moment more and she plunged us both into matching darkness.

And, settling by my side, said: "I think I'll go insane if all I'm allowed to do is listen."

After a moment, I said, "Me, too."

She nestled a little closer. "You won't take it too personally, will you? If we do something to pass the time?"

"Not if you won't."

I was a slinger, after all. And slingers were all about enjoying sensations without allowing themselves to be touched by them.

111

# 7.

What was it like with her? Considering that it was our first time, and the second was a decade away?

I'd like to say that we took it as more than a moment's distraction from the magnitude of the parting taking place a few short meters away. But I'd be lying. The truth was that neither of us was really there. I was accustomed to considering every sensation, every moment of experience, as an element in a larger story, that needed proper manipulation in order for all the proper notes to be played. I may have thought I liked her, but like all slingers I lived in the service of novelty, considered it my stock in trade, and was too detached, too jaded, to see my few moments with Ch'tpok as much more than that.

As for Ch'tpok, I don't think she really cared about me being there at all: I was just a useful emotional anesthetic that didn't work as well as expectations. I tasted the anger in the form of the tears on her cheeks, and though I could not understand the Riirgaan phrases she whispered both during and afterward, I could still tell they were not directed toward me. I would later wonder if they were words she wished Dalmo could hear, but I don't think that's what they were. They were curses, muttered by the lost.

Much later on, when we were both floating on the edges of sleep, and the sounds from outside the sleepcube had faded, Ch'tpok placed a hand on my chest and murmured another Riirgaan word: "Darrr'pakh."

I didn't open my eyes. "What?"

"Riirgaan word. Means teacher. A very special kind of teacher." Her index finger found a hair on my chest, played curling games with it. "He teaches a lesson that all Riirgaan children need to learn, and learn well, in order to earn the rights of a free adult in their society. It's a difficult lesson, I understand; it takes a full year, by their calendar, and some children fail. I won't say what happens to them, except to say that their productive lives are, essentially, over; they don't get educations, they don't get jobs, they don't mix with the general population, they don't have futures. They don't get a second chance."

A breeze from somewhere cooled sweat on my forehead.

"Did you take the course, Chuppock?"

"Of course. I was legally Riirgaan, and bound by Riirgaan tradition."

"And?"

She tapped my chest again. "I was also a human being, and I failed."

The regret in her voice was so palpable I searched for her other hand, found it, gave her a reassuring squeeze. "But you're here. They didn't do . . . whatever they do to the others."

"That's because I'm human. They knew that I couldn't. They couldn't penalize me for that. But they also knew that I could never be Riirgaan too unless I was at least given the chance to try. The end result is that I'm one of them all right . . . but I'm also the only one who never had to meet the one sacred standard that otherwise allowed no exceptions. So I'm also always apart."

I groped for something to say about that. "Maybe it's not the right place for you."

"Maybe." She let that hang for a while, perhaps challenging me to come up with something more relevant to say . . . then accepted my silence and sat up, facing the sleepcube wall as if hoping to see what was happening on the other side. I reached for her but she was just out of reach; and when I didn't try to pull her back, she moved still farther away, re-

113

ceding into shadow. Her profile became a distant crescent floating in darkness, like the narrowest phase of a moon searching for the place it was meant to orbit.

# 8.

I never got my interview. I never learned Shalakan's real name, or where she came from, or how she'd reached the decision that this one ritual was more important than any human endeavor. I probably shouldn't have expected to do so; in those early years of the Human-Vlhani connection, the dancers made a point of rejecting their pasts. Like her predecessors Isadora and Gabriel and Xavis, who had taken this journey before her, or Melaniherz, whose own infamous performance would follow, Shalakan admitted to nothing but humanity . . . and she entered the dance knowing that ten thousand worlds would pretend to be her birthplace.

By the time I woke up the next morning, staring through a thin layer of sleepcube canvas at a sun still bright enough to glare, she and the Vlhani had already fled for the Ballet, now only four days away. I lifted the still-sleeping Ch'tpok's arm off my chest, fell back into the same clothes from the night before, and emerged from the sleepcube to find the desert bright, stiflingly hot, and empty but for one. That one, Dalmo, sat cross-legged on the ground, staring at a horizon that had probably swallowed his departing wife hours before. Though his eyes were dry, his hands still drew obsessive patterns in the dirt.

I might have thrown a fit about broken promises, but there wasn't any point. This man, misguided or not, had just lost a lot more. So I sat down beside him, and for a minute or so shared a companionable silence. In this light, it was easy to see that he was just a kid, not much older than Shalakan, but his hollow cheeks and sunken eyes and the sense of unavoidable loss made him look ancient, as well: like a man who had progressed from childhood to dotage without a stop in between.

I asked, "Are you all right?"

"She's not gone," Dalmo said, his fingertip tracing a loop-de-loop in the desert. "She'll never be gone."

He sounded like every other self-deluded fanatic I'd ever heard, but it was not the time to make a point of that either. "Did she say anything before she went?"

"You mean," he flashed a grim smile, "anything meant for you?"

"Anything you don't mind me quoting."

"No. At the end everything she said was between us." He flashed a smile which betrayed no sense of loss whatsoever, then stabbed the earth with another fingertip. "What about you and Ch'tpok? We heard the two of you in there. We were surprised but happy for you. I hope you don't plan on including any of that in your playback."

For a moment, just a moment, I felt like smacking him. Then I got his point: none of your business. It was a sentiment that never had much success among those of us employed in exporting the personal business of other people to the masses, but I'd rarely had it so skillfully thrown in my face.

He relented before I could figure out what to say next. "You want commentary? The Ballet's her commentary. She'll speak volumes there."

"Before she dies."

"Yes," he said. "Before she dies."

"Doesn't that bother you?"

For the first time in our association he showed a little human annoyance at being pricked about his bereavement. "Of course it does. But you people all focus on that aspect,

like it's the only detail that matters. You don't see the performance that leads up to it. Or everything she'll leave behind
when she's gone."

I couldn't resist pushing him a little further. "Like yourself, for instance."

He erased his meaningless dirt-drawing with a sweep of
his hand, creating a fresh canvas, before starting again with
another pattern of interlocking swirls. "You want commentary, Mr. Royko? All right. Here's your commentary. I'm
going to mourn my wife. I'll miss her. But I'm just a person,
you know. A little sack of bones and flesh. An organism with
insight. The Ballet is something much larger."

I had already spent three days mingling with some of the
freshest arrivals, and heard a lot of what sounded like
pseudomystical profundity from kids desperate to justify the
obsession that had swallowed their lives whole. I wiped perspiration from my forehead and asked him the question I'd
asked them: "How?"

"Well. You know that the Ballet doesn't start fresh, every
year? That each year's performance is actually a continuation
of the performance from the year before? All going back thousands of years?"

That information had been provided by Isadora. "Yes."

"Well, it goes on from here, too. The role Shal plays this
year affects what the next set of dancers have to do next year.
And what the next set of dancers have to do the year after
that. Come back ten thousand years from now, after watching
every Ballet between now and then, and you'll be able to pick
out some of the themes she introduced, some of the sub-
routines she helped evolve." He drew another set of lines over
the first, eradicating the pattern he'd produced with another
just as meaningless to my eyes. "It's complicated, but it all
follows certain rules. Seen from the right viewpoint—the

viewpoint of a future Vlhani, for instance—you're able to read not only the meaning of those movements, but also how they must have been developed. With enough patience, you'll be able to piece together the specific refinements of all the generations that came before . . . working your way back, one Ballet at a time . . . until at long last you reconstruct how they must have started with a single dancer very much like her, playing a part very much like hers." He drew a third pattern in the same patch of dirt, and said: "If you understood the Ballet at all, you would know just how intricate an epic it is—how every single dancer who ever played a part, in all of its thousands of years of history, was a vital participant in the choreography of all the years to come. And someday, when it reaches its conclusion, and accomplishes everything the Vlhani know it can do, everybody involved in its evolution will have been a part of something transcendent. That's not dying, Mr. Royko. That's a little bit like living forever."

I asked the question that haunted everybody who had ever seen the Vlhani dance. "But for what purpose?"

He turned toward me, making direct eye contact for the first time. I expected him to be devastated, possibly even torn to pieces by denial. What I saw in his eyes was far worse: a deep, abiding faith in the Ballet, and an equally overwhelming pity for me, the outsider who would always be unable to appreciate it.

He said, "I wish you had enough of a vocabulary to understand. I wish human speech provided me with enough of a vocabulary to explain it. I wish I could dance it, even once, just to show you. I wish I could work out all the problems and let everybody know what I see, just once. It's just . . . too goddamned important. Not just for them. But for everybody. Everywhere."

He spoke as a man who knew the world was burning and

couldn't find anybody willing to listen to the warnings.

Maybe it was the moment. But I noticed something then that I hadn't noticed before: that we weren't alone after all. There were a pair of Vlhani a few hundred meters away, each standing still as distant from each other as they were from us. I didn't have to turn around to know that if I scanned the other direction I would probably find more. Sentries? Lookouts?

An Honor Guard?

My heart thumped. "Dalmo . . . why is Ch'tpok studying you? Why did she and Shalakan call you the dance? Why were those spiders making such a fuss over you, last night? Why do they think you're so special?"

He closed his eyes tight enough to make my own burn.

"Because I see it, Mr. Royko. Not just the little bits and pieces most of my fellow Pilgrims see . . . but all of it. Everything the dance means. Everything it's ever going to mean. Everything that has to be done to bring out its real potential. I just can't do enough to make it happen."

I struggled for words. "Shalakan said . . . something about her dance being your accomplishment, not hers. I almost thought that was just love talking . . ."

He shook his head. "Shal loved me for what I could give her."

"And you?"

"I loved her so much I let her have it."

He rose and walked into the desert, his right leg dragging. Partial paralysis, even now. Whatever he'd gained from the Enhancements cost him the pleasure of walking with confidence. I considered going after him, lest he freeze up again, somewhere out of sight, and end up baking his brainpan beneath the heat of the broiling midday sun. Somehow, it seemed like a bad idea. He may have been a damaged thing who would never accomplish that which he'd changed himself to do—but for this moment, he had earned a few minutes away from my eyes.

It also occurred to me, too late, that my link was still off. I hadn't archived a single damn word he'd said.

It was the first commandment drummed into the head of every neurec slinger: Don't Miss Anything. The turnoff option was a courtesy provided those occasional slingers who liked to have personal lives in between bouts of professional sensation, who may have wanted to eat meals or take shits or make love without the queasiness that comes from sharing the most intimate moments with millions of future voyeurs. Not all slingers used it; I knew a couple so burned out that they remained linked all their waking hours. I wasn't that far gone, fortunately—I liked being able to relate to people—but I was still pretty good about catching everything important. Missing the first conversation with the grieving, disabled husband was a professional gaffe of the highest order.

At the moment, I couldn't have cared less.

I returned to Ch'tpok, who had curled into a fetal position. (That was human, at least; I recalled reading somewhere that her adopted folks the Riirgaans grew their fetuses in straight lines.) The frown built into her face was even more pronounced now, but she looked peaceful anyway. I knelt beside her and put a hand on her shoulder.

She came awake with a nova-intensity smile. "Slinger Man."

"Riirgaan Lady," I said, brushing a strand of hair from her face. "Good morning."

"Is it morning?"

"Don't kill me for this, dear Chuppock, but it's more than morning. We overslept."

Her eyebrows knit tighter. "She's gone?"

"They both are."

A moment of discontinuity, as she processed that. "Dalmo too?"

"Yes."

She sat up in a hurry, clutching at the discarded clothing of the night before. "Goddammit, why didn't you tell me? You saw the way he is, you know he can't take care of himself! If he wanders too far, and freezes up again . . ."

I took her by the shoulders. "Not a chance. The Vlhani posted nursemaids. They know what he's worth."

She almost fought me, but then the message sank in, and she relaxed all at once, the panic giving way to a sadness so deep it almost qualified as mourning. I knew something else, then: something I'd already suspected but had not confirmed until now—that she loved him.

I hadn't invested any emotional permanence to our one night, but it still stung.

The angle of the sun seemed to change several degrees in the time it took her to face me. When she did, her eyes were defiant. "Do you understand how important he is?"

"Yes," I said. "I've seen it before."

# 9.

Even neurec slingers have childhoods. Mine had been seventy-five light years away, on a wheelworld called Eden.

You don't need to know the nasty details, but the place name was false advertising of the cruelest kind. The owners didn't want it to be pleasant, or even livable—just survivable. The indentures who sold off the months and years in their lives in exchange for one-way passage there discovered that the promises of a better life were just empty propaganda, produced by backers less interested in the creation of a self-sustained community than they were in exploiting the trapped tenants of a one-factory town. Intended as a slum from the moment it was commissioned, it wasn't called Eden by the people who had to live and work there. I won't repeat the name they did use. I follow the promise I made to myself, on getting out, to never utter the epithet again.

But while I was still imprisoned there, believing I'd die a wasted old man at forty years Mercantile standard, chol was one of the few forms of recreation we had. It was an indigenous song style, performed *a capella* and produced so deep in the throat that one visitor who heard it for the first time characterized it as a unique form of musical wheeze. Chol compositions were short, but soulful; joyous, but filled with the desperation of the trapped; tonal, but as expressive as any combination of words. More conventional singing styles were sometimes used to add clarifying lyrics. It didn't happen often. Chol didn't really need it, and it wasn't a great idea, in any environment patrolled by company police, to let those in power know what the songs were actually about. It was enough that we knew, and that we were able to take comfort in giving our pain a voice.

Everybody I grew up with performed chol, if they were any good. Most weren't. But there was one kid who happened to be better than good. Better than genius. Better, even, than magical. The sounds that came out of him had no business coming out of a human being; they stretched not only what was physically possible to sing, but also what was emotionally possible to say. He used to climb up to the rafters in the dormitories where everybody our age was housed, position himself at the junction of two cross-beams, and improvise music that immediately called Time-Out on all the casual brutalities we inflicted upon each other the rest of the time. Sometimes he sang, too. He was not bad at that. But he was unparalleled at chol; it was an art form that existed nowhere else, and he had a gift for it. Even now, a lifetime away, I think about the sounds he made and I remain convinced that, had he escaped with his instrument intact, he would have been known forever.

Alas, one major risk of the industry we trained for was degenerative lung damage, and this kid got it early. It didn't kill him outright. But his windpipe coarsened, his air capacity shriveled, and he lost the sounds he was able to make earlier in youth. I stayed too long to prevent it from happening to him, and I died inside the night he tried to perform anyway, producing a series of gasps and squeaks all the more pathetic for its recognizable connection to the music he was determined to make. The music itself wasn't gone. He knew which notes he wanted to phrase. By any standard of raw talent, he was exactly as great as he had ever been. He was even greater, thanks to the pain that had tempered him and given him so much more to say. But he was not able to call any of it forth. The music was now forever trapped inside him, like any other clawed thing that could scar the walls of its cage but would never be able to rip its way free.

I wasn't that boy any more. I was just the boy who had escaped not to achieve freedom, but to avoid the pity of those who had known him.

And who knew enough to recognize Dalmo as part of the same sad fraternity.

Dalmo wasn't merely a vital participant, like Shalakan or Gabriel or even Isadora had been. He had come up with insights even the Vlhani themselves had never been able to produce. He understood the ultimate point of the Ballet, appreciated what it meant, and saw the purpose of this thing the Vlhani and now their human acolytes had spilled so much of their own blood trying to construct. He even knew the special contribution only he was gifted enough to make, the contribution that, to hear him say it, might bring this single evolving work of art to fruition . . . and it was all a waste; his limitless talent just refused to connect with the limited tools he'd been given to express it.

Da Vinci with his hands cut off is still Da Vinci. Just Da Vinci in hell.

And Dalmo possessed just enough ability to let the Vlhani and his fellow pilgrims know it.

# 10.

Even with what I'd been through in my own life, I still didn't appreciate just how much the obsession cost him. But I got an idea two hours later, when he returned pale, drawn, and shaking. Three Vlhani came with him, hovering like nurses worried about the well-being of a patient who shouldn't have been out of bed. He didn't look at them, but then he didn't really look at Ch'tpok and me, either. He faced us, even saw us, but gazed only at something behind us, greater than us, that loomed untold lifetimes away.

"That was a bad one," he murmured.

Ch'tpok moved right past the Vlhani bodyguards and braced him. "It's all right, Dal. I'm here."

"Are you? Are any of us? Do you have any idea what the Ballet has to say about what it means to be anywhere?" His knees buckled and the Vlhani surged forward to help Ch'tpok support his weight. They moved so quickly that my own impulse to catch him came after the others were well on their way to carrying him back inside. "I . . . oh, hell . . . oh, damn . . ."

I followed, feeling useless. The interior was now pretty crowded, with three Hom.Sap and three Vlhani; the spiders, who needed ample space for gesturing and were effectively gagged by the low ceiling, held their whips close, their heads bobbing about with the restlessness of hyperactive human children struggling to obey a parental Shut Up. Dalmo lay on the ground, his pain-wracked form speckled with desert sand. His legs writhed like angry snakes. He must have clawed Ch'tpok, who knelt beside him fumbling with sedatives from her kit. I don't know how she could even see with that angry gash in her forehead oozing scarlet into her eyes. As for me, I did the only thing neurec slingers have ever been equipped to do: I stood there and watched.

He spotted me, though. "Mr. Royko! Are you there?"

I didn't move. "Yes, Dalmo. I'm here."

"I loved her! Do you see that, Mr. Royko? Do you believe me?"

I might have hesitated if not for Ch'tpok's eyes, beseeching me as Vlhani arms held Dalmo down. "Yes. I believe you."

"Then come to the Ballet! Make sure you watch!"

It was an unnecessary promise; Shalakan's dance was after all a major part of the spectacle I'd traveled so far to capture. But even if Dalmo hadn't been convulsing with the need to hear the actual words, Ch'tpok's eyes raged just as hot. I gave the answer they wanted. "I'll watch, Dalmo. I promise."

She put him down. He sank to the cube floor, his arms and legs unfurling like banners robbed of all motivating wind. The Vlhani bobbed over him, tapped their big black heads together in a gesture that might have been their equivalent of a distraught group hug, then moved past me to the exit.

Ch'tpok held Dalmo's head in her lap and sang. I can only suppose that's what she was doing, since the sound itself was more Riirgaan than human. It bubbled with glottal stops and atonal whistles, and was beautiful enough, though few human audiences would have been able to discern a lullaby.

It had the desired effect, because once his eyes closed he seemed to have found some kind of peace. It was a temporary peace, and the last I would ever see him have, but it was there nevertheless.

It was not at all reflected by the loss I saw in Ch'tpok's eyes.

She murmured, "God Damn It."

Thinking of chol, I said: "Yeah. God Damn It."

We may have been tired of using it, but sometimes no other phrase will do.

I watched her tend to him for maybe twenty minutes. Then I went outside and used my pocket hytex to signal the Riirgaan Embassy for a ride back. The skimmer arrived while Ch'tpok was still inside with Dalmo. I hopped aboard and left without saying goodbye, already thinking of the show to come.

# 11.

This year's Vlhani Ballet came together in the same natural amphitheatre that had hosted millennia of ballets before it. The hundred thousand chosen Vlhani swarmed out of the hills. The entire landscape turned black from them, the world dappling from the sunlight that reflected off their great mirrored heads. Avoiding only the northern rim, where the diplomats and observers from seven separate offworld species traditionally gathered to watch, they approached from every other compass point at once, moving in clean orderly sweeps over the edge and toward the killing ground where so many before them had died. Some stayed behind on the southern rim, as eager to watch as we were. Between them, millions of serpentine whips twirled above their heads in the kind of gestures that might have been prayers and might have been their equivalent of the excruciatingly banal small talk that has always dominated the last conversations before long-anticipated ceremonies.

They took their positions, milled about in the seeming chaos that Riirgaan exolinguists called the Primary Ascension, then began to move faster. Black heads bobbed up and down like bubbles floating on a sea of writhing snakes, only to descend again, beneath carpets of intertwined black whips caressing each other in ebony knots. The dancers came together, separated, leaped into the sky in waves, slowed down just long enough to provide contrast, then sped up, becoming blurs, turning the performance into a blur of undifferentiated motion. There were times when all of them were synchronized, times when they seemed about as well-organized as a riot, and times when all of the dancers made enough room for a single Vlhani to step forward and punctuate the performance with a solo that elaborated on themes visible in the Ballet as a whole.

It turned out to be one of the longest Ballets the Vlhani had given in recorded history. Some had lasted only a few hours, others a couple of days. This one was epic. It went on longer than any normal human spectator could have been expected to follow it. Even those offworlders known for their endurance had trouble staying for the whole thing. My fellow Hom.Saps, the naked Ambassador Croyd included, all attended in dour shifts. The Riirgaans came and went with enthusiasm, seeing nothing but beauty even as the first few deaths bloodied the floor of the valley below. Among the organics, the Tchi probably stayed awake longest, but they were so busy complaining about the lack of discernment on the part of the other delegations that they probably saw nothing at all. Only the hovering AIsource flatscreens stayed for the whole thing, recording billions of nano-movements in precisely detailed increments.

The limitations of human observation being what they are, most of the neural records provided at the time were fragmentary. They had to be pieced together, and well supplemented with AIsource data and the far more inclusive holos taken by the instruments the various offworlders traditionally set up around the site. Nobody saw it all, even if they were destined to spend years picking it apart.

I stayed for the whole thing.

It was an Enhancement I'd been provided by the linkcaster. Strictly temporary, good for one-time only: an implant that cleansed blood toxins and divorced me from any need for sleep for the entirety of the seven days it took this year's dance to progress from first step to last death. I couldn't see everything, of course; no human mind, Enhanced or not, could follow everything that happened on that one teeming stage. But I took in as much of it as any one person could, following not only the show before me but also the reactions of the various diplomats behind me.

I followed Shalakan's performance with special interest; she threaded in and out of everything that happened around her with an elegance that tried but failed to transcend the terrible, scarlet moment when the whips of her dance partners sectioned her into pieces. Too much has been written about how beautiful she was during that performance: the same things that were written the first year when Isadora fell, and would be written the next year when Melaniherz fell. If you want to know what it felt like to watch her die, you don't have to ask me. My neurec's still available for those who need to isolate the moment when one more piece of my soul chipped off and died. The bit analysis is available for those who want the moment-by-moment coverage.

No, I want to talk about the part that came after that, which few people noticed. The part that you don't know about because it got edited out; the part that should have been the real story.

# 12.

It happened on the southern rim, opposite the vantage point traditionally taken by offworld spectators, among the sizeable gathering of Vlhani who had come to this place to watch their brethren struggle and dance and die. There were usually a large number of Dance Pilgrims among them as well, but they had moved away over the past few hours, either retreating into the desert or drifting to other outlooks along the rim. Their exodus had been so gradual that, in the face of the far more spectacular show taking place down below, nobody had noticed the stage being set for a sideshow. Few saw it even when one row of Vlhani all lined up side by side, each extending a pair of long black whips in a gesture that reminded me of a formal salute. The whips all came down and stabbed the dirt together, forming a barrier which almost immediately rose to reveal a single human form, emerging from their midst.

I had been alone for the majority of the Ballet. That was good. Paying attention was my job. Distractions would have marred the playback. But Ch'tpok, whom I hadn't seen since the failed interview in the desert, now sought me out, snuck up behind me, and whispered in my ear: "Now."

I heard her voice but couldn't afford to turn around to see her. The recording would have been damaged.

I understood why she said it. She wanted to make sure I knew he was starting. But the reminder was unnecessary. I'd been waiting for this. I took the rangeviewers from my jacket pocket and watched the scene at full magnification.

It was a man, pale, naked, trembling, and not extraordinary in any way. He limped, dragging one leg, hardly seeming to notice as the Vlhani parted before him. He had eyes for nothing but the dirt.

When he reached the circle of open ground they had reserved for him, he just stood there, blinking, as if lost in their adulation.

His arms extended. He spread them wide, as if claiming the whole universe above him. He arched back, doubling over, making a knot of himself. He drew himself in, wrapping himself tight, forming a little personal universe with himself as its own citizen. He seemed capable of shrinking still further, retreating so far that he became a singularity, about to disappear in a single dot of compressed misery.

Then he uncurled, opening himself up, turning his back on wherever he had been a few short seconds before. He kept this up a long time, longer than just the increased flexibility of a Dance Pilgrim should have permitted. He made it seem that, however much he uncurled, however tall he managed to stand, there was still a part of himself huddled in the dirt. He bloomed and he continued to bloom and he made it a drive that would never be able to satisfy, and he did this in the midst of hundreds of Vlhani who for that moment all seemed willing to defer to him. And then he raised his pale ribbonlike arms and allowed the opening movements of his great unperformed dance to ripple down those arms in the sine waves that have always been the densest form of Vlhani communication.

It would be nice to report that his dance was brilliant, that in these hours after the death of his wife, his heartbreak allowed him to overcome all of his physical limitations and give a performance that dwarfed anything taking place in the amphitheatre below.

I would like to report that because for those few minutes at least, it actually seemed about to happen.

I would like to report it happened because it's what I was hoping would happen.

But the grace he showed was fleeting, the brilliance he

129

demonstrated was pretty much all untapped potential, and the masterpiece he seemed about to perform never took place.

Instead, his limitations came back into play. He froze in mid-gesture. Paralyzed, imprisoned by the moment, probably screaming silent frustration at the mutiny of his nervous system, he stood in place, his body contorted, his eulogy undelivered.

The tableau lasted for an endless few seconds before the Vlhani nearest him surged forward, shielding him from view, mercifully drawing the curtain with their own bodies.

I don't think any of the other observers paid the incident any special notice.

The rest of the Ballet lasted forever. One hundred thousand Marionettes and one altered human woman died for no cause I could fathom. Conscious of my responsibilities toward my audience, I willed myself to feel the glory. I'm told I was persuasive. Nobody enjoying the playback ever complained about my lack of sincerity.

When the Ballet was over, Ch'tpok was gone.

# 13.

The aftermath, on the offworlder side, was always the same in those days. The Riirgaans and the Bursteeni and the Tchi all scurried off to their embassies, to pore over the playback, in the vain hope that their translation programs had succeeded in furthering their understanding another percentile point or two. The Hom.Sap analysts did much the same, though not without muttering about the loss of another human life. The AIsource flitted about making no pronouncements at all, releasing no information beyond a strict accounting of the volume of data retrieved. Many representatives of many races expressed awe at the beauty they had seen. Some pretended understanding.

Nobody produced an actual explanation.

I forwarded my file to the network via hytex, hitched a ride back to the human compound, found an unclaimed bunk in the common room, and slept for fourteen hours.

Giving Ambassador Croyd all due credit, he waited until I woke naturally before having his two largest and most intimidating aides drag me to his office. They weren't very large and were way too soft at the edges to be intimidating: call them faux-thugs. There wasn't room for three on the tiny couch, but they still sat down on either side of me, their elbows resting against invisible notches in my ribs in a laughable effort to rattle my personal space. Croyd sat on the opposite side of his desk, his eyes red and shadowed, his shock of white hair now a wild starburst. Not only was he still naked, but he'd had something bready to eat recently: I could tell from the crumbs scattered in his thatches of chest hair. He tapped a drumbeat against the top of the desk, waiting for me to break the silence first.

When I didn't, he said: "I had an friend in the our first embassy to Vlhan. The one the spiders attacked when my predecessor tried to keep Isadora out of the Ballet. He said that the dirt was muddy with blood, that there were some people torn into so many pieces that the cleanup detail had to freeze the parts in cryofoam cubes. After that, he gave up thinking that the Ballet was art. He called it a mass suicide and wished only that there was something he could do to get every single Vlhani to participate at once."

I said nothing.

"She died horribly. She was torn to pieces. And all over Confederate Space, morons with nothing better to do are patching into your neurec, thinking they can see something beautiful and profound in that. Some will want to follow where she led. No doubt one or two will even die the way she died. Does that bother you at all, Royko? Even a little?"

I tried to speak, found my throat too dry to make a sound. After a moment I managed it. "A little."

"Too bad," he said. "That's not nearly enough to qualify as human. You're still a vampire. Did you find out anything about the Enhancements?"

"No."

"Nothing at all?"

"Nothing," I said.

He might have pressed it, but then he lowered his weary eyes and made a dismissive gesture at the two faux-thugs, too fed up the night after such a bloodletting to continue with the empty charade of personal fearsomeness. They rose on either side of me with such smooth simultaneity that there might have been an invisible string connecting them, and strolled out the door together. Croyd watched their backs recede with all the sadness of a man watching the departure of the only two friends he had in this world. When the door closed behind them, he shook his head. "You have colluded with a great evil, but there's no law against that on this world, so here's the best I can do. You'll be transporting out of here in seven days. Between now and then I don't want to see you, I don't want to hear you, and I sure as hell don't want to smell you. You will not receive any amenities from my staff beyond the bare minimum necessary to support your worthless life, and then you will get the hell out of here and never come back. Does that leave you with any questions?"

All my instincts warned to say nothing.

There was no reason to say anything, anyway. I'd sent my recording off. I had finished the assignment. I had no official remaining interest in the madness of everyday life on Vlhan.

So I rose from the couch and headed toward the door. But something stopped me just before I left—a sense of questions unanswered, business unfinished—and I found myself turning to face the ambassador's glare once again. "Sir . . . what do you know about a woman named Ch'tpok?"

He looked surprised. "That Riirgaan girl who was doing the study on Shalakan?"

"Yes. Except she's human, not Riirgaan."

His surprise turned to annoyance. "You know who I mean. What about her?"

"Tell me what you know."

He next tried dubiousness on for size. "Are you attracted to her, Royko? Is this supposed to be a dating service I'm running here?"

I waited.

Ultimately, he sighed. "If you've met her, you know almost everything we do. Her family defected a long time ago, over some piddling political reason or another. Then they defected from Riirgaan too, leaving her there to grow up with the lizards. From what I understand, she went through their education system, their coming-of-age rituals, their religious instruction, even this sort of sexless ritual marriage thing they do, and is quite open about believing in none of it. Their Ambassador, Hurrr'poth, considers her the Riirgaan equivalent of an adopted daughter. We've offered to repatriate, but she says she's not interested. Told me, the time we met, that she prefers her biological species from the outside; says we're more entertaining that way. Even chittered that annoying laugh the Riirgaans have. And why did I waste even that much time out of my day telling you this?"

"Because I need to talk to her again," I said.

He stared at me, not knowing how to read what he saw.

Then he scowled. "I don't like you, Royko. I'm not interested in your infatuations. I just want you off this world as soon as possible."

He was right, of course. I had nothing more to say to her, or to Dalmo.

But finding them still required less than a day.

# 14.

The Riirgaans had established their embassy by a lake in one of the wispy, ethereal forests that dotted Vlhan's temperate zone, a place as quiet as an unspoken thought that nevertheless constantly teased the eye with tiny flying things that darted from one hiding place to the next whenever they imagined themselves unobserved. The air was cool and misty, the cabins of the Riirgaan rustic in style but far too sturdy to have anything to do with the region's fragile wood. The embassy personnel drifted from cabin to cabin in twos and threes, chittering away in a variety of languages ranging from their own to Hom.Sap Mercantile; they noticed my arrival, in a skimmer I'd borrowed from a contact among the Bursteeni, but only one changed his routines to investigate me.

That one led me to their Ambassador Hurrr'poth, who gave me certain things I needed and had me escorted to their on-site hospital facility, and a certain bright green room where I found two figures lying in utter silence.

Ch'tpok lay curled on a mattress that had curled into a crescent to mimic the position of her body. Her eyebrows were knit with that special species of worry that occurs only in troubled sleep.

The object of her dreams drifted on his back on the surface of a flotation pool, staring open-eyed at the ceiling. The proportions of his arms and legs were uneven, but close to mainline human; a sign of his Enhanced anatomy, contracting to the positions it assumed at rest.

I wanted to wake Ch'tpok, but Dalmo sensed my presence first. His eyes twitched. "Don't disturb her. She needs her rest; she's been fussing over me all day."

The Riirgaans had provided me with a stool capable of housing the Hom.Sap posterior. Carrying it in, I parked myself beside the pool and looked down at Dalmo. "She cares about you."

Dalmo's body twitched and bobbed, forming ripples in the amber liquid. "No. She's like Shalakan. She cares about the Dance."

Was that bitterness? "You're also a man."

Were he not paralyzed, he might have shrugged; he managed to express the gesture with an eye-twitch. "I sometimes think so. I sometimes wish not."

There was nothing I could say to that.

We remained silent for a while, listening to the ripples in the flotation tank and the whispering rasp of Ch'tpok's breath. Then he said: "I wanted to dance for Shalakan. I wanted to pay tribute to her. I froze up. I fell mute."

"The message got through," I assured him.

"Don't humor me!" he said.

"I'm not. It looked good."

"You're blind," he said.

More silence.

And then: "You know, Shalakan and I met in surgery. Not before or after our surgery. Not in recovery from our surgery. During our surgery."

"You mean, while getting your Enhancements?"

A wry, if lopsided grin. "I'm not about to tell you who did it, or where it was done. I can't, you know. Silence on the subject is one of the changes they built in."

"Tell me what you can."

He coughed, without really needing to; Enhanced lungs knew no congestion. It was just the delaying tactic of a man trying to put off what needed to be said. "You have to

135

imagine what it was like. I was just a strange, lonely kid who thought he saw something in a pirated neurec of the Ballet, and was so driven by that understanding that I was willing to re-invent myself to become part of it. Contacting the Engineers was easy. They found me. But nobody told me how much the change would cost."

"What did it cost, Dalmo?"

"The body has to be rebuilt, practically cell by cell. The nervous system has to be rewired, given a new race memory. I won't insult you or the Ballet by saying how much pain is involved. But it takes two full Mercantile years, with the machines working on you every moment. You're only pieces for most of it. And you're awake throughout; you need a normal sleep cycle for the neural restructuring to take. The Engineers understand that human beings need company to endure it. Shalakan and I were given each other."

I tried to comprehend what it must have been like. "That must have been a comfort."

He was far away, now, reliving the tortures of a time now dead. "No. I was too weak. From the first day I screamed for it to stop. She was the strong one. She only screamed some of the time. She told me she loved me before I could speak a single sane word. But by the time I was able to give her anything, I loved her too. It was the only thing that got us through the recovery. That . . . and talking about the Ballet. Which we both knew would always be far more important to both of us than we could ever be to each other."

They were words that should have been drowned in tears, but his eyes remained dry. I leaned in close: "And then?"

"You know what then. She proved more compatible. She became a dancer. I became," he groped for a phrase, "a marionette with tangled strings."

"But she still stayed with you, Dalmo."

"She had to. Because while she had the physical ability . . . her understanding of the Ballet itself was only mediocre. She didn't meet Vlhani standards. She didn't have the right insights. Without me, there would have been no chance of her ever being chosen." He closed his eyes, keeping them shut for so long that I wondered if he'd fallen asleep. Then he spoke again, his words even softer than they'd been before. "So I taught her."

It was a good thing my neurec had already been sent to the publisher, because the weight of what I'd just been told might have burned out the playback. The blood pounding in my ears, I said: "What?"

"The only woman I've ever loved. Probably the only woman I ever will love. And I'll never be sure she really loved me, because we spent years giving her everything she needed in order to leave me." His eyes popped open and stared at the ceiling again. They were not quite aligned with each other, the way human eyes ought to be, with the one on the left trying hard to retreat beneath a droopy lid. Neither seemed to see me at all. He whispered: "If I didn't know what the Ballet is for, I'd hate it. If I didn't know what I still have left to do, I'd kill myself. But I don't have those options." His words became thick, sludgy. "Art speaks to art, Mr. Royko. The Ballet will never be complete if what I know stays in my head. I have to find another way. Get Enhanced again. Changed Again. And Again after that. Make them invent the right procedures for me, if they have to. Anything that's Necessary. It's that important."

"And Ch'tpok?"

"It's not love. At least not for me. But she's still the one who'll get me where I need to go."

I thought about waking her. I thought about dragging her off the amoeboid mattress and hauling her away from this literally damned man before she was forced to pay a price as great as he had paid. I wrote ten separate scripts for the eloquent things I could have said to make her see reason. But she was a Riirgaan who only happened to look human; I was a neurec slinger whose feelings were his stock in trade; and we were both on Vlhan, where sacrificing yourself to the cause of the great Ballet was not a sick abnormality but a religious calling.

Call it cowardice. Call it sympathy from a crippled artist who knew exactly how Dalmo felt. Call it even the curse of a neurec slinger, so accustomed to experiencing life as a spectator that concrete action of any kind requires more will than I had.

But once again I turned my back without speaking. I left the room, and Vlhan, and did not see her again for ten years Hom.Sap Mercantile.

# 15.

They were the ten busiest years of my professional life.

I traveled from system to system, covering the empathy drought, the search for the beast Magrison, the unveiling of the Michelard Colossus, the riot at the latest Vossoff funeral, even the banquet held at a house of an unremarkable old Hom.Sap couple worshipped by a cult of interstellar cargo loaders. I saw all the things I was supposed to see and felt all the things I was supposed to feel and even made myself a little reputation for the intensity of my coverage, which didn't quite make up for the sensation of dying inside, one piece at a time, as it came to mean less and less.

I didn't go out of my way to follow developments on Vlhan. It was, after all, a place I'd visited for less than two weeks, covering one story out of many—even if it happened to be one story that sometimes left me gasping after dreams I barely remembered.

But you couldn't live in Hom.Sap civilization without hearing more about the Ballet. It remained a sensation, despite the Confederacy's efforts to paint it as a monstrosity. The source of the pilgrim Enhancements remained a mystery despite the entire system treasuries the Confederacy poured into tracking down those responsible. The neurecs went on-line, the analyses flew back and forth by hytex, the human dancers who participated became celebrities and then gods. There were novels and vids about star-crossed romances with the Ballet as a backdrop, even a few that told the tale of Shalakan in terms that substituted sensation for insight. (Two of those theorized that she had survived somehow, and set up housekeeping with Isadora and Melaniherz and all the dancers who came before and after, none of whom died as we had seen them die; the fictitious bungalow grew awfully crowded by the time the number of humans approved for the Ballet exceeded a dozen per performance.)

I felt a chill the year the Dance Pilgrims training on Vlhan exceeded one million. Few of those were ever chosen for the performance, of course, but the Confederacy still cried genocide the first and only year more than a thousand humans danced and died. By then the celebrity phase of the movement was over, of course. By then the humans were almost as faceless in their numbers as the Vlhani.

The updates on Dalmo arrived without my invitation, waiting for me at every new destination. I heard when he married again, to Moralia, a second pilgrim woman who also used his help to qualify for the Ballet. I heard when she died. I heard when he became a teacher guiding other chosen toward their own final performances. I heard when he disappeared, and when he returned to Vlhan with even more radical Enhancements, intended to take him closer to the time when he'd be able to join the Ballet himself. The holo I have of him as he appeared at that time shows an emaciated male torso that sprouts half a dozen long black whips uncompromised by any resemblance to human arms and legs. The face is Dalmo's, but it's slack-jawed, heavy-lidded, idiot in its lack of emotional affect. The whips move in painful spasms, occasionally leavened by grace. The Vlhani surrounding him move with such comparative ease that they're like giants, unwittingly mocking the clumsy visitor on stilts. Ch'tpok's there, too: a shadowy observer in their midst, absorbing everything she sees with inscrutable rapture.

I never liked the updates. As a slinger I saw more than my share of tragedy, but the Dalmo updates felt different: like dispatches in the evolution of a skimmer crash occurring before me in slow motion.

Still, I might have spent my entire life going from disaster to disaster, feeling none of them, never stirring myself to a moment of genuine participation . . . were it not for the summons that called me back.

It didn't come from Ch'tpok. I was about forty light years away, returning from a sensational murder case involving defendants of four separate species, and a victim who remained conscious despite passing all of the clinical definitions of death, when my sponsors diverted my latest transport to Vlhan. They wanted me to cover Rafael, a young man whose charm and magnetism and passion for the Vlhani Ballet had rendered him the first Chosen dancer to capture the imagination of the Hom.Sap public in three years Mercantile. And while I did my job, and spoke to him and watched him perform and saw him die, he was not the real story any more than Shalakan had been.

# 16.

The growing Pilgrim city known as Nureyev occupied a stark expanse of shoreline between one of Vlhan's many deserts and one of its rarer freshwater seas. Why the pilgrims had chosen that particular spot for their promised land was anybody's guess. Maybe the Vlhani themselves dictated the site. Or maybe, like most fanatics, the pilgrims believed they could ennoble their cause with suffering.

Established soon after Isadora's dance as a handful of ragged tents, huddled defiantly against both the dry desert winds and the diplomatic firestorms that had greeted their arrival, Nureyev had grown into a boom town, with many square kilometers of cramped cubehouses arrayed in as disorganized a grid as possible. There were still a few battered tents scattered around the perimeter, a phenomenon common to many frontiers that attract new citizens faster than the old can be housed. It was in no way a self-sufficient community; the pilgrims grew only a little food and produced even fewer goods, surviving mostly on the support of the various alien embassies who continued to supply them with staples despite the Hom.Sap Confederacy's increasingly shrill protests that this only encouraged more pilgrims to show up.

There were about eighty thousand Hom.Saps in Nureyev, most of them Enhanced. There was also always a scattering of aliens, visiting from their respective delegations, sometimes mingling with each other, sometimes keeping to themselves, always observing the mysteries of Vlhan with a fascination that transcended species.

And Vlhani, of course. Whether alone or in groups, they moved among their followers with the self-assurance of gods on daily errands. Or if not gods, then something else: for as my skimmer banked over the central marketplace, the thousands of undulating whips on display resembled nothing so much as an inferno of writhing snakes.

Ch'tpok was, as promised, waiting at a table outside one of Nureyev's slapdash bars. Years of desert conditions, without compensatory rejuvenation by AIsource Medical, had aged her more than time could have. She was grayer, browner, more leathery about the eyes. She wore battered old Hom.Sap gear instead of the Riirgaan uniform she'd affected years ago. The frown built into her features now looked more like a scowl. But the weariness lightened when she saw me, and she flashed the same dazzling smile I remembered from so long ago. She didn't stand to greet me, but instead just raised her beer in a salute. "Mr. Royko. Been a lot of years."

"Not so many you can't still call me Paul," I said, as I took the seat opposite hers.

"Um," she said. "I did call you Paul, didn't I?"

"For a while," I said.

"I remember," she said, and for a moment we both smiled. "You know, you made the best recording that day. Some of the young ones, pilgrims I mean, tell me how inspiring they found it."

My expression must have been complicated. "Thank you."

"I'll call you Paul."

"And I'm still willing to try to pronounce Chuppock."

Her eyes darkened, lowered, and found something intensely interesting to study on the surface of her beer. The moment was fleeting, though; before the clouds had a chance to gather the sunlight broke through, revealing a determined cheer that must have taken her some effort to maintain. "My," she said. "We really have been out of touch for a while, haven't we?—That's not my name anymore. A while back I had a misunderstanding with my adopted species and was forced to renounce my affiliation."

That was a stunner. "You're not Riirgaan anymore?"

"Never was," she said, taking dark enjoyment in my reaction.

"I mean, legally. What are you, Hom.Sap now?"

"Wish I could say I was; it would be awfully convenient sometimes." There was another flash of darkness, dispelled just as quickly. "No. The Confederacy said it wouldn't let me reclaim Hom.Sap citizenship without first making a public statement renouncing my support for the Ballet. So I'm legally nothing."

I thought of what it must have been like to have no home, not even in theory; to have fewer rights than a representative of a species not yet judged Sentient or Animal, to have the closest thing to a consensus government in a thousand human worlds decide that the entire race would turn its back on her.

My reaction must have shown on my face, because she laughed out loud. "Don't look so damn stricken. People have been without countries before. And while I may not have rights anywhere else, the Vlhani don't care about stupid concepts like citizenship and species loyalty."

It was still exile, and it had taken more out of her than she evidently liked to pretend, but I declined to say so. "What can I call you?"

She made a Vlhani gesture, her right arm looping around itself in an uneven spiral. The move was lyrical, beautiful, and so fleeting that until she repeated it twice I wasn't sure I'd seen it at all. "That's what they call me."

Damn. She'd obtained Enhancements of her own. I wondered if she harbored any dreams of giving her life for the Ballet, and felt a pang at the idea: as brief as our past encounter had been, I still remembered her with too much

143

fondness to wish such an end for her. Wanting to protest, I tried to imitate her new name with a flappy arm movement and failed.

Another grin. "Call me Chuppock, if you must. This time it can even be the correct pronunciation."

"All right," I said. "Chuppock."

The pause between us lasted as long as some entire Vlhani Ballets, with nothing filling it except for mutual anticipation. A number of Marionettes and pilgrims passed by, limbs flailing in communication many times more frenzied but not any more articulate than our silence. There were any number of things I could have said to break the moment, but I just asked, "Where is he, Chuppock?"

She looked away, studied the rough wood surface of the table, and drummed her fingertips against the grain. "Is it just for a story, or do you really want to know?"

My answer was no answer at all. "What do you think?"

I wouldn't have blamed her for refusing to tell me. We really didn't know each other well, and the media have been disregarding pledges of secrecy since before the bygone era of paper.

But if there was one thing that personified all questions about the Vlhani Ballet, it was the genuine need to know . . . and if there was one thing that characterized humanity it was the equal, and compensatory, need to tell.

After a long time, she said: "Dalmo always said he'd see you again."

# 17.

The clinic was dim and humid and filled with a smoky something that wasn't exactly breathable but didn't have the courtesy to suffocate you either. The walls echoed with the cries of other patients, some of which sounded human enough but made no coherent sense. All of those interred here had been damaged beyond repair by the Enhancement technology; none had any hope of getting better.

The figure in the hammock was the worst. Neither Vlhani or human or the hybrid pilgrim Enhancements were meant to achieve, he was just a failure, twitching and writhing from his inability to achieve any of those lost but exalted states.

The torso I'd seen in the holo was gone. It had been simplified, streamlined, reduced to a knotty cable that might have begun existence as a human spinal column. Bags of moist something clung to the cable by straps. So did a human head, still recognizable as the man I'd met, but robbed of his passion and intelligence. Even the eyes were blind, clouded. I would have thought him brain-dead were it not for the hovering AIsource monitor busily translating every neural jolt into screens of data.

Behind me, Ch'tpok said: "They kept trying. They never did it for anybody else, but they kept taking him back to try again. Six, seven stages already: all making him a little less human, all in search of a system capable of expressing the choreography locked inside his head."

It was monstrous. It made me want to vomit. I choked: "And he wants it this way?"

"He isn't driven by what he wants," she said. "He's driven by what he needs to do."

I moved closer to the damaged creature in the hammock, not knowing what to say, not knowing what to think. I felt horror, awe, repugnance, amazement, and for a moment, the ghost of another feeling I couldn't identify. Retrospect, much later on, allowed me to identify that feeling as understanding. Maybe my own exposure to the Ballet had given me some awareness of the Vlhani plan; maybe I couldn't tell what that plan was all about but still understood that it was about something. Maybe my first glimpse of what Dalmo had become gave me some sense of progress toward the realization of what they wanted.

Or maybe it was just plain pity for the idiot who had damned himself to hell for a belief. "Can I talk to him?"

"He doesn't make much sense these days. But the monitor will translate." She spoke up: "Amplify, please."

The flatscreen obliged, flashing the words in Hom.Sap Mercantile while simultaneously speaking the words in a simulation of Dalmo's voice: "Dance. Future. Dance. Time. Heat. Vlhani. Dance. Spin. Leap. Dance. Death. Life. Dance. Hate. Danger. Death. Time. Dance. Love. Dance. Ch'tpok. Dance. Fear. Fear. Pain. Dance. More. Dance." It went on like that, the only pattern frequent repetition of the word "Dance." The tone was insistent, even desperate, underlaid with the kind of irritation that comes with explaining something to somebody too stupid to get it.

Ch'tpok said, "That's in Mercantile, of course. It doesn't have enough of a common vocabulary to express what Dalmo's getting at. Unfortunately, there's not much more for those of us who understand the dance. We play the neurecs and get something useful to the Vlhani once every three or four days."

"Is that enough?"

"No," she said. "He needs to move. He won't be able to do much the way he is now."

"Meaning more Enhancements," I said.

"Another generation. Maybe two. Yes."

I could see it, then: more years in torment, more disfigurement, more pain and exile. Was it even something he was still capable of wanting? Or were Ch'tpok, and whoever else she included in the mysterious "we," just torturing a lost soul whose potential, if any, had been lost several operations back? I opened my mouth to ask, realized while still forming the question that there was no way to phrase it without striking the barrier called faith, and shut my mouth, feeling trapped.

She seemed unsurprised. "You don't believe I love him?"

I turned, to confront eyes glowing with conviction. "I believe you love what you think he is. I don't know if that means doing what's best for him."

"Unfortunately," she said, her smile becoming downright broad, "we can't all meet here in a few thousand years, take a look around us, and know who was right."

"No," I said. "We can't."

She took me by the wrist and led me down the stinking corridor, past an array of other failed pilgrims in other states of degeneration. I allowed myself to be pulled along less out of faith that she'd take me someplace meaningful, than hope she'd take me away from so much wasted pain. She brought me outside and she led me across a bright sunlit plain to a sleepcube much like the one where I'd found her so long ago.

This one was empty but for a neural playback unit. She sat me down beside it, plugged me in, and placed a hand on my shoulder. "Paul? Do you remember, a long time ago, I told you about the Riirgaan Darrr'pakh?"

There were many things she'd spoken to me about, that were now lost; but that particular detail had stuck. "Yes."

"Well, mine said something to me, once, not long after I accepted that I'd never learn what he had to teach. He said that no piece of paper can bear words unless it's the right color to provide contrast with the ink. He said that just because the human mind was incompatible with his particular curriculum, didn't keep it from being receptive to other things. Even harder things." She took a deep breath, and gave the machine a glance that suggested she resented it. "Dalmo said that you'd understand. He said that if you ever came back I would have to show this to you."

I stared at the playback leads. "What?"

"Art," she said. "Speaking to art. A little gift from him to you."

I might have hesitated.

But then I plugged in—

# 18.

It was a recording of chol.

The neurec had been made by a genius at the peak of his abilities, capturing another whose sounds should have been entirely alien to any concerns involving the Vlhani Ballet. I had no idea how Dalmo knew that they would speak to me, or how he commissioned the performance. I can only say that the voice I heard was infinitely greater than I had been even on the best day of my life, that the tears sprung from my eyes within the first few notes, and that by the time I calmed down enough to listen I had discovered it was possible to miss hell if hell was the place where you were at your best.

And one other thing.

For the duration of that song, at least, I understood everything the Vlhani had been trying to express. I saw what Isadora and Shalakan and Dalmo had seen, what the pilgrims were desperate to create, what lesser visionaries like Ch'tpok and myself could appreciate only in fragments. I saw the millennia of Ballet performances as a single unified whole, creating a single, complex, exhaustively-annotated image. I saw what the image conveyed and I knew why the message had to be delivered and I understood why the Vlhani and all the humans who had begun to join them felt their own lives of minor consequence in the face of the ways everything would change upon the day of the final performance. I saw who in power harbored the secrets of the Enhancement engineers and I saw how those secrets were being kept and I understood the great colossal joke that was being played on the Confederate Dip Corps and its futile ambition to shut the Ballet down.

I saw all this and for a few moments I persuaded myself that I could use this knowledge to blackmail the engineers into inflicting their Enhancements upon me, so I could dance where all those others had danced before me. But that urge lasted less than a second. Almost as soon as it struck I knew that it was impossible. Even if I endured the surgeries, I didn't have what Dalmo had, or what Shalakan had. I didn't even have what Ch'tpok had. I could hear the music, for now—even if, like most complex melodies, its precise structure would no doubt fade from memory the second I stopped listening—but I would never be able to play the song.

It was a feeling I had felt before, upon losing chol.

The performance built to a crescendo. I saw the final Ballet, being performed on a Vlhani plain more than ten thousand years from now. It involved every single Vlhani alive at that time, gathered together from horizon to horizon, giving their all for the climax of the performance that had consumed their racial history. I saw, not thousands, but millions of altered humans among them. I sensed others, too far away for me to see: entire civilized worlds which had dedicated their entire populations to dancing these last few moments. I saw no indication that anybody would die in this last performance. I sensed only what all those sentients sensed as they raised their limbs for the last flourish.

And one other thing:

I saw that the Vlhani conception was flawed. That they were flailing about in a vacuum. That they'd never accomplish what they wanted to accomplish unless Dalmo pointed the way for them.

149

Why a human? Since it made no sense for a human to be able to accomplish what creatures evolved for this dance could not?

I saw the reason for that, too.

And it was the only part that frightened me.

As the song ended, I found myself on my hands and knees, shaking. Ch'tpok had her Enhanced arms curled around me in a sort of harness, holding me tightly and murmuring soft reassurances as I passed through the various stages of hysteria.

I said, "Thousands of years." Destroyed that I'd never see it. "Thousands."

Ch'tpok held me, and kissed me on the back on the neck. "But we'll get him there."

We, I thought. And knew it was true.

I would never dance.

But the rest of my life would be about making that final dance happen.

# 19.

Travel to a certain isolated plateau, in the southern hemisphere of the planet Vlhan, and you'll find the statue: a representation of a lone Vlhani, its whips contorted in expansive, frozen curls.

You'll wonder what it signifies, and you'll decide that it means nothing. After all, Vlhani Dance requires movement. A static moment like this means nothing to them, without the choreography that carries one position to the next. It's realistic enough, even lifelike, but utterly without meaning, to anybody interested in decoding the great Vlhani Ballet.

Chances are that you'll describe it a curiosity and walk away.

Chances are that you won't return at some later date.

Chances are that if you do you won't notice the subtle differences between its position now and its position then. Those changes involve millimeters over a series of years—each micro-movement carefully planned, and laboriously plotted by the one part of this enhanced creature that still belongs to a lonely and tormented human being. You wouldn't see anything if you came back a year from now. Or even a century from now. But give it time. Sooner or later, with all its movements plotted and memorized, all its calculations finished and all its plans made, the thing will come to life and perform its dance at the proper speed. Sooner or later, it will tell the Vlhani what they need to know.

That, Ch'tpok tells me, is when everything will change.

Until then, it's just a statue.

You might consider it a monument.

But you won't guess which kind.

# Unseen Demons

## 1.

The other monster sat at the edge of his cot, staring at the floor of his immaculate white cell. He held his hands clasped between his knees in a manner that might have signified despair in another prisoner, but which in his case seemed to be an obscene lack of concern instead. He showed no fear, no guilt, no uncertainty. He did seem bored, but not like he was oppressed by that boredom; rather, like he considered his confinement a welcome vacation from his more pressing responsibilities.

The other monster was a pleasant-looking young man, of average height and unremarkable build. He had pale blue eyes, sandy brown hair, and a corn-fed complexion. There was nothing about him that suggested hidden depths, of depravity or anything else. There was instead an undeveloped element of charm in his half-smile, and in the way he hummed currently popular love songs as he waited for his hour of judgment.

Andrea Cort stood at the entranceway of a meeting room elsewhere in the embassy compound, studying the other monster's projected image. Several times life-size, it dominated the space above the long conference table, haunting the forms of two dozen desperately unhappy indentured diplomats who had been haunted by the deeds of the real man for months now. They had reserved a chair for Cort at that table, but she remained the only person in the room still standing. It

153

had been her way, since early in life; as long as there was any way to avoid it, she tried not to sit in the presence of other people. Or eat. Or sleep.

As a monster herself, she was acutely aware that she had more in common with this other monster than she did with them.

The man in the projected image shook his head, as if enjoying Cort's self-consciousness.

Her brown eyes narrowed to slits. "This a real-time image?"

"Linked to his cell," one of the diplomats said.

They all avoided looking at the other monster's image themselves, as if afraid his madness might prove infectious. They also avoided looking at Cort, though whether that was because they'd learned of her own monstrousness, or because they feared catching some of the blame for this particular fiasco, was hard to say.

She hated having to read them; she wanted to be the enigma herself. She wanted them to see her as a whip-lean bureaucrat in black, professional with every breath, human only on occasion and then only by oversight. She wanted them to worry themselves into knots wondering what she was going to do. To this end, she kept her comportment severe. She wore sharp but functional gray clothing; she kept her hair buzz-cropped but for a single band that dangled at shoulder-length; she kept her expression blank and her voice distant, eschewing any attempt at charm. If this assignment went like all her others, the locals would soon call her bitch behind her back. That was, of course, exactly the way she needed it: not just on the job but everywhere else.

She gnawed the tip of her thumb, taking herself past the threshold of pain. "Does he know you're monitoring him?"

"Yes."

"Does he know we're watching right now?"

"We monitor him constantly. If you mean, does he know the Advocate's getting her first look at him right now, the answer's no."

Ambassador Lowrey himself, a dull career man whose true level of expertise was probably inversely proportional to his self-importance, muttered: "Not that he gives a damn."

"You have been holding him in almost complete isolation for six months standard," Cort pointed out. "I would have been surprised if a certain amount of apathy hadn't set in by now."

"But look at him. That's not apathy—that's not giving a damn."

She conceded the point with a nod. "What was he like before his arrest?"

The indentured diplomats around the table glanced at each other, silently negotiating the appointment of a spokesperson. A slender young woman in her early twenties provided the officially sanctioned shrug. "Polite. Well-behaved. Friendly."

"Dull," another of the diplomats said.

"That's it," the young woman said. "Dull. Not the kind of guy you get close to."

"No real personality at all," said another.

Behind that remark was the unspoken thought: Like You.

She appreciated that.

Ambassador Lowrey said: "I've heard his guards say he's put on a little attitude since."

"What kind of attitude?" Cort asked.

"The kind that comes from spending six months in a cell, waiting for the Advocate to arrive from Third London."

Third London was a wheelworld complex in Hom.Sap

space, the home of billions, which happened to house many human communities and the central offices of the Confederacy Dip Corps. An austere apartment in the administrative complex was as close as Cort had ever permitted herself to having a permanent home. She wasn't there much.

She clicked her thumbnail against her teeth. "He didn't seem upset when he was caught?"

"No," the young woman said, "he was smiling, just like that."

There was a chorus of general agreement, and Cort said: "Is it possible he doesn't comprehend what he did? There's still room in the Protocols for insanity exemptions."

"We thought of that while you were still enroute," said Roman Whalekiller. Whalekiller, her official liaison here on Catarkhus, was despite his fierce-sounding name a innocuous, round-shouldered stuffed animal of a man whose bright round face did not easily accommodate expressions of moral revulsion. His dislike of the other monster was so extreme that he managed it anyway. Aware of Cort's appraisal, he rubbed the back of his neck, sharing with her the degree of his aggravation. "We even promised him his choice of treatment facilities if he just helped us support the claim. But he wouldn't go for it. He said he knew exactly what he was doing, and would do it again in a heartbeat."

"Cocky little bastard is right, then," Cort said.

"And why not? He knows nothing's going to happen to him. —Frankly, Counselor, I think he considers this situation he's put us in half the fun."

Cort, who suspected the same thing, worried her thumb a little bit more. "You think that might have been the point? Embarrassing us in front of all the alien delegations?"

"That occurred to me, too; it wouldn't be the first time. But the slug doesn't have a political bone in his body. He's just having a good time watching us run around in circles trying to clean up the mess he made."

"A lover of slapstick comedy, huh?"

"And a genuine pathological sadist," Whalekiller agreed. "Never a good combination, Counselor."

"Especially not among diplomats," Cort said.

"And definitely," one of the embassy indentures said, "not during First-Contact missions."

Ambassador Lowrey muttered a disgusted, "The Bastard."

Cort wished the man would shut up if he couldn't progress to anything more helpful. She coped by directing another question to Whalekiller, who at least seemed to know what he was doing: "And what about all the alien delegations? What have they been saying about this?"

"Unofficially? They think he's right. He is going to get away with murder. They're not stupid; they understand the locals have limitations; they know why handing him over to them won't work. But that hasn't stopped them from painting us as co-conspirators trying to cover up the latest in a long series of atrocities."

Cort grimaced at the thought. The long history of human relations with alien civilizations, both within and outside the species, had always been a study in trying to live down the crimes of the past. Crimes like those committed by the man in the cell—among others—provided plenty of ammunition to those who said Hom.Saps had squandered the last of its second chances. Feeling tired, she murmured: "Are they at least going to give me enough room to work?"

"They'll make a show of it," said Whalekiller. "But they'll be on your back before you've been here twenty-four hours. Not much longer after that, they'll be portraying you like you're as big a monster as he is."

Cort remembered a night filled with warring shrieks, and thought: I am.

It just didn't make the task ahead of her any less impossible.

# 2.

Catarkhus was just another lumpy rock, dominated by deserts but seasoned with a mixture of inland seas and rainforests that formed a verdant belt around its equator. Andrea Cort had seen enough to sate her before leaving orbit. The skimmer tour Whalekiller had insisted on providing her on the way to the briefing hadn't served to endear the place to her any further. Nor did the scent of the air, which was neither acrid nor perfumed, but the kind of instantly noticeable tinge that every new biosphere manufactured for its very own. Folks who liked worldhopping cooed that such grace notes gave each new planet a special signature. Cort had always found that they gave her a headache.

She couldn't help it. She hated worlds. Having spent all but the first few years of her childhood in a safe wheelworld habitat, and having devoted the majority of her legal career to constantly untangling the disasters that inevitably took place wherever human beings were allowed to interact with naturally evolving life-systems, she far preferred artificial environments. They at least could be forced to make sense. Worlds, by contrast, repelled her—and First Contact nexus or not, this one seemed more repugnant than most. As far as she was concerned, the other monster had lent it what little distinction it had by murdering several of the natives.

His name was Emil Sandburg; the file she'd been provided contained all the empty facts about his life without explaining why he would decide to start slicing up alien sentients as a hobby. He'd lived twenty-four years Old Earth Standard, an economic refugee from some failed industrial cooperative on the edge of Confederate Space. His indenture screening had listed him low normal in empathy, low normal in charisma, low normal in imagination; a determined nonentity who just happened to score extremely high normal in inductive thinking. He had been on Catarkhus for three years, forming distant but entirely cordial relationships with the rest of the embassy staff; he was reported to be reasonably competent at cooperative relations with the representatives of the seven other spacefaring species maintaining first-contact Embassies here.

Everybody had liked him, in the sense that everybody always likes people who don't get in the way. Nobody could claim to know him. They had called him bland, forgettable, free of personality. Dull. They had seen no indications that he was in any way deranged. But now it seemed that on at least six separate occasions during his tour of duty here, he had descended into the underground colonies of the native sentients, isolated random individuals among the population, and taken his time cutting them to pieces. He might have indulged this hobby indefinitely if a representative from the Riirgaan delegation hadn't discovered one of Sandburg's murders in progress.

Cort was scheduled to talk to the Riirgaan in question later this afternoon, and she was supposed to have a meeting with the local interspecies council as soon as she produced her recommendations; if she was lucky, and the council was feeling sufficiently charitable, she might be able to establish some moral distance between this one demented human and the rest of the species that had spawned him. But it was going to be tough. After the Hossti debacle, and the (*Tone*)-Shtok crisis, and the embassy massacre on Vlhan—(three spectacular diplomatic incidents that had within the past year left interspecies confidence in the good faith of human beings at an all-time low)—the diplomatic community wasn't exactly motivated to give the perpetually bumbling Hom.Saps the benefit of the doubt again.

# 3.

The Hom.Sap Embassy had no jail facilities, so Sandburg's cell was a hastily-converted quarantine booth tucked away in the embassy's on-site clinic. The one guard was a skinny, and somewhat sheepish, first-year indenture armed with nothing but a cryogenic foamer; even so, he wasn't trained for security work, and the pretense at high security rendered him almost apologetic as he dampened the door field to allow her admittance. Having won her argument with her security-minded escort Whalekiller, she went in alone, noting a handful of real books and a scan-only hytex before the figure on the bed had time to demonstrate how he was going to react to her arrival.

It turned out to be with a shy smile and an extended hand. "Hello."

"Hello," she said, without returning either.

Sandburg let his hand remained extended for five full seconds before dropping it with a fatalistic shrug. "You're a new one."

"Just landed." There was no place to sit other than the cot, which she wouldn't have wanted to share with him, so she remained standing. "I've traveled a long way to see you, Emil."

He flashed a tentative grin, forcing her to upgrade her assessment of the smile: it was not warm so much as insolent. "Oooh. Officialdom."

"Andrea Cort. Legal Counsel for the Dip Corps Judge Advocate."

"Big-time officialdom," he said, his grin acquiring several

additional degrees of off-center tilt. "Took you long enough to get here, ma'am."

Cort, who had spent the last two subjective months of her life being sick to her stomach at high g, didn't particularly need to be reminded. "Well, I'm here now."

He appraised her. "I don't know whether I ought to be real happy about that, ma'am. I mean, you are a pretty lady and all, and I love your legs, but you were sent here to make sure I get a proper lynching, weren't you?"

This was the man cited as bereft of personality? His current persona was obnoxious, but that was as far from bland as he could get. "I'm not your prosecutor, Emil."

"Maybe not, but I can sure as hell see in your eyes that you wish you were part of the jury." He chuckled without bitterness at that, thus establishing himself as a man who expected to be hated but didn't give a shit. He patted the mattress beside him. "It's not a sexual overture, pretty lady, but I really do wish you'd sit down. Otherwise, I'm going to get a crick in my neck just talking to you."

He meant it to be disarming, but just being in the same room with him was enough to raise the acid levels in her belly. "There's a solution to that, Bondsman. You can stand. In fact, I'm going to require you to."

Sandburg rolled his eyes, but clapped his hands against his knees and rose to his feet with the air of a long-suffering martyr. "Yes, ma'am."

Cort wished she had a paper to look at, a docreader to scan, even a colleague to pull off to one side and consult; anything to delay the rest of the interview by the two or three beats she needed to compose herself. "I'm told that you were caught in the act of disemboweling a Catarkhan whose limbs you had already amputated; that in the time since your initial arrest you have confessed to committing the same crime at least half a dozen times in the past. I have also been told that you say you did this for no reason other than your own personal recreation. Is all of this accurate, Emil?"

"They've briefed you real well, ma'am."

She went nose-to-nose, so her words could burst against his skin in puffs of breath: "You enjoy killing things, Emil?"

His eyes remained amused. "Sometimes."

"Torturing them?"

"That's the fun part."

"You tortured the Catarkhans?"

"Not sure the word applies in this case, ma'am. Not with this species."

Neither was she, damn him. That was part of the problem.

"For the sake of the argument: you enjoy slow kills."

"Sometimes, ma'am."

"Do you only do it to Catarkhans? Or have you ever practiced this particular hobby on other sentients?"

He showed teeth. "None of your damn business, ma'am."

She knew then, as she was meant to know, that he had; that somewhere in his past, on some other world he'd known, there'd been other bodies left behind in dark places. He had probably enjoyed the usual childhood experimentation on animals, and might have taken down a few human beings before hitching his star to the Dip Corps, which gave him the opportunity to indulge himself with a wider variety of sentients. Maybe she could link him to some unsolved crimes in his past, wrest jurisdiction from the locals, and resolve her current dilemma that way—but somehow, she already knew that she would find nothing. A monster like Sandburg wouldn't be so playful if he thought the game was going to be that easy for her. So she smiled back at him, with equal unpleasantness. "All right. This is a Catarkhan matter. I'll confine my inquiries to the matter of the dead Catarkhans."

He nodded. "That should save us some time, ma'am."

"Why did you do it, Emil?"

"You ever stomp on bugs, ma'am?"

(She remembered a shattered and bleeding alien form, unable to rise, trying to ward her off with imploring hands: the face behind those hands so swollen from previous beating that it was nearly unrecognizable, the eyes still clearly those of a being she had once considered a second father.)

"You find that an appropriate description of what you've done?"

"Pretty much, yeah. Watch them for a while and tell me it's not."

"These so-called bugs were sentient beings."

"That's what you people keep telling me," he said, without any particular heat. The crooked smile came back. "Personally, I don't see it."

"Is that your defense? That they weren't sentient?"

"I don't know if they are or not. I just don't see it, that's all."

The bastard wasn't intimidated; he wasn't even worried. He knew that all diplomatic precedent placed him outside the reach of human punishment. He also knew that the very nature of the creatures he'd killed probably placed him outside the reach of their punishment as well. She had to hand it to him; he'd chosen a perfect species to victimize. But she moved closer to him and said: "You committed six murders, Emil. If you think I find anything cute or endearing about that, or have any interest in what you see or don't see, you're even sicker than I thought you were. I promise you, I will see you pay for that."

"A lot more than six," he said, still without any particular heat. "And yes, I did enjoy myself doing it; it's really not like there was anything better to do on this rock. But if you want me to pay for it, you do have a problem, don't you?"

"One I'll solve. You can be confident about that."

He yawned in her face. "Yeah. Right. I think we're done with this conversation, ma'am. I need a nap."

He sat down on the bed, rolled over on his side, and began loud, theatrical snoring.

Cort stood there staring at his back for a while, contemplating the attractions of pure, unadulterated sociopathy. Her work had placed her in close proximity with several specimens of this type over the years (as many behind desks as behind bars), and her reaction had always been the same: the instinctive, natural revulsion almost matched by something else she had come to acknowledge as envy. She tried to imagine what it was like, for people like Sandburg, being able to live their lives with absolutely no internal governors, to be able to do anything they could manage to get away with without later feeling shame or regret or even embarrassment at the worst of what that meant. It must have been an interesting form of freedom. Not one she liked being able to recognize as human, and not one that she would ever want to live herself, even if it made it easier to bear the blood on her own hands—but one as compelling, in its own way, as any other alien form of life. Which was just one of the many good reasons she was determined to destroy him.

She turned and headed toward the exit.

He called before she got there. "Oh, one last thing? Andrea?"

Unwillingly, she turned. "Yes?"

His smile was now broad, confident, hateful.

"Good luck finding yourself a judge and jury."

# 4.

Roman Whalekiller was smart enough to recognize Cort wanted silence and professional enough to give it to her for almost five minutes. They were on their way out of the embassy hospital when he demonstrated that he wasn't going to let it last forever. "Are you all right?"

"Yes." Her tone underlined just how much she resented the condescension.

"I'm sorry. It's just that you look a little shaken . . ."

"It's the air; a little thinner, here, than I'm used to. Get me down to the plains where your aboriginals live and I'm sure I'll look a lot better."

"If you say so," Whalekiller said, providing official agreement wedded to the texture of denial—always a diplomatic specialty.

It irked her. "He's not my first murderer, Bondsman."

Whalekiller stiffened at the title, reminder of the gulf between his mortgaged status and her freewoman rank. "I know that. I'm sure you've known many of them."

She shot him a glare, certain she heard rank accusation in his words—then realized he had been referring to the people she met in her role as Advocate. "A few," she said. Then, seeing she'd already shown a little too much arrogance, and knowing it would do her no good to pointlessly alienate this man, she retreated: "I can't say it's something I've ever gotten used to."

"That's good," Whalekiller said, his tone so dry it was impossible to determine whether it was conciliatory or sarcastic.

They left the embassy hospital, then crossed the quad, a cheery acre the Dip Corps indentures had gone to far too much effort designing. With offworld flora a forbidden element, they'd transplanted trees and shrubs and grass-

165

analogues from all over Catarkhus and arranged them in oval plots set off with arrays of polished white glowstones, with a Dip Corps flag fluttering atop a pole in their midst. The overall effect was neither human soil nor Catarkhan, but some uneasy graph position that lay midway between the two extremes. There weren't many people visible; even now, with the crimes of Emil Sandburg still casting its pall over the human presence here, most of the research personnel had better reason to be elsewhere on the planet. But a group of three young indentures who were sharing lunch and buzzpops under the warm Catarkhan sun did look up as she and Whalekiller passed, with something like morbid fascination in their eyes: *That's her, that's the Advocate, that's the one they sent to deal with the Sandburg Problem.*

She was afraid they'd try to delay her with conversation, but they were too well-trained; they knew urgency when they saw it. They let her and Whalekiller pass.

She thought that meant she was home free.

Then Whalekiller led her through the arched corridor that bisected the staff dormitory, rounded a long white structure of uncertain purpose, saw what was waiting for them by the vehicle hangar, and muttered a long, eloquent: "Shit."

The four aliens waiting for them by the entrance to the hangar—a squat little Bursteeni, a cadaverous long-necked Tchi, an gravely expressionless Riirgaan, and a hovering flatscreen representative of the AIsource—were no doubt officially visiting the Hom.Sap Embassy Compound for reasons that had nothing to do with Cort's still-embryonic investigation. After all, first-contact delegations did have to share their data from time to time, and some of that information exchange was best performed on-site. But it was still convenient for these four, appearing here at this time, on this day, representing such a neat cross-section of the interspecies mission to Catarkhus, to so carefully position themselves in Cort's path. Whatever they had been talking about, if it was anything other than concocting a common excuse for their presence, they immediately stopped and converged on Cort and Whalekiller.

"You don't have to speak to them now," Whalekiller said. "You haven't even been out in the field yet."

Cort, of course, knew that; but she also knew that as the official charged with settling the Sandburg problem, she was also bound to function as the whetstone necessary for the grinding of certain axes. "Don't worry about it. We're going to have to get this out of the way sometime."

The Tchi, an angular string of a creature topped with a thatch of curly gray hair, was the first to accost her. He raised his patrician chin and murmured, "Excuse. You are the Hom.Sap legal counsel known as AndreaCort?"

She wondered how her name had circulated so quickly. "Yes. Can I help you?"

The round little Bursteeni, demonstrating its species' tendency toward excessive enthusiasm, bounced up and down with excitement. "It is an honor to meet you, Counselor Cort. I am Mekile Nom of the Bursteeni delegation, and I understand that you have had a long and distinguished career dealing with questions of legal jurisdiction—"

"A career," the Tchi said, its dust-dry air of innate superiority immediately cutting its friendlier colleague off in midsentence, "that achieved such impressiveness mostly because her species has provided her since her very early childhood with many opportunities to investigate criminal acts on alien soil. No doubt, if her people continue to wreak havoc among aboriginals, she will have many more chances to display her talents—a state of affairs that, demanding as it might be for her, still presents what has to be seen as a remarkably ugly display by humanity. Your weak standards betray you here, Mekile; I myself would hesitate to call that excellence." It turned a measuring gaze toward Cort, and said: "Allow me to introduce myself. I am Counselor Gayre Rhaig, of the Tchi Republic's own Committee on First-Contact violations. I arrived on-world twenty-two local days ago, and have been busily conducting my own investigation as insurance against the expected human attempt to subvert justice in this matter."

Cort did not smile, but she didn't raise her voice either. "I can assure you, Mr. Rhaig: subverting justice is absolutely the last thing the Hom.Sap Confederacy has in mind."

"Your own presence here provides strong evidence to the contrary. I have already established from my own research that you supported human over native jurisprudence in at least sixty percent of the cases you've investigated. How do you intend to justify such gross misuse of your power in this case?"

This was another diplomatic specialty that some representatives of the Tchi had always been able to practice with special skill: the kind of question that, like "When did you stop beating your wife?" allowed no non-incriminating answer. Cort hid her annoyance behind a content-free: "I'll be happy to answer your questions when I've completed my investigation."

"Of course," Rhaig said. "Given the poisonous extent of Hom.Sap chauvinism, you first have to determine whether they're sufficiently similar to your own species before you decide whether you can be forced to acknowledge the grievous sins committed against them."

Whalekiller broke in: "Well, that shows real impartiality, Goodsir . . ."

Though sharing his anger, Cort deferred the remainder of

his words with a gesture. She said: "We don't need to be forced, Mr. Rhaig. Nobody, except possibly Sandburg himself, minimizes the seriousness of his crimes."

"Then why is he still in Hom.Sap custody, except to deny the indigenous people of this planet an opportunity to judge him?"

"You know why," Whalekiller said.

"I know the reason alleged to be why. I have yet to see proof that the Hom.Sap Embassy intends on using at anything more than a convenient excuse."

Cort said: "We need to establish that the Catarkhans have the capacity to judge him."

"Ah," said Rhaig. "And if you determine they have no capacity? Given the demented history of your own species, what makes you believe that you possess such capacity yourselves?"

There were any number of answers Cort could have given to that: the diplomatic answer, the legal answer, the defensive answer, even the angry answer. None of them qualified as the definitive answer; none of them provided anything like a sufficient rebuttal to all the human history Cort knew to be written in spilled blood; none of them erased her own vivid memory of bodies falling on a clear, sun-dappled morning.

Before she could speak, the representative from the Riirgaan delegation cut in, with the high-pitched trilling that provided his species' closest equivalent to laughter. "Indeed. None of us envy your task, Counselor. It is difficult to come up with answers to questions that do not permit the existence of any. But it is your fellow human Sandburg who has placed you in that position."

"He certainly did," said Cort. "But I will find the answers."

"Then we will all no doubt be very interested in hearing your proposals."

The flatscreen from the AIsource flashed agreement: WE ARE ALL MOST INTERESTED IN JUSTICE.

In context, it sounded as challenging, and as threatening, as the monster Sandburg's crack about finding a jury.

After all, as she'd been told again and again, justice on Catarkhus was probably not a possibility.

But then, she was used to that.

# 5.

As Whalekiller piloted their skimmer high over the Catarkhan desert, the paucity of cloud cover ensured a constant, clear view of the streaked landscape below; it was a dull pattern of light brown against slightly darker brown, with the darker areas representing cultivated sections farmed by the oft-discussed aboriginals. On their first flight over, Whalekiller had rhapsodized about how beautiful it was. Cort couldn't see it. Maybe it was as magnificent as he said, and maybe (as she suspected), people who got assigned to the same world for too long became so starved for beauty that they created some out of their own heads.

Timing was all. No sooner had she registered Whalekiller's appraising look than he opened his big mouth again. "I hate Tchi."

She glanced at him. "Odd thing for a diplomat to say."

"I know. By contract, I'm supposed to respect everybody. And I really try. I like the Riirgaans, I like the Bursteeni, I even enjoy playing logic games with AIsource . . . but the Tchi, and their air of incessant superiority, make me want to bang my head against a wall. Does that make me a bigot, Counselor?"

"No," she said. "It makes you what the Tchi want you to be.—They do it on purpose, you know."

"What? Act obnoxious?"

"That does happen to be one way of putting it, but their culture teaches them to treat most social interactions as a series of verbal challenges; they tend to keep upping the ante until their opponents either overcome them or back down. They're very aggressive about it, particularly against those they imagine capable of pushing back . . . which makes it hard to tell whether somebody like Rhaig is just following protocol or preparing to be a real threat."

He glanced at her. "And here I thought they were just assholes."

"Most of them are," she said, with spooky calm. "But culturally so."

"And what do you make of Rhaig, specifically? Is he just giving you the closest Tchi equivalent to a friendly hello, or is he really going to be a problem?"

"I'm not sure yet," she said. But she was already thinking: A problem.

He blinked at her. "Something else I picked up during that meeting. You don't like aliens much, do you?"

Cort clicked her thumbnail against her incisors. "They're all right."

"You're uncomfortable around them."

Another click. "I'm uncomfortable around everybody."

Whalekiller's brow furrowed. "Shyness, Counselor? I wouldn't have believed it in a woman capable of rising to your position."

"It's not shyness, but preference. I just don't have a very high opinion of sentient life in general."

The furrows grew more furrows. "All sentient life?"

"That's right. Human, Alien, AI, In-Betweeners, Combinants. You show me something that can think, and I'll show you something that can't be trusted."

Whalekiller's mouth worked in ways common among

people trying to determine just how seriously they should take her. "But you can think, Counselor."

"I can think, I'm sentient, and I don't count myself as an exception."

"Ummm. Leaves you with a limited number of choices as far as friends are concerned, doesn't it?"

"One reason," she said, making sure he received the eye contact, "that I've never been particularly interested in looking for any."

He turned away from her and studied the empty airspace ahead of them—a pretense of active involvement in the skimmer's flight that might have been persuasive if she hadn't seen him load their destination. After a while, not looking at her, he said: "Would you be very offended if I told you I found that sad?"

"No," she said. "You can find it any way you like."

Whalekiller left it at that, fortunately. Had he questioned her further, she might have been forced to explain that she'd derived her opinion honestly, from years of personal and professional experience. She might have said that she'd seen genocide close up as a child; she might have said that she'd seen madness as an adult; she might have said that she'd seen brutality as an Advocate. She might have said that for the ability to think carried with it the potential for joy, but also the potential for self-torment. She might have said that it made bad things happen, and that any species capable of sustained abstract thought spent much of its existence piling those thoughts into rickety, unwieldy, top-heavy structures . . . some of which made sense, some of which were downright brilliant, and some of which were top-heavy nonsense that needed constant attention to keep from collapsing under their own weight. She might have concluded that while sentience was the source of all human and alien civilization, it was also where all evil and madness came from. It was, after all, where people liked Emil Sandburg came from. In the end, she might have said all that, and found herself unable to hold back all the other places those dark, damnable, never-silent thoughts had taken her.

Maybe ten minutes passed before Whalekiller, who probably felt as oppressed by the silence as she did, cleared his throat. "Counselor?"

"Yes?"

"I've got to ask you: that thing the Tchi said, about you favoring humans in so many jurisdiction disputes? Is that true?"

Relieved to be distracted by business again, she brushed a strand of black hair away from her face, and said: "No. It's a gross distortion."

"I figured as much," Whalekiller said, in a tone that testified to long personal experience with diplomatic carping. "What precisely did he leave out?"

"The fact that none of the cases I managed to flip to human courts were ever about crimes committed against native sentients. They may have been committed on alien soil, but they were all human-on-human crimes—disputes between Dip Corps personnel, ranging from petty theft to one particularly stupid murder. The indigenes were always entitled to jurisdiction if they wanted it, but I was always able to persuade them that humanity was the injured party and therefore entitled to our own justice. If they agreed to extradition, it was because they were relieved they could."

"Wish you could manage that in this case," said Whalekiller.

"So do I," Cort said. "It would make things a lot easier."

He hesitated. "You ever surrender somebody like Sandburg to the locals?"

"Somebody like Sandburg? No. I've never had anybody like Sandburg." The unwanted thought: *I've had worse; I've been worse.* "But I had a case not too long ago: some indenture hiking cross-country got caught in a rainstorm, hid out in a cave, took a leak in there while he was at it. Some pilgrim saw him doing it and accused him of desecrating a holy tomb. The punishment was public flogging followed by banishment. We didn't even fight that one: the guy was a real do-his-duty type, said he could take ten lashes if it meant honoring native law. We gave him something to deaden the pain, fixed him up afterward, then re-assigned him. It probably helped his career, actually. I think he's now an ambassador somewhere."

"But he didn't really feel the punishment."

"We didn't think he deserved any," Cort said. "The site wasn't marked and hadn't been mentioned before. He just did what came naturally, and handing him over kept the indigenes happy without doing him any permanent damage. Sandburg, on the other hand—"

She let the sentence trail off.

He finished it for her. "—deserves anything they could possibly do to him."

She nodded. "Did you know him, Bondsman? I mean, before?"

"Know him? I think it's pretty clear that nobody knew him. If we'd known him, we would have shipped him off-world before the damage was done."

"But did you think you knew him?"

Whalekiller considered that. "I think I tried talking to him three, four times. Casual conversation. He was polite enough. He tried to be friendly. But the man had nothing to say. Everything he said was just . . . empty. Like everything he said was being edited by a committee intent on making sure that nothing of any real content ever escaped his mouth." He shivered. "I don't know. Maybe that was as close as he could come to normal. Maybe the only alternative to being a nobody was revealing what a sick bastard he was every time he opened his mouth."

"Maybe," she said, trying to reconcile that with the cocky Sandburg she'd interviewed.

"One thing's for sure, Counselor: whatever's in this head of his is downright evil. The Riirgaans provided footage of what he did, and it's enough to make you ashamed to be human." He closed his eyes, shook his head, and said: "It's too bad. About our problem, I mean. Too bad the Catarkhans don't have laws."

"Yes. It certainly is."

She fell into silence as she watched the endless brown of the Catarkhan desert passing by far below. It would indeed be easier if Sandburg could only be extradited. The Dip Corps would have made damn sure he received the maximum punishment for his crimes—if not out of moral outrage, then at least out of concern for its own reputation. But Emil Sandburg's offense had been a crime of violence against locals, a distinction that, under the First Contact Protocols supported by all the major spacefaring races, required trial under the local version of justice.

It didn't matter a whit that in this case, there was no local version of justice, or of crime, or of right and wrong. Nor did it matter at all that there was no way, short of warfare, that adherence to the policy could be practically enforced against any spacefaring race that decided in any given situation to ignore it. The policy was still seen, and treated, as an inviolate rule, one which all the major spacefaring races had instituted to minimize the kind of disasters that so frequently occur when one culture decides the run roughshod over another. Failing to honor it, even here, would seriously damage humanity's prestige and moral capital and whatever right it had to claim that the worst of its sins was in the past.

The locals had to provide judge and jury.

Even if they had no such thing. Even if they had no even distant equivalent.

Even if, as in this case, they might have been incapable of ever understanding that a crime had been committed.

# 6.

One of the worlds Cort's work had inflicted upon her in the past boasted a herbivore the local aboriginals had given a name that sounded like a slow air leak. The closest human analogue to the sound was a sibilant sssssss, pronounced in a barely audible whisper. The abos called it that because the beast moved at a rate that seemed about as fast as erosion, blinking maybe once an hour, breathing about twice that much, reacting to everything that happened in its vicinity half an hour after it had passed into the realm of history. The beast was fortunate to be as stupid as a brick, since any creature with greater intelligence would have been driven insane by the boredom of its own existence.

The Catarkhans were downright manic by comparison, in that when excited they moved at roughly half the rate of human beings assaying a relaxed walk. They were sluggish, but just enough to seem more deliberate than decrepit. Had they shown any awareness of anything happening anywhere around them, the trait might have been endearing. But they were easily as oblivious as the sibilant-s herbivores Cort remembered; the world around them was simply not part of their equation.

"They have no justice system," Whalekiller explained, soon after they landed. "They have no laws, no societal structure, no philosophy, no religion, no rituals, no real sense of the individual, and no behaviors that seem independent of whatever's hardwired into their genes."

Cort's thumb was starting to ache from all the nibbling. "Have we ever been able to conduct any kind of communication with them at all?"

"Are you kidding? We haven't even been able to alert them we're here."

The Catarkhans were gray, but not elephant-gray; elephants have character, and Catarkhans had nothing of the kind. Imagine a gray that was not just the absence but the thoroughgoing rejection of color. Imagine a gently-curved kidney of a torso about three-quarters of a meter in length; an inverted cone of a head that would have been entirely featureless if it didn't provide space for a brain and didn't have a thicket of perpetually-writhing cilia around the perpetually-open mouth. Imagine no teeth and no tongue and no fixed jaw, just a solid funnel leading right down the gullet. There were six limbs, each articulated with two knees apiece, the lower set lined with a layer of cilia somewhat finer than that which bracketed the mouth. There were clumsy grasping appendages, a compromise between hands and feet, at the bottom of those limbs; they were just strong enough to pick up and manipulate small objects, which usually meant the globby mash Catarkhans directed toward that cavernous mouth.

Catarkhans could dig, and in fact they lived in hives. But the excavation took forever and required the constant effort of hundreds in order for any real progress to be made. Individuals were very weak in relation to their size, and weighed about as much as a bubbles of hollow flesh—one of the main reasons Emil Sandburg would have had no problem overpowering one. A small human child probably could. But that wasn't the least of their shortcomings.

The greatest of those was that they were practically insensate. They were islands unto themselves. They perceived almost nothing. They were blind and deaf because they had no accommodation for eyes and ears; they had an at-best rudimentary sense of smell thanks to the chemical receptors in their cilia, but that was just enough to recognize food, and perhaps smell it, certainly not enough to distinguish tastes. Nor was their any pain center in their brains; shoot them, cripple them, shatter their limbs, set fire to their skins, and they just blundered on, dragging the nonfunctional parts of themselves out of sheer inability to recognize their injuries. The only sense they had in functional quantities was tactile, and that on only a relatively small part of their body—the cilia that lined the limbs below each second knee. If they were removed or incapacitated, the Catarkhans were cut off from the rest of the universe, reduced to bubbles of empty consciousness, unaware even that there was anything around them subject to awareness. It was no wonder their life-support behaviors needed to be hardwired; otherwise, they would have survived as a species only as long as it took the entire population to starve.

Cort found standing in the midst of thousands of them, who inched along the ground in multiple files as they headed toward the cultivated farms that surrounded their hive in concentric circles, a lot like not existing at all.

It was her first encounter with the creatures the law had so perversely designated her jury pool.

After about ten minutes of silent observation, she said, "Shit."

"You're beginning to see the size of your problem."

"I saw it before, Whalekiller; I'm just now beginning to feel it. There's no way to interact with them at all?"

"Try it, why don't you."

Hesitating only a moment, Cort reached out and pulled one of the deaf-and-blind marchers from its parade. The hardest thing about that was figuring out where it was safe to touch one; they had no real offensive capabilities, so there was no possibility of it being able to hurt her, but she had no intention of hurting it and therefore ending up another diplomatic nightmare occupying the cell next to Emil Sandburg. She settled on placing her palms on either side of its bean-shaped torso to gently steer its progress away from its parade and toward her. The degree of pressure she needed in order to influence its course was so negligible she might have been manipulating a balloon, or a toy boat. The Catarkhan meekly turned away from its fellows, moved toward Cort, then stopped, either paralyzed by its unexpected detour, or confident that she would soon provide it additional guidance.

The Catarkhans who had been marching along behind the one she'd captured did not follow. They ignored the disruption and continued their march without interruption. As far as Cort could tell, there was no way of telling whether this was obliviousness, deliberate judgment, or robotlike devotion to their previous programming.

The one she had pulled from its place on line just stood there, waiting. It didn't see her at all. She wasn't there. She may have been an incomprehensible natural force capable of producing changes in its daily routine, but she was still as invisible as a spirit.

"Or a Demon," she said, thinking of Emil Sandburg.

Whalekiller said, "What?"

"Nothing."

The cilia around the Catarkhan's wide-open mouth writhed like anemones, the only indication that it was trying to perceive anything other than itself. Engaged in perceiving anything other than itself, they too looked deaf and blind—

aware that something was happening, but forever unable to determine exactly what. Cort tried and failed discern patterns in the way they danced. "Can I touch those?"

"For all the good it will do," Whalekiller said.

Cort was wearing the gloves she usually wore for planet work; the risk of getting dirt, real planetary dirt, on her fingers was just one of the many things she didn't appreciate about worlds. She doffed the right one and touched those undulating little worms with the tip of her index finger. They weren't slimy, as expected; they had a sandpapery, feverish warmth that didn't feel organic at all, but more like some kind of fabric that had been stored under hot conditions. They didn't react to her touch at all, and neither did their host.

She glanced at Whalekiller. "Nothing?"

"It doesn't have taste receptors for anything you're made of," Whalekiller said.

"So I'm still invisible to it."

"That's right. It can't sense you at all."

"Doesn't it have any idea what's happening?"

"To know how much it understands, we first have to get into its head, and to date, nobody, not even the Riirgaans, has ever succeeded in doing that."

Cort's grimace grew broader. "Then how the hell do we know it's sentient?"

"The same way we know the Vlhani or the Thlane or the Farsh are sentient."

They were three pre-technological species who had presented particularly tough first-contact problems. They were all clearly sentient, but they were all so alien, not only by the standards of human beings but also by the standards of all the other known spacefaring species, that the task of establishing some form of substantive communication with them had been dragging on for years. But the comparison was not perfect, because while little communication with the Vlhani and the Thlane and the Farsh had progressed beyond the equivalent of baby talk, all three species had at least noticed that somebody was trying to talk to them. The Vlhani had even progressed to the point of allowing human beings to participate in their most sacred rituals—and in raising holy hell when the idiot human ambassador tried to interfere. But seven earth-standard years of constant study had left the Catarkhans still cut off, disconnected, oblivious.

She said: "How do we know? Wishful thinking?"

If Whalekiller was offended by her sarcasm, he did not show it; instead, he launched into a speech so polished that he must have honed it during many previous briefings. "By measuring the data content of their interpersonal communication."

"There is some?"

"It all takes place in the hive. There's an incredibly complex language that has to do with how many cilia they touch or refrain from touching at any one time—I don't get most of it myself, but the Riirgaans, who made the breakthrough, mapped the informational traffic, and found grammatical structure, consistent themes, individuality, complex repeated sequences, and even regional accents. It's as dense as an AI stream. It's definitely sentient communication. But nothing in it seems affected by anything they do in their daily lives—it feels as abstract as philosophy or religion or poetry, and it's totally inaccessible to us without some kind of clear way in."

"I don't know, Whalekiller. Sentience implies a certain minimal level of free will, and I don't see any of that in their behavior."

"They have plenty of free will—as far as talking to each other is concerned. They just don't need any to handle their behavior. Their behavior is hardwired."

"Instinct," she said. "Or reflex."

"Something like that. See, Counselor, Catarkhus has such a stable ecosystem it's ridiculous. They don't have any predators. They don't have any enemies. They don't have any seismic activity. They don't have any heavy weather. They only have a limited number of contagious diseases. They never needed the capability to react to unforeseen circumstances. They never needed a wide array of senses to provide constant data about a unstable and potentially dangerous environment. They never needed pain to teach them which things were bad to do. And they never needed individual variation to provide their population with a complementary and competitive skills. They just needed food gathering and reproductive instincts, and primitive tactile and olfactory senses to help them out on those rare occasions where that wouldn't be enough. They didn't need brains this evolved, or a communication system this complex. That's all devoted to higher thinking. —In fact," he added, as if just remembering it at right that very moment, "there's a school of thought, among many of the exolinguists here, that says the Catarkhan mind isn't really aware of what the body does at all—that the intelligence they possess is totally disconnected from a daily life run by their involuntary nervous system. It would explain a lot. But either way, their adaptations made them totally helpless when something genuinely alien did enter their environment."

"Ourselves," Cort said.

"Well," Whalekiller shrugged, "the Bursteeni first. They discovered the species and named the planet. Then the Riirgaans, who established Catarkhan sentience. Then a couple of others, and then us. We were the last to join this particular Contact mission. But we're all alien here . . . and we're all new concepts to a creature biologically incapable of perceiving new concepts."

Nodding, dazzled by the size of it, Cort murmured: "We're non-happenings. Rumors."

"Not even rumors," Whalekiller said. "Invisible demons."

There was that word again. It applied uncannily well to Emil Sandburg. The Catarkhans he'd torn apart hadn't known that anything was happening to them; they hadn't suffered in pain, or in terror, or in sheer rage that the universe would select them for such torments. The ones he'd left behind, the ones he hadn't had time to touch, probably didn't even know that any of their number were missing. For them, the crimes of Emil Sandburg had been non-events in an existence so unchanging that even ten thousand generations would not provide one sentence of actual history.

It hadn't touched them at all.

"What?" Whalekiller asked.

"Did I say something?" Cort said.

"No. But you're smiling."

"No, I'm not."

"Believe me, you are," Whalekiller said. "It's the first time I've seen you do that since I ferried you down from orbit."

That surprised her. She so rarely smiled. But now that it had been pointed out to her, she could feel the telltale tension in her cheeks. She fought down the feeling, buried it, and drove a stake through its heart. "Come on. We still have a lot to do."

# 7.

They caught up with the Riirgaan witness, one Goodsir Vighinis Mukh'thav, at their own Embassy Compound on the edges of a Catarkhan temperate rainforest. Like most of the other embassies, it was a site far removed from the habitat of the indigenous sentient species; it was a standing policy instituted to avoid con-

taminating the culture of the locals with excessive exposure to
offworld technology, but the truth was that the Riirgaans might
have picked it anyway. They just enjoyed environments like
that, for some reason beyond Cort's comprehension; though
their own world wasn't anything at all like that, and they seemed
far too intelligent to enjoy nasty things like bugs and venomous
plants and mud under their feet all the time, they considered the
hothouse jungle a paradise. They even liked swimming, which
had always struck Cort as, war excepted, the most insane habit
that any sentient race had ever cultivated for itself; after all,
people drowned in water. It's a planet thing, she supposed. And
as a species that seemed to enjoy ferreting out and establishing
contact with the most unlikely alien sentients imaginable, they
would have had to harbor a fair degree of tolerance for planet
things.

Mukh'thav was, according to Whalekiller, what the
Riirgaans call a First Contact Prime, a position which should
have kept him out in the field living as close to the natives as
possible. But now they had him assigned to full-time vehicle
maintenance, a job that kept him securely within their embassy perimeter. He explained why as the three of them sat
together at an outdoor table the Riirgaans had carved into
one of the ornate historical friezes that decorated so much of
their artifacts, Cort and Whalekiller drinking the hot coffee
the Riirgaans had been kind enough to provide, Mukh'thav
lowering his flat, masklike features to inhale the vapors from
some kind of fermented mush that bubbled and roiled in a
bowl set before him. "I am polluted," Mukh'thav said, with a
sadness that broke through the infamous Riirgaan reserve. "I
have seen an atrocity, and I still feel the filth on my skin. I am
here, performing menial labor instead of the work I trained
for, because I do not know if I will ever feel clean again."

"You were not responsible," Whalekiller said.

Mukh'thav cocked his head in the unreadable Riirgaan manner that could have been any emotion from annoyance to affection to distaste to warmth. "Do you expect me to take comfort in that? Is that the way you Hom.Saps think? That if a terrible crime occurs when you are not present to stop it, you are not at heart responsible? It is no wonder you have historically always been able to live in comfort and complacency when others of your people conducted genocides in other parts of your habitat. My people find such detachment profoundly alien. But I suppose that, given your tendencies, many of you cultivate the knack in order to remain sane."

Cort's voice was very tight and very controlled. "I'm not detached from this, Mr. Mukh'thav."

The Riirgaan made the kind of noise that seemed to concede the point while simultaneously establishing that nothing had been conceded at all. "Forgive me, AndreaCort: I am sure you believe that. But you are also a bureaucrat, well-used to professing deep personal compassion as a matter of policy. It is still not real to you."

"Real enough to feel polluted; to still feel the filth on my skin; to know that I'll never feel clean again. Think what you want of us in general, Goodsir, but I am not detached."

What followed was a noticeable pause, as Riirgaan and Human faced each other, like a pair of imperfect reflections recognizing the face on the other side of the glass.

It was not telepathy; neither individual was wired for it. But some knowledge is so shattering that people who share it can recognize each other. In Cort's case it took the form of a night filled with screams. In Mukh'thav's, it was the sight of Emil Sandburg plying his deadly hobby. They were different lessons, learned in different places—but while the particulars were different, the resonances were still great enough to fill the air between them.

Whalekiller, abandoned somewhere outside the loop, glanced from one impassive face to the other, saw the moment of clear understanding that passed between them—and seemed terribly frustrated by his own inability to partake of it. He hesitated only a second or two longer before breaking the silence: "None of us approve of what Sandburg did, Goodsir. We all want justice."

Mukh'thav turned toward him, as if reminded of his presence. "Yes. Justice." He slumped. "As if that's even possible in this case."

"I intend to make it possible," Cort said.

"I did not expect to believe you, AndreaCort, but I suppose I do, now. Will you require me to describe what I saw?"

Cort held off responding long enough to take another sip of coffee and set it down on the mat the Riirgaans had provided to protect their intricately carved wood. "No particular need for that; your testimony has been recorded, and the crime itself has already been established to our satisfaction. Sandburg himself admits it. What hasn't been established, at least in my mind, is just what the crime was."

There was a moment of silence. The impassive, inexpressive Riirgaan face, locked as it was in one blank mask, nevertheless seemed to change aspect four times in the interval before Mukh'thav's answer. "You know very well it was murder."

"I do," Cort said, keeping her face as unreadable as Mukh'thav's own. "I am wondering whether you believe it was also torture."

Mukh'thav considered that for what seemed a small eternity before raising his face out of the thickest vapors, leaning back, and linking hands in a gesture so deliberate that the fingers seemed to knit in slow motion. "It is an interesting question, AndreaCort. Is it also an important one?"

"I'm just collecting data," said Cort.

"Very well, then." Mukh'thav's head cocked again; this time, she experienced no difficulty interpreting the reaction as the expansiveness of an any expert enjoying the opportunity to show off his knowledge. "The victim was a Catarkhan. It wasn't capable of being tortured. It wasn't in pain. It wasn't afraid. It wasn't even aware. It was a creature being violated that had no sense of violation; a being ripped apart which wasn't equipped with the senses it needed to understand what being ripped apart meant; a conscious, thinking creature that couldn't hear its executioner's laughter. Death, when it came, wasn't a blessing or a surprise; if the Catarkhans have an afterlife, they may not even notice the passage." He lowered his head to the vaporous bowl one more time; when he raised his head, bits of smoke roiled around his carapace, making him resemble a demon who had just emerged from one of the hotter pits in hell. "If it is your Hom.Sap intention to argue that this small mercy somehow diminishes the crime . . ."

"Not at all, Goodsir." She picked up the coffee cup again, emptied it to the dregs, and placed it down again, before rising and gesturing for Whalekiller to do the same. "I'm just establishing what the crime really is. And what it is not."

Whalekiller was about to suffer a hernia withholding his curiosity.

Mukh'thav's face roiled with vapors. "You are done?"

"Not even close," said Cort.

# 8.

The Tchi Embassy was a snow-white pylon stabbing the sky from somewhere in the most inhospitable wastelands of the Catarkhan polar region; it was the very vessel which had brought them here, imbedded in ice, facing the sky as if it might have been thinking it never expected to see the stars again. The minimal living space within the vessel itself was supplemented by about a dozen small inflatable structures that sprouted from the surrounding glacier like mushrooms, and one big transparent dome that rested on the pylon's flat summit. The dome, which turned out to be one of their bubblewall inflatables, was as warm as toast, comfortably furnished, perfumed with a fertilizer scent Cort assumed to be an import from the Tchi homeworld, and wholly insulated from its constant assault by the most hostile landscape Catarkhus had to offer. The Tchi did everything they could to see to the physical well-being of their guests Whalekiller and Cort, bringing refreshments, inquiring after their comfort, and even altering the humidity level on request—but Cort was still miserable there; every time a gust of wind lashed the bubblewalls with snow, she gripped her couch reflexively, certain that their precariously-balanced platform was about to break off and spiral away into the distance.

Really, she didn't understand anybody who liked planets one bit.

They were there for about one hour, waiting, before Whalekiller, who had been pretending to be engrossed in the view, broke away with an explosion of hoarded breath. "Counselor . . . I know I'm supposed to give you room to work, here . . . but just what the hell was going on, there, between you and Mukh'thav?"

Cort avoided his eyes. "Nothing unexpected, Bondsman. Just evidence-gathering, nothing more."

"I don't mean your line of questioning," he said. "I'm sure you have something in mind. I mean that moment earlier on, when you took all his contempt for us and flung it back in his face. He saw something in you that I didn't. What was it?"

She gave him a look. "Empathy."

The muscles in his face twitched. "I'm going to figure you out sooner or later."

"Let me know when you manage it," she said.

After a moment, he nodded and returned to the edge of the bubblewall, where he could lose himself in the ice-fields of the Catarkhan north.

Cort was grateful to be left alone, if only for a few minutes, but genuine peace eluded her; the second she permitted her mind to drift, it came across the image of Emil Sandburg, slicing away at a Catarkhan victim. Her mind refused to reconstruct what Emil had done—if only because she still didn't know what a Catarkhan looked like beneath its skin—but it showed real enthusiasm imagining the face he'd worn during the act. Possibilities paraded themselves before her: the dispassionate killer, the gleeful killer, the leering killer, the orgasmic killer, the killer who didn't seem to know what he was doing. None of them made any immediate sense. By the time she gave him a face filled with fear, she realized that the image in her mind was not Sandburg's face at all . . . and that the Catarkhans she imagined were not the funnel-faced hive-creatures Whalekiller had shown her. No, these were more humanoid. They were mammalian, they were humanoid enough to possess human expressions, they had bright green eyes filled with humor and curiosity, and their screams were resonant baritone rumbles, backed by a chorus of more human cries.

She opened her eyes and discovered that Whalekiller, still standing against a backdrop of frozen wasteland, was now staring at her with frank concern.

She blanked her expression and stared back until he looked away.

It was an eternity before Haat Vayl, the Tchi exolinguist they'd come to see, arrived for the interview. Thin even by the slight standard of his species, an attribute which might have been a measure of advanced age, Vayl was also marked by an air of deliberate gravity and a set of forlorn, droopy eyes that together made him resemble the most unctuous bureaucrat ever to take secret pleasure in giving bad news. He wore a long diaphanous robe so delicate that it seemed about to tear with every step he took.

Unfortunately, Counselor Rhaig, the Tchi who had accosted Cort earlier, was with him, and considering himself in charge. His pale skin reddened from wind-burn, his fringe of curly gray hair frizzed with moisture, he nevertheless bustled across the chamber with an easy grace that left his more feeble colleague Vayl far behind. "Forgive us the delay, Counselor—but I was out in the field, observing the indigenes."

"You didn't have to cut your observations short for us," Cort said. "We were here to see Dr. Vayl."

"I'm aware of that," Rhaig said, as he claimed a seat opposite her, "but the doctor here thought it wise not to speak with you unless I was personally here to advise him on his answers."

Cort would have bet a considerable sum that the policy was not Haat Vayl's personal idea. "That isn't necessary, Counselor. The Doctor isn't a defendant in danger of incriminating himself."

"He most certainly is not," Rhaig said, "but since humans are universally recognized as masters at the art of the malleable misquote, he did consider it prudent to have an advisor at hand."

Overstepping his bounds, Whalekiller said: "You really do go out of your way to be unpleasant, don't you? What kind of distortion could you possibly be afraid of, here?"

Rhaig fixed him with a cool glare. "If I truly wanted to be

unpleasant toward you, Mr. Whalekiller, I would make obvious remarks about the irony inherent in your having a name that so aptly commemorates one of your species' most infamous past acts of xenocide. But my determination to treat you with basic civility will not prevent me from doing everything I can to counter the human tendency toward gross revisionism."

Whalekiller collapsed into the chair beside Cort. "You'll notice he didn't answer the question."

Cort, who had indeed noticed, addressed Rhaig: "Do you have a personal problem with human beings, Counselor?"

"It is not a personal problem at all. I have dealt with several tolerable members of your species. The best of you seem to mean well, even if your inborn inadequacies prevent you from accomplishing it. Alas, the best of you constitute only a small percentage of your population—and the collected mass of you refuses all responsibility for the acts of the worst. I think that makes you dangerous. I think it makes you something that should be contained."

"Like a disease," Whalekiller said.

"Precisely," said Rhaig. "There's nothing wrong with human beings that a good military quarantine couldn't cure."

Cort's own dislike of the Tchi Counselor was so intense she almost wanted the argument to run its course, but her time here was limited, and she had another agenda to pursue. So she addressed her next words to the weary, silently-waiting exobiologist who had just taken a seat at Rhaig's side. "Goodsir. Forgive us. You are a scientist caught in an argument between bureaucrats."

"I've noticed this," Vayl said, in the craggy, desert-wind tones of any human old man. He was frail, all right; the very effort of speech seemed to diminish him.

"My name is Andrea Cort; I'm here to help determine the

issue of jurisdiction in the Emil Sandburg case. What I need from you, as the ranking researcher here, is your perspective on the Catarkhans. You do agree with the accepted judgment, that the Catarkhans are sentient?"

Vayl's voice was a rasp that barely traveled the short distance to Cort's ears. "I do."

"A very learned human once defined sentients as creatures capable of unpredictable behavior."

Rhaig cut in: "I will not allow you to use a human definition for the sake of human convenience."

Vayl lowered his head. "I will accept it for the sake of discussion, Counselor. Continue."

Cort resisted the temptation to stick out her tongue at Rhaig. "Once, a long long time ago, I had a puppy who met that standard. That's a small domesticated animal some human beings have as pets; they're pretty rambunctious and hard to control when they're young. There is never any way to predict what they're going to do, and they do show a fair degree of skill at problem-solving, in things that matter to them—issues such as, let's say, getting into a cabinet filled with food, or evading capture when it's time to put them back in their pens. Puppies pass the Turing test, but nobody would ever declare them sentient."

Rhaig, who had been rolling his eyes throughout, now heaved a heavy sigh. "Is this another example of the way human beings think? Demeaning murder victims by comparing them to domestic animals?"

"No," Vayl said, silencing the Tchi counselor with a gesture. "I'll answer that." A tiny pink tongue emerged from his beaklike lips, performed a full circuit of his mouth, and then retreated. He addressed Cort: "I can see where you're going with this, Counselor, but this Turing of yours provided a very unreliable means of measurement. Certainly, there are high-ranking officials among both our peoples who would never pass it—hidebound personalities whose responses are fixed in stone by their prejudices but who yet remain sentient by every measurable standard." He made a point of glancing at Rhaig, who blinked several times before Vayl continued: "The same is true for the Catarkhans, but only more so. Their regimented existence may provide them with a limited range of responses we can understand, but every single analysis done so far establishes that they have a wide range of responses when communicating with each other."

"You are absolutely certain of that?" Cort asked.

"Yes I am. But whether we will ever be able to establish any form of communication with them, or how you're going to provide them the means to prosecute your murderer, remains to be seen."

"Thank you," Cort said. She lowered her gaze to the floor, took a deep breath, and continued: "I have one more question."

"Perhaps a relevant one this time," Rhaig suggested.

She ignored him. "Assume for the sake of argument that your own people had never experienced any previous contact with human beings. Assume that we hadn't agreed on a common diplomatic language, assume that you knew nothing of us except that we had been judged sentient by somebody whose expertise you trusted. Assume that we were now meeting for the first time. Assume I now marched in, crossed the room, and without any previous provocation punched Mr. Rhaig here in the mouth." (Rhaig's head rose a little higher on his neck at that one.) "Eliminating all interspecies chauvinism, would that gesture communicate to Mr. Rhaig the message that I don't like him?"

Dr. Vayl's eyes narrowed enough to suggest that he was either deeply offended or deeply enthralled by the image; his sudden animation seemed to suggest the latter. "I would be inclined to believe so, myself, but bereft of data I would also have to admit the possibility that human beings always said hello to other sentients that way."

"Too often they have," Rhaig said.

Whalekiller, giving the devil his due, actually chuckled at that.

Cort only had eyes for Dr. Vayl. "All right, then. Forget meaning. Would it qualify as any kind of message at all?"

Vayl's eyes were almost closed, now. "I would have to say so."

Whalekiller, whose own enjoyment of the turn the conversation had taken had lit up his face like sunrise, seemed almost giddy.

"So what you're saying is—inflicting pain qualifies as communication."

"Not in any articulate manner, of course—but yes, I would have to say so. In fact, at the bare minimum, pain is the body's message to itself. Unfortunately, I don't see how that's relevant here; as I'm sure you've been told by now, the Catarkhans—"

"—don't feel pain. I know." Cort stood, bowed, and signaled the still-goggling Whalekiller that the interview was over. "Thank you very much, Goodsir Vayl, Goodsir Rhaig; I have all I need for now."

# 9.

That night, back at the embassy, Cort sat on the edge of her bed; that was the only item of furniture in the small cubicle she had been provided. It was her second set of quarters; the first had been the local equivalent of VIP accommodations, tiny by the standards of some official residences where she'd stayed but downright palatial in light of the limited resources available to most first-contact embassies. There was room to pace, a desk, a soft chair, a dry-flotation mattress on the bed, a sleep inducer, full sonics in the bath, and a full-sensory hytex link. She would have been absurdly comfortable there; the inducer alone would have ensured the kind of dreamless full night's sleep that she rarely achieved in a lifetime of nights too often interrupted by bad dreams and cold sweats. But she had wanted a smaller room with fewer amenities, and had successfully fought Ambassador Lowrey's protests to the effect that an important visitor like her clearly deserved the best.

These second quarters were even smaller than the medical isolation cell provided to Emil Sandburg—the only item of furniture was a bed that folded up into the wall, and the only amenity was a sonic shower tucked away in one corner. The idea of pacing, in that small amount of floor space that remained, was a joke; any observer would have thought she was merely spinning in circles. It was very much like being in prison, which was precisely what Cort liked most about it. Let other VIPs have rooms large enough to get lost in. Cort didn't approve of rooms she could get lost in any more than she approved of planets. Quarters this small reduced everything to its bare minimum: herself, and her task. As far as she was concerned, there was nothing more. Everything else was static, and an invitation to unwanted dreams.

She'd rejected an invitation to dinner with Lowrey and the rest of his command staff, eating in the room as she pored over the life story of Emil Sandburg. It was, strictly speaking, irrelevant to the case she was putting together—interspecies law didn't allow for sympathy based on cruel childhoods— but it provided an interesting picture. Or rather, the lack of one.

His parents were nonentities, zeroes in political affiliation, religious background, and lateral economic movement. He had gone through thirteen years of schooling without distinguishing himself in the locally mandated intelligence tests, personality profiles, socialization ratings, and emotional intelligence scores. None of the tests had indicated either antisocial activity or any kind of personality at all. His Dip Corps Psych Evaluation described him as dull and humorless but worth signing because of a compensatory drive to succeed; it was even noted that he wouldn't be popular among his fellow indentures but wouldn't be a noticeable irritant either. (It was, she noted with grim humor, pretty much what the same required evaluation had said about her.) There had been no sign of murderous tendencies or the arrogance he had shown in his meeting with Cort. Maybe he'd been repressing his true personality. Or maybe the personality he showed now was the put-on . . . ? Maybe he enjoyed being a monster?

It was not a point of view she could share; being a monster had blighted her life. But then her monstrousness had come early, reducing everything she'd done since to expiation. Sandburg's monstrousness—or at least, the discovery of it—had come late, as if it was something he'd needed to work hard to achieve. Maybe he saw it as an accomplishment, something to be proud of . . . ?

Something resonated there. She flagged the question for later perusal.

From there she moved on to historical and legal precedent, examining the stories of historical crimes against natives on a flatview image projected against the plain white wall. She went back centuries, back to the old single-system days, even back to the single-planet days, and was depressed by just how many there were, though there were of course many more in the days when the Confederacy was still trying to be a colonial power, and understanding the aboriginals was not nearly as great a priority as making sure they were subjugated. It was such a litany of human madness that it made even Cort, who was already familiar with much of it, nauseated at the sheer waste.

Habit, and masochism, led her to call up the well-worn story about the massacres at Bocai. It was an old tale, and one she knew by heart; she didn't need to read the file. But she did spend some time examining the one image known to have survived the event: a stillshot of the ragged survivors being loaded into a rescue shuttle. It was not the best neurec image of all time: a poor signal had blurred the captured memory and turned the finer details into mush. But even so, it was easy to tell that the survivors were traumatized to the edge of sanity; their faces looked vacant, uncomprehending. One, a little girl who stood alone by the edge of the frame, staring at nothing in particular, had pale eyes old enough to have witnessed the shattering of worlds.

*Don't trust anything sentient,* she thought.

Then the hytex image scrambled with a voice message that the ambassador needed to see her in his office immediately.

She found him dressed for bed and pacing in circles like a man who believed the floor to be mined and who was so irritated at the inconvenience that he was trying to set one off just for spite. He had worked himself into some kind of serious frenzy; his forehead was a spotlight, and his hair an explosion of greasy thickets. Whalekiller, who must have caught some of the shrapnel already, stood just outside Lowrey's orbit, studying the floor so intently that he might have subscribed to the mine theory himself.

The ambassador stopped in mid-circle the instant he saw Cort. He glared at her, his eyes round, his face the color of blood. "Counselor. I was assured that you were good at your job. I was told that you were a professional."

Cort answered with perfect calm. "I am."

"I just spent the last three-quarters of an hour calming the Tchi Ambassador. He says you threatened violence against their man Rhaig. Is it typical Tchi bullshit or is he telling the truth?"

"He might think he is," Cort said.

That broadsided Lowrey; clearly, he'd expected a flat denial. He approached and faced her from less than a meter away. "And just what the hell is that supposed to mean?"

"It means that since their ambassador wasn't personally present when we met with Rhaig, he only knows what Rhaig told him. He might not be a part of the lie."

Lowrey studied her eyes as if expecting the answer to scroll across them in readable type. "Rhaig says you threatened to punch him."

"I did not. I just presented a hypothetical first-contact situation that included me punching him in the face. I never said that I intended to do it, or even that I wanted to. I just used it to set up my question for Dr. Vayl."

Lowrey's cheeks twitched. "Rhaig says that you were trying to intimidate him into ceasing his support of the Catarkhans."

"Rhaig has yet to accomplish one damn thing for the Catarkhans. And he was sitting next to another member of the Tchi delegation who had absolutely no trouble understanding the difference between a hypothetical question and a genuine threat."

Lowrey's anger was fading, now; but like most people who have felt anger slipping away, he used the tools he had to try to prevent it from leaving. "He says Dr. Vayl will testify for him."

Cort met his look with a far steadier one. "I'm not fond of the Tchi. But unless I hear that from Dr. Vayl himself, who I would consider a reliable witness, I would have to consider the Counselor a bigot, a paranoid, and a liar."

The ambassador absorbed that, then gave a barely perceptible nod and retreated to the safety of his desk, collapsing in his seat with the suddenness of a man yanked down by invisible strings. "Shit," he said, patting the desktop. "Shit. Shit. Shit." And then, several seconds afterward: "Shit." The bluster of a few seconds earlier was completely gone now, replaced with a weariness so palpable it seemed to be what he had instead of blood. His features sagged, and his eyes aged about ten thousand years, and he said, "Do you know why the Dip Corps assigned me to this place, Counselor? Not because I'm good at First Contact; I'm not. I never have been. They gave me this job because seniority demanded it. They figured I couldn't mess things up too badly on a planet of beings blind, deaf, and dumb. Nobody saw how I could possibly manage a diplomatic incident out of that. Nobody ever thought that anything on this rock could possibly be that important." He sighed. "But one thing even I know is that if you don't know how alien cultures think, you run the risk of making matters worse."

Cort moved to one of the chairs and sat down. "With all due respect, sir, I've spent my career arbitrating legal disputes with alien cultures. And I strongly suspect this particular misinterpretation has less to do with Counselor Rhaig being a Tchi than it does with Counselor Rhaig being a flaming asshole."

Forgotten in his corner of the room, Whalekiller tried very hard to stifle a laugh.

Lowrey, shooting him a look, and trying equally hard to remain stern when his own ability to maintain a straight face hung by a thread, said: "He's going to hurt us for this, Counselor. He's going to demand sanctions."

"Not a loss, sir. He was going to try to do that anyway. He

had it planned when he got here. It's his agenda. He practically admitted as much—he's thrown in with those who want us censured and crippled by a total diplomatic quarantine. Unless I'm wrong, he really believes he can use this situation to cut us off from all influence in matters of interspecies policy."

Lowrey blanched. "And can he?"

"Of course not. It's a fringe-group opinion; he doesn't have nearly enough influence, even among his own people, to push through what would essentially be an act of war. He can only use our failure here—if we fail—to build some additional support for his cause. And I won't let him, because I have no intention of failing. I'm going to make justice happen here, whether the Catarkhans are capable of providing it or not."

Lowrey almost looked afraid, now; he wore the same paralyzed-rabbit expression that his indentures had shown during this morning's briefing. "I think you're taking bigger risks than you think. He's got more influence than you think."

"Then it's twice as important to settle this. And I intend to."

The ambassador sighed, linked his fingertips, and examined her like a man who had just boarded a ride he couldn't leave. "How?"

She turned toward Whalekiller. "Something you said earlier—about the Catarkhans not having many contagious diseases."

"That's right. They're very simple organisms, on a cellular level. They—"

"I don't need that much detail. It just occurs to me that saying they don't have many contagious diseases is another way of saying that they do have some."

Whalekiller immediately looked wary. "And?"

"Any fatal ones?"

"We've catalogued a few. Why?"

"I want to see what Catarkhans do when they're dying."

# 10.

The void the skimmer traveled was not the vacuum of space, but it could have been. It was night on a world without artificial light, a condition that rendered the landscape below them effectively invisible; it was a stabilized vehicle so unbuffeted by local weather conditions she could pretend she wasn't moving at all; it was filled with air so filtered that even her hypersensitive nose couldn't discern any of the annoying local smells. Cort found that comforting, in a way: but for the trace level of unease she always felt in the presence of other sentients, it was pleasantly like being safe in an egg. It was amazing, she thought, just how much the absence of anything involving planets or other people improved the general ambience of things.

Whalekiller naturally did his best to disrupt that ambience, banging around an equipment locker in the rear of the skimmer as if all human civilization depended on his ability to make percussion noises with every tool in his inventory. Worse, he insisted on chatting: "I know it's night here, but we're going to make things easy on ourselves. We're going to hop hemispheres, pick a hive someplace where it's mid-day."

"Fine," said Cort.

"It really doesn't matter one way or the other, of course. There's no natural light underground; wherever we go, we'll still have to carry in helmet lights. But most people exploring downside feel more comfortable knowing that there's still a sun burning somewhere up above." More clanking and clanging; a muffled curse. "I don't know why that is. Psychological, I suppose."

"Fine," Cort said again.

Whalekiller backed out on his hands and knees. Then he

sealed the locker, stood, arched his back in a manner that suggested a dedicated project to realign each and every verte-brae, then collapsed into the seat beside Cort. Collapsed was the precise word; he didn't so much lower himself into the chair as permit gravity to pull him there. His weariness showed in the dark circles lining his eyes. "Of course, waiting till tomorrow would have been good, too."

"Sorry. I figured we were up anyway. Might as well get the job done."

"Up and exhausted, and the job could have waited. Or don't you ever sleep?"

"As little as possible," Cort said.

He raised an eyebrow. "Bad dreams?"

"Better things to do."

He accepted that, and pretended to consult the display, which was now projecting a miniature topographical map of the dark regions passing by far below. With the course laid in, the map was at best a formality, designed to provide a pilot the illusion of having something to do with actually control-ling the vehicle; it was rendered even more irrelevant by the exaggerated vertical scale, a sop to clarity that turned even the gentlest foothills into jagged Himalayan spires. As a navi-gation resource, it was next to useless; as reassurance that the vehicle remained in charge, it was invaluable. But Whalekiller's expression as he regarded it seemed lost in more ways than one . . . and more tired than mere physical weariness could have accounted for.

He didn't look at her when he said it. "Bocai, right?"

A lump of molten lead, composed of equal parts anger, embarrassment, shame, and fear, materialized all at once in the center of her chest. She wanted to kill him. "You've been investigating me."

He still wouldn't face her, so deeply engaged in the navigation display that it might have been offering him a life-sized landscape in which to hide. "It didn't take much, Counselor. I didn't have to read anything classified. It's all in your Dip Corps profile—maybe a couple of levels deeper than most searches would penetrate, but nevertheless available for any sufficiently interested person to find."

Cort didn't buy that; she'd been through every line and every link in her profile, and she knew just how deeply the Bocai material was buried. A casual search wouldn't have turned it up; Whalekiller would have had to conduct genuine in-depth research. Her voice dropped about forty degrees as she said: "Nobody invited you to be interested."

Whalekiller's eyes flickered toward her. "I know, but I'm an exopsychologist. Poking my nose into alien minds is what I do."

Cort felt more violated with every word he spoke. "I'm not an alien, mister. And I'm not a mystery put here for you to solve."

He looked at her, and though his own eyes were as dry as hers, the sadness she saw there seemed, like hers, far too great to have accumulated in only one lifetime. "Everybody's an alien, Counselor. And everybody's a mystery. We weren't necessarily put here to understand—but we were sure as hell put here to try." He let that hang for a heartbeat, as if believing that it might be enough—then apparently saw that it wasn't, and shrugged, providing the ultimate inexpressive gesture for the ultimate inexpressive moment. He regarded the nav display again, and said: "It makes no sense. Two small communities. One human, one indigenous sentient. Living together, in a remote region of the indigenes' homeworld, in what seems like perfect harmony for twenty years O.E.S. The two species trading, communicating, participating in each others' festivals, so psychologically compatible that they fool themselves into believing they're also psychologically identical. So pleased with how they get along that two families, acting with the approval of their respective leaders, experiment with raising each others' young. And then, with no warning—" He shook his head. "Do you even remember what set it off? What would make both sides go after each other with such hatred? And why would—"

She cut him off with the most acidic voice she could muster. "I've answered these questions before, Bondsman."

But Whalekiller remained unfazed. "You've said you don't remember. From what I could see, none of the other survivors did, either. Oh, they told plenty of horror stories about what the Bocai did to the humans, and what the humans did to the Bocai . . . but nobody's ever said word one about what started the killing. Nobody's even come up with a workable theory. All I can tell is that one little girl with one foot in both worlds walked away saying she hated humans and Riirgaans both. That she would never trust sentients again." He looked away from the nav screen, and bored his eyes into hers. "It's what you said to me. You're a bigger mystery than Sandburg, you know that?"

"I was eight years old," she said, hating the defensiveness that always came over her whenever she was questioned about the hated summer. "It was a long time ago."

"No, it wasn't. I just have to look at you to know it's still happening."

Cort wanted to rip the prying son of a bitch a new asshole, but for the life of her she couldn't think of anything to say.

He astonished her with what he said next: "You'd be surprised how much we have in common . . ."

# 11.

The hive Whalekiller had selected ("Calcutta," he said), was nestled in a chain of remote rust-colored hills somewhere in the temperate band of Catarkhus' southern hemisphere. It occupied pebbly ground that crunched with every step they took—the kind of terrain that would have rendered stealth impossible on any world where the deafness of the natives wouldn't have rendered stealth irrelevant. The vegetation was so sparse and scrubby it seemed to have established a toehold here out of obstinacy alone. The main entrance to the Catarkhan hive was a spiral funnel, sinking diagonally into the earth. There were a handful of Catarkhan footprints near the entrance, but otherwise no sign that anything lived below.

Cort hesitated when, taking her first step into the tunnel, she sank up to her ankles into soft sand, considerably more yielding than the desert terrain she had just left. She was not yet ready to forgive Whalekiller enough to speak to him, but necessity obliged her: "Just how stable is this place?"

Whalekiller saw she was about to stumble, and steadied her with a tug on her upper arm. "Very stable, Counselor. The walls aren't made of this stuff, fortunately; they would collapse in a second if they were. This is just flooring the Catarkhans carry from a sand quarry about seven klicks away. The walls themselves come from some tougher kind of gravel the locals gather somewhere else; they do something biological to it that makes it liquefy into a kind of malleable cement. It's an entirely different kind of construction than that used by their cousins in the other hive I showed you—but that was half a world away, where they have a different set of raw materials."

She pulled free of Whalekiller, tested her footing with another step, and decided that it seemed safe enough, if a clumsy medium for human feet. Several steps further in, her eyes narrowed: "So their behavior isn't all hardwired, after all."

"Not entirely. They're sentient, after all; they can override instinct when they absolutely have to. But it's not so much creative thinking or the ability to learn as it is a facility for re-writing survival behaviors on a group-by group basis. For in-stance, the guys down here don't have any decent farmland, like their cousins up north; they'd starve if they tried to sup-port themselves that way. So they subsist on some kind of foul-smelling yeasty stuff they cultivate in ground water cis-terns about half a kilometer straight down. It's nasty, but it sustains life."

"Which shows a certain degree of adaptability," Cort said.

"Within a very narrow range. If you took a bunch of random Catarkhans from this hive and transplanted them to the location I showed you before, most of them would starve to death; a few of them would rewrite their personal software to match the new paradigm, and thrive up there while be-coming totally helpless here. None of that equips them to deal with a truly random factor, like a cave-in, an offworld maniac cutting them up for fun, or . . ."

"Jury duty," Cort said.

He nodded. "Yes."

It was, after all, the problem at hand.

They descended deeper into the hive, leaving even the ghost of daylight. Their portable lights provided poor alter-native. They were bright enough, but something about the congealed stone burrows openly rejected illumination; the little circles of daylight Whalekiller and Cort carried with them seemed tentative and afraid in this place, as if recog-nizing how unwelcome they were and unwilling to completely banish the darkest of the shadows. Things didn't get any better when Whalekiller and Cort traveled far enough to encounter their first residents, a parade of Catarkhans who marched along in single file, intent on their robotic errand and oblivious of the two invaders who had just landed in their midst.

"This is as close to the surface as these guys usually get," Whalekiller explained. "No topside farms to tend. They'll go up for building materials, but not for much more than that. I'd call it a cultural difference if I was willing to think culture had anything to do with it."

Cort considered just how often the various diplomats here were reduced to disparaging the limitations of the natives. She didn't blame them; the more she heard about this species, the more she found herself thinking of them as a locked door with no available key.

They descended still further, into realms where the air started to deteriorate. They passed more Catarkhans conducting errands, immobile Catarkhans who seemed to be sleeping, and communicating Catarkhans who knelt funnel-face to funnel-face, linking the cilia on their lower legs. Every pair of communicating Catarkhans she encountered looked like every other pair; she knew she'd been assured how intricate and complex their conversations were, but there was nothing else in the Catarkhan demeanor to provide a context capable of allowing her human eyes to see those conversations as prayers, negotiations, ironic banter, dirty jokes, heated arguments, or any combination of the above. Still, the stiff robotic regimentation she had encountered on the upper levels seemed absent in those encounters; whatever these particular Catarkhans might have been saying, they were in the residential district, and they gave the impression of being at leisure. That might not have been recognizable sentience, but it was a start.

"I call this the Main Boulevard," Whalekiller said. "It's a section common to most hives, where they have what passes for their social life."

"When do we find a dying one?" Cort asked.

"It's not all that easy, most hives. Like I said before, Catarkhans don't seem to get sick much; disease isn't totally unheard-of, but they usually just wear out when they get too old."

"And this hive is different?"

"Yep. The stuff these particular folks cook in the cisterns has a tendency to turn septic if allowed to sit too long. They're susceptible to the infections. The death rate here is much higher here than anything you'd find elsewhere on-world. As it happens, I've been here a few times and I've seen what they do to the afflicted.—Down this way."

Whalekiller led her through another series of tunnels. The Catarkhan traffic, crowded in the busier sections of the hive, here grew sparse, then nonexistent. The air got worse, and they switched to oxygen distillers, with masks worn over nose and mouth. They descended another set of tunnels: a nearly vertical shaft they had to descend on ropes. Cort reeled, wondering just how far the hive extended, and how it endured the weight of all the earth pressing down upon it. But just as she began to doubt that Whalekiller really knew where he was leading her, they came to the place he called The Sick Ward.

# 12.

It was a long, narrow chamber stuffed with a huge writhing sea of Catarkhans giving their all for the right to occupy the same space at the same time. They all wanted to be at the center; they all wanted to be surrounded by all the others. The result was a lot like watching maggots swarm over something recently dead; there were so many of them, in such a constricted space, that they literally swam in a sea of each others' bodies, submerging when they could, emerging when the struggle taking place all around them ejected them from the composite bodymass. Some of those she saw on the surface were clearly dead, but she couldn't keep her eyes off one twitching specimen whose limbs had been broken by the eternal struggle. Constantly hurled free of the fight, he just as constantly struggled back, managing a return to the Sick Ward only to be flung free once again.

Andrea Cort had seen sentient beings slaughter each other. She had seen people she loved, meaning only to protect her, commit acts that had poisoned the very memory of their faces. She had visited worlds wracked by poverty, and worlds where war and starvation and disease had ripped across entire populations in waves, leaving hollow-eyed survivors whose only deliverance was to stand weak and defenseless against whatever came next. She had hardened her skin in a vain attempt to become unshockable, but she had found that there were always fresh horrors capable of touching the soft spots between the scabs. This was one of them. "What are they doing?"

"Are you all right?"

"No, I'm not. What are they doing?"

"Quarantining themselves. There's almost no infectious disease among the Catarkhans—they seem largely immune to it, and most of the researchers here have never seen any—but what little they do have prompts a quarantine response. Most of the hives we've explored have a special chamber set aside for just that purpose; we don't usually find more than three or four residents. Sometimes they get better, and rejoin the hive; sometimes they die, only to be walled in where they drop."

"But that's not the way it's working here."

"Clearly," Whalekiller said. "No, unfortunately for these fellas, the little food-poisoning problem of theirs activates the quarantining instinct—and they're too ruled by their hardwiring to build larger chambers for increased demand. They'll keep jamming themselves into this space until they reduce each other to fruit squeezed of its juice."

Cort winced at the phrase. "It's horrible."

"It's the way they are."

She watched a little while longer and wondered whether she should revise her feelings about sentience. True, it offered tremendous capacity for evil and madness; it was the soil which nurtured tragedies like Vlhan and Bocai; but instinct, raw robotic instinct, was potentially even worse. Instinct could never be reasoned with. Worse still was the idea of sentient creatures so chained by instinct that they were incapable of ever making any decisions for themselves. She didn't want to know if the Catarkhans before her now had any idea what they were doing; both possibilities struck her as equally terrible.

"What happens if there's an infected Catarkhan too sick to move?"

"They tend to realize they're sick before they show symptoms. But if they don't come down here on their own, they get dragged or carried."

She found herself focusing on one Catarkhan in particular—an emaciated, bloody thing with only three functioning limbs out of the original six, the others so bloodied and broken that they hung from its torso like flexible ropes. Banished by weakness to the outer edges of the Sick Ward, unable to fight its way deeper into the place where it was obliged to lie down and die, it seemed to be spending most of its passage from this life stumbling, falling over, struggling to stand, attacking the wall of writhing bodies, and then stumbling once again. It was pathetic and it was trapped and it was incapable of giving up, even when another of its limbs snapped, and it fell back, twitching and trembling and gathering up the will for another go.

Surprising herself, Cort bolted from Whalekiller's side, seized the prone Catarkhan by its hindlimbs, and began to drag it away from the riot at the threshold to the Sick Ward. As if in protest, it dug two of its forelimbs into the tunnel floor, clawing deep gouges in the sand as she pulled it farther from the impossible destination its hardwiring demanded. The gesture seemed less reluctance than reflex. Beyond that, the Catarkhan didn't particularly seem to mind; it didn't struggle or grow frantic or slash at her in its eagerness to escape. It just continued trying to crawl forward, with a typical Catarkhan lack of awareness that anything was interfering with its progress.

Whalekiller rushed to her side and grabbed the Catarkhan too. "Please tell me what you think you're doing."

"I'm taking a look," Cort said.

"You don't actually think you can help this guy? —Look at him. He's holding on to life like it's just a bad habit he's ready to drop."

"I see that," Cort said. "But hold on to him anyway. I want to figure out something." She passed the Catarkhan's hind legs to Whalekiller, then scrambled around its body to face the hollow, unmoving funnel up front. Even now, after years of dealing with aliens, after a career spent teaching herself that facial expressions were just illusory anthropomorphic structures that couldn't even be considered reliable windows to the soul on human beings, and meant even less when used to judge sentients from elsewhere, she found herself searching that eyeless noseless faceless face for how it regarded such a violation. She waved that thought away and grabbed the edges of its funnel-mouth with both hands.

Whalekiller held the Catarkhan in place with no difficulty.

211

"Again, Counselor: what are you doing?"

"Taking a message."

The cilia at the edges of the creature's funnel-mouth were slimy with blood and other bodily excretions, and gritty with sand from the tunnel floor. She thought of human equivalents and gagged, but brushed her hands through the little undulating fingers anyway. She circled the funnel-mouth twice, then knelt, grabbed the forelimbs seeking purchase in the sand and brushed her hands through the limb cilia as well. They were, if anything, even more moist; when she pulled her hands away, her gloves glistened in the glow of Whalekiller's lamp. So did Whalekiller's.

Then she stood, and stepped out of the way. "I'm done. You can let it go, now."

Whalekiller released the Catarkhan's hindlegs. It hit the ground and immediately began to thrash its broken limbs, struggling with every ounce of strength in its possession to reach the Sick Ward that had expelled it so many times. At its current speed and apparent stamina, it might have managed to get there in an hour or so; Cort was not willing to place any bets about the journey being at all worth the effort. She said, "I really do wish there was something we could do for him. For all of them."

Joining her, Whalekiller said: "You've already been given one impossible job on this planet. You don't really want to try for two."

"It doesn't stop me from wanting it," she said, with sadness so palpable that her voice cracked from the weight of it. "I don't like death."

"I don't either," he said—and the sympathy in his voice, while real, was like a knife cutting into old wounds. "But sometimes, if you've seen enough of it, you stop feeling it. It was like that where I came from. And down here, with the

Catarkhans, you get clinical. You stop feeling. There's a—"

"Get me the hell out of here," she said, cutting him off.

He blinked, taken off guard by the return of the iron in her voice. For a moment, he looked like he was going to insist on showering her with his empathy. But then he straightened, nodded, and began the task of leading her out.

But then they were attacked by Catarkhans on their way out.

# 13.

Both before and after Mankind met its first alien sentients, Hom.Sap popular culture was filled with scenarios where heroic human protagonists withstood assault by wave after wave of marauding monsters.

All of those scenarios presupposed that the marauding monsters in question would be dangerous in some way.

Cort and Whalekiller were several minutes into this attack before either one of them realized that the Catarkhans were not just blindly blundering into them by accident, but ramming them with deliberate intent. The Catarkhans moved so slowly it was more like an organized jostling than a riot. It caused the two humans no damage whatsoever, and rendered escaping the hive just like struggling through any other large crowd. The greatest hardship Cort and Whalekiller suffered was tempering the force of their own struggle to escape enough to avoid doing the delicate Catarkhans any harm.

Whalekiller said: "I don't believe this. They've noticed us."

Cort had suspected they might. "We can get past them, right?"

"I don't think getting past them's going to be our biggest problem."

A Catarkhan rammed its head into Whalekiller's chest,

not inconveniencing him at all. Another grabbed hold of his arm and tugged; he flexed, and easily lifted the feeble creature off the ground. It lost hold and tumbled to the tunnel floor in a scramble of arms and legs, with still more Catarkhans, moving no faster than molasses, already scrambling over its body for another attack. He pressed himself against a tunnel wall and said: "You get it? We're like heroes out of myth in here. As long as the tunnel prevents them from coming after us in numbers, we can knock down hundreds of these guys. The problem's going to be getting past them without harming any. Kill one, and we start sharing a cell with Sandburg."

"That would amuse him," Cort said.

"Yeah, well, amusing multiple murderers is not one of my life's greatest ambitions."

They inched along the wall, all but impervious to the assaults of Catarkhans trying to drive them back by the sheer weight of their massed bodies. Slow as they were, the Catarkhans seemed frantic, even desperate—maddened by the need to keep the two humans from leaving; but it might have been an attack by origami animals, incapable of wreaking harm despite all the ferocity they could muster. Cort had a memory-flash of the massacres at Bocai, but the thought was a mere reflex, with no real weight behind it. At Bocai, two species of equivalent strength had turned upon each other in spasms of equivalent madness; the war had been like many wars, filled with hundreds of life-or-death dramas where the only real factor in who lived and who died had been who was fast enough to strike the killing blow first. This was something else. This was total war fought against a blind enemy that possessed all the strength of a soft breeze brushing against exposed skin. This was not violence, so much as delusion.

Then one of the Catarkhans, launching itself against Whalekiller, scraped a forelimb against his face. He yowled, shoved it aside, and fell back, clutching at his eyes. "Shit!"

"What happened?"

"Lucky shot—poked my eye. Bastard could have blinded me if it had known what it was doing. Hurts like hell."

"You all right?" Cort shouted.

"Can't see out of the thing, if that's what you mean! Watch your face!"

The Catarkhans swarmed even more thickly now, clogging the tunnel up ahead, forming a wall of their own bodies. There was no question of ever being able to get past them now—not without smashing their fragile forms to pieces. It was still more comical than frightening; Cort couldn't look at the way their funnels craned toward the two humans without picturing an orchestra filled with angry trumpets. She had the crazy thought that if all those musical instruments blared at once, they'd all play a single note with perfect pitch—one so distinguished by its absolute clarity that it would explain everything all the exolinguists assigned to the world had never been able to understand. But the thought died, replaced by another: that if the silent Catarkhans had been able to make any noise at all, they would have been screeching with rage.

These Catarkhans hated them. As intruders.

Or as invisible demons.

She shouted: "Fall back! Get to the Sick Ward!"

"We'll be trapped in there!"

"That's the point! Do it!"

Whalekiller would have argued, but the wall of bodies the Catarkhans had built to prevent him from moving further down the tunnel had transformed from a wall to a tidal wave, breaking down on top of him. It was still like being pelted with creatures made of paper, but he was being buried in them, and their sheer persistence was driving him back anyway. He cursed, reached for Cort, found her hand, and allowed her to pull him out of the densest part of the Catarkhan mob, and back toward the Sick Ward. The Catarkhans who had driven them back followed, but not in the manner of creatures who wanted to overtake them; rather, they were more like shepherds herding a wayward flock back into a pen. Whalekiller and Cort outdistanced them with ease.

Whalekiller, still holding his eye, grunted in fresh dismay.

"What?" Cort asked.

"I think the little fuck blinded me."

"That can be fixed." Even with the eye a complete loss, the embassy clinic could grow a new one overnight.

"But it still hurts like hell," he said. It didn't need to be said; his walk had become an agonized lurch, dependent on Cort's support.

They descended closer to the side-tunnel that housed the Sick Ward. Their pursuers fell back, giving them room, leaving them alone as long as they continued their retreat. At one point Whalekiller's knees buckled; Catarkhan shadows loomed on all sides; Cort forced him back to his feet and pulled him further along the tunnel; the shadows retreated. It was hard to tell, when Catarkhan fury was so hard to discern, but what there was calmed to something like casual interest.

Just outside the Sick Ward, only a few meters from the site where dying Catarkhans fought to bury themselves in the bodies of other dying Catarkhans, she and Whalekiller sank to the tunnel floor, their breaths reduced to ragged gasps.

"Just . . . my luck," he managed. "Hundreds . . . of diplomats . . . running all . . . over this . . . mudball . . . without ever . . . getting noticed . . . and I happen . . . to be the bastard . . . who . . . finally . . . makes contact . . ."

Cort lurched to her feet, wobbled, held her head, and

faced the threshold, where dozens of ailing Catarkhans warred to fit themselves into a space too small to accommodate them. Their bodies, illuminated by her helmet lights, glistened with the blood pouring from their wounds they had inflicted upon each other fighting in that pointless war. The ground beneath them was sodden with it. She focused on that blood now, forcing herself to remember a similar sea of spilled blood; it would have been just another pointless way to upset herself, had she not wanted to be upset, had she not needed the strength that came from being angry. "Have you been able to call for a rescue team?"

Whalekiller tapped his throat mike. "Doing it now." Two minutes of anguished subvocalization later, he reported: "ETA three hours, if Lowrey . . . can scramble his team quickly. Maybe less than that . . . if one of the alien field teams intercept. We'll be okay if the bugs don't swarm us again."

"They won't," she said. "Tell them to bring isolation suits and we'll be okay getting out, too."

He froze then, regarding her for long minutes through his one intact eye. The look was cold, appraising, and a churning cauldron of emotions ranging from pity to disgust; the kind of look one gives other human beings only after deciding that they are not human beings after all, but representatives of an older and more predatory species that should have died out before the first human beings carved the first club out of bone.

Cort had no trouble facing that expression, mostly because she'd been encountering it, off and on, for most of her life. She'd first seen it in a rescue worker's eyes when she was eight years old. She couldn't pretend it didn't bother her. But it was what she had to work with.

Whalekiller's voice was hurt, betrayed. "You knew this

would happen, didn't you? You expected it."

"I expected something like it. It solves a lot of problems."

"And you didn't let me in on it?"

"I wasn't sure," she said. "And I didn't want to be wrong."

He grimaced, more out of revulsion than pain, but relayed the message.

She sat down again, her back to the tunnel wall, descending into a silence disturbed only by the sound of Catarkhans, mobbing each other for the right to die in splendid quarantine.

# 14.

The Catarkhans didn't bother them again. As long as the two humans stayed within a certain distance of the Sick Ward, they were left alone, to stew in their separate flavors of misery.

Whalekiller was silent at first, but when he injected himself with an anesthetic to dull the pain, it made hash of his prior decision to ostracize her. It didn't put him out, or render him any less rational, but it did unleash a flow of words, and gave them a distracted, otherworldly quality, like dispatches from another country so distant that its nature was of interest to serious scholars only. He talked a little about his homeworld, Greeve, a place so dominated by ocean that only a few speckled islands emerged above the usually placid surface; and about his name, a reference to the massive ocean-dwelling beasts who occasionally entered the shallows long enough to provide the colonists there with the one source of food they didn't have to synthesize, grow themselves, or import from somewhere offworld. Perhaps because his tongue had been loosened by the neural block, or perhaps because he couldn't forget that he was in the presence of a Dip Corps advocate, he told her about twenty times that these whales had been named for their extinct terrestrial counterpart only because of their physical resemblance. They were not sentient. They were not even possibly sentient. They were not endangered. They were not even close to endangered. Harvesting them was not a crime. They were mobile meat. They were nothing more.

He was innocent. He was. They all were. Greeve was a good place: a paradise. Really.

But then the nonsentient classification had been challenged in the light of new evidence—and it now seemed clear that the whale hunting on Greeve had been another in a long line of Hom.Sap crimes against thinking beings.

"I didn't know," Whalekiller murmured. And then, "It was my home."

She didn't point out that he had sold himself into the Dip Corps to escape it. She had no business criticizing; in a sense, it had been what she had done, too. She may have been a freewoman, but she had been fleeing her guilt too long to believe that anybody ever truly enjoyed that condition.

At one point during the wait of several hours, Whalekiller said that his injured eye was showing a lot of sensitivity to light. He asked if she had any problems with sitting in the dark a while. She said she had none, and they turned off their lamps. Darkness descended. The sounds of sick and dying Catarkhans mobbing each other at the entrance to the Sick Ward continued; they were moist sounds, violent sounds; sickening sounds. Cort, who was sitting cross-legged against the tunnel wall, immediately found herself covering her ears with both hands, blocking out not the sound of Catarkhan fighting but the even more immediate sound of humans and Bocai tearing each other to pieces in another place, worlds and lifetimes ago.

Whalekiller had been wrong about how much she remembered. She remembered hating them, that's all. She had been eight years old, and a living symbol of interspecies harmony, and she played with the Bocai young, and she ate at the Bocai feasts, and she amused her human parents with how well she had learned the Bocai songs. She even had a Bocai name, emblem of her honorary adoption into a Bocai family, a name she had impossibly even learned how to speak perfectly, despite the harsh differences between the human and Bocai vocal apparatus, which had always rendered their interspecies parley such a comic-opera litany of malapropisms and mispronunciations. She had loved them as much as she had loved her own family and she had been loved as much by them in return, but then she'd hated them, and they had hated her, and she had been too small to participate in the fighting, the killing, the burning, the two-way war of annihilation erupting for no conceivable reason one day like any other. Her father's head had been smashed to jelly beneath Bocai farming implements suddenly transformed to clubs, her mother had been torn to pieces beneath Bocai hands suddenly transformed into claws. Andrea, too small to participate, and too afraid of the monsters overpowering and destroying her, had hid in a dark alcove, watching, listening, hating, waiting for her moment, emerging only as her Bocai second father crawled away from the fighting, lay there helpless, bleeding, sobbing, helpless. And she had emerged from her little dark place and looked down at the being who had called her his daughter and she had hated him, hated the very idea of him, wanting to expunge him, to erase him, to free the universe of the very idea of his existence. He had pleaded with her, that being, in his last moments. Perhaps the madness that had rocked his people and hers had already passed from him. But it had not passed from her.

After that day she had wanted no family. Not any more. She wanted no world. Not any more. She had wanted no friends. Not any more. She had harbored no trust for senti-ents, of any species, not even her own. Not any more.

She just wanted to fight the monsters.

It was the only way to atone for having been one of them.

To not remember her own little hands, driving the cutting blade into her Bocai father's face.

She closed her eyes, and pressed her hands harder against her ears, and retreated into a private place where there was no such thing as time or blood until, lifetimes later, she felt something or somebody shaking her by the shoulders. For one terrible instant her heart spasmed in her chest, as she half-expected it to be a Catarkhan, fully aware of her pres-ence, wanting her awake so it could make her pay for the crimes of Emil Sandburg. Or worse, a Bocai, arriving here from across the years, to hold her accountable for the crimes she'd committed once upon a time. But then she opened her eyes and saw that it was neither. It was a Tchi: not one of the ones she'd met so far, but a younger, shorter individual, whose gray eyes had narrowed in frank confusion.

"Are you injured, Counselor?"

She looked past him: saw a petite human woman tending to Whalekiller, a grave Riirgaan staring open-mouthed at the perpetual riot that raged at the mouth of the Sick Ward, and a flatscreen from the AIsource hovering between them, flashing its symbols for fascination and dismay.

The Tchi asked her again: "Are you injured?"

She felt herself twitch at the corners of her mouth. "Not . . . recently." Allowing the Tchi to help her to her feet, she said: "And Whalekiller?"

"He has sustained an injury to the eye. Painful, but not as bad as it looks; it will probably not require replacement. He suffers from shock, nothing more."

"That's good," she said, oddly surprised to find that she

meant it. "Did they give you any trouble getting this far? The Catarkhans, I mean?"

"The Catarkhans were Catarkhans. They didn't even notice us. I will be interested in learning why they provided such an impediment to you."

She said: "They'll be an impediment again unless you brought isolation suits."

"Your call for help specified you'd be needing them. They're here."

"Good," she said.

The Tchi said, "It will be interesting to see if you're right."

"I am," she said.

She was referring to more than the suits, but she didn't let him know that.

# 15.

The meeting of the local interspecies council was held five days later.

It was not a trial. Nobody here could have gotten away with calling it a trial. Trials imply the right to hold them. Nobody wanted to call it a hearing either, as even that term seemed to impart official weight to any conclusions it happened to draw. It was a meeting, nothing more.

The Bursteeni, who had discovered and named Catarkhus, as well as the first to suggest that its inhabitants might be sentient, hosted the inquiry in their own embassy, which they'd constructed in a salt desert. It was a graceless, windowless block with a flat roof and an interior empty enough to qualify as cavernous. There was nothing about it that seemed to reflect the Bursteeni character; they were traditionally lovers of luxury at home and in the field. But here, in their planetary base of operations, they behaved differently; they kept almost no equipment and absolutely no furnishings here, but instead stored the things they really needed at various drop points around the planet, and conducted the day-to-day business of their embassy at this hall so large it would have seemed almost as empty if it were allowed to house everything they possessed. Nobody had been able to explain this to Andrea Cort, who in the end just wrote it off as one of those maddening alien-psychology quirks that, like the mysteries of the Catarkhans themselves, seemed to exist only to twist the brain of human observers into Gordian knots.

Regardless: the site's nondescript flavor made it infinitely adaptable to any purpose, and therefore perfect for those rare occasions where the various first-contact teams on Catarkhus all needed to meet in one place. Each of the various alien races on-world brought their own native version of furniture to accommodate themselves—the Hom.Saps their functional tables and chairs, the Tchi their imposing portable stages, the Riirgaans their ornately-carved reclining benches, the various other races odder artifacts ranging from hammocks to poles with protrusions to dangle from. The Bursteeni sat on the floor and a flatscreen representative from the AI hovered two meters above it all, its usually-colorful surface now projecting a studiedly neutral black. They were all gathered in an approximate circle, creating an empty stage at the center where the various presentations would be made.

Almost all the human beings on Catarkhus attended, but most of those at the outer fringes of the audience. There were only three people seated at the table provided for the Hom.Sap contingent—Ambassador Lowrey, the fully-healed Roman Whalekiller, and, confined to a paralysis chair for security reasons, the cause of all this bother, Emil Sandburg himself. He managed to look chipper despite his temporary, artificially-induced state of quadriplegia; he was cheerful enough to catch Cort's eye, and smile at her. At that, he was friendlier than Whalekiller, who had refused to accept her visit during his stay at the Embassy Clinic, and had been nothing but chilly and professional to her since his return to duty, eliminating all the affability that had previously made him such a trial for somebody with Cort's reserve.

Cort, who had as per her usual habit rejected a seat of her own, stood by herself until Sandburg winked at her. Then she crossed the stage to stand before him. "Still enjoying yourself, I see."

Sandburg beamed. It was the look of a man in control, who expected to remain in control. "Why shouldn't I be? I love theatre."

"And that's all this is to you."

"I'll be more specific. It's not just theatre; it's farce. It's just a bunch of sentients who wish they could take me out back and shoot me, but are too hamstrung by their own rules to do anything but cluck."

"You're not worried, then. You're that certain the Catarkhans can't judge you?"

He sneered. "The Catarkhans can't judge anything."

She nodded, not because it might have been literally true, but because she recognized the nature of Sandburg's anger. It crystallized something she'd come to realize about his crimes—something that rendered the most basic assumptions about them a lie.

Whalekiller, who was seated beside Sandburg, grimaced. "There's that smile again."

A few days earlier, during her investigation, the words would have reeked of wry affection; now, nothing informed them but resentment.

She confronted it head on. "I've got to watch that. I wouldn't want to get obvious. How's the eye?"

"Fine. You got this handled?"

"It's handled," said Cort.

Lowrey lowered his head and spoke with soft urgency. "It's not going to be that easy, you know; I've been told that Rhaig's lying in wait for you."

"We already knew that."

"We knew his agenda. We also knew that he's been wanting to politicize this since day one. We suspected, but didn't know for sure, until now, that he was going to aim much of his attack against you."

"And how do you know that?"

Wringing his hands so tightly that he might have been trying to remove them at the wrists, Lowrey said: "Rhaig went to the Riirgaans to try to recruit supporters for his side. He figured they'd want to support him; they were after all key in cleaning up the ambassador's screwups during the Vlhani mess last year. But we still have a supporter or two over there, and one of those called to let us know that he's ready to cut you off at the knees."

"So he's making this about me," Cort said.

"What else did you expect, when you insulted him to his face?"

And she smiled again, without any warmth at all, making sure it was clearly visible to everybody in sight.

"I expected him to make this about me," she said.

At precisely the moment the schedule dictated, Mekile Nom of the Bursteeni called the meeting to order by praising every race represented there at excessive length. He was, he assured everybody in turn, a longtime admirer of all their cultures, all their accomplishments, and all of their efforts in the allied fields of Exosociology, Exolinguistics, and Exodiplomacy. He praised them further for the spirit of cooperation that occasioned this hearing, expressed his extreme gratification that so many distinguished sentients had chosen to participate, and conveyed his approval of the conclusions that were about to be reached, whatever they were going to turn out to be. He seemed so pleased by the sheer wonderfulness of everything that the hearing might as well have been a party with himself as the guest of honor. That was the Bursteeni; they tended to get carried away with their enthusiasm. By the time Nom relinquished the floor to Cort, so she could give her report, she felt like she'd won half the battle just by curbing the tidal wave of superlatives.

But she had barely begun her first sentence when Rhaig stepped forward and said: "Excuse me—but with all due respect to the purpose that brought us here today, I must raise serious objections to this woman's presence here."

The general murmur that greeted this statement was punctuated by a few angry shouts, most of those human. The cries of protest from Ambassador Lowrey were especially loud; unfortunately, so were the hoots of laughter from Emil Sandburg. Cort herself said nothing, content to let the next few seconds play themselves out.

Nom's face wrinkled with a series of dumbfounded blinks. "Her presence? On the grounds?"

"On the grounds that the real issue here today isn't the psychological aberration of one diseased individual, but the habitual Hom.Sap arrogance toward less developed peoples." Rhaig's words boomed across the chamber, dominating the assemblage despite the dull roar that began to swell before he was even finished with his sentence. He didn't wait for the tumult to subside, but instead spoke louder, riding out the spectator reaction, beating it down, and finally conquering it. "Justice isn't about punishing crimes, or even about providing victimized peoples the means to fight for justice; it's about taking steps to ensure that such crimes never happen again. To do that, in this case, we must recognize where these crimes are coming from. To do that, we must recognize that the human species has been committing such crimes with monotonous regularity since they first climbed down from the trees—and that they haven't slowed down after finding their way to the stars. It's a constant, with these people." He gestured at Andrea Cort. "Even with our colleague, the learned Counselor from the Hom.Sap Confederacy. That's why I protest her involvement: because she has a history of participating in crimes just as heinous."

The roar erupted again: a tidal wave of noise, overwhelming the decorum of the proceedings, turning the room into a polyglot of shouted words in a dozen separate languages. Even the AIsource flatscreens, which usually communicated only in raw fact, scrolled their text so frantically that the flashing effect made them seem to be shouting. Andrea Cort, still keeping her own counsel, noted only that Whalekiller was among those shouting . . . and that the smiling Emil Sandburg was not.

Rhaig continued: "It happened a long time ago, so you might not all know the facts of the case—but many years ago, on a world called Bocai, a small colony of Hom.Sap settlers turned on the indigenes who had been living alongside them in peace with a savagery that outdid anything the demented Mr. Sandburg has done. From all reliable ports, every able human being in the colony participated—even the children—and the peaceful Bocai needed to resort to violence themselves in order to defend their families. One of the human criminals, caught with Bocai blood beneath her fingernails and between her teeth, was a young child only eight years of age by the human O.E.S. scale; a child who sane justice would have condemned as a threat to everything to lived, but who was instead rewarded—REWARDED!" he shouted, with sudden rage—"with adoption by the Confederacy Diplomatic Corps and training in a career with their Judge Advocate! Do we want to honor their hypocrisy by allowing such a creature to speak? Do we?"

The roar that had filled the chamber now engaged in pitched battle with itself, the universal desire to shout louder, to protest louder, to be louder, acting as natural enemy to the simultaneous need to choke back all that noise and hear whatever Andrea Cort had to say in response. Cort did not make the amateur mistake of trying to answer the Tchi's charges too soon; instead, she just remained silent, her face impassive, her demeanor calm, her attitude that of a woman in no particular hurry to be heard.

It was an open dare to Counselor Rhaig, to continue haranguing her.

But Rhaig, who had evidently expected the kind of fight that would have permitted him to shout her down, had peaked too early. He had nowhere else to go. He had to fall as silent as everybody else, awaiting either Cort's reaction or the reaction of whoever stepped forward to defend her.

The roar died to a murmur. Then a moment of hoarded breath.

Cort did not rush to fill the silence. She just waited, one two three beats, while the mood of the gathering evolved moved from anticipation to out-and-out worry.

Mekile Nom leaned forward. "Counselor Cort? Do you have any response to that?"

She held the silence one more heartbeat, and said, "Yes."

She stepped forward, speaking in a soft murmur that commanded attention from all the sentients who otherwise might have been moved to drown her out. "Counselor Rhaig is correct. I was at the Bocai Massacre. I participated in the Bocai Massacre. I—" She paused to allow the renewed hubbub another second or two to die down. "I was a child at the time. I will further point out that the incident in question involved not one, but two, separate communities both erupting in unmotivated violence against each other for no apparent reason. The madness they shared was so savage and so unmotivated that debate has raged for years over the possible existence of an organic or environmental factor beyond their conscious control. No independent investigation has ever succeeded in determining the cause. Even the Bocai themselves have refused to fix blame, and it was after all their world."

"And their fear of human reprisals had nothing to do with that?" Rhaig said. "Counselor! Really!"

Cort proceeded as if he hadn't spoken. "If anybody present here today wishes to review the facts to determine whether I'm truly as guilty of great crimes as Counselor Rhaig claims, please feel free; I personally agree with him, and I've taken the precaution of sending the full text of the interspecies investigation on Bocai to each of your embassies by hytex. But regardless of how you ultimately judge me, NONE," she said, repeating the word for emphasis, "NONE of what you decide to believe about me should affect what I came here to say; the facts I offer cannot be changed by the character of the sentient who speaks them. The implication that they might has more to do with Counselor Rhaig's private agenda, and his own complete shamelessness, than it does with the reason we're here."

She let that thought sink in, and scanned the room for reaction; she saw sympathy, disgust, admiration, loathing, anger, and even sheer confusion. But they were all listening. They were, if anything, paying closer attention than they might have if Rhaig hadn't smeared her. She spotted Mukh'thav among the Riirgaans and Haat Vayl among the Tchi; neither had shown her particular sympathy during their interviews, but they were both rapt as hungry men offered their first meals after long enforced fasts. She glanced at the Hom.Sap contingent next, and saw that (the grinning Sandburg aside) they'd all been affected the same way—but then they couldn't be blamed for such a reaction after Rhaig had attempted to magnify the issue here into a judgment on the entire human race. She had their support, for whatever that may have been worth.

She certainly had Whalekiller's. Though still seated, he resembled a coiled spring about to leap. His eyes flickered toward Rhaig, then caught hers. She could not quite read what she saw there, but anger on her behalf was part of it.

She allowed her lips to twitch, and moved on: "However, one thing Mr. Rhaig said is relevant to my point; he cited what he called the human attitude toward less developed peoples. I liked that phrase. Less developed peoples. It says less about human beings than it does about the assumptions that brought us here today. Our assumptions toward the very people whom this hearing is supposed to be about." Addressing Rhaig, she asked: "Is it your belief that the Catarkhans are inadequate in some way? That they need to be developed? That they'd be developed, in part, by the ability to communicate with us?"

Rhaig feigned nausea. "The Counselor is twisting my words—"

There was more, but she rode over it, reclaiming the floor as easily as he'd claimed it for his previous attack on her. "I am pointing out that the First Contact Protocols which have served us so ably elsewhere are less than appropriate for this species. As much as all our own races have benefited from our mutual association, from our cultural and technological exchanges, from our free trade and from the opportunity to see existence through differently evolved perspectives, we all have to admit that the Catarkhans were doing just fine by themselves before we came along. Maybe all of our attempts to contact them have just been an exercise in gratifying our own egos. Maybe we think we can elevate them by finding some way to make them notice us. And that's not true. We can't make them notice us. We can only disturb them in ways they're not evolved to handle."

"Ways that include murders committed by humans," Rhaig said.

"By a single diseased human," Cort said, "but yes.—And what about our insistence on including them in our efforts to seek justice for crimes committed on their soil? It's well-meaning enough, and it's perfectly appropriate when we're dealing with species capable of understanding concepts like crime, but isn't it perverse to require Catarkhan input when providing input of any kind seems utterly alien to their fundamental nature? Doesn't that say more about what we need from them, than what they need from us?"

Rhaig, who had been staring at her throughout her speech, unable to determine where she was going with this, took another shot: "You all see where the Hom.Sap counselor is going with this. She is making excuses . . ."

"No, I'm not," she said, with an insistence that immediately shut him up again. She turned as she spoke, addressing all of the gathered sentients in turn. "There are no excuses here. I want Mr. Sandburg to face justice as much as you all do. But I'm asking you to recognize that requiring him to be judged by Catarkhan standards is by definition requiring them to develop standards. That's defining them by our rules. That's denying them protection from people like Mr. Sandburg, because we have trouble living with the awareness that they don't need the rest of us either. And that," she said, directing her last words to Mekile Nom, "is a crime, just as surely as anything Mr. Sandburg did."

That disturbed the little Bursteeni. Silencing Rhaig, who had a no-doubt outraged response to this, with an outstretched hand, he regarded Cort through eyes turned grey with moral exhaustion. "These are not exactly startling arguments," he said, "and they don't change anything about the essential problem here. The First Contact Protocols—"

". . . don't apply here," Cort said.

That caused a stir. A small one, that didn't even begin to match the response to Rhaig's revelations about her, but a stir nevertheless. All around her, the chamber turned electric with the knowledge of a net about to draw tight.

Nom, wary but unable to anticipate her intent, said, "The last thing I heard, Counselor, this was supposed to be a First Contact mission."

She directed her next words not at the presiding chairman but at the entire chamber: "Then, why, precisely, aren't there any Catarkhans attending?"

Silence.

"They're not here," Cort said, "because it makes no sense for them to be here. They wouldn't participate. They wouldn't pay attention. They wouldn't understand. They wouldn't care. They wouldn't even know that any of this was happening. Oh, we could bring some here by force, but they wouldn't be ambassadors—they'd be prisoners. Or worse—specimens."

"That doesn't excuse killing them!" Rhaig shouted.

"No, sir, it does not. But it does change the nature of the crime, and it does simplify the issue of finding justice. It eliminates the need to shackle ourselves with the Protocols for First Contact."

Rhaig practically exploded at that. "How?"

"The Catarkhans," she said, smiling broadly now, "have not been contacted."

# 16.

The pandemonium that followed arrived in slow-motion. It was Nom who got it first. Typically, for a member of his species, he reacted with effusive appreciation, bobbing up and down in his seat like a cork, waggling his fingers with glee. "Oh, very good, AndreaCort! Very good!" The Hom.Sap contingent erupted with gasps and muttered damns. Emil Sandburg woo-hooed, the AIsource flatscreen flashed A FINE ARGUMENT in Hom.Sap. standard lettering, the Riirgaans exploded with frenzied consultation, and then the shock just rippled through the room in waves, turning the gathering into a babble of voices demanding to know if it could possibly be as simple as all that.

Rhaig attempted to reclaim the floor: "I fail to understand how my colleagues can celebrate such a self-serving Hom.Sap tactic."

"They celebrate it," Cort said, "because they felt as trapped by the seeming confines of the law as we did. They knew there was no way Sandburg could be judged by the Catarkhans. They just didn't see, until now, how we were going to get around that fact."

"Justice," Rhaig said, "is not an inconvenience to be . . . gotten around."

"Nor is it something to be penned behind false barriers," Cort said. "That was in danger of happening here. You believed that because you were here on first-contact missions, that this was a first-contact situation—while the facts quite clearly illustrate that it's nothing of the kind. It can't be. First contact hasn't been made yet."

"I would call murdering sentients in their homes a pretty definitive form of contact, Counselor."

"I would, too—but then my human perspective, and your Tchi viewpoint, are both totally beside the point here. That's

233

why I spent so much time during my investigation consulting so many of you, confirming that Mr. Sandburg's crimes didn't constitute a form of contact." She addressed Rhaig: "Remember, Counselor? When I asked your expert Dr. Vayl if punching you in the face would qualify as a form of communication?" The gathering rippled with laughter, some of it from Dr. Vayl. She continued: "Vayl said yes, even if the differences between our species prevented you from knowing what that punch signified. He said that inflicting pain qualifies as communication. A low form of communication, he said, but communication nevertheless. And I agree, it does. If the Catarkhans victimized by Mr. Sandburg had been able to suffer pain, then the First Contact protocols would be in force now.

"But Dr. Mukh'thav of the Riirgaans assured me that Mr. Sandburg's crimes, brutal as they were, did not include torture, because it was utterly impossible for the Catarkhans to have felt pain, or even to know what was happening to them. A message may have been sent, all right . . . but none was received. Therefore, no First Contact.

"I'll even cite a precedent. There was a case, several years ago, where a starship from a species I won't name jettisoned waste radioactives in an inhabited system. It was a stupid and irresponsible thing to do, and it resulted in serious environmental damage when the radioactives entered the gravity well of the world with sentient aboriginals. There were arguments, then, that the criminals in question should have been judged by the aboriginals they had so grievously harmed. This would have presented serious difficulties, as there had been no actual physical contact, and explaining the nature of the crime to the aboriginals would have required first making contact, then establishing communication, then explaining radioactivity and space travel to them first. It was judged that the crime itself did not constitute First Contact, and that the crime could be dealt with by existing interspecies law. So, too, with this."

"That was accidental contamination!" Rhaig shouted. "This was deliberate murder! You can't compare the two!"

"I don't intend to," Cort said, "since, as it turns out, assigning jurisdiction doesn't really matter here anyway. There's yet another issue."

Whereupon she told them what they should have known all along.

# 17.

The closing statement of Counselor Andrea Cort, edited to remove various ineffectual interruptions by the Tchi Gayre Rhaig:

A. CORT: Ironically, even if this hearing eventually finds against this argument, and concludes that the First Contact Protocols still apply in this case—that still has no bearing on what we ought to decide.

Politics aside, interspecies resentments aside, our decision on the matter of Emil Sandburg turns out to be an obvious one; we just haven't examined the situation closely enough to recognize the inevitable even as it looms before us waiting for us to notice it.

But when the story of this case is told, the students of interstellar law will note that there were really, always, only a limited number of ways we could have dealt with Sandburg.

If you eliminate letting him get away with his crimes—an option we must all as civilized peoples reject with total revulsion—there are, in fact, only three.

We could have judged him by our best approximation of Catarkhan law.

We could have deferred the question, until we were able to establish communication with the Catarkhans and find out for sure what they wanted.

Or we could have judged him by Human law, since Sandburg also broke the laws of the Corps he was supposed to represent.

Three possible approaches.

All equally legitimate; our wrangle over jurisdiction has prevented any one of them from being chosen.

But let us examine their implications.

Deferring judgment would delay this case for years, maybe even lifetimes. Mr. Sandburg would have to be imprisoned until he could be judged. If we never establish contact, it amounts to a life sentence.

This is conveniently enough the same thing human judgment would want.

As for Catarkhan Law, that's a little more difficult to determine—especially since I've been told time and time again that the Catarkhans don't have laws. But that's nonsense. They do have laws, and we all know they have laws. They have laws so strict that they never even think of breaking them.

Except we don't think of them as laws, because we call them instincts instead. They may be hardwired in the genetic code, but they're definitely rules of conduct—which Catarkhans follow with absolute dedication.

Who ever said we couldn't consult those laws to see what a Catarkhan would do to somebody like Mr. Sandburg?

We can't be exact, of course; Catarkhans don't have murderers. But they do have analogous situations. Specifically their way of dealing with diseased individuals who threaten the rest of the community. They quarantine such individuals in special chambers where they can't endanger the rest of the hive with their sickness. They keep those individuals imprisoned as long as the threat remains real. Of course, sick Catarkhans quarantine themselves voluntarily—but, as I recently arranged for Mr. Whalekiller and myself to confirm, when we saturated ourselves with the secretions of one desperately ill individual, sick Catarkhans who don't quarantine themselves have quarantine forced upon them by the rest of the community. In short, they're isolated until the illness runs its course, or until they die . . . whichever comes first.

Mr. Sandburg is a diseased individual whose presence threatens the rest of his community. By human law, he should be imprisoned; by Catarkhan law, he should be quarantined. The difference between that and the human solution is a semantic one, but this is a diplomatic issue; we're willing to use the word you prefer.

That's what I meant when I said it doesn't matter. Because we were all in perfect agreement all along. We just weren't paying enough attention to see it.

# 18.

The Council went for it, of course. They had no other choice; denying her logic would have meant perpetuating the deadlock that prevented Sandburg from being tried. Nobody wanted that, not even those who would have preferred to keep the shame on Mankind's shoulders.

The Cort Compromise, as it would come to be called, would be painted a triumph of interspecies diplomacy; her argument would be quoted, analyzed, fussed over, and dissected long after the words themselves became dead things, drained of meaning by their very overuse. In the years to come, they would even be abused, by advocates seeking to overturn local sovereignty in cases of crimes committed by off-worlders; they were applied, with questionable accuracy, to cases of crimes committed against locals far more receptive to communication than the Catarkhans. Andrea Cort's precedent was as vilified in those cases as it was praised now.

In a subsequent hearing, the Interspecies Council ruled in favor of life imprisonment for Emil Sandburg, that sentence subject to future alteration by Catarkhan authorities—a circumstance that, given the apparent impossibility of communicating with Catarkhan authorities, nobody really expected. Arrangements were made for Sandburg's transport to a maximum-security facility on New Pylthothus, the same prison housing the convicted culprits in previous diplomatic crimes on Hossti and Vlhan.

An attempt by Counselor Rhaig to bring censure proceedings against Andrea Cort, on the basis of her physical threats against his person, met with a resounding lack of interest; indeed, the Hom.Sap Embassy forwarded to her several messages from other embassies that had dealt with Rhaig and empathized with the urge. Even so, Rhaig announced his attention to file his complaint with the Dip Corps Judge Advocate. Cort would probably have to face some minor disciplinary action, which wouldn't bother her all that much; she had always been considered a problematic personality, whose reputation had been soiled beyond repair long before the first day she had ever spent on the job. It didn't matter when she still got the job done.

Ambassador Lowrey praised her at length for her brilliance; so did Mekile Nom of the Bursteeni, Goodsir Mukh'thav of the Riirgaans, and Haat Vayl of the Tchi. She accepted the compliments without much response, not trusting them to mean what they were supposed to mean on the surface. Politics was after all the creation of sentience. She did what she had to do to respect protocol, and then retreated as soon as possible.

Cort received word of another crime on alien soil—this one a bored embassy worker who had become quite prosperous selling his co-workers the sacred hallucinogens the local indigenes reserved for their honored priesthood. The aliens were willing to settle things by declaring the idiot in question an honorary member of their clergy, but he was desperate to avoid the mandatory gender realignment surgery. It may have been a shit case, as such things go, but Cort found herself looking forward to it; after Catarkhus, it would be a relief dealing with a crime that involved no savagery, and indigenes capable of arguing their own interests.

Everybody thought the matter was settled.

Everybody except Andrea Cort.

When the Hom.Sap Embassy held a victory celebration—one that could not be called a victory celebration without offending the other embassies, but which served precisely that function nevertheless—she declined to attend. Habit would have made her stay away anyway, but there was more to it this time—enough that, as she stood outside the compound walls, buffeted by wind and the sound of distant music, she often trembled despite the warmth of the night. Sometimes she stared into the empty air around her, and asked it questions beneath her breath.

Whalekiller came out, dressed in his formals, carrying a drink for her. He said: "It occurred to me that I ought to stop being mad at you."

She didn't take the drink. "That's your choice."

"You didn't know that the Catarkhans would react as violently as they did. You expected a reaction, but not one that extreme."

"If you say so," she said.

Whalekiller waited for more, closed his eyes in brief frustration, and spread his hands like a man casting cards upon a table. "You could make a pretense of giving a damn."

"It wouldn't be a pretense," she said. "I'm not a robot."

"You make a big show of trying to be," he said.

"Maybe I have to. Maybe that's what I'm left with."

There was just enough bitterness in her voice for Whalekiller to assume he knew what she was talking about. He sighed, put the drink down on a post beside her, and said: "And maybe that's just self-serving bullshit. Maybe we all have garbage in our pasts—some of it petty next to yours, some of it just as bad as yours, some of it downright worse. Maybe some of us throw away that garbage while some hold on to it like it's a family heirloom too valuable to lose. Maybe that says less about how painful that garbage was, than about how much we deserve to stay there alone."

"Maybe," she said, her gaze level. "And maybe I'm not even close to being alone. Maybe I've been surrounded all along. Maybe I'm surrounded now."

His eyebrows knit. "You lost me with that one, Counselor."

His incomprehension left her tired. He really thought everything was settled. But if such an intelligent man, who had devoted his entire career to communicating with alien minds, could spend so much time with the Catarkhans and not see the deeper implications, how much of a chance did she have persuading the rest of humanity? For a moment, she wondered if she'd be better off just giving up . . .

Unfortunately, giving up had never been in her nature.

She accepted the drink he'd offered and swallowed it in one gulp. "You're a good man, Goodsir Whalekiller. I just hope you find a way to live with it before it breaks your heart."

"Thank you," he said. "And I believe you're a good woman, Counselor Cort. I just hope you find a way to believe it while it can still make a difference for you."

She wanted to argue the point. But instead she nodded and returned to her quarters without speaking even one more word to anybody.

# 19.

Early the next morning, she arranged admission to Emil Sandburg's cell. She knew as soon as she entered that the other monster had experienced a night almost as bad as her own; the arrogance and sarcastic affability that had distinguished their first meeting was now completely gone, replaced with a red-eyed desperation that his keepers had misdiagnosed as a mere psychotic mood swing. Fear that he might try to hurt himself, or attack one of his infrequent visitors, had led them to fix him up with partial nerve block; it didn't paralyze him all the way, like the chair that had imprisoned him during his trial, but it did lend every move he made a curious slow-motion quality, as if the very air around him had been thickened to the consistency of gelatin. There was nothing slow about his trembling, though. The man was terrified.

A funny thing she noticed at once: with the fear upon him, the arrogance he affected was easy to see as the mask that it was. The bland and unformed personality his fellow indentures had seen now stood out in sharp relief, revealing a man without distinction, without edges, without blood beneath the skin. He was, as his Dip Corps profile had indicated, a nobody. A void. One who had been able to reap the dubious benefits of infamy for a short interval, but nevertheless, still just a void.

She tried to fight feelings of sympathy for him, and failed. After a moment she pulled over a stool that somebody had left in his cell and broke longstanding personal policy by sitting down in the presence of another human being. "Hello, Emil."

"Hello, Pretty Lady." He attempted to energize his smile with some of his old arrogance, but failed. He was a man trying to reclaim a vocabulary he had possessed for a short time, but which had been lost as completely as his freedom. "Come to gloat?"

"I don't gloat," Cort said.

"You probably don't. You don't laugh, either. Or cry. Or do much of anything else, I guess. Leftover trauma from your violent childhood, I suppose? Did you enjoy killing as much as I did?"

She wanted to respond with the same sternness she had shown toward him during their first interview, but there was no point; he was already defeated, and this was just bravado. Needing more of him than that, she took a small spherical device from her pocket, flourished it before Sandburg, and placed it on the cell's pull-down tray table. Depressing a thumb-sized cavity at one end of the device, she said: "There. That'll scramble the monitor system. Nothing you or I say to each other in the next few minutes will ever be seen or heard by anybody else."

He licked his lips. "That leaves you awfully vulnerable if I decide to kill you."

It was a weak threat, uttered because he seemed to think it was expected of him; there was little he could do in light of what the nerve block had done to his reaction time. But she treated it at face value anyway: "You're free to try, Emil. But as you're so fond of noting, you're not the only monster in this room. Provoking me to violence would be a very bad idea."

An acknowledging tired nod. "So what do you want?"

"I wanted to speak to you one last time about your crimes."

He seemed infinitely tired. "Maybe we should talk about yours."

"That's all right," she said. "I don't really want to have a conversation with you, Emil; your gamesmanship is too boring for that. I just wanted to let you know that I figured out your secret. I know what you're all about."

"Well, la-de-da."

"It took a while to see it, mostly because your co-workers here, human and alien, have all been so busily painting you as a sadistic killer."

"I am."

"Maybe you are and maybe you're not. You certainly enjoy having people think you are. You've played the role very well, Emil; so well, in fact, that for a while, dealing with you, I had trouble seeing the empty, faceless little man your co-workers described. It must have been fun, being somebody. Even a monster. At the very least it must have been a novelty for you."

"Shut up."

"You never came out and said it, but you did everything you could to make us believe that you committed murders before Catarkhus. You encouraged anything that bolstered your image as a sadistic monster. It couldn't have been hard. It even seemed reasonable in context. After all, killing is such a messy business that it takes genuine enthusiasm for anybody to make a regular habit of it. Sadism would be a good explanation for that kind of thing, and the pleasure you took in taunting us seems to argue for that. Except," she hesitated, then pressed on: "it doesn't enter into the killings here, does it, Emil? It couldn't have. These were Catarkhans. They didn't feel pain; they didn't even feel fear. You had to have some other reason for going back to them time and time again."

"Maybe I have a rich fantasy life," he said.

"I thought of that; killing Catarkhans, who won't notice

and won't complain, is a safer alternative to carving on Tchi or Bursteeni or even your fellow Hom.Saps, all of whom would tend to raise more of a fuss. If you wanted to indulge a compulsion at minimal risk, killing Catarkhans would be the way to go. Except—if you really were driven to inflict pain, killing Catarkhans wouldn't satisfy you for long, would it? A connoisseur of pain, driven by his love of pain, would soon find torturing them about as enjoyable as chewing paper."

"I know people who chew paper," Sandburg said. "Disgusting habit."

"So's killing," Cort said, "even in the absence of sadism."

Sandburg closed his eyes, looked away from her, and began to hum a vapid love song currently popular on the nets. It was, Cort realized, the same song he'd been humming during her first onworld briefing, when the diplomatic staff had shown her the real-time images of his imprisonment. His rendition of it had not improved. But the meaning of it had changed. Back then humming it had seemed the arrogance of a man who didn't care what happened to him, and now it was just a pathetic series of sounds made by a soul desperate to block out the truth he did not want to hear.

Cort, driven by her own wounds, was the last sentient alive capable of showing him mercy. "A nobody," she said. "A deficient personality. Low charisma, low empathy. Utterly forgettable. Leaving no impression anywhere he went. Joining the Dip Corps to make contact with something. Anything. Not succeeding even there. Cruelly assigned to establish contact with creatures incapable of even acknowledging his presence."

He hummed louder; he even started rocking back and forth, like an autistic child desperate to retreat into a world of his own.

She leaned forward and yanked his hands away from his

ears. The move took him totally by surprise. He emitted a little squeak, and flinched; a big bad monster, trembling like tissue under a gale-force wind, not afraid of being struck, but terrified beyond reason at the simple threat of being understood.

She whispered it: "You can't stand being invisible, can you, Emil?"

He yanked his hands free, hugged himself, and faced the floor again.

She said: "You took your time killing them—because you were willing to do anything you needed to do to get them to notice you."

He said nothing, and did nothing.

"In your own desperate way," she said, "you were actually attempting First Contact."

Again, he responded in no obvious way. But without moving a millimeter, without making a sound any of the monitors would record, he succeeded in answering her anyway. She could see the answer in the way all the strength seemed to drain from his bones.

She watched him for several minutes, taking his measure in the weight of his silence. She had thought him another monster, and painted him large enough to fit the role; but there was nothing large about him, nothing substantial that deserved all the time and effort that had been devoted to his case. He had just been the sum total of his illusions, and nothing else. Now that she'd stripped even those away, there was nothing left. It deflated him, reduced him to the nonentity that he had been before and would now be again. Just before she left him for the last time, she could almost imagine she saw his flesh going the way of his pretenses, his skin and bones and muscle turning transparent as what little substance he had dissipated into the recirculated air of his cell.

Prison would destroy him. He would disappear into a population of true monsters, who would either victimize him or ignore him. Either way, he had nothing to look forward to. Nobody would ever pay any special attention to him ever again.

But he had made a difference, without knowing it.

He said: "Go away."

She said: "Not yet, Bondsman. There is one other thing I want to share with you. It has to do with what happened at Bocai."

He murmured: "I wasn't there."

"It erupted out of nothing, Emil—there were no resentments fueling it, no unresolved conflicts motivating it. There was just pure, savage hatred, arriving as if by spontaneous generation in the midst of two communities who had committed to living in peace. I never thought I stood a chance of understanding it . . . until I saw what you did to the Catarkhans."

He met her gaze again, and this time his despair was mixed with a dose of sheer incomprehension. She didn't blame him; there was no way he could help her with this part. But he was the only other monster present, and therefore the only other person who deserved a share of it.

She said, "We walk among them, talk to them, move them around against their will, get aggravated and—in your case— even murderous because they refuse to notice us. But what makes us think we're any better? Why are we so sure we're seeing and feeling and hearing everything there is to see? How do we know there aren't other First Contact teams, from species we're not equipped to sense ourselves? How do we know that they're not all around us? In fact, how do we know that they're not just like you, frustrated to the point of madness because we don't have what it takes to notice them?"

Sandburg stirred. "Invisible Demons." A little of the monster's previous arrogance came back to him, then. "You're crazier than I am."

"And if some imaginative Catarkhan told his friends that there were invisible people walking around among them, trying to get them to pay attention? What would they say to that?"

He looked past her, through her, through even the walls of his cell, seeing not the shape of his cage but the shape of the idea that was forming. His lips twitched, the look of a man fed an exotic treat who was trying to decide whether he liked it.

Cort said: "Maybe it's the kind of idea you have to be crazy to imagine. Maybe it's the kind of idea you can only believe if you're desperate for some kind of absolution. But that doesn't mean it's a bad idea—just an old one we thought we could safely outgrow. Maybe the demons who we used to believe influenced all our worst impulses actually do exist—and we were only wrong about what they were and where they come from. Maybe they come from all around us, and we're just not equipped to see them. Maybe that frustrates them so much they get even by pulling our strings." She took such a deep breath that the rest of her words emerged in a half-hysterical shudder: "Maybe one was with us on Bocai. Maybe one was with you here."

For a moment, Sandburg seemed desperately anxious to believe it. Then he shook his head and delivered the verdict with as much contempt as he could: "And maybe this is just you, seizing on any explanation that frees you from the ultimate responsibility for what you did."

"I thought of that, too," Cort said. "I just don't believe it anymore."

The black rage bubbled up in him, then, dispelling—at least for the moment—any remaining sense of defeat in his bearing. His face contorted in a grimace, his hands curled into fists, and he stood so suddenly that she winced, imagining imminent violence—but no; the nerve block was still in place. It was disgust and not bloodlust that had returned some semblance of power to his limbs. "Then I'm better than you, Counselor. Because I know I did what I did, and I don't look for excuses. If you must, you should listen to Rhaig and read a history book sometime. Because we don't need Demons to act the way we act."

"Maybe," she said, facing his anger with an equally dangerous calm. "And the hell of it is, you're almost certainly right. But from this moment on, my life's about finding out one way or the other."

She stood, and placed her hand on the scrambler device, resting her thumb on the activation switch, but not yet applying the miniscule degree of pressure that would once again allow Sandburg's warders access to everything that was said and done in this room. She wanted to press it now; strictly speaking, she even should. But part of her resisted, knowing that once she did she'd have to return to the greater world outside, a place where she would once again be infinitely more alone than she ever could be here, in the presence of another monster.

Sandburg, who perhaps sensed the same thing, and maybe even sympathized with her against his will, simply glared at her, waiting.

She smiled at him before she left: the same smile Whalekiller had seen and come to dread. And made her promise:

"And if I do find them, I'm going to make damn sure they're properly judged."

*This one's for Joey and Debbie Green.*

# The Magic Bullet Theory

I don't know why Beauregard Finch picked me to partner with. Maybe he just liked my face. Or maybe he approved of the initiative I showed by stealing that lunger's boots.

It was a cold spring morning about twenty years back, around eighteen-eighty something, just outside the Hotel Excelsior, at that time the best (and only) accommodations available in Sticky Tar, New Mexico. I needed the lunger's boots because I'd just five minutes before been forced at gunfight to surrender my own in lieu of payment for the previous night's stay. This was a heinous miscarriage of justice, I felt, since I hadn't ever made it to my lumpy, termite-infested bed anyway—although I'd checked in early the night before, I'd woken up with empty pockets early this morning after a long night passed out in the alley between Miss Veronica's Social Club and Doc Early's Painless Dentistry. The way I did the math, it worked out that since I used the alley, I shouldn't have had to pay for the room. Clete at the front desk didn't agree, and he had a Remington backing him up. Worse, he took not one but both my own boots, even though I tried to persuade him that a night spent, or not spent, in the breeding farm he called a bed shouldn't have cost me more than the left one with the broken heel.

He was helpful about it, though. When I asked him just how in tarnation I was supposed to get around the dusty streets of Sticky Tar, with not even a single good boot to hop around in, he suggested I appropriate the lunger's.

He didn't say the lunger's name, of course. The lunger had one, but nobody around town knew it. Nobody talked to him because nobody wanted the fella to cough and give us a face full of what he had. So we just called him the lunger. He was the only lunger we had, so there was no real source of confusion.

So I went to get the boots. The lunger was lying face-down, half-on and half-off the plank sidewalk, with his face half-buried in a souvenir left behind by somebody's palomino. They were tight boots, and to stand a chance getting them off I had to get down on the planks with him, pulling with both hands while I braced my right foot against his rear end for leverage. Some of the folks passing by on the street cried out words of encouragement as I grunted and heaved and yanked on those boots with all the strength I had.

The stranger who came by around about then was the only one to actually volunteer his services. He was a tall, well-dressed fella—too well-dressed for Sticky Tar, where most of the folks, men and women, seemed to upgrade their wardrobes using the same method I was attempting. He had an all-black suit with a bolo tie and a wide-brimmed black hat, all of it a mite grayed just from walking around town, but clean enough to look like he'd only been wearing it a week or two. He also had a thick black moustache, eyes that looked like squinty little apostrophes punctuating the big protruding letter O he had for a nose, and a smile containing more of his own teeth than any three of Clete's hotel guests, myself included. I don't know where he was headed before he saw me struggling with the lunger, but he seemed to have given up on getting there until I was done; instead, he just rolled a cigarette, leaned an elbow on Clete's hitching post, and stood there blowing smoke as I struggled to obtain my footwear.

After a while, I said, "You got a problem?"

"Not particularly," the Stranger said, in an accent that screamed Somewhere Back East.

"You just watchin', then?"

He nodded slightly. "You can't put on a spectacle without inviting spectators."

"I ain't exactly doin' this for your amusement."

"That's all right," the Stranger said. "I'll accept the amusement as an incidental side benefit. Won't this poor individual miss his boots when he wakes up?"

"He can always take 'em back."

"Except," the Stranger said, "that being unconscious at the moment, he won't have any way to know who you are and where you've absconded with his footwear."

I grunted. "I cain't spend all day worrying about his problems."

"Ahhh," the Stranger said.

"You ain't thinkin' of stopping me, are you?"

"No, you're entitled to warm feet, I suppose. But perhaps you can use some help?"

The offer testified that he hadn't been in Sticky Tar for long. If it was the kind of town where nobody stopped to rescue some poor lunger, found himself face-down in horse dung on a cold winter morning, it also wasn't the kind of place where folks stopped to help folks with good lungs and no boots innocently trying to make the best of the situation. It occurred to me, briefly, that maybe he wanted the boots for himself, but then I looked at his and saw that they were new and shiny and about fifty times better than what the lunger had on anyway. I said, "I'd much appreciate that, mister," and the stranger clamped his teeth on his smoke and ambled on over to the lunger's outstretched arms and grabbed hold of the fella's two toothpick wrists, and said, "One, Two, Three, Pull."

It still took us a couple of minutes, and we must have got the poor lunger stretched a couple of vertebrae taller before a couple of kindly boys in town to spend their paychecks from the Lazy T saw what we were doing and rushed on over to help us pull. We got the lunger lifted up out of the dung and waltzed him around the street for a while, spinning him around once or twice as we pulled on both ends, and for a while it looked like the four of us were going to spend the whole damn day doing just that, but then the object of our tug of war shuddered, let out a cough and a piece of lung, asked us with no small amount of irritation just what in tarnation we all thought we were doing, and relaxed his feet long enough to let his boots fly. I fell backwards and the stranger fell backwards and the helpful cowboys fell backwards and the lunger fell to the ground and got knocked out, poorer the boots but richer in not having his face in horse dung any more.

The cowboys went off in search of Miss Veronica's Social Club, the stranger considerately dragged the lunger over to the sidewalk so he wouldn't get tramped by any of Sticky Tar's famous nearsighted horses, and I retired back to the sidewalk in front of the Hotel to try on my brand new boots.

I was just discovering that they were two lefts when the stranger came back, relit his now-mangled cigarette, and blew out a cloud of deeply amused smoke. "Beauregard T. Finch, at your service."

"Jared Wallop," I said. "Likewise."

He shook hands with me, and said, "Jared, don't take this too personally or anything, but it strikes me that most folks would have to be pretty desperate, to want to steal a lunger's boots."

"They're okay," I said, scowling as I forced my right foot into the extra left boot. "They ain't infected or nothing. It ain't like even a lunger breathes through his toes. Besides, if they're warm and dry and don't got nothing living in them I can't safely mash to a paste with my own feet, they're still better than stockings with holes in 'em."

"Excellent logic," he said.

"Wish I had a nickel to buy you a whiskey by way of thanks."

"That's all right. I didn't get the impression you were prosperous, so I never had my hopes up." He blew out a long cloud of smoke, which billowed around his chin for a second or so, like it had too much affection for him to leave. "Interested in a job?"

I kicked the horse trough, first with one foot, then the other, to see if the boots had any give to them. The left one felt okay, the right like I was already losing circulation in the toes. "I hope it don't involve any hard work."

"Not especially," Finch said. "I'm just going to be in town for a while, working on a unique money-making opportunity, and I need somebody to watch my back."

I squinted at him, searching for little invisible hash-marks behind his eyes. "You ain't a hired gun, I know that much. Ain't nobody in town worth killing. Hell, there ain't nobody in town worth spittin' on in a fire."

He shook his head. "No, I don't want to shoot anyone. Far from it; I came here because the Shooting's been done already."

Which is how I found out he was here for the Magic Bullet.

Now, it's probably going to seem peculiar to folks hearing this story for the very first time, especially considering what the Bullet had been doing, or not doing, for the better part of the previous two years, but Beauregard T. Finch was the first fella who ever bothered to pay it any special mind. I mean, everybody in Sticky Tar knew that the Bullet's behavior wasn't normal, but the kind of folks who wound up in these parts, at least at that particular point in history, were also the kind of folks who looked at a miracle like the Bullet, said "Huh!" and then went back to the more serious business of picking pockets, shooting preachers, and whacking folks with whiskey bottles. The Bullet was just an inconvenience that had to be dealt with, like bedbugs or horseflies or Feeney the town barber who sometimes got twitchy and sliced off a cheek or two. As long as we stayed out of its way we just didn't see any reason to pay attention.

Finch didn't see it that way, though. And then he dragged me off to Mamie's, where he outbid a fella with green teeth for the morning's one fresh egg. After telling Mamie to scramble it for me, taking care to specify that she had to go all-out and use a clean pan, he lit a fresh cigar and contributed to the overall murk. "Tell me," he said.

My stomach growled from the novel concept of solid food for breakfast. "I don't reckon I can tell you anything you don't already know. You seen the thing?"

"First place I went when I rode into town: had to know it was real, and not just some whimsical rumor. It's quite impressive. I was almost tempted to touch it."

"Good way to lose a hand," I opined. "Or a finger, one."

"Oh, I haven't tried it, don't worry," Finch said, though I hadn't; I was sure I would have already noticed a thing like a pool of blood collecting under the table. "The gentleman who pointed me this way made sure I knew all the pitfalls. No, I just want to know if the local version of its provenance matches the story that one-eyed bible salesman told me in Kansas City. Were you there when it was fired?"

"Nope. I was pinned beneath a gutshot stallion out on the llano. Didn't get rescued till a week later, when a couple of skinners came by for the hide. But I heard about it, when they dragged me back to town."

"Tell me what you heard," he said.

And there wasn't much to tell, but I obliged.

It had been a hot day. That much I could vouch for. The sun was pounding down like a angry kid in a sailor suit using his Sunday shoes to make splatter-dots of a bunch of ants. It was the kind of Sticky Tar afternoon when you didn't move around much, since even the air was too ornery to like getting out of your way. It was so hot that when Singing Jackson took out his fool guitar in the saloon, to sing one of his cheerful songs about all the playful animals out on the range, Rufus Foster only walloped him over the head with it six or seven times before losing interest—which is saying a lot, since Foster was the kind of fella apt to make a whole day out of that kind of activity. It was pretty bad for me, since as I said I was out on the llano seeing thirst-visions under the weight of the gutshot stallion, but even as bad as that sounds, I still wasn't much better off than the folks still in town with food and water and no horses on 'em. Because it was the kind of day that weighs you down whether you got a horse on you or not.

So I don't know how much of this is really what happened and how much was just the drunk and sun-addled citizens of Sticky Tar getting their fool stories wrong like always. But the way I heard it, later, these big angry coal-black storm clouds rolled in from the east in no time flat, covering the sky like it was something they wanted to steal when we weren't looking. They say lightning struck about fifty times over by the Black Hills, and about sixty times out by Jake Forrester's spread, and just once right in the center of town, blasting poor Agatha Thompson right out of her sensible shoes and over the roof of Miss Veronica's. And they figured that Sticky Tar was about to get its very first twister, which was fine with them since it was the kind of town that had always had two of everything else, and even the overall season of destruction could rightly benefit from a little variety.

But there wasn't any twister, and there wasn't any rain. Instead there was just this tolerable old fella with a long white beard, a thin pointed nose and eyes like a pair of Apache arrowheads glinting red from just being carved out of somebody's liver. He rode in on a blood-red camel, wearing nothing but a big black tent of a thing with stars and eyeballs and little dancing men on it, and a big pointed dunce cap with pretty much more of the same, only smaller, and the kind of expression you usually only see on folks when they're bone-stupid crazy or sick as walking mange. The folks of Sticky Tar, watching behind curtains if they had curtains, or behind barrels if they happened to be sleeping in alleys instead, or from right out in the open if they weren't the clever and perceptive types who'd already figured out from the general flavor of things that Main Street was going to be right unhealthy for the foreseeable future, were all united in the shared impression that the fella on the camel was both—as crazy as an armless man with an itch, and as sick as a pony express rider transporting an anthill in his shorts.

"Deke Watson says the guy was Chinese," I told Beauregard Finch. "But Deke thinks everybody is Chinese. He got these big bug eyes, Deke; they stick out ahead of him like a couple of extra testicles on his face, and he figures everybody else with normal-shaped eyes is Chinese by comparison. So he thinks he's the only white guy in the world, if you follow."

"Yes, I do. But—"

"Yeah, he got himself some funny ideas, that Deke. One time, he—"

"Later," said Beauregard Finch. "After you finish telling me about the man on the camel."

256

The fella rode his camel right past the various businesses and amenities of Sticky Tar, right past the whorehouse and the saloon and the tobacconist and the barrelmaker and the painless dentist and the house belonging to Ole Widow Ramsey, who spent her days sitting on her porch with a sawed-off just in case the husband she'd used it on the first time came crawling back from Boot Hill requiring her to use it a second time. And for a while it looked like he was going to ride right out of town, which would have suited everybody just fine. But then he stopped right at the far western end of Main Street, right at the threshold where the almost-nothing of Sticky Tar becomes the absolutely-nothing of the desert beyond, and he turned that big ugly beast of his around, and he sat there staring at the town, as if noticing for the very first time that it had been a town, and not a patch of unusually detailed high grass with windows and hitching posts and ugly old women clutching shotguns on front porches.

"And then?" Finch prompted, the excitement growing in his little black eyes.

I used a thumbnail to scrape leftover egg off my beard, sucked it off noisily, and used the tip of my tongue to excavate the lingering remnants from the three teeth on the left and the four teeth on the right. "And then he decided he was mad, I guess. He hopped down off the camel, drew his revolver, and fired a single shot down the center of Main Street."

"The very same Bullet," Finch noted, "that still hovers motionless four feet off the ground, in the middle of the street, on the western side of town, at the very same spot where it was fired."

I nodded vigorously. "Well, not the very same spot; we figure it's moved about six inches or so, last two years. But that's the one, all right. The funny-looking fella fires it, looks pissed off, gets back on his camel, and rides the rest of the way out of town. We figure he gone riding back to his outfitter to complain about the laziness of his ammunition; get caught out in Indian country with nothing but a gun full of that, and I promise you you'll have time to be captured and fed to ants about a thousand times over before your best shot even moves as far as a halfway decent fart."

"And nobody ever tried to do anything about it?"

"Why? It ain't exactly going nowhere in a hurry, and it's pretty harmless as long as you leave it alone. Oh, every once in a while some jasper comes galloping in from the west, don't see that Bullet hangin' there in his way, and ends up flat on his face 'cause he just accidentally drilled a hole through his horse. And sometimes a drunk not watching where he's going stumbles into it and ends up with a jaw connected by only one hinge. And once upon a time somebody tries to pluck the thing right out of the air bare-handed—like Mose Wilson done, which is why they call him Two-Fingers now. But mostly, it's just the kinda thing you gotta get used to. Like, in this other town I lived once—"

Beauregard said: "That's enough, Jared." He drummed his fingers on the table, cocked his head thoughtfully, and said: "Has anybody ever considered building a fence around it, to avoid such unfortunate accidents?"

"Been jawed about. Nobody wants to do the work."

He drummed his fingers some more, then removed a wad of bills from his jacket pocket and said: "Do you know why I'm in this town?"

"Uh, no. I don't think you ever mentioned."

"I'm in this town," he said, "because I'm in dire need of a new career. The old one wasn't really working out."

I blinked a number of times.

And Beauregard said, "Who do I see in this town about purchasing some land?"

★ ★ ★ ★ ★

Now, nobody can ever accuse the citizens of a town like Sticky Tar of being swift; George Peterson once stumbled into the same drainage ditch five times five days in a row, Two-Nose MacDougal never quite figured out what shoes were for, and Ed Colton required a week of going about his daily business before he realized the reason his wife was still in bed and by that time not smelling too good. But folks thereabouts did have a special talent for spreading rumors. They had to be: it was the only form of free entertainment. Sometimes we spent entire winters whispering made-up bullshit into each other's ears, just to see how much it changed by the time it came back to us; like the time I told some drunks around a poker table that Zeke Callahan had four thousand dollars in gold buried beneath some floorboards in his cabin, and the story got around, and by the time anybody got around to saying it was crap, three folks had drowned diving for the same treasure in the brackish soup at the bottom of his well. Nobody ever pulled up any of Zeke's floorboards and nobody ever remembered the story came from me; the survivors tarred and feathered Zeke instead. And that was just one made-up story. Whenever there was something real to talk about, like the news that some fool stranger had just paid good money for a twenty-foot plot of land in the middle of the street with nothing worth looking at but the magical floating Bullet in the middle of it, it moved through the population faster than greased buckshot through a goose.

By lunchtime, Beauregard Finch had gathered quite a large audience for himself, building a corral round his Bullet. Folks had stopped getting drunk indoors and brought their whiskey bottles out on the porches so they could call Finch about two dozen different words for Stupid as he finished the fence, then started on the framework for a tent with the Bullet in its center. By the time Finch hung his tent and went back to the saloon to purchase one of their stools, they'd stopped calling him Stupid and Fool and Idjit and Numbskull and started in on a series of imaginative metaphors for Shit—a subject the good citizens of Sticky Tar had a history of attacking with particular gusto.

Then he put up his sign: THE MAN WHO CHEATS DEATH 10 CENTS! and they all got in line.

Red Elder wasn't the first one in line, originally, but he beat up the four folks standing in front of him so he could have first honors.

Now, you can't understand Red Elder unless you picture yourself an ant and Elder a big flat rock being dropped in your vicinity from about four feet up. It might land on you; it might not. If it lands on you that's the end of the story; if it doesn't then you hear the nearby thump, see the rock, and figure, okay, can't do nothing about it except be happy I wasn't one of the fools standing there. Red was okay, most of the time, which is why folks felt so safe disrespecting him to his face, but he went through whole days and weeks where he turned mean enough to make John Wesley Hardin look like your local parson's sweet baby sister. On those days it didn't even matter whether you were nice to him or not; stand in the wrong place and he'd shoot you because it was easier than breaking up his momentum. Any other town, Red Elder would have had a hangman's noose tied for him long ago. But in Sticky Tar folks just didn't want to bother.

It helped Red Elder that he was an unnaturally big fella— with a chest as big as a barrel and a head that bumped doorways if he didn't stoop some when entering a room. It helped too that his eyes didn't quite agree with each other about which direction to face. And it helped some that the nickname Red had nothing to do with his hair, which was the kind of scraggly blond as transparent as a windowpane. Red was his skin color—which is to say that though he was a white man, he was that kind of white man who's always a bit scarlet around the face, like a fella keeping a major tantrum on hold just in case he's about to need one.

"I want to see this fool myself," he said.

I was standing out in front of the tent flap with an old spittoon Finch had drafted for use as cashbox. "That's ten cents."

"I don't got to pay ten cents to see a fool! I see fools all the time for free!"

"I know that. I done met your brothers." (There were six of those, all as mean as Red, but none as big or tough. They started as many fights, but ended most of them on the floor spitting blood. They didn't have an iguana's brain or a mouthful of teeth still left between them.) "But the show's still ten cents."

"I have half a mind to just turn around and say the hell with it."

Now, you know and I know that for as long as there have been folks inclined to say that they had half a mind to do something, there have also been folks inclined to tell the first folks they had half a mind, period. I point this out at this particular juncture just to establish that I had enough sense of self-preservation to avoid going down that road. "Ten cents."

"You must be twice as dumb as he is," Elder said.

I allowed as how I wasn't sure of the precise ratio.

Elder made a few more vague noises about how god-forsakenedly dumb I was, saying about how I didn't have as much brains as this or even half the sense of that, but it wasn't long before he ran out of metaphors and begrudgingly counted out eleven pennies, that precise sum being the result of getting temporarily lost somewhere in the vicinity of six. I took the coins, pocketed one myself as a fringe benefit of being the guy at the front gate, and parted the tent flap so he and Beauregard could have a jaw.

Now, I wasn't in there with them, since I had all I could handle standing at the front gate making sure that the good citizens of Sticky Tar stayed ruly while they waited, but since I knew the way Beauregard had himself set up in there, and I was close enough to hear every word he and Red Elder said, I can still tell you pretty much exactly what it was like.

Beauregard Finch was sitting calmly on a stiff-backed wooden chair, his eyes focused on The Bullet as it hovered about two inches away, threatening a point of impact right between his eyes. It was right smack in front of him, almost touching the bridge of his nose, barely far enough to keep his eyes from crossing. Itching to blow the top of his head clean off, one eyeblink of normal speed away from decorating the tent canvas behind him with bits of bone and blood and brain, it was more clearly a little piece of death waiting to happen than it ever had been before Beauregard had the vision to wrap it up in a tent and a corral and a ten-cent admission.

Beauregard sat in that chair, eye to eye with that round, and didn't even break a sweat.

Red Elder, who'd purchased his admission intending to spend his five minutes telling Beauregard Finch he didn't have the sense the Good Lord gave a cowflop in a high wind, just about naturally felt the back of his mouth going dry. He said: "Why you doin' this?"

Beauregard Finch put a cigar to his mouth and took a drag. He said: "I do this because I hate Death. Because I tease Death. Because I spit in the face of Death. Because I will wrestle Death to the ground every day of the week. Because it makes me feel alive. Because I am a Man."

Elder felt some of his courage coming back. "I think you're just plain stupid."

"That's another possible explanation," allowed Beauregard Finch.

"Your Mama know you're this stupid?"

"My mother," Beauregard Finch said, "died to save me from a ravenous Siberian tiger when I was four months old. It happened in India, near the temple of Ali Apu Apa. The tiger leaped from the foliage, scanned the crowd for an appetizer, spotted me in my stroller, and pounced. My mother threw herself in its path, seized it by its powerful jaws, and held on with her bare hands until some soldiers with muskets could intervene. Alas, the strain was too much for her poor noble heart. She died that evening. Her last words were to spend my life taking vengeance on the Reaper." He pointed his cigar at the Bullet. "That is what I am doing here, sir. I am mocking Death. Ridiculing it. Teaching it that, try as it might, it will never conquer a Finch."

I had to admit this much: whatever Beauregard did before he came here, it had certainly left him with a harmonious tongue. Elder needed three or four attempts to successfully locate his voice. " 'Ceptin' your Ma, I guess."

And Beauregard chuckled. " 'Ceptin her."

Elder didn't say much after that: just stood there staring at Beauregard, tilting his big oddly-shaped head first one way and then the next, like a dog trying to figure out the source of a high-pitched noise. Beauregard said later that he figured Elder was trying to let the knowledge percolate to the rest of his seven brain cells. I didn't know what that meant then, but I know what it meant now: that something in the bone-stupid mad-dog-mean sponge he had inside that skull of his had just picked up a little taste of poison it hadn't had before. It wasn't going to be easy to see for a while; but it was there.

Then Elder said something entirely unexpected: "I want to sit in your chair."

Beauregard said: "What?"

"I want you to get up and let me sit in your chair. I want to face that there Bullet and let it know it ain't gonna conquer me."

"Your paid admission doesn't cover—"

"You own this tent. You don't own the Bullet. I want five minutes alone with that Bullet. You give me that, I'll leave. But I want that five minutes."

Beauregard said later that he wanted to argue against it, but couldn't; Red Elder was wearing the kind of expression that made his face a Magic Bullet in its own right. It was facing him all still and quiet-like, but it had a peculiar kind of tension behind it, like it was just a canvas bag filled with gunpowder waiting for just one wrong word to provide the wrong kind of spark. Beauregard later said that he felt closer to death, just looking at that face, than he ever felt with the Bullet drawing an invisible line between itself and the back of his skull. He might be telling the truth; Red Elder was a scary fella, even before the Bullet did what it done to him. Or he might have been lying, Beauregard Finch being the kind of guy who always to put his own special signature on every story. Either way, he did get up from his chair, and let Red Elder take five minutes staring down the miraculous ammo.

When Red Elder got up, his eyes were shining, in the manner of a man who had just courted his one and only love.

"It's a woman," he murmured. "A woman."

Then he walked off, and Beauregard still thought he was done with it.

But that night, during a Poker Game at Mamie's, Red Elder got mad at a guy who drew an inside straight. He stood up, reached out with both hands, grabbed the guy's ears, and without saying a word gave them both a wicked but perfectly synchronized twist that popped them both right off the man's head. The newly earless guy was so stunned he passed out, also without saying a word. Red Elder scooped up the fella's money and stomped out, still without saying anything. It was a pretty serious moment, even for Red Elder, but not so out of the ordinary that we thought anything was up.

The man without the ears fell off his horse twice, riding out of town the next day. It wasn't that he was in pain and shock, but because he couldn't see where he was going; his hat kept slipping down over his eyes. He never got to see what happened between Red Elder and Beauregard Finch; which I suppose made him a lucky man, more or less.

Now, granted, it's a pretty remarkable thing when a grown man decides to face death in the eye ten hours a day, seven days a week, and it's even more remarkable when the death in question doesn't make any sense to begin with, and for a while there Beauregard and I did a pretty tolerable repeat business, with most of the good folks of Sticky Tar getting on line about a dozen times or more, just to sneak themselves another gander at the crazy fella. They got on line even after they saw what he looked like and what he was going to say; they got on line even though they could see him for free every night when he spent their dimes on whiskey and women and (twice in that first week alone) fresh bathwater guaranteed not to have known more than twenty or thirty backsides before him. It wasn't that they didn't know he was the same guy. Each night he walked into Mamie's all duded up despite a long hard day spent as the innermost concentric circle on a target, folks quit spitting and cussing and passing out long enough to wave and cheer and invite him over to buy them drinks. They asked him if he was gonna go out and do that darn fool thing again tomorrow, and he always said only if he couldn't think up anything better to do, and they always laughed, and they always got on line again to watch him staring at the Bullet again the next day. It got to the point where I began to count the dimes in my own pocket, which were sometimes as much as four or five dollars worth at a time, more money than I ever had at any one time before, and think that just maybe taking tickets at the front gate of Beauregard's Crazy Man exhibit just might be the respectable law-abiding career my poor departed Daddy always said I should have. Another few months of this, I thought, and I might even be able to give some thought to maybe running for public office as one of Sticky Tar's few steadily employed.

It felt good to have Beauregard as a friend, too. I don't mind telling you that. It wasn't the absolute first time, for me, but a couple of winters earlier my other one and I had gotten stuck in the mountains without food, and he'd lost the coin toss, so there you go. Having a friend who could actually set me up in a career was even better.

But when I mentioned it to Beauregard, he just laughed at me. "It won't last that long, Jared. Folks have a saturation point for miracles. Why, if I walked outside right now, reached into the sky, stretched real hard, grabbed the moon, pulled it down, and used it for a monocle, folks around here might stare at me for a while, but they'd get used to it sooner or later; and before long they'd get to the point where whenever somebody from out of town came by and asked, holy mother of tarnation, how is it that that man over there is using the moon for a monocle, they'd just look bored and say, 'Waal, that's just Beau, don't you pay him no mind.' The good folks of Sticky Tar are going to start feeling that way about the Bullet again, and soon; way before I earn back my investment."

I scratched my head. "Then what are you doing here?"

"Establishing ownership," he said.

"Of the Magic Bullet?"

"Of the Magic Bullet," he confirmed. "Jared, this town may be the kind of place that only sprung up because folks on their way to better places just got themselves tired of walking, but there are folks moving into these parts, and they'll be more folks coming after them, and not long after that there'll be roads and carpetbaggers and lawyers and families and, holding them all together, money; enough to bury this town, and the closest fifteen towns besides. When all that gets here, the kind of folks who come with it are gonna be the kind of folks willing to throw their money around amusing themselves. And I'm going to be ready for them when they get here. That Magic Bullet, Jared, is going to be the main attraction of a permanent sideshow, with dozens of other acts, which I'm going to set up right here, in the center of Main Street. Whole families are going to travel here from all over the West just to see it. And this whole town's going to get rich, feeding them and housing them and selling them keepsakes and robbing them. Just you see."

This didn't make all that much sense to me—a small town in the middle of nowhere, setting itself up as some kind of magic kingdom for the benefit of jaspers who have nothing better to do than to drag their wives and kids halfway across the country to look at a bunch of nonsense like that—but right now we were raking in the dimes, so I let it be. Besides, I had something else to talk to him about. Namely: "Long as you're answering questions . . . don't it bother you none? Lookin' that Bullet in the eye all day long?"

Beauregard just sighed and said: "Sure it does, Jared. I look at that Bullet and I see Death so close that I can feel its fingers closing on my heart. I know it can come for me at any

time, without a moment's warning; that when it does I probably won't even have time to see it coming."

"How do you keep it from driving you crazy?"

He took another sip of his beer. "By loving it."

I figured, then, that the answer was he really was crazy.
"Lovin' it? You sound like Red Elder, when he called it a
woman."

"Well," Beauregard chuckled. "Maybe I don't love it as
intensely as that poor deluded individual. But nevertheless, I
look at that Bullet and every time I feel the size of it, the inevitability of it, start setting little brushfires around the corners
of my sanity, I think, well, hell, I'm not scared of that. I won't
let myself be scared of it. Instead, I'll love it. I'll love everything about it. I'll love it because it's perfect and it's beautiful
and it's all set waiting for the proper moment to kill me and it
continues to hang there, as harmless as a daisy, letting me
live, and paying my bar bill in the process. I'll love it and I'll
forget to be scared of it. That's a fine thing, one worthy of
loving—and the day you understand what I mean by that is
the day you figure out how I can sit out there, letting it stare
back."

Like most things Beauregard said, it sure sounded good. I
resolved right then and there to devote some effort to figuring
out what it meant.

But then I never really had the chance, because it's just
about then that Red Elder upped the ante.

Elder started with Victoria Sue, the half-a-whore. We
called her half-a-whore because she had one eye and one leg
and was also missing the front half of her nose. I don't know
about how she lost the eye or the leg but I was there the night
she lost the nose; some drunken cowboy in the next room
over got so excited about getting the most important part of

his business done that he fired his six-shooter for emphasis. Victoria Sue didn't know whether to be pissed off or relieved by the result; pissed-off because she figured she couldn't make a decent whore's living with only a fraction of a nose, relieved because that first bullet was followed by at least four more which missed her entirely, striking instead the drunken cowboy's best friend, who she'd been about to service at the time and who lost something a lot more personal than his nose. As it happened, though, Victoria Sue didn't have to worry much about her livelihood; half-a-whore or not, the folks of Sticky Tar were open-minded about this sort of thing, and most of the men around town remained dearly in love with her red hair and her laugh and her beautiful blue eye.

Until the day that Red Elder ponied up his quarter and went upstairs with her.

I dunno exactly what he did with her; I've asked the folks that got to see and they just look at me kinda funny, like it's something I have to be just as bad as Red Elder just to ask. But Zeke Callahan, who was playing piano at the time, said that the sounds coming from the top of the stairs sounded a lot like a bunch of skinned horses tumbling head-first into hell . . . and George Peterson, who kicked down the door to help her, said he never saw nothing quite so awful . . . and Two-Nose MacDougal, who had the bad luck to be buttoning his pants in the hallway when Elder burst from the room with spit on his lips and blood on his hands and nothing on his mind but committing harm against everybody in his path, took one look at Elder's eyes and never spoke another word in his whole life. As for Victoria Sue herself, she lived long enough to heal up and leave town. Folks in the know said she was now closer to one-quarter to one-third a whore now. Some days I wish I knew what that meant; some days I'm just as happy I don't.

In any event, Red Elder came out of that perfumed room laughing like he'd just been told the funniest joke anybody ever heard. He barreled past Peterson and MacDougal and found his way blocked by Spooner Watts, who was by remarkable coincidence both too deaf to have heard the screams and too nearsighted to tell that Elder was anything other than just another customer losing his head from poison rotgut. Spooner, a friendly fella who said hi to everybody, tried to say hi to Elder. Elder cupped his right hand around the top of Spooner's head and twisted it like a doorknob. Spooner weighed so little that his whole body turned with the twist, a stroke of luck that spared his neck but gave Red Elder no reason to throw him aside; by the time Elder left the saloon, still dragging the unfortunate Spooner by the top of his head, the man was dead as a dead cat anyway from being swung like a club against every stick of furniture in Miss Veronica's, most of which was now as broken up as Spooner.

I did show up in time to see what happened when Elder reached the street, and that was by far the worst of it, since by then almost everybody in town knew that a massacre was going on, and everybody figured to be the one to take care of it. About fourteen folks all opened fire on him, from about fourteen different angles. They included the Widow Ramsey, who fired her shotgun at him from the second floor of the General Store, the new Preacher, who whipped out a Derringer and opened it into his back; and Stinking Jasper, who stumbled from the Saloon screaming like a coyote with its tail on fire and emptied both his revolvers at Elder's head. And more. There should have been pieces of Elder all over that dirty street. But all fourteen rounds all took detours around him and spun in the air a bit and went on to take out the same fourteen folks who'd fired them. Elder yelled something about Death loving him too much; I don't know what it was. But I was so glad my revolver was strapped in too tight to draw that I didn't even mind shooting off two toes right through the leather of my stolen boots. There are some times when you just don't want to do your civic duty.

I was not part of the posse that rode up to the Elder farm, to ask his brothers for their help in finding him. But I didn't miss much. Elder's brothers weren't saying anything . . . and I hear it was a real messy job, matching up all their severed arms and legs so they could be properly buried.

Not long after that, it started raining and didn't stop.

Sometime that night, Beauregard Finch came to visit me in my room on the top floor of the Excelsior. By then, I could have used the cheering up; a regular army of bugs had vacated my mattress to investigate the leaking bandage around my foot; they were pretty thorough investigators, too, continuing their inquiries long after normal bugs would have considered themselves experts on the subject. Also, this being the top floor, it was raining several places in the room, too, including over by the dresser and over by the stove and over by the place where the bed had been before I got tired of the drip-drip-drip against my forehead and bribed Clete to move me closer to the window; he'd put down buckets to spare me the puddles, but the room was still damp as a sponge, which is one thing the bone-dry climate of Sticky Tar never got. I'd drunk my way through half the unbroken liquor salvaged from Miss Veronica's just to console myself, and it wasn't working, not really. Beauregard didn't seem to have much to say about any of it. He just sat by the side of my bed and worried the rim of his big black hat for about ten minutes or so before he finally came out with the words:

"This doesn't have to be bad for business, you know."

I slurred an unhappy: "What?"

"The remarkable Mr. Elder has done us a favor," Beauregard said. "In one bloody rampage, he has established himself as a one-of-a-kind figure, a larger-than-life monster of the sort that populates the dime novels and the Wild West shows. He has rendered himself an icon. His grave—or, better yet, his stuffed and mounted corpse—can provide us with a secondary attraction almost as popular as the Magic Bullet itself."

I was just drunk enough to consider scolding Beauregard for exploiting a tragedy so fresh that the bodies ain't even been planted yet. That was pretty damn drunk, since when I was sober I didn't have thoughts like that at all. After a moment, I slurred some more: "You really think folks are gonna pay money to see that?"

"A couple of years back," Beauregard said expansively, "while I was still involved with my old line of work, I drifted through a town in Mexico where the main attraction was a baby with another face growing out of his ear. Pitifully inbred place, Jared, which is how I suppose you'd account for it. They had no other industry there: no agriculture, no live-stock, no military garrison, not even a decent whorehouse. Just a bunch of brothers and sisters acting like husbands and wives, and a cute tot marked by another cute tot in perpetual profile. They'd even taught it, the extra face, I mean, to smoke cigars. I'm not kidding you here: they'd stuff a cigar between its little lips and it would just sit there—I suppose that's what you'd call it, sit there—puffing away. It was defi-nitely a sight, but it was the only sight in three hundred miles, and in a perfect world folks would have just stayed at home figuring that any three hundred miles that ended with that was a three-hundred mile trip you might be better off skip-ping. But they didn't skip it; they came. They rode their horses and their wagons right out into the middle of nowhere, right through the devil's own acres, just to get themselves a look. If folks are willing to ride that far to get a look at that, then I wager you they'd be willing to ride ten times as far just to catch a glimpse of a man who did what Red Elder's done. Put his stuffed corpse next to the Magic Bullet and we have not one, but two separate fortunes just begging to be made."

I was in no mood to admit that I would have been one of the folks riding three hundred miles to see the kid with the two faces. So I said: "Only problem is, last I heard, the man ain't dead."

"Sometimes, an entrepreneur has to make his opportunities."

I swigged some more watered-down whatever-it-was, and said: "I ain't all that certain this particular opportunity wants to cooperate."

"Entrepreneurs," Beauregard said, "take charge of their opportunities."

I almost told him I didn't see what his religion had to do with it. "Even those opportunities bullets don't want to hit?"

"Especially those opportunities," said Beauregard.

"You gotta find him before you kill him."

Beauregard smiled. "No need. He'll find me."

"And then you gotta kill him before he kills you."

"A minor detail," he said. And then he put on his hat and got out of there, leaving me to the rotgut and the sound of rain plinking in buckets.

I didn't hear much more about the situation for most of that night; the Doc came in once or twice, to cluck over my feet and shoo away some of the bigger flies; Clete came in, to rifle through my pockets for the rainbucket rental fee; then about midnight the lunger came in to wheeze at me, spit lung into my bucket, and steal back his somewhat damaged boots.

I didn't think I was gonna sleep, but somehow, despite all that and the rain hammering against the window like a thousand hysterical savages insisting on a way in, I must have drifted off from fever or exhaustion—because I slept right through all the commotion when the Church burnt down just up the street. The folks still alive and awake to see it say that it went up all at once, top to bottom, from the warped front steps to the slightly off-kilter steeple; they say that the fire didn't seem to mind the rain at all, let alone the comparatively puny contributions of the bucket brigade Clete formed from the Ladies Auxiliary and Miss Veronica's surviving whores. They also say that the Church burned for the better part of an hour before the cheap tinderbox wood even started to show the effects of the flame; but that when the walls finally turned black and the Church fell in on itself, the screams coming from inside sounded an awful lot like all the folks who died shooting at Red Elder earlier that day. Again, I don't know how much of this is true; I wasn't there.

Nor was I there in any of the houses Red Elder visited that night. There were a lot of them, I know that; to hear tell of it, it was pretty much every house in town. There wasn't a family or a passel of saddle tramps in town, that didn't get themselves a right unfriendly visit from a hulking red-haired maniac determined to leave at least one body and one terrified witness every place he went. Sometimes he used his guns; sometimes he used his bare hands. Once, I'm told, he used a pair of shoelaces—and when I heard just how he used them, I had to shake my head, because I never knew you could do serious damage to a fella that way. And though some folks tried to negotiate, to get him to stop by asking him what he wanted, he didn't say what he wanted. Where Beauregard Finch was, while all of this was going on, I don't know; maybe he was sleeping and maybe he was drunk and maybe he was waiting for Elder to get tired and maybe it just took him a lot of hiding before he was able to make himself ready to take on whatever had become of Red Elder. I don't think he was just letting the killing go on as long as possible, to drive up the value of his planned sideshow attraction; I don't want to think it. But maybe he was. You had to give the man that. He certainly did have a head for business.

Whatever the explanation, I woke up in the darkest part of the night gagging from the taste of Red Elder's shotgun, rammed against the back of my mouth.

It was dark. There weren't any candles or lamps. The rain outside still sounded like the end of the world. I shouldn't have been able to see anything. But there's something about having a shotgun shoved down your throat that tends the focus your vision. I may not have been able to see the ugly striped-duck wallpaper or the bugs in my bandages or the buckets filled with rainwater and tobacco juice and spit-up Lunger lung, but I was able to follow the twin black barrels all the way to the darker patch of blackness that stood gripping the stock at the other end. I knew it was Red Elder, and without being able to make out a single detail of his face I still knew he was grinning, and that in good light he would have been shiny with sweat, and that if I'd been able to see him his eyes would have been like a pair of poisoned water holes reflecting the cold dead moon back at the black sky it came from.

What with all the rotgut I'd had, and the barrels touching the back of my throat and all, I very badly wanted to throw up. I only avoided it because I knew that if I gave in to the urge, Elder would squeeze the trigger and make of me something for somebody else to throw up about later. On the other hand, if I held it in, he might let me live.

That's what I thought, anyways.

I said the only thing I could. "Mmmmmmmmph!"

Somewhere in the dark, Red Elder muttered: "You were the bastard that sold me the ticket."

I almost did throw up, then.

But before I could, he blew my brains right out the back of my head.

Now, I know that's got to surprise some of you, hearing all of this for the first time. After all, I'm the fella telling you the story, and the fella telling you the story is usually expected to live all the way through the story, even if the very last thing that happens before the end is some kind of horrible death that comes up on him by surprise. You might be wondering about how I got to hear all the things various folks reported about the things Red Elder did while I wasn't around; but that ain't too hard to explain—if I didn't hear it a thousand times just hanging around as they drank themselves silly in saloons for the rest of their lives, then I heard it sooner or later when they caught up with where I was and got a chance to fill me in personally. Trust me, the subject of Red Elder and Beauregard Finch came up in conversation a lot, for years and years, no matter where it was or how hot it may have been for the fellas telling it.

And if you think this turn of events was unexpected, then just imagine how I took it. I was standing there at the foot of the bed, in a drippy room stinking of blood and gunpowder and things bodies have a habit of letting go, looking down at a spattered mess that used to be me, and is now just an unshaven, unwashed sack of shit leaking from both ends. Dark as the room was, I could see it perfectly, and all I could think is that I never saw a sorrier, more pathetic-looking sight in my whole life, and that I should have gone into Dentistry like my Mama wanted. Then I saw that the army of bugs investigating my bandaged foot had a wealth of material to research now, up around where my face had been, and that they were losing no time rushing to pursue these new avenues of inquiry, and it occurred to me for the very first time that this must have meant I was Dead.

I yelped the natural response. "Red Elder, you bastard!"

Elder didn't hear me, of course. He just put down the shotgun, went over to the body, my body, and started rummaging around in its pockets. It irritated me that a man as crazy as he was by then was still able to give a damn about money, and even more that when he emerged with a silver dollar he bit to make sure it was real.

Under the circumstances, that struck me as awfully petty.

I could have followed him out the door when he left, just to see where he went next. But it honestly didn't occur to me. I'd been through a lot, and wasn't very motivated.

I just sat down on the edge of the bed and tried not to notice that the mattress didn't sag a bit under my weight. I thought of all the things I'd wanted to have in my life, which one blast from a shotgun had forever denied me. I'd always wanted a clean hat, for one; and I'd always wanted a pair of long johns with no holes in them, for another. Most of all I'd always wanted to spend just one night sleeping in a class place where the pattern on the rug wasn't a mixture of dirt and tobacco stains. I'd never had any of those things, so I really had no idea what they were like, but they all sounded pretty damn fine, and I regretted knowing that I'd never have a taste of them, not even for a moment, not even briefly. That, or sing opera. I'd always wanted to do that, too.

But it wasn't a total loss, I supposed. Once, between towns, I came across a half-mad old jasper gnawing toothlessly on a buzzard who said to me, "You know, all any man can ever really expect out of life is one true friend and one deadly enemy." I'd never really had a true friend before, unless you count that fella in the mountains who went along with the coin toss so I could eat him; and though I'd had more than my share of hateful sons-of-bitches shooting at me I'd never really had anybody taking it personal enough to be called a deadly enemy either. I'd just had a whole bunch of folks wandering around in the middle, who weren't really important enough to be one or the other. Now, at long last, I had to admit that, by the old jasper's definition at least, I'd found both—one fella mean enough to shoot me dead just for selling him a ticket to something he'd wanted to see in the first place, and one fella who I knew for a fact was going to bend heaven and earth just to put that right.

By the time Beauregard came in, I was downright smiling.

He was drenched from the rain, his black suit dripping and squishing and leaving puddles with every step he took. He had a soggy cigar drooping from his lips. He stopped when he saw my dead body, stood there dripping for a second or two as he took in the sight, then without saying a word or even changing his expression shuffled over to the bed so he could kneel beside me.

Then he started rifling through my pockets.

That didn't bother me, particularly. I hadn't expected prayer. And since we were partners, it only made sense that any funds I had on me at the moment of my untimely death get plowed back into our mutual business, for what Beauregard would have called Research and Development purposes. If he'd been the one Red Elder had shot, I would have done the same thing. It's part of what being partners means. All things being equal, I could only respect him for denying the full weight of his emotions long enough to attend to the needs of business like a professional. I was just sorry Red Elder had taken the money before Beauregard got his chance.

After a moment, finding my pockets empty, Beauregard leaned in closer and looked at what was left of my face. He stayed silent for a spell, thinking. And then he closed his eyes, and shuddered.

I dearly hoped he wasn't going to cry.

But he wasn't closing his eyes to cry; he just had a chill from all the rain outside, that's all. He just reared back and let out one of the most walloping sneezes I ever saw anybody ah-choo, right there in my dead face, without covering his mouth or anything. It was just about the only thing he could have done that would have invested my poor death with a little less dignity. And that one thing I might have resented a mite—if I hadn't thought about it a little and decided that in this partic-ular case keeping his germs to himself wasn't really an issue anymore. Besides, he had the right. It was cold.

Then he said, "I'll get him, Jared. This career might not be working out, either, but I'll do this much right. I'll get him."

He got up, and went out, without wiping his nose or mine.

I followed him out, leaving all my earthlies behind.

Now, I don't know how Sticky Tar got its name, origi-nally, but it earned that appellation on the night of the show-down between Red Elder and Beauregard Finch. The streets, which were just a collection of dirt and manure at the best of times, had spent the last few hours sucking up raindrops the size of apples, transforming into something thicker and nas-tier than normal old everyday mud. It was now the kind of ground that, for living folks at least if not ghosts like me who could float serenely above it all, swallowed your legs all the way up to your knees, and didn't let them go unless you sur-rendered your boots first. And it was dark, too; unless you were dead, which I was, you couldn't see anything but a bunch of blackness that kept stinging your eyes with rainwater hard enough to puff up your eyelids like gourds filled with coo-coo juice. I saw a street filled with shattered windows both upstairs and downstairs, a half-crazy horse trying to smash an overturned buckboard to kindling, a man with a hole in his back bent face-down in a water trough, and a fella with no teeth sucking away at a bottle while trying to ward off the storm with a lady's parasol. I saw no limit of scared folks staring out through whatever the night had left of their windows. I don't know how much Beauregard Finch saw; it couldn't have been much, because just as he stepped off the plank sidewalk of the Excelsior Hotel he tripped on a splintered spot in the board and tumbled face-first into the goo—and even after he got up, looking like a fella who'd just taken a swim in somebody else's soiled unmentionables, he stumbled through the muck and the slime like a blind man on the third day of a six-day whiskey drunk.

It didn't look very heroic. I have to tell you that.

He wasn't appearing any more deft as he approached the place where his tent-show had advertised THE MAN WHO CHEATS DEATH 10 CENTS! It was windswept and abandoned, and though the fence was still up, there wasn't a tent there anymore: either the storm, or Red Elder, had ripped it to shreds which blew like loose streamers in the wind, lashing Beauregard in the face and arms as he drove himself toward the place where it had been. The loss of the tent reduced the fenced-in area to nothing but a very small, very empty corral. Beauregard's stool sat in the center of that corral, and the hulking, storm-drenched figure of Red Elder sat perched on top of it, clutching the same shotgun he'd just used to kill me, and staring with endless fascination at the familiar, motionless black dot hovering six inches from his eyes.

Elder heard Beauregard coming, of course. There was no way to avoid hearing him—not with every step a splash and a splish and a sucking splot in the swamp the street had become. He didn't turn around or say anything or clutch his shotgun a little closer to his chest; he just sat there and waited, lost in the static glory of the Bullet hovering just a couple of inches before his eyes.

As for Beauregard, he was so blinded by all the wind and rain in his eyes that he didn't even notice the half-dozen bodies lying face-down half-buried in the mud. Some of them I recognized by their faces, and some I knew only by the clothes they wore: Jake Forrester, Ed Colton, Zeke Callahan, Singing Jackson, some fella whose name I'd never gotten around to asking, and a strange-looking fella in a domino mask and powder-blue trail outfit. They all lay sprawled near their own guns, and though I appreciated the guts they'd shown in trying to take Elder down, I didn't need to have seen the last attempt to bushwhack him to know that even those who'd been given a chance had only wasted their bullets and their lives. It had been a massacre, pure and simple . . . and Beauregard, walking right into the center of it, didn't even notice.

Instead, he just wiped the water from his eyes and called out: "Hey!"

Red Elder didn't answer.

Beauregard had to shout to be heard over the rain, but there was nothing at all hysterical or afraid about his voice. "I said Hey! Elder! I do believe you're on my land!"

Red Elder grunted, and spoke softly, without raising his voice at all. "You think you can claim it, boy?"

"I already did claim it!" Beauregard stepped forward, the wind choosing that moment to churn up, making even that step a fight he needed to win. "I signed a paper in the land office! Had it notarized and everything! Everything as legal as legal can be! The land inside that corral is mine!"

"And if I burn every building and every piece of paper in this town? And stay right here, on your land, with the only thing that ever loved me? What are you going to do about that, boy?"

Beauregard took another step; the wind churned up again, whipping his mud-spattered black jacket around his shoulders, and nearly turning him all the way around. He had to blink several times before he found Elder again. "If you persist in trespassing," he cried, "then you will be shot!"

It seemed to me, standing there all dead and all, not feeling the wind or the rain but fresh enough to remember what it would have felt like if I hadn't left my earthlies back at the room, that Beauregard must have lost whatever sense he had.

Red Elder must have felt the same way, because he smiled a little, and spoke quieter still, his words whispers that rang out over the storm. "That's a hot one," he said softly. "You can't shoot me. That Bullet loves me too much. It won't let any other Bullet touch me."

Beauregard Finch shouted back: "I know! It told me!"

"Yeah, it said you talked to it. It even likes you. But it doesn't love you the same way it loves me. It won't protect you."

"No!" Beauregard shouted mournfully. "That's what it said!"

"I could just cut you down like a mangy dog, right here."

"I expect you could," shouted Beauregard. "You could even do worse! But right now, I'm just wondering why you haven't done so already!"

Red Elder hesitated a little before answering. I don't know why. Maybe there was some part of him that didn't like what he'd done and wanted to stop; maybe he just sensed a little unexpected confidence in Beauregard's voice and wished he knew just what my business partner was up to. (Standing there, watching invisibly, I realized, with something like amazement, that he was a little scared of Beauregard—which made no sense to me, but was still the most encouraging news I'd gotten since he blew out the back of my head). But then he said: "Maybe I just want to hurt you too much to kill you."

"Then why don't you try?"

Again, Elder didn't answer right away. He seemed to consider his options, weighing them for trap doors set to plunge him into the basement; and then he sighed, more tiredly than any man I'd ever heard, and stood up. I will say that "Stood Up" ain't adequate to describe it. He had always been a tall cuss, but he seemed taller now than he'd ever been—so tall that his knees took forever just straightening his back and lifting that red face of his all the way up to full height. Then he turned, and stepped off the platform Beauregard and I had built, and strode through the rain to the spot where Beauregard stood waiting for him.

It would be nice to report, here, that Beauregard turned out to be a real hero in a scrap, and that he laid out Red Elder with no trouble at all.

But Beauregard had the dirty-fighting skills of a temperance crusader. He didn't even get his fists up. Red Elder just clapped his right hand around the top of Beauregard's head, and twisted that head around so fast that Beauregard had to spin his whole body to avoid having his neck broken. Then, not even feeling the weak punches and kicks bouncing off his side, probably insulted by them, Elder used all the strength in that one arm to bend my poor partner all the way down to muddy ground, not stopping until he'd shoved all of Beauregard's head under the muck. He held Beauregard there easily, not straining at all even as Beauregard inhaled his first full breath of Sticky Tar real estate and started to kick and thrash for something more conducive to life. For a couple of seconds there, I feared that Red Elder intended to keep this up until Beauregard drowned.

But maybe he'd had enough killing for one night, or maybe he felt some loyalty for the fella who'd been kind enough to introduce him to the Bullet, or some of that fear I'd imagined he felt for Beauregard came back in time to give him pause. Because, whatever the explanation, Elder waited only a minute or so before he yanked Beauregard's face out of the muck, pulled him to a kneeling position, and glared at him nose-to-nose. "That Bullet's mine," he said.

Beauregard coughed and choked and spat out clods of soggy dirt—but without understanding why, I thought I saw a smile there. "Is . . . that the way you feel?"

"I thought I was clear about that."

Beauregard coughed some more, and seemed about to lose his last few breakfasts and lunches, but then he got himself under control, and spoke in a voice that sounded like he'd had about a dozen rotgut whiskeys too many. "You really . . . do love that Bullet . . . don't you?"

"I do," Red Elder said.

"And it loves you?"

"It does."

That was definitely a smile on Beauregard's face now; Elder probably thought it was a grimace. He coughed again, spat out some more dirt, and spoke in the clearest voice he'd managed since sucking mud: "You ever noticed how good I am with words, Elder?"

"I noticed you jaw a lot."

"You know what I did before I came to Sticky Tar, to find a new career?"

"I don't care," said Red Elder.

"I was a preacher!" cried Beauregard Finch. "And I now

pronounce you Man and Wife!"

I saw it coming, then. I couldn't believe what I saw, but I saw it.

The sky exploded with lightning as Beauregard went on: "You may kiss the bride!"

Red Elder's face underwent at least five separate facial expressions in the instant of life left to him. The first was annoyance. The second confusion. The third concern. The fourth sudden understanding. The fifth terror. He whirled to face the love of his life. I don't think you can call the way he looked when the bottom half of his face disintegrated an expression, but I do know this: it redefined the phrase big wet sloppy kiss. The blur of tiny gray-black passion bored lovingly against his lips, grinding everything it touched to chopped meat and pieces of grit, just like any faster Bullet would, except so slowly and, I guess, tenderly, that the guy being shot in the face could follow its progress inch by inch by increasingly messy inch. Elder threw himself backward, to escape its affections, but it kept digging into him, coloring the rain with a shower of blood and bone and shattered teeth; he shook his head, as if trying to tell it No, but that just whipped his cheeks back and forth across the damned thing's path, making holes and turning that foul tongue of his to thick tobacco-flavored goo.

About the time his jaw exploded he lost his grip on Beauregard's head. Beauregard gasped and dove for safety, landing flat on his belly and sliding halfway across the street before the mud slowed him down enough to stop. But he didn't need to try that hard; the Bullet just wasn't after him at all. It was after Red Elder, who by this point deserved that nickname for a whole bunch of other reasons. He'd slipped forward a little, allowing the Bullet to slip up through his palate and out through the bridge of what had been his nose.

His eyes reddened, turned to beet soup, and disappeared. He slipped forward some more and the back of his head popped off like the lid of a boiling pot; I never would have given him much credit for having any kind of a brain, but there it was, churning and bubbling and spitting up little pieces of itself as a little gray-black something zipped back and forth across its shapeless blood-red acreage, plowing furrows as if in preparation for a crop.

This went on for longer than I want to talk about—at least ten minutes, before the Bullet decided it was tired and zipped back to its place at the center of Beauregard's corral. Red Elder was alive for what seemed like most of it.

I suppose, being his murder victim and all, I should have taken some satisfaction in watching it.

But I can tell you this: one of the dearest advantages of being a ghost is that you can avoid the sensation of throwing up.

For about a week after that, I worried about Beauregard. Oh, he pitched in at all the funerals, and even spoke at a couple of them—though promises that from now on, admission to THE MAN WHO CHEATS DEATH! would be offered at a special half price discount for citizens of Sticky Tar didn't endear him much to the widows and orphans and wounded. And he put on a good show of still being the most popular fella at Mamie's, buying drinks for the house, playing cards, and sometimes even saying that if she wanted to use a dirty pan it was all right with him. He even defended himself from folks who blamed him for everything and kept trying to shoot him—though he wasn't much better at fighting than he'd been the night of his showdown with Red Elder, and the number of folks who wanted to see him taste mud again numbered in the double digits.

I thought things were looking up when he pitched a new tent, put up a new sign, and started staring at the Bullet from six inches away again. But the only folks who bought tickets did so because they wanted to punch him in the mouth—and by the time they all had their fill of it, everybody knew that there wasn't any point in it anyway. The act had gone wrong. There was no defiance in it anymore, no style: just an unshaven fool sitting in a chair drinking whiskey straight from the bottle, while regarding that Bullet with first one eye and then the other, as if trying to figure it out. Sometimes he mumbled to himself, sometimes he laughed, sometimes he passed wind, and sometimes he laughed for passing wind. What he didn't do, was eat.

Sometimes I wondered if he was just going to continue sitting there until he starved or drank himself to death. I kept telling him to snap out of it, but of course I was dead and he didn't listen to me.

And then one day he took down the tent, dismantled the corral, got himself a bath and a new set of clothes, and came to see my grave over at the local Boot Hill, which in Sticky Tar wasn't even a hill.

He held his black hat in his hands and looked down at my gravestone. It read JARRED, which was either a stupid misspelling of my name or an inaccurate cause of death. He smiled a bit and said: "Well. I tried, Jared. I guess I could stick around a little longer and see if those circuses and showmen and East Coast investors I wrote to ever come around to help me develop the attraction. But folks around here have had enough, and after sitting in that chair again another day or two, I realized I pretty much have too. It's a pretty stupid way to want to earn a living, if you think of it— even stupider than my last one, and that's saying a lot." He fingered his hat, brightened a little, and said: "Besides, I heard about a town some three hundred miles north of here, that has itself a real live three-headed cow . . . and that cow's not getting any younger, not while I'm sitting here still acting in a show that nobody wants to see. So I'm going to head on.—Sorry you're dead."

"That's all right," I said, though of course he didn't hear me. It hadn't made all that much difference in my life, after all. Nobody had ever paid attention to me before and nobody had ever paid attention to me now. At least now, I didn't have to worry about finding myself a fresh pair of boots.

He put on his hat, tipped it, then got on his horse and rode off, past the edge of town, where I found the limitations of my ghosthood wouldn't let me go. I wished him well: a fella like Beauregard Finch doesn't come along all that often, and it would be nice to think that he finally found the business opportunity that made him as rich as he wanted to be.

But somehow, I don't think so.

Because just a couple of days after that, the Bullet started moving.

Not all that fast; not at first. Nobody living noticed, because nobody still alive wanted to look at it any more. Like Beauregard had said, they'd had enough of Magic Bullets and Men Who Cheated Death. But Me, being a Man Who Hadn't Cheated Death, a man who didn't have much to do except stand around watching things happen, I noticed right away. So I saw the inch it moved the first day, the two inches it moved the second, the three it moved on the third. By the fourth day, when it sped up so dramatically that it moved past the confines of Beauregard's corral entirely, its progress was so obvious that even the living saw it—though I was still the only one paying enough attention to note slight changes in its course. I didn't even have to think hard to figure that it was constantly re-aiming itself, like a compass needle pointing at wherever Beauregard was at any given moment.

A week and a half after Beauregard Finch left town, it was moving at a slow walk, a couple of miles west of town.

The last person who saw it was a prospector who had his mule shot out from underneath him. It was still headed West, at a rate faster than the fastest horse can gallop. There's a mountain about seventeen miles out beyond that, that has a hole drilled all the way through it; some folks like to look through it, though they can't see the other side and a lot of folks said it would be just like the damned thing to surprise some fool taking a peek by coming back the same way to say Hi.

I figure it reached regular bullet speed by the end of the month.

I don't know where and when it caught up with Beauregard. I don't know whether it took vengeance on him for depriving it of Red Elder, or greeted him joyfully as the only other man it had ever loved.

But I do know this: either way, it probably didn't make all that much of a difference to him.

# Sunday Night Yams at Minnie and Earl's

Frontiers never die. They just become theme parks.

I spent must of my shuttle ride to Nearside mulling sour thoughts about that. It's the kind of thing that only bothers lonely and nostalgic old men, especially when we're old enough to remember the days when a trip to Luna was not a routine commuter run, but instead a never-ending series of course corrections, system checks, best-and-worst case simulations, and random unexpected crises ranging from ominous burning smells to the surreal balls of floating upchuck that got into everywhere if we didn't get over your nausea fast enough to clean them up. Folks of my vintage remember what it was to spend half their lives in passionate competition with dozens of other frighteningly qualified people, just to earn themselves seats on cramped rigs outfitted by the lowest corporate bidders—and then to look down at the ragged landscape of Sister Moon and know that the sight itself was a privilege well worth the effort. But that's old news now: before the first development crews gave way to the first settlements; before the first settlements became large enough to be called the first cities; before the first city held a parade in honor of its first confirmed mugging; before Independence and the Corporate Communities and the opening of Lunar Disney on the Sea of Tranquility. These days, the moon itself is no big deal except for rubes and old-timers. Nobody looks out the windows; they're far too interested in their sims, or their virts, or their newspads, or (for a vanishingly literate few) their paperback novels to care about the sight of the airless world waxing large in the darkness outside.

I wanted to shout at them. I wanted to make a great big eloquent speech about what they were missing by taking it all for granted, and about their total failure to appreciate what others had gone through to pave the way. But that wouldn't have moved anybody. It just would have established me as just another boring old fart.

So I stayed quiet until we landed, and then I rolled my overnighter down the aisle, and I made my way through the vast carpeted terminal at Armstrong Interplanetary (thinking all the while: *Carpet, carpet, why is there carpet; dammit, there shouldn't be carpeting on the moon*). Then I hopped a tram to my hotel, and I confirmed that the front desk had followed instructions and provided me one of their few (hideously expensive) rooms with an Outside View. Then I went upstairs and thought it all again when I saw that the view was just an alien distortion of the moon I had known. Though it was night, and the landscape was as dark as the constellations of manmade illumination peppered across its cratered surface would now ever allow it to be, I still saw marquee-sized advertisements for soy houses, strip clubs, rotating restaurants, golden arches, miniature golf courses, and the one-sixth-g Biggest Rollercoaster In the Solar System. The Earth, with Europe and Africa centered, hung silently above the blight.

I tried to imagine two gentle old people, and a golden retriever dog, wandering around somewhere in the garish paradise framed by that window.

I failed.

I wondered whether it felt good or bad to be here. I wasn't tired, which I supposed I could attribute to the sensation of renewed strength and vigor that older people are supposed to feel after making the transition to lower gravities. Certainly, my knees, which had been bothering me for more than a decade now, weren't giving me a single twinge here. But I was also here alone, a decade after burying my dear wife—and though I'd traveled around a little, in the last few years, I had never really grown used to the way the silence of a strange room, experienced alone, tastes like the death that waited for me too.

After about half an hour of feeling sorry for myself, I dressed in one of my best blue suits—an old one Claire had picked out in better days, with a cut now two styles out of date—and went to the lobby to see the concierge. I found him in the center of a lobby occupied not by adventurers or pioneers but by businessmen and tourists. He was a sallow-faced young man seated behind a flat slab of a desk, constructed from some material made to resemble polished black marble. It might have been intended to represent a Kubrick monolith lying on its side, a touch that would have been appropriate enough for the moon but might have given the decorator too much credit for classical allusions. I found more Kubrick material in the man himself, in that he was a typical hotel functionary: courteous, professional, friendly, and as cold as a plain white wall. Beaming, he said: "Can I help you, sir?"

"I'm looking for Minnie and Earl," I told him.

His smile was an unfaltering, professional thing, that might have been scissored out of a magazine ad and scotch-taped to the bottom half of his face. "Do you have their full names, sir?"

"Those are their full names." I confess I smiled with reminiscence. "They're both one of a kind."

"I see. And they're registered at the hotel?"

"I doubt it," I said. "They're lunar residents. I just don't have their address."

"Did you try the directory?"

"I tried that before I left Earth," I said. "They're not listed. Didn't expect them to be, either."

He hesitated a fraction of a second before continuing: "I'm not sure I know what to suggest, then—"

"I'm sure you don't," I said, unwillingly raising my voice just enough to give him a little taste of the anger and frustration and dire need that had fueled this entire trip. Being a true professional, used to dealing with obnoxious and arrogant tourists, the concierge didn't react at all: just politely waited for me to get on with it. I, on the other hand, winced before continuing: "They're before your time. Probably way before your time. But there have to be people around—old people, mostly—who know who I'm talking about. Maybe you can ask around for me? Just a little? And pass around the word that I need to talk?"

The professional smile did not change a whit, but it still acquired a distinctively dubious flavor. "Minnie and Earl, sir?"

"Minnie and Earl." I then showed him the size of the tip he'd earn if he accomplished it—big enough to make certain that he'd take the request seriously, but not so large that he'd be tempted to concoct false leads. It impressed him exactly as much as I needed it to. Too bad there was almost no chance of it accomplishing anything; I'd been making inquiries about the old folks for years. But the chances of me giving up were even smaller: not when I now knew I only had a few months left before the heart stopped beating in my chest.

They were Minnie and Earl, dammit.

And anybody who wasn't there in the early days couldn't possibly understand how much that meant.

It's a funny thing, about frontiers: they're not as enchanting as the folks who work them like you to believe. And there was a lot that they didn't tell the early recruits about the joys of working on the moon.

They didn't tell you that the air systems gave off a nasal hum that kept you from sleeping soundly at any point during your first six weeks on rotation; that the vents were considerately located directly above the bunks to eliminate any way of shutting it out; that just when you found yourself actually needing that hum to sleep something in the circulators decided to change the pitch, rendering it just a tad higher or lower so that instead of lying in bed begging that hum to shut up shut up SHUT UP you sat there instead wondering if the new version denoted a serious mechanical difficulty capable of asphyxiating you in your sleep.

They didn't tell you that the recycled air was a paradise for bacteria, which kept any cold or flu or ear infection constantly circulating between you and your co-workers; that the disinfectants regularly released into the atmosphere smelled bad but otherwise did nothing; that when you started sneezing and coughing it was a sure bet that everybody around you would soon be sneezing and coughing; and that it was not just colds but stomach viruses, contagious rashes, and even more unpleasant things that got shared as generously as a bottle of a wine at one of the parties you had time to go to back on Earth when you were able to work only sixty or seventy hours a week. They didn't tell you that work took so very much of your time that the pleasures and concerns of normal life were no longer valid experiential input; that without that input you eventually ran out of non-work-related subjects to talk about, and found your personality withering away like an atrophied limb.

They didn't tell you about the whimsical supply drops and the ensuing shortages of staples like toothpaste and toilet paper. They didn't tell you about the days when all the systems seemed to conk out at once and your deadening routine suddenly became hours of all-out frantic terror. They didn't tell you that after a while you forgot you were on the moon and stopped sneaking looks at the battered blue marble. They didn't tell you that after a while it stopped being a dream and became instead just a dirty and backbreaking job; one that drained you of your enthusiasm faster than you could possibly guess, and one that replaced your ambitions of building a new future with more mundane longings, like feeling once again what it was like to stand unencumbered beneath a midday sun, breathing air that tasted like air and not canned sweat.

They waited until you were done learning all of this on your own before they told you about Minnie and Earl.

I learned on a Sunday—not that I had any reason to keep track of the day; the early development teams were way too short-staffed to enjoy luxuries like days off. There were instead days when you got the shitty jobs and the days when you got the jobs slightly less shitty than the others. On that particular Sunday I had repair duty, the worst job on the moon but for another twenty or thirty possible candidates. It involved, among them, inspecting, cleaning, and replacing the panels on the solar collectors. There were a lot of panels, since the early collector fields were five kilometers on a side, and each panel was only half a meter square. They tended to collect meteor dust (at best) and get scarred and pitted from micrometeor impacts (at worst). We'd just lost a number of them from heavier rock precipitation, which meant that in addition to replacing those I had to examine even those that remained intact. Since the panels swiveled to follow the sun across the sky, even a small amount of dust debris threatened to fall through the joints into the machinery below. There was never a lot of dust—sometimes it was not even visible. But it had to be removed one panel at a time.

To overhaul the assembly, you spent the whole day on your belly, crawling along the catwalks between them, removing each panel in turn, inspecting them beneath a canopy with nothing but suit light, magnifiers and micro-thin air jet. (A vacuum, of course, would have been redundant.) You replaced the panels pitted beyond repair, brought the ruined ones back to the sled for disposal, and then started all over again.

The romance of space travel? Try nine hours of hideously tedious stoop labor, in a moonsuit. Try hating every minute of it. Try hating where you are and what you're doing and how hard you worked to qualify for this privilege. Try also hating yourself just for feeling that way—but not having any idea how to turn those feelings off.

I was muttering to myself, conjugating some of the more colorful expressions for excrement, when Phil Jacoby called. He was one of the more annoying people on the moon: a perpetual smiler who always looked on the bright side of things and refused to react to even the most acidic sarcasm. Appropriately enough, his carrot hair and freckled cheeks always made him look like a ventriloquist's dummy. He might have been our morale officer, if we'd possessed enough bad taste to have somebody with that job title; but that would have made him even more the kind of guy you grow to hate when you really want to be in a bad mood. I dearly appreciated how distant his voice sounded, as he called my name over the radio: "Max! You bored yet, Max?"

"Sorry," I said tiredly. "Max went home."

"Home as in his quarters? Or Home as on Earth?"

"There is no home here," I said. "Of course Home as on Earth."

"No return shuttles today," Phil noted. "Or any time this

month. How would he manage that trick?"

"He was so fed up he decided to walk."

"Hope he took a picnic lunch or four. That's got to be a major hike."

In another mood, I might have smiled. "What's the bad news, Phil?"

"Why? You expecting bad news?"

There was a hidden glee to his tone that sounded excessive even from Jacoby. "Surprise me."

"You're quitting early. The barge will be by to pick you up in five minutes."

According to the digital readout inside my helmet, it was only 13:38 LT. The news that I wouldn't have to devote another three hours to painstaking cleanup should have cheered me considerably; instead, it rendered me about twenty times more suspicious. I said, "Phil, it will take me at least three times that long just to secure—"

"A relief shift will arrive on another barge within the hour. Don't do another minute of work. Just go back to the sled and wait for pickup. That's an order."

Which was especially strange because Jacoby was not technically my superior. Sure, he'd been on the moon all of one hundred and twenty days longer than me—and sure, that meant any advice he had to give me needed to be treated like an order, if I wanted to do my job—but even so, he was not the kind of guy who ever ended anything with an authoritarian *That's An Order*. My first reaction was the certainty that I must have been in some kind of serious trouble. Somewhere, sometime, I forgot or neglected one of the safety protocols, and did something suicidally, crazily wrong—the kind of thing that once discovered would lead to me being relieved for incompetence. But I was still new on the moon, and I couldn't think of any recent occasion where I'd been given enough responsibility for that to be a factor. My next words were especially cautious: "Uh, Phil, did I—"

"Go to the sled," he repeated, even more sternly this time. "And, Max?"

"What?" I asked.

The ebullient side of his personality returned. "I envy you, man."

The connection clicked off before I could ask him why.

A lunar barge was a lot like its terrestrial equivalent, in that it had no motive power of its very own, but needed to be pulled by another vehicle. Ours were pulled by tractors. They had no atmospheric enclosures, since ninety percent of the time they were just used for the slow-motion hauling of construction equipment; whenever they were needed to move personnel, we bolted in a number of forward-facing seats with oxygen feeds and canvas straps to prevent folks imprisoned by clumsy moonsuits from being knocked out of their chairs every time the flatbed dipped in the terrain. It was an extremely low-tech method of travel, not much faster than a human being could sprint, and we didn't often use it for long distances.

There were four other passengers on this one, all identical behind mirrored facemasks; I had to read their nametags to see who they were. Nikki Hollander, Oscar Desalvo, George Peterson, and Carrie Aldrin No Relation (the last two words a nigh-permanent part of her name, up here). All four of them had been on-site at least a year more than I had, and to my eyes had always seemed to be dealing with a routine a lot better than I had been. As I strapped in, and the tractor started up, and the barge began its glacial progress toward a set of lumpy peaks on the horizon, I wished my co-workers had something other than distorted reflections of the lunar landscape for faces; it would be nice to be able to judge from their expressions just what was going on here. I said: "So what's the story, people? Where we headed?"

Then Carrie Aldrin No Relation began to sing: "Over the river and through the woods to grandmother's house we go . . ."

George Peterson snorted. Oscar Desalvo, a man not known for his giddy sense of humor, who was in fact even grimmer than me most of the time—not from disenchantment with his work, but out of personal inclination—giggled; it was like watching one of the figures on Mount Rushmore stick its tongue out. Nikki Hollander joined in, her considerably less-than-perfect pitch turning the rest of the song into a nails-on-blackboard cacophony. The helmet speakers, which distorted anyway, did not help.

I said, "Excuse me?"

Nikki Hollander said something so blatantly ridiculous that I couldn't force myself to believe I'd heard her correctly.

"Come again? I lost that."

"No you didn't." Her voice seemed strained, almost hysterical.

One of the men was choking with poorly repressed laughter. I couldn't tell who.

"You want to know if I like yams?"

Nikki's response was a burlesque parody of astronautic stoicism. "That's an a-ffirmative, Houston."

"Yams, the vegetable yams?"

"A-ffirmative." The A emphasized and italicized so broadly that it was not so much a separate syllable as a sovereign country.

This time I recognized the strangulated noises. They were coming from George Peterson, and they were the sounds made by a man who was trying very hard not to laugh. It was several seconds before I could summon enough dignity to answer. "Yeah, I like yams. How is that relevant?"

"Classified," she said, and then her signal cut off.

In fact, all their signals cut off, though I could tell from the red indicators on my internal display that they were all still broadcasting.

That was not unusual. Coded frequencies were one of the few genuine amenities allowed us; they allowed those of us who absolutely needed a few seconds to discuss personal matters with co-workers to do so without sharing their affairs with anybody else who might be listening. We're not supposed to spend more than a couple of minutes at a time on those channels because it's safer to stay monitored. Being shut out of four signals simultaneously—in a manner that could only mean raucous laughter at my expense—was unprecedented, and it pissed me off. Hell, I'll freely admit that it did more than that; it frightened me. I was on the verge of suspecting brain damage caused by something wrong with the air supply.

Then George Peterson's voice clicked: "Sorry about that, old buddy." (I'd never been his old buddy.) "We usually do a better job keeping a straight face."

"At what? Mind telling me what's going on here?"

"One minute." He performed the series of maneuvers necessary to cut off the oxygen provided by the barge, and restore his dependence on the supply contained in his suit, then unstrapped his harnesses, stood, and moved toward me, swaying slightly from the bumps and jars of our imperfectly smooth ride across the lunar surface.

It was, of course, against all safety regulations for him to be on his feet while the barge was in motion; after all, even as glacially slow as that was, it wouldn't have taken all that great an imperfection in the road before us to knock him down and perhaps inflict the kind of hairline puncture capable of leaving him with a slight case of death. We had all disobeyed that particular rule from time to time; there were just too many practical advantages in being able to move around at will, without first ordering the tractor to stop. But it made no sense for him to come over now, just to talk, as if it really made a difference for us to be face-to-face. After all, we weren't faces. We were a pair of convex mirrors, reflecting each other while the men behind them spoke on radios too powerful to be noticeably improved by a few less meters of distance.

Even so, he sat down on a steel crate lashed to the deck before me, and positioned his faceplate opposite mine, his body language suggesting meaningful eye contact. He held that position for almost a minute, not saying anything, not moving, behaving exactly like a man who believed he was staring me down.

It made no sense. I could have gone to sleep and he wouldn't have noticed.

Instead, I said: "What?"

He spoke quietly: "Am I correct in observing that you've felt less than, shall we say . . . 'inspired,' by your responsibilities here?"

Oh, Christ. This was about something I'd done.

"Is there some kind of problem?"

George's helmet trembled enough to suggest a man theatrically shaking his head inside it. "Lighten up, Max. Nobody has any complaints about your work. We think you're one of the best people we have here, and your next evaluation is going to give you straight A's in every department . . . except enthusiasm. You just don't seem to believe in the work anymore."

As much as I tried to avoid it, my answer still reeked with

denial. "I believe in it."

"You believe in the idea of it," George said. "But the reality has worn you down."

I was stiff, proper, absolutely correct, and absolutely transparent. "I was trained. I spent a full year in simulation, doing all the same jobs. I knew what it was going to be like. I knew what to expect."

"No amount of training can prepare you for the moment when you think you can't feel the magic anymore."

"And you can?" I asked, unable to keep the scorn from my voice.

The speakers inside lunar helmets were still pretty tinny, in those days; they no longer transformed everything we said into the monotones that once upon a time helped get an entire country fed up with the forced badinage of Apollo, but neither were they much good at conveying the most precise of emotional cues. And yet I was able to pick up something in George's tone that was, given my mood, capable of profoundly disturbing me: a strange, transcendent joy. "Oh, yes. Max. I can."

I was just unnerved enough to ask: "How?"

"I'm swimming in it," he said—and even as long as he'd been part of the secret, his voice still quavered, as if there was some seven-year-old part of him that remained unwilling to believe that it could possibly be. "We're all swimming in it."

"I'm not."

And he laughed out loud. "Don't worry. We're going to gang up and shove you into the deep end of the pool."

That was seventy years ago.

Seventy years. I think about how old that makes me and I cringe. Seventy years ago, the vast majority of old farts who somehow managed to make it to the age I am now were almost always living on the outer edges of decrepitude. The physical problems were nothing compared with the senility. What's that? You don't remember senile dementia? Really? I guess there's a joke in there somewhere, but it's not that funny for those of us who can remember actually considering it a possible future. Trust me, it was a nightmare. And the day they licked that one was one hell of an advertisement for progress.

But still, seventy years. You want to know how long ago that was? Seventy years ago it was still possible to find people who had heard of Bruce Springsteen. There were even some who remembered the Beatles. Stephen King was still coming out with his last few books, Kate Emma Brenner hadn't yet come out with any, Exxon was still in business, the reconstruction of the ice packs hadn't even been proposed, India and Pakistan hadn't reconciled, and the idea of astronauts going out into space to blow up a giant asteroid before it impacted with Earth was not an anecdote from recent history but a half-remembered image from a movie your father talked about going to see when he was a kid. Seventy years ago the most pressing headlines had to do with the worldwide ecological threat posed by the population explosion among escaped sugar gliders.

Seventy years ago, I hadn't met Claire. She was still married to her first husband, the one she described as the nice mistake. She had no idea I was anywhere in her future. I had no idea she was anywhere in mine. The void hadn't been defined yet, let alone filled. (Nor had it been cruelly emptied again—and wasn't it sad how the void I'd lived with for so long seemed a lot larger, once I needed to endure it again?)

Seventy years ago I thought Faisal Awad was an old man. He may have been in his mid-thirties then, at most ten years older than I was. That, to me, was old. These days it seems one step removed from the crib.

I haven't mentioned Faisal yet; he wasn't along the day George and the others picked me up in the barge, and we didn't become friends till later. But he was a major member of the development team, back then—the kind of fixitall adventurer who could use the coffee machine in the common room to repair the heating system in the clinic. If you don't think that's a valuable skill, try living under 24-7 life support in a hostile environment where any requisitions for spare parts had to be debated and voted upon by a government committee during election years. It's the time of my life when I first developed my deep abiding hatred of Senators. Faisal was our life-saver, our miracle worker, and our biggest local authority on the works of Gilbert and Sullivan, though back then we were all too busy to listen to music and much more likely to listen to that fifteen-minute wonder Polka Thug anyway. After I left the moon, and the decades of my life fluttered by faster than I once could have imagined possible, I used to think about Faisal and decide that I really ought to look him up, someday, maybe, as soon as I had the chance. But he had stayed on Luna, and I had gone back to Earth, and what with one thing or another that resolution had worked out as well as such oughtas always do: a lesson that old men have learned too late for as long as there have been old men to learn it.

I didn't even know how long he'd been dead until I heard it from his granddaughter Janine Seuss, a third-generation lunar I was able to track down with the help of the Selene Historical Society. She was a slightly-built thirty-seven year-old with stylishly mismatched eye color and hair micro-styled into infinitesimal pixels that, when combed correctly, formed the famous old black-and-white news photograph of that doomed young girl giving the finger to the cops at the San

Diego riots of some thirty years ago. Though she had graciously agreed to meet me, she hadn't had time to arrange her hair properly, and the photo was eerily distorted, like an image captured and then distorted on putty. She served coffee, which I can't drink anymore but which I accepted anyway, then sat down on her couch with the frantically meowing Siamese.

"There were still blowouts then," she said. "Some genuine accidents, some bombings arranged by the Flat-Mooners. It was one of the Flat-Mooners who got Poppy. He was taking Mermer—our name for Grandma—to the movies up on topside; back then, they used to project them on this big white screen a couple of kilometers outside, though it was always some damn thing fifty or a hundred years old with dialogue that didn't make sense and stories you had to be older than Moses to appreciate. Anyway, the commuter tram they were riding just went boom and opened up into pure vacuum. Poppy and Mermer and about fourteen others got sucked out." She took a deep breath, then let it out all at once. "That was almost twenty years ago."

What else can you say, when you hear a story like that? "I'm sorry."

She acknowledged that with an equally ritual response. "Thanks."

"Did they catch the people responsible?"

"Right away. They were a bunch of losers. Unemployed idiots."

I remembered the days when the only idiots on the moon were highly-educated and overworked ones. After a moment, I said: "Did he ever talk about the early days? The development teams?"

She smiled. "Ever? It was practically all he ever did talk about. You kids don't, bleh bleh bleh. He used to get mad at the vids that made it look like a time of sheriffs and saloons and gunfights—he guessed they probably made good stories for kids who didn't know any better, but kept complaining that life back then wasn't anything like that. He said there was always too much work to do to strap on six-guns and go gunning for each other."

"He was right," I said. (There was a grand total of one gunfight in the first thirty years of lunar settlement—and it's not part of this story.)

"Most of his stories about those days had to do with things breaking down and him being the only person who could fix them in the nick of time. He told reconditioned-software anecdotes. Finding the rotten air filter anecdotes. Improvised joint-lubricant anecdotes. Lots of them."

"That was Faisal."

She petted the cat. (It was a heavy-lidded, meatloaf-shaped thing that probably bestirred itself only at the sound of a can opener: we'd tamed the moon so utterly that people like Janine were able to spare some pampering for their pets.) "Bleh. I prefer the gunfights."

I leaned forward and asked the important question. "Did he ever mention anybody named Minnie and Earl?"

"Were those a couple of folks from way back then?"

"You could say that."

"No last names?"

"None they ever used."

She thought about that, and said: "Would they have been folks he knew only slightly? Or important people?"

"Very important people," I said. "It's vital that I reach them."

She frowned. "It was a long time ago. Can you be sure they're still alive?"

"Absolutely," I said.

307

She considered that for a second. "No, I'm sorry. But you have to realize it was a long time ago for me too. I don't remember him mentioning anybody."

Faisal was the last of the people I'd known from my days on the moon. There were a couple on Earth, but both had flatly denied any knowledge of Minnie and Earl. Casting about for last straws, I said: "Do you have anything that belonged to him?"

"No, I don't. But I know where you can go to look further."

Seventy years ago, after being picked up by the barge:

Nobody spoke to me again for forty-five minutes, which only fueled my suspicions of mass insanity.

The barge itself made slow but steady progress, following a generally uphill course of the only kind possible in that era, in that place, on the moon: which was to say, serpentine. The landscape here was rough, pocked with craters and jagged outcroppings, in no place willing to respect how convenient it might have been to allow us to proceed in something approaching a straight line. There were places where we had to turn almost a hundred and eighty degrees, double back a while, then turn again, to head in an entirely different direction; it was the kind of route that looks random from one minute to the next but gradually reveals progress in one direction or another. It was clearly a route that my colleagues had traveled many times before; nobody seemed impatient. But for the one guy who had absolutely no idea where we were going, and who wasn't in fact certain that we were headed anywhere at all, it was torture.

We would have managed the trip in maybe one-tenth the time in one of our fliers, but I later learned that the very laboriousness of the journey was, for first-timers at least, a traditional part of the show. It gave us time to speculate, to anticipate. This was useful for unlimbering the mind, ironing the kinks out of the imagination, getting us used to the idea that we were headed someplace important enough to be worth the trip. The buildup couldn't possibly be enough—the view over that last ridge was still going to hit us with the force of a sledgehammer to the brain—but I remember how hard it hit and I'm still thankful the shock was cushioned even as inadequately as it was.

We followed a long boring ridge for the better part of fifteen minutes . . . then began to climb a slope that bore the rutty look of lunar ground that had known tractor-treads hundreds of times before. Some of my fellow journeyers hummed ominous, horror-movie soundtrack music in my ear, but George's voice overrode them all: "Max? Did Phil tell you he envied you this moment?"

I was really nervous now. "Yes."

"He's full of crap. You're not going to enjoy this next bit instead in retrospect. Later on you'll think of it as the best moment of your life—and it might even be—but it won't feel like that when it happens. It'll feel big and frightening and insane when it happens. Trust me now when I tell you that it will get better, and quickly . . . and that everything will be explained, if not completely, then at least as much as it needs to be."

It was an odd turn of phrase. "As much as it needs to be? What's that supposed to—"

That's when the barge reached the top of the rise, providing us a nice panoramic view of what awaited us in the shallow depression on the other side.

My ability to form coherent sentences became a distant rumor.

It was the kind of moment when the entire universe seems

to become a wobbly thing, propped up by scaffolding and held together with the cheapest brand of hardware-store nails. The kind of moment when gravity just turns sideways beneath you, and the whole world turns on its edge, and the only thing that prevents you from just jetting off into space to spontaneously combust is the compensatory total stoppage of time. I don't know the first thing I said. I'm glad nobody ever played me the recordings that got filed away in the permanent mission archives . . . and I'm equally sure that the reason they didn't is that anybody actually on the moon to listen to them must have also had their own equally aghast reactions also saved for posterity. I got to hear such sounds many times, from others I would later escort over that ridge myself—and I can absolutely assure you that they're the sounds made by intelligent, educated people who first think they've gone insane, and who then realize it doesn't help to know that they haven't.

It was the only possible immediate reaction to the first sight of Minnie and Earl's.

What I saw, as we crested the top of that ridge, was this:

In the center of a typically barren lunar landscape, surrounded on all sides by impact craters, rocks, more rocks, and the suffocating emptiness of vacuum—

—a dark landscape, mind you, one imprisoned by lunar night, and illuminated only by the gibbous Earth hanging high above us—

—a rectangle of color and light, in the form of four square acres of freshly-watered, freshly moved lawn.

With a house on it.

Not a prefab box of the kind we dropped all over the lunar landscape for storage and emergency air stops.

A house.

A clapboard family home, painted a homey yellow, with a

wraparound porch three steps off the ground, a canopy to keep off the sun, a screen door leading inside, and a bug-zapper over the threshold. There was a porch swing with cushions in a big yellow daisy pattern, and a wall of neatly-trimmed hedges around the house, obscuring the latticework that enclosed the crawlspace underneath. It was so over-the-top middle American that even in that first moment I half-crazily expected the scent of lemonade to cross the vacuum and enter my suit. (That didn't happen, but lemonade was waiting.) The lawn was completely surrounded with a white picket fence with an open gate; there was even an old-fashioned mailbox at the gate, with its flag up. All of it was lit, from nowhere, like a bright summer afternoon. The house itself had two stories, plus a sloping shingled roof high enough to hide a respectable attic; as we drew closer I saw that there were pull-down shades, not Venetian blinds, in the pane-glass windows. Closer still, and I spotted the golden re-triever that lay on the porch, its head resting between muddy paws as it followed our approach; it was definitely a lazy dog, since it did not get up to investigate us, but it was also a friendly one, whose big red tail thumped against the porch in greeting. Closer still, and I made various consonant noises as a venerable old lady in gardening overalls came around the side of the house, spotted us, and broke into the kind of smile native only to contented old ladies seeing good friends or grandchildren after too long away. When my fellow astro-nauts all waved back, I almost followed their lead, but for some reason my arms wouldn't move.

Somewhere in there I murmured, "This is impossible."

"Clearly not," George said. "If it were impossible it wouldn't be happening. The more accurate word is inexpli-cable."

"What the hell is—"

311

"Come on, goofball." This from Carrie Aldrin No Relation. "You're acting like you never saw a house before."

Sometimes, knowing when to keep your mouth shut is the most eloquent expression of wisdom. I shut up.

It took about a million and a half years—or five minutes if you go by merely chronological time—for the tractor to descend the shallow slope and bring us to a stop some twenty meters from the front gate. By then an old man had joined the old woman at the fence. He was a lean old codger with bright blue eyes, a nose like a hawk, a smile that suggested he'd just heard a whopper of a joke, and the kind of forehead some very old men have—the kind that by all rights ought to have been glistening with sweat, like most bald heads, but instead seemed perpetually dry, in a way that suggested a sophisticated system for the redistribution of excess moisture. He had the leathery look of old men who had spent much of their lives working in the sun. He wore neatly-pressed tan pants, sandals, and a white button-down shirt open at the collar, all of which was slightly loose on him—not enough to make him look comical or pathetic, but enough to suggest that he'd been a somewhat bigger man before age had diminished him, and was still used to buying the larger sizes. (That is, I thought, if there was any possibility of him finding a good place to shop around here.)

His wife, if that's who she was, was half a head shorter and slightly stouter; she had blue eyes and a bright smile, like him, but a soft and rounded face that provided a pleasant complement to his lean and angular one. She was just overweight enough to provide her with the homey accoutrements of chubby cheeks and double chin; unlike her weathered, bone-dry husband, she was smooth-skinned and shiny-faced and very much a creature the sun had left untouched (though she evidently spent time there; at least, she wore gardener's gloves, and carried a spade).

They were, in short, vaguely reminiscent of the old folks standing before the farmhouse in that famous old painting "American Gothic." You know the one I mean—the constipated old guy with the pitchfork next to the wife who seems mortified by his very presence? These two were those two after they cheered up enough to be worth meeting.

Except, of course, that this couldn't possibly be happening.

My colleagues unstrapped themselves, lowered the stairway, and disembarked. The tractor driver, whoever he was, emerged from its cab and joined them. George stayed with me, watching my every move, as I proved capable of climbing down a set of three steps without demonstrating my total incapacitation from shock. When my boots crunched lunar gravel—a texture I could feel right through the treads of my boots, and which served at that moment to reconnect me to ordinary physical reality—Carrie, Oscar, and Nikki patted me on the back, a gesture that felt like half-congratulation and, half-commiseration. The driver came by, too; I saw from the markings on his suit that he was Pete Rawlik, who was assigned to some kind of classified biochemical research in one of our outlabs; he had always been too busy to mix much, and I'd met him maybe twice by that point, but he still clapped my shoulder like an old friend. As for George, he made a wait gesture and went back up the steps.

In the thirty seconds we stood there waiting for him, I looked up at the picket fence, just to confirm that the impossible old couple was still there, and I saw that the golden retriever, which had joined its masters at the gate, was barking silently. That was good. If the sound had carried in vacuum, I might have been worried. That would have been just plain crazy.

Then George came back, carrying an airtight metal cylinder just about big enough to hold a soccer ball. I hadn't seen any vacuum boxes of that particular shape and size before, but any confusion I might have felt about that was just about the last thing I needed to worry about. He addressed the others: "How's he doing?"

A babble of noncommittal okays dueled for broadcast supremacy. Then the voices resolved into individuals.

Nikki Hollander said: "Well, at least he's not babbling anymore."

Oscar Desalvo snorted: "I attribute that to brain-lock."

"You weren't any better," said Carrie Aldrin No Relation. "Worse. If I recall correctly, you made a mess in your suit."

"I'm not claiming any position of false superiority, hon. Just giving my considered diagnosis."

"Whatever," said Pete Rawlik. "Let's just cross the fenceline, already. I have an itch."

"In a second," George said. His mirrored faceplate turned toward mine, aping eye-contact. "Max? You getting this?"

"Barely," I managed.

"Outstanding. You're doing fine. But I need you with me a hundred percent while I cover our most important ground rule. Namely—everything inside that picket fence is a temperate-climate, sea-level, terrestrial environment. You don't have to worry about air filtration, temperature levels, or anything else. It's totally safe to suit down, as long as you're inside the perimeter—and in a few minutes, we will all be doing just that. But once you're inside that enclosure, the picket fence itself marks the beginning of lunar vacuum, lunar temperatures, and everything that implies. You do not, repeat not, do anything to test the differential. Even sticking a finger out between the slats is enough to get you bounced from the program, with no possibility of reprieve. Is that clear?"

"Yes, but—"

"Rule Two," he said, handing me the sealed metal box. "You're the new guy. You carry the pie."

I regarded the cylinder. Pie?

I kept waiting for the other shoe to drop, but it never did.

The instant we passed through the front gate, the dead world this should have been surrendered to a living one. Sound returned between one step and the next. The welcoming cries of the two old people—and the barking of their friendly golden retriever dog—may have been muffled by my helmet, but they were still identifiable enough to present touches of personality. The old man's voice was gruff in a manner that implied a past flavored by whiskey and cigars, but there was also a sing-song quality to it, that instantly manifested itself as a tendency to end his sentences at higher registers. The old woman's voice was soft and breathy, with only the vaguest suggestion of an old-age quaver and a compensatory tinge of the purest Georgia Peach. The dog's barks were like little frenzied explosions, that might have been threatening if they hadn't all trailed off into quizzical whines. It was a symphony of various sounds that could be made for hello: laughs, cries, yips, and delighted shouts of "George! Oscar! Nikki! Carrie! Pete! So glad you could make it! How are you?"

It was enough to return me to statue mode. I didn't even move when the others disengaged their helmet locks, doffed their headgear, and began oohing and aahing themselves. I just spent the next couple of minutes watching, physically in their midst but mentally somewhere very far away, as the parade of impossibilities passed on by. I noted that Carrie Aldrin No Relation, who usually wore her long red hair beneath the tightest of protective nets, was today styled in pig-tails with big pink bows; that Oscar, who was habitually scraggly-haired and two days into a beard, was today per-fectly kempt and freshly shaven; that George giggled like a five-year-old when the dog stood up on its hind legs to slobber all over his face; and that Pete engaged with a little mock wrestling match with the old man that almost left him toppling backward onto the grass. I saw the women whisper to each other, then bound up the porch steps into the house, so excitedly that they reminded me of schoolgirls skipping off to the playground—a gait that should have been impossible to simulate in a bulky moonsuit, but which they pulled off with perfect flair. I saw Pete and Oscar follow along behind them, laughing at a shared joke.

I was totally ignored until the dog stood up on its hind legs to sniff at, then snort nasal condensation on, my faceplate. His ears went back. He whined, then scratched at his reflec-tion, then looked over his shoulder at the rest of his pack, long pink tongue lolling plaintively. *Look, guys. There's somebody in this thing.*

I didn't know I was going to take the leap of faith until I ac-tually placed the cake cylinder on the ground, then reached up and undid my helmet locks. The hiss of escaping air made my blood freeze in my chest; for a second I was absolutely certain that all of this was a hallucination brought on by oxygen deprivation, and that I'd just committed suicide by opening my suit to vacuum. But the hiss subsided, and I real-ized that it was just pressure equalization; the atmosphere in this environment must have been slightly less than that pro-vided by the suit. A second later, as I removed my helmet, I tasted golden retriever breath as the dog leaned in close and said hello by licking me on the lips. I also smelled freshly mowed grass and the perfume of nearby flowers: I heard a bird not too far away go whoot-toot-toot-weet; and I felt direct sunlight on my face, even though the sun itself was nowhere to be seen. The air itself was pleasantly warm, like summer before it gets obnoxious with heat and humidity.

"Miles!" the old man said. "Get down!"

The dog gave me one last lick for the road and sat down, gazing up at me with that species of tongue-lolling amusement known only to large canines.

The old woman clutched the elbow of George's suit. "Oh, you didn't tell me you were bringing somebody new this time! How wonderful!"

"What is this place?" I managed.

The old man raised his eyebrows. "It's our front yard, son. What does it look like?"

The old woman slapped his hand lightly. "Be nice, dear. You can see he's taking it hard."

He grunted. "Always did beat me how you can tell what a guy's thinking and feeling just by looking at him."

She patted his arm again. "It's not all that unusual, apricot. I'm a woman."

George ambled on over, pulling the two oldsters along. "All right, I'll get it started. Max Fischer, I want you to meet two of the best people on this world or any other—Minnie and Earl. Minnie and Earl, I want you to meet a guy who's not quite as hopeless as he probably seems on first impression—Max Fischer. You'll like him."

"I like him already," Minnie said. "I've yet to dislike anybody the dog took such an immediate shine to. Hi, Max."

"Hello," I said. After a moment: "Minnie. Earl."

"Wonderful to meet you, young man. Your friends have said so much about you."

"Thanks." Shock lent honesty to my response: "They've said absolutely nothing about you."

"They never do," she said, with infinite sadness, as George smirked at me over her back. She glanced down at the metal cylinder at my feet, and cooed: "Is that cake?"

Suddenly, absurdly, the first rule of family visits popped unbidden into my head, blaring its commandment in flaming letters twenty miles high: THOU SHALT NOT PUT THE CAKE YOU BROUGHT ON THE GROUND—ESPECIALLY NOT WHEN A DOG IS PRESENT. Never mind that the container was sealed against vacuum, and that the dog would have needed twenty minutes to get in with an industrial drill: the lessons of everyday American socialization still applied. I picked it up and handed it to her; she took it with her bare hands, reacting not at all to what hindsight later informed me should have been a painfully cold exterior. I said: "Sorry."

"It's pie," said George. "Deep-dish apple pie. Direct from my grandma's orchard."

"Oh, that's sweet of her. She still having those back problems?"

"She's getting on in years," George allowed. "But she says that soup of yours really helped."

"I'm glad," she said, her smile as sunny as the entire month of July. "Meanwhile, why don't you take your friend upstairs and get him out of that horrid suit? I'm sure he'll feel a lot better once he's had a chance to freshen up. Earl can have a drink set for him by the time you come down."

"I'll fix a Sea of Tranquility," Earl said, with enthusiasm.

"Maybe once he has his feet under him. A beer should be fine for now."

"All rightee," said Earl, with the kind of wink that established he knew quite well I was going to need something a lot more substantial than beer.

As for Minnie, she seized my hand, and said: "It'll be all

right, apricot. Once you get past this stage, I'm sure we're all going to be great friends."

"Um," I replied, with perfect eloquence.

Wondering just what stage I was being expected to pass. Sanity?

Dying inside, I did what seemed to be appropriate. I followed George through the front door (first stamping my moonboots on the mat, as he specified) and up the narrow, creaky wooden staircase.

You ever go to parties where the guests leave their coats in a heap on the bed of the master bedroom? Minnie and Earl's was like that. Except it wasn't a pile of coats, but a pile of disassembled moonsuits. There were actually two bedrooms upstairs—the women changed in the master bedroom that evidently belonged to the oldsters themselves, the men in a smaller room that felt like it belonged to a teenage boy. The wallpaper was a pattern of galloping horses, and the bookcases were filled with mint-edition paperback thrillers that must have been a hundred years old even then. (Or more: there was a complete collection of the hardcover *Hardy Boys Mysteries*, by Franklin W. Dixon.) The desk was a genuine antique rolltop, with a green blotter; no computer or hytex. The bed was just big enough to hold one gangly teenager, or three moonsuits disassembled into their component parts, with a special towel provided so our boots wouldn't get moondust all over the bedspread. By the time George and I got up there, Oscar and Pete had already changed into slacks, dress shoes with black socks, and button-down shirts with red bowties; Pete had even put some shiny gunk in his hair to slick it back. They winked at me as they left.

I didn't change, not immediately; nor did I speak, not even as George doffed his own moonsuit and jumpers in favor of a similarly earthbound outfit he blithely salvaged from the closet. The conviction that I was being tested, somehow, was so overwhelming that the interior of my suit must have been a puddle of flop sweat.

Then George said: "You going to be comfortable, dressed like that all night?"

I stirred. "Clothes?"

He pulled an outfit my size from the closet—tan pants, a blue short-sleeved button-down shirt, gleaming black shoes, and a red bowtie identical to the ones Oscar and Pete had donned. "No problem borrowing. Minnie keeps an ample supply. You don't like the selection, you want to pick something more your style, you can always have something snazzier sent up on the next supply drop. I promise you, she'll appreciate the extra effort. It makes her day when—"

"George," I said softly.

"Have trouble with bowties? No problem. They're optional. You can—"

"George," I said again, and this time my voice was a little louder, a little deeper, a little more *For Christ's Sake Shut Up I'm Sick Of This Shit.*

He batted his eyes, all innocence and naiveté. "Yes, Max?"

My look, by contrast, must have been half-murderous. "Tell me."

"Tell you what?"

It was very hard not to yell. "You know what!"

He fingered an old issue of some garishly-colored turn-of-the-millennium science fiction magazine. "Oh. That mixed drink Earl mentioned. The Sea of Tranquility. It's his own invention, and he calls it that because your first sip is one small step for Man, and your second is one giant leap for Mankind. There's peppermint in it. Give it a try and I promise you

you'll be on his good side for life. He—"

I squeezed the words through clenched teeth. "I. Don't. Care. About. The. Bloody. Drink."

"Then I'm afraid I don't see your problem."

"My problem," I said, slowly, and with carefully repressed frustration, "is that all of this is downright impossible."

"Apparently not," he noted.

"I want to know who these people are, and what they're doing here."

"They're Minnie and Earl, and they're having some friends over for dinner."

If I'd been five years old, I might have pouted and stamped my foot. (Sometimes, remembering, I think I did anyway.) "Dammit, George!"

He remained supernaturally calm. "No cursing in this house, Max. Minnie doesn't like it. She won't throw you out for doing it—she's too nice for that—but it does make her uncomfortable."

This is the point where I absolutely know I stamped my foot. "That makes HER uncomfortable!?"

He put down the skiffy magazine. "Really. I don't see why you're having such a problem with this. They're just this great old couple who happen to live in a little country house on the moon, and their favorite thing is getting together with friends, and we're here to have Sunday night dinner with them. Easy to understand . . . especially if you accept that it's all there is."

"That can't be all there is!" I cried, my exasperation reaching critical mass.

"Why not? Can't 'Just Because' qualify as a proper scientific theory?"

"No! It doesn't!—How come you never told me about this place before?"

"You never asked before." He adjusted his tie, glanced at the outfit laid out for me on the bed, and went to the door. "Don't worry; it didn't for me, either. Something close to an explanation is forthcoming. Just get dressed and come downstairs already. We don't want the folks to think you're antisocial . . ."

I'd been exasperated, way back then, because Minnie and Earl were there and had no right to be. I was exasperated now because the more I looked the more impossible it became to find any indication that they'd ever been there at all.

I had started looking for them, if only in a desultory, abstracted way, shortly after Claire died. She'd been the only person on Earth who had ever believed my stories about them. Even now, I think it's a small miracle that she did. I had told her the story of Minnie and Earl before we even became man and wife—sometime after I knew I was going to propose, but before I found the right time and place for the question. I was just back from a couple of years of Outer-System work, had grown weary of the life, and had met this spectacularly kind and funny and beautiful person whose interests were all on Earth, and who had no real desire to go out into space herself. That was just fine with me. It was what I wanted too. And of course I rarely talked to her about my years in space, because I didn't want to become an old bore with a suitcase full of old stories. Even so, I still knew, at the beginning, that knowing about a real-life miracle and not mentioning it to her, ever, just because she was not likely to believe me, was tantamount to cheating. So I sat her down one day, even before the proposal, and told her about Minnie and Earl. And she believed me. She didn't humor me. She didn't just say she believed me. She didn't just believe me to be nice. She believed me. She said she always knew when I was shoveling manure and when I was not—a boast that turned out to be an integral strength of her marriage—and that it was impossible for her to hear me tell the story without knowing that Minnie and Earl were real. She said that if we had children I would have to tell the story to them, too, to pass it on.

That was one of the special things about Claire: she had faith when faith was needed.

But our son and our daughter, and later the grandkids, outgrew believing me. For them, Minnie and Earl were whimsical space-age versions of Santa.

I didn't mind that, not really.

But when she died, finding Minnie and Earl again seemed very important.

It wasn't just that their house was gone, or that Minnie and Earl seemed to have departed for regions unknown; and it wasn't just that the official histories of the early development teams now completely omitted any mention of the secret hoarded by everybody who had ever spent time on the moon in those days. It wasn't just that the classified files I had read and eventually contributed to had disappeared, flushed down the same hole that sends all embarrassing government secrets down the pipe to their final resting place in the sea. But for more years than I'd ever wanted to count, Minnie and Earl had been the secret history nobody ever talked about. I had spoken to those of my old colleagues who still remained alive, and they had all said, what are you talking about, what do you mean, are you feeling all right, nothing like that ever happened.

It was tempting to believe that my kids were right: that it had been a fairy tale: a little harmless personal fantasy I'd been carrying around with me for most of my life.

But I knew it wasn't.

Because Claire had believed me.

Because whenever I did drag out the old stories one more time, she always said, "I wish I'd known them." Not like an indulgent wife allowing the old man his delusions, but like a woman well acquainted with miracles. And because even if I was getting too old to always trust my own judgment, nothing would ever make me doubt hers.

I searched with phone calls, with letters, with hytex research, with the calling-in of old favors, with every tool available to me. I found nothing.

And then one day I was told that I didn't have much more time to look. It wasn't a tragedy; I'd lived a long and happy life. And it wasn't as bad as it could have been; I'd been assured that there wouldn't be much pain. But I did have that one little unresolved question still hanging over my head.

That was the day I overcame decades of resistance and booked return passage to the world I had once helped to build.

The day after I spoke to Janine Seuss, I followed her advice and took a commuter tram to the Michael Collins Museum of Early Lunar Settlement. It was a popular tourist spot with all the tableaus and reenactments and, you should only excuse the expression, cheesy souvenirs you'd expect from such an establishment; I'd avoided it up until now mostly because I'd seen and heard most of it before, and much of what was left was the kind of crowd-pleasing foofaraw that tames and diminishes the actual experience I lived through for the consumption of folks who are primarily interested in tiring out their hyperactive kids. The dumbest of those was a pile of real Earth rocks, replacing the weight various early astronauts had taken from the moon; ha ha ha, stop, I'm dying here. The most offensive was a kids' exhibit narrated by a cartoon-character early development engineer; he spoke with a cornball rural accident, had comic-opera patches on the knees of his moonsuit, and seemed to have an I.Q. of about five.

Another annoying thing about frontiers: when they're not frontiers anymore, the civilizations that move in like to think that the people who came first were stupid.

But when I found pictures of myself, in an exhibit on the development programs, and pointed them out to an attendant, it was fairly easy to talk the curators into letting me into their archives for a look at certain other materials that hadn't seen the light of day for almost twenty years. They were taped interviews, thirty years old now, with a number of the old guys and gals, talking about their experiences in the days of early development: the majority of those had been conducted here on the moon, but others had taken place on Earth or Mars or wherever else any of those old farts ended up. I felt vaguely insulted that they hadn't tried to contact me; maybe they had, and my wife, anticipating my reluctance, had turned them away. I wondered if I should have felt annoyed by that. I wondered too if my annoyance at the taming of the moon had something to do with the disquieting sensation of becoming ancient history while you're still alive to remember it.

There were about ten thousand hours of interviews; even if my health remained stable long enough for me to listen to them all, my savings would run out far sooner. But they were indexed, and audio-search is a wonderful thing. I typed in "Minnie" and got several dozen references to small things, almost as many references to Mickey's rodent girlfriend, and a bunch of stories about a project engineer, from after my time, who had also been blessed with that particular first name. (To believe the transcripts, she spent all her waking hours saying impossibly cute things that her friends and colleagues would remember and be compelled to repeat decades later; what a bloody pixie.) I typed in "Earl" and, though it felt silly, "Miles," and got a similar collection of irrelevancies—many many references to miles, thus proving conclusively that as recently as thirty years ago the adoption of the metric system hadn't yet succeeded in wiping out any less-elegant but still fondly-remembered forms of measurement. After that, temporarily stuck, I typed in my own name, first and last, and was rewarded with a fine selection of embarrassing anecdotes from folks who recalled what a humorless little pissant I had been way back then. All of this took hours; I had to listen to each of these references, if only for a second or two, just to know for sure what was being talked about, and I confess that, in between a number of bathroom breaks I would have considered unlikely as a younger man, I more than once forgot what I was supposedly looking for long enough to enjoy a few moments with old voices I hadn't heard for longer than most lunar residents had been alive.

I then cross-referenced by the names of the various people who were along on that first Sunday night trip to Minnie and Earl's. "George Peterson" got me nothing of obvious value. "Carrie Aldrin" and "Peter Rawlik," ditto. Nor did the other names. There were references, but nothing I particularly needed.

Feeling tired, I sat there drumming my fingertips on the tabletop. The museum was closing soon. The research had exhausted my limited stores of strength; I didn't think I could do this many days in a row. But I knew there was something here. There had to be. Even if there was a conspiracy of silence—organized or accidental—the mere existence of that unassuming little house had left too great a footprint on our lives.

I thought about details that Claire had found particularly affecting.

And then I typed "Yams."

★ ★ ★ ★ ★

Seventy years ago, suffering from a truly epic sense of dislocation that made everything happening to me seem like bits of stage business performed by actors in a play whose author had taken care to omit all the important exposition, I descended a creaky flight of wooden stairs, to join my colleagues in Minnie and Earl's living room. I was the last to come down, of course; everybody else was already gathered around the three flowery-print sofas, munching on finger foods as they chatted up a storm. The women were in soft cottony dresses, the men in starched trousers and button-downs. They all clapped and cheered as I made my appearance, a reaction that brought an unwelcome blush to my cheeks. It was no wonder; I was a little withdrawn to begin with, back then, and the impossible context had me so off-center that all my defenses had turned to powder.

It was a homey place, though: brightly lit, with a burning fireplace, an array of glass shelving covered with a selection of home-made pottery, plants and flowers in every available nook, an upright piano, a bar that did not dominate the room, and an array of framed photographs on the wall behind the couch. There was no TV or hytex. I glanced at the photographs and moved toward them, hungry for data.

Then Earl rose from his easy chair and came around the coffee table, with a gruff, "Plenty of time to look around, son. Let me take care of you."

"That's—" I said. I was still not managing complete sentences, most of the time.

He took me by the arm, brought me over to the bar, and sat me down on a stool. "Like I said, plenty of time. You're like most first-timers, you're probably in dire need of a drink. We can take care of that first and then get acquainted." He moved around the bar, slung a towel over his shoulder, and said: "What'll it be, Pilgrim?"

Thank God I recognized the reference. If I hadn't—if it had just been another inexplicable element of a day already crammed with them—my head would have exploded from the effort of figuring out why I was being called a Pilgrim. "A . . . Sea of Tranquility?"

"Man after my own heart," Earl said, flashing a grin as he compiled an impressive array of ingredients in a blender. "Always drink the local drink, son. As my Daddy put it, there's no point in going anywhere if you just get drunk the same way you can at home.—Which is where, by the way?"

I said, "What?"

"You missed the segue. I was asking you where you were from."

It seemed a perfect opportunity. "You first."

He chuckled. "Oh, the wife and I been here long enough, you might as well say we're from here. Great place to retire, isn't it? The old big blue marble hanging up there all day and all night?"

"I suppose," I said.

"You suppose," he said, raising an eyebrow at the concoction taking shape in his blender. "That's awful noncommittal of you. Can't you even admit to liking the view?"

"I admit to it," I said.

"But you're not enthused. You know, there's an old joke about a fella from New York and a fella from New Jersey. And the fella from New York is always bragging on his town, talking about Broadway, and the Empire State Building, and Central Park, and so on, and just as often saying terrible things about how ugly things are on the Jersey side of the river. And the fella from Jersey finally gets fed up, and says, 'All right, I've had enough of this, I want you to say one thing, just one thing, about New Jersey that's better than anything you can say about Manhattan.' And the fella from New York says, 'No problem. The view.' "

I didn't laugh, but I did smile.

"That's what's so great about this place," he concluded. "The view. Moon's pretty nice to look at for folks on Earth—and a godsend for bad poets, too, what with June-moon-spoon and all—but as views go, it can't hold a candle to the one we have, looking back. So don't give me any supposes. Own up to what you think."

"It's a great view," I said, this time with conviction, as he handed my drink. Then I asked the big question another way: "How did you arrange it?"

"You ought to know better than that, son. We didn't arrange it. We just took advantage of it. Nothing like a scenic overlook to give zip to your real estate—So answer me. Where are you from?"

Acutely aware that more than a minute had passed since I'd asked him the same question, and that no answer seemed to be forthcoming, I was also too trapped by simple courtesy to press the issue. "San Francisco."

He whistled. "I've seen pictures of San Francisco. Looks like a beautiful town."

"It is," I said.

"You actually climb those hills in Earth gravity?"

"I used to run up Hyde every morning at dawn."

"Hyde's the big steep one that heads down to the bay?"

"One of them," I said.

"And you ran up that hill? At dawn? Every day?"

"Yup."

"You have a really obsessive personality, don't you, son?"

I shrugged. "About some things, I suppose."

"Only about some things?"

"That's what being obsessive means, right?"

"Ah, well. Nothing wrong about being obsessive, as long as you're not a fanatic about it. Want me to freshen up that drink?"

I felt absolutely no alcoholic effect at all. "Maybe you better."

I tried to turn the conversation back to where he was from, but somehow I didn't get a chance, because that's when Minnie took me by the hand and dragged me over to the wall of family photos. There were pictures of them smiling on the couch, pictures of them lounging together in the backyard, pictures of them standing proudly before their home. There were a large number of photos that used Earth as a backdrop. Only four photos showed them with other people, all from the last century: in one, they sat at their dining table with a surprised-looking Neil Armstrong and Buzz Aldrin; in another, they sat on their porch swing chatting with Carl Sagan; in a third, Minnie was being enthusiastically hugged by Isaac Asimov; the fourth showed Earl playing the upright piano while Minnie sat beside him and a tall, thin blonde man with androgynous features and two differently-colored eyes serenaded them both. The last figure was the only one I didn't recognize immediately; by the time somebody finally clued me in, several visits later, I would be far too jaded to engage in the spit-take it would have merited any other time.

I wanted to ask Minnie about the photos with the people I recognized, but then Peter and Earl dragged me downstairs to take a look at Earl's model train set, a rural landscape incorporating four lines and six separate small towns. It was a remarkably detailed piece of work, but I was most impressed with the small miracle of engineering that induced four heavy chains to pull it out of the way whenever Earl pulled a small cord. This handily revealed the pool table. Earl whipped Peter two games out of three, then challenged me; I'm fairly good at pool, but I was understandably off my game that afternoon, and missed every single shot. When Carrie Aldrin No Relation came down to challenge Earl, he mimed terror. It was a genial hour, totally devoted to content-free conversation—and any attempt I made to bring up the questions that burned in my breast was terminated without apparent malice.

Back upstairs. The dog nosing at my hand. Minnie noting that he liked me. Minnie saying anything about the son whose room we'd changed in, the one who'd died "in the war." A very real heartbreak about the way her eyes grew distant at that moment. I asked which war, and she smiled sadly: "There's only been one war, dear—and it doesn't really matter what you call it." Maxine patting her hand. Oscar telling a mildly funny anecdote from his childhood, Minnie asking him to tell her the one about the next-door neighbors again. I brought up the photo of Minnie and Earl with Neal Armstrong and Buzz Aldrin, and Minnie clucked that they had been such nice boys.

Paranoia hit. "Ever hear of Ray Bradbury?"

She smiled with real affection. "Oh, yes. We only met him once or twice, but he was genuinely sweet. I miss him."

"So you met him, too."

"We've met a lot of people, apricot. Why? Is he a relation?"

"Just an old-time writer I like," I said.

"Ahhhhhh."

"In fact," I said, "one story of his I particularly like was called 'Mars is Heaven.' "

She sipped her tea. "Don't know that one."

"It's about a manned expedition to Mars—written while that was still in the future, you understand. And when the astronauts get there they discover a charming, rustic, old-fashioned American small town, filled with sweet old folks

331

they remember from their childhoods. It's the last thing they expect, but after a while they grow comfortable with it. They even jump to the conclusion that Mars is the site of the afterlife. Except it's not. The sweet old folks are aliens in disguise, and they're lulling all these gullible earthlings into a false sense of security so they can be killed at leisure."

My words had been hesitantly spoken, less out of concern for Minnie's feelings than those of my colleagues. Their faces were blank, unreadable, masking emotions that could have been anything from anger to amusement. I will admit that for a split second there, my paranoia reaching heights it had never known before (or thank God, since), I half-expected George and Oscar and Maxine to morph into the hideously tentacled bug-eyed monsters who had taken their places immediately after eating their brains. Then the moment passed, and the silence continued to hang heavily in the room, and any genuine apprehension I might have felt gave way to an embarrassment of more mundane proportions. After all—whatever the explanation for all this might have been—I'd just been unforgivably rude to a person who had only been gracious and charming toward me.

She showed no anger, no sign that she took it personally. "I remember that one now, honey. I'm afraid I didn't like it as much as some of Ray's other efforts. Among other things, it seemed pretty unreasonable to me that critters advanced enough to pull off that kind of masquerade would have nothing better to do with their lives to eat nice folks who came calling.—But then, he also wrote a story about a baby that starts killing as soon as it leaves the womb, and I prefer to believe that infants, given sufficient understanding and affection, soon learn that the universe outside the womb isn't that dark and cold a place after all. Given half a chance, they might even grow up . . . and it's a wonderful process to watch."

I had nothing to say to that.

She sipped her tea again, one pinky finger extended in the most un-self-conscious manner imaginable, just as if she couldn't fathom drinking her tea any other way, then, spoke brightly, with perfect timing: "But if you stay the night, I'll be sure to put you in the room with all the pods."

There was a moment of silence, with every face in the room—including those of Earl and Peter and Carrie, who had just come up from downstairs—as distinguishedly impassive as a granite bust of some forefather you had never heard of.

Then I averted my eyes, trying to hide the smile as it began to spread on my face.

Then somebody made a helpless noise, and we all exploded with laughter.

Seventy years later:

If every land ever settled by human beings has its garden spots, then every land ever settled by human beings has its hovels. This is true even of frontiers that have become theme parks. I had spent much of this return to the world I had once known wandering through a brightly-lit, comfortably-upholstered tourist paradise—the kind of ersatz environment common to all overdeveloped places, that is less an expression of local character than a determined struggle to ensure the total eradication of anything resembling local character. But now I was headed toward a place that would never be printed on a postcard, that would never be on the tours, that existed on tourist maps only as the first, best sign that those looking for easy traveling have just made a disastrous wrong turn.

It was on Farside, of course. Most tourist destinations, and higher-end habitats, are on Nearside, which comes equipped with a nice blue planet to look at. Granted that even on Nearside the view is considered a thing for tourists, and that most folks who live here live underground and like to brag to each other about how long they've gone without Earthgazing—our ancestral ties are still part of us, and the mere presence of Earth, seen or unseen, is so inherently comforting that most normal people with a choice pick Nearside. Farside, by comparison, caters almost exclusively to hazardous industries and folks who don't want that nice blue planet messing up the stark emptiness of their sky—a select group of people that includes a small number of astronomers at the Frank Drake Observatory, and a large number of assorted perverts and geeks and misanthropes. The wild frontier of the fantasies comes closest to being a reality here—the hemisphere has some heavy-industry settlements that advertise their crime rates as a matter of civic pride.

And then there are the haunts of those who find even those places too civilized for their tastes. The mountains and craters of Farside are dotted with the little boxy single-person habitats of folks who have turned their back not only on the home planet but also the rest of humanity as well. Some of those huddle inside their self-imposed solitary confinement for weeks or months on end, emerging only to retrieve their supply drops or enforce the warning their radios transmit on infinite loop: that they don't want visitors and that all trespassers should expect to be shot. They're all eccentric, but some are crazy and a significant percentage of them are clinically insane. They're not the kind of folks the sane visit just for local color.

I landed my rented skimmer on a ridge overlooking an oblong metal box with a roof marked by a glowing ten-digit registration number. It was night here, and nobody who lived in such a glorified house trailer would have been considerate enough to provide any outside lighting for visitors, so those lit digits provided the only ground-level rebuttal to starfield up above; it was an inadequate rebuttal at best, which left the ground on all sides an ocean of undifferentiated inky blackness. I could carry my own lamp, of course, but I didn't want to negotiate the walk from my skimmer to the habitat's front door if the reception I met there required a hasty retreat; I wasn't very capable of hasty retreats, these days.

So I just sat in my skimmer and transmit the repeating loop: Walter Stearns. I desperately need to speak to Walter Stearns. Walter Stearns. I desperately need to speak to Walter Stearns. Walter Stearns. I desperately need to speak to Walter Stearns. Walter Stearns. I desperately need to speak to Walter Stearns. It was the emergency frequency that all of these live-alones are required to keep open 24-7, but there was no guarantee Stearns was listening—and since I was not in distress, I was not really legally entitled to use it. But I didn't care; Stearns was the best lead I had yet.

It was only two hours before a voice like a mouth full of steel wool finally responded: "Go away."

"I won't be long, Mr. Stearns. We need to talk."

"You need to talk. I need you to go away."

"It's about Minnie and Earl, Mr. Stearns."

There was a pause. "Who?"

The pause had seemed a hair too long to mean mere puzzlement. "Minnie and Earl. From the development days. You remember them, don't you?"

"I never knew any Minnie and Earl," he said. "Go away."

"I listened to the tapes you made for the Museum, Mr. Stearns."

The anger in his hoarse, dusty old voice was still building. "I made those tapes when I was still talking to people. And there's nothing in them about any Minnie or Earl."

"No," I said, "there's not. Nobody mentioned Minnie and

Earl by name, not you, and not anybody else who participated. But you still remember them. It took me several days
to track you down, Mr. Stearns. We weren't here at the same
time, but we still had Minnie and Earl in common."

"I have nothing to say to you," he said, with a new shrill-
ness in his voice. "I'm an old man. I don't want to be bothered. Go away."

My cheeks ached from the size of my triumphant grin. "I
brought yams."

There was nothing on the other end but the sibilant hiss of
background radiation. It lasted just long enough to persuade
me that my trump card had been nothing of the kind; he had
shut down or smashed his receiver, or simply turned his back
to it, so he could sit there in his little cage waiting for the big
bad outsider to get tired and leave.

Then he said: "Yams."

Twenty-four percent of the people who contributed to
the Museum's oral history had mentioned yams at least
once. They had talked about the processing of basic food
shipments from home, and slipped yams into their lists of
the kind of items received; they had conversely cited yams as
the kind of food that the folks back home had never once
thought of sending; they had related anecdotes about funny
things this co-worker or that co-worker had said at dinner,
over a nice steaming plate of yams. They had mentioned
yams and they had moved on, behaving as if it was just another background detail mentioned only to provide their
colorful reminiscences the right degree of persuasive veri-
similitude. Anybody not from those days who noticed the
strange recurring theme might have imagined it a statistical
oddity or an in-joke of some kind. For anybody who had
been to Minnie and Earl's—and tasted the delicately seasoned yams she served so frequently—it was something

more: a strange form of confirmation.

When Stearns spoke again, his voice still rasped of disuse, but it also possessed a light quality that hadn't been there before. "They've been gone a long time. I'm not sure I know what to tell you."

"I checked your records," I said. "You've been on the moon continuously since those days; you went straight from the development teams to the early settlements to the colonies that followed. You've probably been here nonstop longer than anybody else living or dead. If anybody can give me an idea what happened to them, it's you."

More silence.

"Please," I said.

And then he muttered a cuss word that had passed out of the vernacular forty years earlier. "All right, damn you. But you won't find them. I don't think anybody will ever find them."


Seventy years earlier:

We were there for about two more hours before George took me aside, said he needed to speak to me in private, and directed me to wait for him in the backyard.

The backyard was nice.

I've always hated that word. Nice. It means nothing. Describing people, it can mean the most distant politeness, or the most compassionate warmth; it can mean civility and it can mean charity and it can mean grace and it can mean friendship. Those things may be similar, but they're not synonyms; when the same word is used to describe all of them, then that word means nothing. It means even less when describing places. So what if the backyard was nice? Was it just comfortable, and well-tended, or was it a place that reinvigorated you with every breath? How can you leave it at "nice" and possibly imagine that you've done the job?

Nice. Feh.

But that's exactly what this backyard was.

It was a couple of acres of trimmed green lawn, bordered by the white picket fence that signaled the beginning of vacuum. A quarter-circle of bright red roses marked each of the two rear corners; between them, bees hovered lazily over a semicircular garden heavy on towering orchids and sun-flowers. The painted white rocks which bordered that garden were arranged in a perfect line, none of them even a milli-meter out of place, none of them irregular enough to shame the conformity that characterized the relationship between all the others. There was a single apple tree, which hugged the rear of the house so tightly that the occupants of the second floor might have been able to reach out their windows and grab their breakfast before they trudged off to the shower; there were enough fallen green apples to look picturesque, but not enough to look sloppy. There was a bench of multi-colored polished stone at the base of the porch steps, dupli-cating the porch swing up above but somehow absolutely right in its position; and as I sat on that bench facing the nice backyard I breathed deep and I smelled things that I had almost forgotten I could smell—not just the distant charcoal reek of neighbors burning hamburgers in their own back-yards, but lilacs, freshly cut grass, horse scent, and a cleansing whiff of rain. I sat there and I spotted squirrels, hummingbirds, monarch butterflies, and a belled calico cat that ran by, stopped, saw me, looked terribly confused in the way cats have, and then went on. I sat there and I breathed and after months of inhaling foot odor and antiseptics I found myself getting a buzz. It was intoxicating. It was invigorating. It was a shot of pure energy. It was joy. God help me, it was Nice.

But it was also surrounded on all sides by a pitiless vacuum that, if real physics meant anything, should have claimed it in an instant. Perhaps it shouldn't have bothered me that much, by then; but it did.

The screen door slammed. Miles the dog bounded down the porch steps and, panting furiously, nudged my folded hands. I scratched him under the ears. He gave me the usual unconditional adoration of the golden retriever—I petted him, therefore I was God. Most panting dogs look like they're smiling (it's a major reason humans react so strongly to the species), but Miles, the canine slave to context, looked like he was enjoying the grand joke that everybody was playing at my expense. Maybe he was. Maybe he wasn't even really a dog . . .

The screen door opened and slammed. This time it was George, carrying a couple of tall glasses filled with pink stuff and ice. He handed me one of the glasses; it was lemonade, of course. He sipped from the other one and said: "Minnie's cooking yams again. She's a miracle worker when it comes to yams. She does something with them, I don't know, but it's really—"

"You," I said wryly, "are enjoying this way too much."

"Aren't you?" he asked.

Miles the dog stared at the lemonade as if it was the most wondrous sight in the universe. George dipped a finger into his drink and held it out so the mutt could have a taste. Miles adored him now. I was so off-center I almost felt betrayed. "Yeah. I guess I am. I like them."

"Pretty hard not to like them. They're nice people."

"But the situation is so insane—"

"Sanity," George said, "is a fluid concept. Think about how nuts relativity sounded, the first time somebody explained it to you. Hell, think back to when you were a kid, and somebody first explained the mechanics of sex."

"George—"

He gave Miles another taste. "I can see you trying like mad to work this out. Compiling data, forming and rejecting theories, even concocting little experiments to test the accuracy of your senses. I know because I was once in your position, when I was brought out here for the first time, and I remember doing all the same things. But I now have a lot of experience in walking people through this, and I can probably save you a great deal of time and energy by completing your data and summarizing all of your likely theories."

I was too tired to glare at him anymore. "You can skip the data and theories and move on to the explanation. I promise you I won't mind."

"Yes, you would," he said, with absolute certainty. "Trust me, dealing with the established lines of inquiry is the only real way to get there.

"First, providing the raw data. One: this little homestead cannot be detected from Earth; our most powerful telescopes see nothing but dead moonscape here. Two: It, and the two old folks, have been here since at least Apollo; those photos of them with Armstrong and Aldrin are genuine. Three: There is nothing you can ask them that will get any kind of straight answer about who or what they are and why they're here. Four: we have no idea how they knew Asimov, Sagan, or Bradbury—but I promise you that those are not the most startling names you will hear them drop if you stick around long enough to get to know them. Five: We don't know how they maintain an earthlike environment in here. Six, about that mailbox: they do get delivery, on a daily basis, though no actual mailman has ever been detected, and none of the mail we've ever managed to sneak a peek at is the slightest bit interesting. It's all senior citizen magazines and grocery store circulars. Seven: they never seem to go shopping, but they always have an ample supply of food and other provisions. Eight (I am up to eight, right?): they haven't noticeably aged, not even the dog. Nine: they do understand every language we've sprung on them, but they give all their answers in Midwestern-American English. And ten: we have a group of folks from our project coming out here to visit just about every night of the week, on a rotating schedule that works out to just about once a week for each of us.

"So much for the raw data. The theories take longer to deal with. Let me go through all the ones you're likely to formulate." He peeled back a finger. "One. This is all just a practical joke perpetrated by your friends and colleagues in an all-out attempt to shock you out of your funk. We put it all together with spit and baling wire and some kind of elaborate special effects trickery that's going to seem ridiculously obvious just as soon as you're done figuring it out. We went to all this effort, and spent the many billions of dollars it would have cost to get all these construction materials here, and developed entirely new technologies capable of holding in an atmosphere, and put it all together while you weren't looking, and along the way brought in a couple of convincing old folks from Central Casting, just so we could enjoy the look on your face. What a zany bunch of folks we are, huh?"

I felt myself blushing. "I'd considered that."

"And why not? It's a legitimate theory. Also a ridiculous one, but let's move on." He peeled back another finger. "Two. This is not a practical joke, but a test or psychological experiment of some kind, arranged by the brain boys back home. They put together all of this trickery, just to see how the average astronaut, isolated from home and normal societal context, reacts to situations that defy easy explanation and cannot be foreseen by even the most exhaustively-planned training. This particular explanation works especially well if you also factor in what we cleverly call the McGoohan Corollary—that is, the idea that we're not really on the moon at all, but somewhere on Earth, possibly underground, where the real practical difficulty would lie in simulating not a quaint rural setting on a warm summer day, but instead the low-g, high-radiation, temperature-extreme vacuum that you gullibly believed you were walking around in, every single time you suited up. This theory is, of course, equally ridiculous, for many reasons—but we did have one guy about a year ago who stubbornly held on to it for almost a full week. Something about his psychological makeup just made it easier for him to accept that, over all the others, and we had to keep a close watch on him to stop him from trying to prove it with a nice unsuited walk. But from the way you're looking at me right now I don't think we're going to have the same problem with you. So . . .

"Assuming that this is not a joke, or a trick, or an experiment, or some lame phenomenon like that, that this situation you're experiencing is precisely what we have represented to you, then we are definitely looking at something beyond all terrestrial experience. Which brings us to Three." He peeled back another finger. "This is a First-Contact situation. Minnie and Earl, and possibly Miles here, are aliens in disguise, or simulations constructed by aliens. They have created a friendly environment inside this picket fence, using technology we can only guess at—let's say an invisible bubble capable of filtering out radiation and retaining a breathable atmosphere while remaining permeable to confused bipeds in big clumsy moonsuits. And they have done so—why? To hide their true nature while they observe our progress? Possibly. But if so, it would be a lot more subtle to place their little farmhouse in Kansas, where it wouldn't seem so crazily out of place. To communicate with us in terms we can accept? Possibly—except that couching those terms in such an insane context seems as counterproductive to genuine communication as their apparent decision to limit the substance of that communication to geriatric small talk. To make us comfortable with something familiar? Possibly—except that this kind of small mid-American home is familiar to only a small fraction of humanity, and it seems downright exotic to the many observers we've shuttled in from China, or India, or Saudi Arabia, or for that matter Manhattan. To present us with a puzzle that we have to solve? Again, possibly—but since Minnie and Earl and Miles won't confirm or deny, it's also a possibility we won't be able to test unless somebody like yourself actually does come up with the great big magic epiphany. I'm not holding my breath. But I do reject any theory that they're hostile, including the 'Mars is Heaven' theory you already cited. Anybody capable of pulling this off must have resources that could mash us flat in the time it takes to sneeze."

Miles woofed. In context it seemed vaguely threatening.

"Four." Another finger. "Minnie and Earl are actually human, and Miles is actually canine. They come here from the future, or from an alternate universe, or from some previously-unknown subset of humanity that's been living among us all this time, hiding great and unfathomable powers that, blaaah blaah blaah, fill in the blank. And they're here, making their presence known—why? All the same sub-theories that applied to alien visitors also apply to human agencies, and all the same objections as well. Nothing explains why they would deliberately couch such a maddening enigma in such, for lack of a more appropriate word, banal terms. It's a little like coming face to face with God and discovering that He really does look like an bearded old white guy in a robe; He might, for all I know, but I'm more religious than you probably think, and there's some part of me that absolutely refuses to believe it. He, or She, if you prefer, could do better than that. And so could anybody, human or alien, whose main purpose in coming here is to study us, or test us, or put on a show for us.

"You still with me?" he inquired.

"Go on," I growled. "I'll let you know if you leave anything out."

He peeled back another finger. "Five. I kind of like this one. Minnie and Earl, and by extension Miles, are not creatures of advanced technology, but of a completely different kind of natural phenomenon—let's say, for the sake of argument, a bizarre jog in the space-time continuum that allows a friendly but otherwise unremarkable couple living in Kansas or Wyoming or someplace like that to continue experiencing life down on the farm while in some way as miraculous to them as it seems to us, projecting an interactive version of themselves to this otherwise barren spot on the moon. Since, as your little conversation with Earl established, they clearly know they're on the moon, we would have to accept that they're unflappable enough to take this phenomenon at face value, but I've known enough Midwesterners to know that this is a genuine possibility.

"Six." Starting now on another hand. "Mentioned only so you can be assured I'm providing you an exhaustive list—a phenomenon one of your predecessors called the Law of Preservation of Home. He theorized that whenever human beings penetrate too far past their own natural habitat, into places sufficiently inhospitable to life, the universe is forced to spontaneously generate something a little more congenial to compensate—the equivalent, I suppose, of magically whomping up a Holiday Inn with a swimming pool, to greet explorers lost in the coldest reaches of Antarctica. He even said that the only reason we hadn't ever received reliable reports of this phenomenon on Earth is that we weren't ever sufficiently far from our natural habitat to activate it . . . but I can tell from the look on your face that you don't exactly buy this one either, so I'll set it aside and let you read the paper he wrote on the subject at your leisure."

"I don't think I will," I said.

"You ought to. It's a real hoot. But if you want to, I'll skip all the way to the end of the list, to the only explanation that ultimately makes any sense. Ready?"

"I'm waiting."

"All right. That explanation is—" he paused dramatically "—it doesn't matter."

There was a moment of pregnant silence.

I didn't explode; I was too shell-shocked to explode. Instead, I just said: "I sat through half a dozen bullshit theories for 'It doesn't matter?' "

"You had to, Max; it's the only way to get there. You had to learn the hard way that all of these propositions are either completely impossible or, for the time being, completely impossible to test—and we know this because the best minds on Earth have been working on the problem for as long as there's been a sustained human presence on the moon. We've taken hair samples from Minnie's hairbrush. We've smuggled out stool samples from the dog. We've recorded our conversations with the old folks and studied every second of every tape from every possible angle. We've monitored the house for years on end, analyzed samples of the food and drink served in there, and exhaustively charted the health of everybody to go in or out. And all it's ever gotten us, in all these years of being frantic about it, is this—that as far as we can determine, Minnie and Earl are just a couple of friendly old folks who like having visitors."

"And that's it?"

"Why can't it be? Whether aliens, time travelers, displaced human beings, or natural phenomena—they're good listeners, and fine people, and they sure serve a good Sunday dinner. And if there must be things in the universe we can't understand—well, then, it's sure comforting to know that some of them just want to be good neighbors. That's what I mean by saying, 'It doesn't matter.' "

He stood up, stretched, took the kind of deep breath people only indulge in when they're truly luxuriating in the freshness of the air around them, and said: "Minnie and Earl expect some of the new folks to be a little pokey, getting used to the idea. They won't mind if you stay out here and smell the roses a while. Maybe when you come in, we'll talk a little more about getting you scheduled for regular visitation. Minnie's already asked me about it—she seems to like you. God knows why." He winked, shot me in the chest with a pair of pretend six-shooters made from the index fingers of both hands, and went back inside, taking the dog with him. And I was alone in the nice backyard, serenaded by birdsong as I tried to decide how to reconcile my own rational hunger for explanations with the unquestioning acceptance that was being required of me.

Eventually, I came to the same conclusion George had; the only conclusion that was possible under the circumstances. It was a genuine phenomenon, that conclusion: a community of skeptics and rationalists and followers of the scientific method deciding that there were some things Man was having too good a time to know. Coming to think of Minnie and Earl as family didn't take much longer than that. For the next three years, until I left for my new job in the

outer system, I went out to their place at least once, sometimes twice a week; I shot pool with Earl and chatted about
relatives back home with Minnie; I'd tussled with Miles and
helped with the dishes and joined them for long all-nighters
talking about nothing in particular. I learned how to bake
with the limited facilities we had at Base, so I could bring my
own cookies to her feasts. I came to revel in standing on a
creaky front porch beneath a bug lamp, sipping grape juice as
I joined Minnie in yet another awful rendition of "Anatevka."
Occasionally I glanced at the big blue cradle of civilization
hanging in the sky, remembered for the fiftieth or sixtieth or
one hundredth time that none of this had any right to be happening, and reminded myself for the fiftieth or sixtieth or one
hundredth time that the only sane response was to continue
carrying the tune. I came to think of Minnie and Earl as the
real reason we were on the moon, and I came to understand
one of the major reasons we were all so bloody careful to keep
it a secret—because the needy masses of Earth, who were at
that point still agitating about all the time and money spent
on the space program, would not have been mollified by the
knowledge that all those billions were being spent, in part, so
that a few of the best and the brightest could indulge themselves in sing-alongs and wiener dog cookouts.

I know it doesn't sound much like a frontier. It wasn't, not
inside the picket fence. Outside, it remained dangerous and
back-breaking work. We lost five separate people while I was
there; two to blowouts, one to a collapsing crane, one to a
careless tumble off a crater rim, and one to suicide (she, alas,
had not been to Minnie and Earl's yet). We had injuries every
week, shortages every day, and crises just about every hour.
Most of the time, we seemed to lose ground—and even when
we didn't, we lived with the knowledge that all of our work
and all of our dedication could be thrown in the toilet the first

time there was a political shift back home. There was no reason for any of us to believe that we were actually accomplishing what we were there to do—but somehow, with Minnie and Earl there, hosting a different group every night, it was impossible to come to any other conclusion. They liked us. They believed in us. They were sure that we were worth their time and effort. And they expected us to be around for a long, long time . . . just like they had been.

I suppose that's another reason why I was so determined to find them now. Because I didn't know what it said about the people we'd become that they weren't around keeping us company anymore.

I was in a jail cell for forty-eight hours once. Never mind why; it's a stupid story. The cell itself wasn't the sort of thing I expected from movies and television; it was brightly lit, free of vermin, and devoid of any steel bars to grip obsessively while cursing the guards and bemoaning the injustice that had brought me there. It was just a locked room with a steel door, a working toilet, a clean sink, a soft bed, and absolutely nothing else. If I had been able to come and go at will it might have been an acceptable cheap hotel room. Since I was stuck there, without anything to do or anybody to talk to, I spent those forty-eight hours going very quietly insane.

The habitat module of Walter Stearns was a lot like that cell, expanded to accommodate a storage closet, a food locker, and a kitchenette; it was that stark, that empty. There were no decorations on the walls, no personal items, no hytex or music system I could see, nothing to read and nothing to do. It lost its charm for me within thirty seconds. Stearns had been living there for sixteen years: a self-imposed prison sentence that might have been expiation for the sin of living past his era.

The man himself moved with what seemed glacial slowness, like a wind-up toy about to stop and fall over. He dragged one leg, but if that was a legacy of a stroke—and an explanation for why he chose to live as he did—there was no telltale slur to his speech to corroborate it. Whatever the reason might have been, I couldn't help regarding him with the embarrassed pity one old man feels toward another the same age who hasn't weathered his own years nearly as well.

He accepted my proffered can of yams with a sour grin and gave me a mug of some foul-smelling brown stuff in return. Then he poured some for himself and shuffled to the edge of his bed and sat down with a grunt. "I'm not a hermit," he said, defensively.

"I didn't use the word," I told him.

"I didn't set out to be a hermit," he went on, as if he hadn't heard me. "Nobody sets out to be a hermit. Nobody turns his back on the damned race unless he has some reason to be fed up. I'm not fed up. I just don't know any alternative. It's the only way I know to let the moon be the moon."

He sipped some of the foul-smelling brown stuff and gestured for me to do the same. Out of politeness, I sipped from my own cup. It tasted worse than it smelled, and had a consistency like sand floating in vinegar. Somehow I didn't choke. "Let the moon be the moon?"

"They opened a casino in Shepardsville. I went to see it. It's a big luxury hotel with a floor show; trained white tigers jumping through flaming hoops for the pleasure of a pretty young trainer in a spangled bra and panties. The casino room is oval-shaped, and the walls are alive with animated holography of wild horses running around and around and around and around, without stop, twenty-four hours a day. There are night clubs with singers and dancers, and an amusement park with rides for the kids. I sat there and I watched the gamblers bent over their tables and the barflies bent over their drinks and I had to remind myself that I was on the moon—that just being here at all was a miracle that would have had most past civilizations consider us gods. But all these people, all around me, couldn't feel it. They'd built a palace in a place where no palace had ever been and they'd sucked all the magic and all the wonder all the way out of it." He took a deep breath, and sipped some more of his contemptible drink. "It scared me. It made me want to live somewhere where I could still feel the moon being the moon. So I wouldn't be some useless . . . relic who didn't know where he was half the time."

The self-pity had wormed its way into his voice so late that I almost didn't catch it. "It must get lonely," I ventured.

"Annnh. Sometimes I put on my moonsuit and go outside, just to stand there. It's so silent there that I can almost hear the breath of God. And I remember that it's the moon—the moon, dammit. Not some five-star hotel. The moon. A little bit of that and I don't mind being a little lonely the rest of the time. Is that crazy? Is that being a hermit?"

I gave the only answer I could. "I don't know."

He made a hmmmph noise, got up, and carried his mug over to the sink. A few moments cleaning it out and he returned, his lips curled into a half-smile, his eyes focused on some far-off time and place. "The breath of God," he murmured.

"Yams," I prompted.

"You caught that, huh? Been a while since somebody caught that. It's not the sort of thing people catch unless they were there. Unless they remember her."

"Was that by design?"

"You mean, was it some kind of fiendish secret code? Naah. More like a shared joke. We knew by then that nobody would believe us if we actually talked about Minnie and Earl.

They were that forgotten. So we dropped yams into our early-settlement stories. A little way of saying, hey, we remember the old lady. She sure did love to cook those yams."

"With her special seasoning." I said. "And those rolls she baked."

"Uh-huh." He licked his lips, and I almost fell into the trap of considering that unutterably sad . . . until I realized that I was doing the same thing. "Used to try to mix one of Earl's special cocktails, but I never could get them right. Got all the ingredients. Mixed 'em the way he showed me. Never got 'em to taste right. Figure he had some kind of technological edge he wasn't showing us. Real alien superscience, applied to bartending. Or maybe I just can't replace the personality of the bartender. But they were good drinks. I've got to give him that."

We sat together in silence for a while, each lost in the sights and sounds of a day long gone. After a long time, I almost whispered it: "Where did they go, Walter?"

His eyes didn't focus: "I don't know where they are. I don't know what happened to them."

"Start with when you last visited them."

"Oh, that was years and years and years ago." He lowered his head and addressed the floor. "But you know how it is. You have relatives, friends, old folks very important to you. Folks you see every week or so, folks who become a major part of who you are. Then you get busy with other things and you lose touch. I lost touch when the settlement boom hit, and there was always some other place to be, some other job that needed to be done; I couldn't spare one night a week gabbing with old folks just because I happened to love them. After all, they'd always be there, right? By the time I thought of looking them up again, it turned out that everybody else had neglected them too. There was no sign of the house and no way of knowing how long they'd been gone."

I was appalled. "So you're saying that Minnie and Earl moved away because of . . . neglect?"

"Naaah. That's only why they didn't say goodbye. I don't think it has a damn thing to do with why they moved away; just why we didn't notice. I guess that's another reason why nobody likes to talk about them. We're all just too damn ashamed."

"Why do you think they moved, Walter?"

He swallowed another mouthful of his vile brew, and addressed the floor some more, not seeing me, not seeing the exile he'd chosen for himself, not seeing anything but a tiny little window of his past. "I keep thinking of that casino," he murmured. "There was a rotating restaurant on the top floor of the hotel. Showed you the landscape, with all the billboards and amusement parks—and above it all, in the place where all the advertisers hope you're going to forget to look, Mother Earth herself. It was a burlesque and it was boring. And I also keep thinking of that little house, out in the middle of nowhere, with the picket fence and the golden retriever dog . . . and the two sweet old people . . . and the more I compare one thought to the other the more I realize that I don't blame them for going away. They saw that, on the moon we were building, they wouldn't be miraculous any more."

"They had a perfectly maintained little environment—"

"We have a perfectly maintained little environment. We have parks with grass. We have roller coasters and golf courses. We have people with dogs. We even got rotating restaurants and magic acts with tigers. Give us a few more years up here and we'll probably work out some kind of magic trick to do away with the domes and the bulkheads and keep in an atmosphere with nothing but a picket fence. We'll have houses like theirs springing up all over the place. The one thing we don't have is the moon being the moon. Why would they want to stay here?" His voice, which had been rising throughout his little tirade, rose to a shriek with that last question; he hurled his mug against the wall, but it was made of some indestructible ceramic that refused to shatter. It just tumbled to the floor, and skittered under the bunk, spinning in place just long enough to mock him for his empty display of anger. He looked at me, focused, and let me know with a look that our audience was over. "What would be left for them?"

I searched some more, tracking down another five or six oldsters still capable of talking about the old days, as well as half a dozen children or grandchildren of same willing to speak to me about the memories the old folks had left behind, but my interview with Walter Stearns was really the end of it; by the time I left his habitat, I knew that my efforts were futile. I saw that even those willing to talk to me weren't going to be able to tell me more than he had . . . and I turned out to be correct about that. Minnie and Earl had moved out, all right, and there was no forwarding address to be had.

I was also tired: bone-weary in a way that could have been just a normal symptom of age and could have been despair that I had not found what I so desperately needed to find and could have been the harbinger of my last remaining days. Whatever it was, I just didn't have the energy to keep going that much longer . . . and I knew that the only real place for me was the bed I had shared with my dear Claire.

On the night before I flew back I had some money left over, so I went to see the musical *CERES* at New Broadway. I confess I found it dreadful—like most old farts, I can't fathom music produced after the first three decades of my life—but it was definitely elaborate, with a cast of lithe and gymnastic young dancers in silvery jumpsuits leaping about in a slow-motion ballet that took full advantage of the special opportunities afforded by lunar gravity. At one point the show even simulated free fall, thanks to invisible filaments that crisscrossed the stage, allowing the dancers to glide from place to place like objects ruled only by their own mass and momentum. The Playbill said that one of the performers, never mind which one, was not a real human being, but a holographic projection artfully integrated with the rest of the performers. I couldn't discern the fake, but I couldn't find it in myself to be impressed. We were a few flimsy bulkheads and half a kilometer from lunar vacuum, and to me, that was the real story . . . even if nobody else in the audience of hundreds could see it.

I moved out of my hotel. I tipped my concierge, who hadn't found me anything about Minnie and Earl but had provided all the other amenities I'd asked for. I bought some stupid souvenirs for the grandchildren, and boarded my flight back to Earth.

After about an hour I went up to the passenger lounge, occupied by two intensely-arguing businesswomen, a child playing a handheld hytex game, and a bored-looking thin man with a shiny head. Nobody was looking out the panoramic window, not even me. I closed my eyes and pretended that the view wasn't there. Instead I thought of the time Earl had decided he wanted to fly a kite. That was a major moment. He built it out of newspapers he got from somewhere, and sat in his backyard letting out more than five hundred meters of line; though the string and the kite extended far beyond the atmospheric picket-fence perimeter, it had still swooped and sailed like an object enjoying the robust winds it would have known, achieving that altitude on Earth. That, of course, had been another impossibility . . . but my colleagues and I had been so inured to such things by then that we simply shrugged and enjoyed the moment as it came.

I badly wanted to fly a kite.

I badly wanted to know that Minnie and Earl had not left thinking poorly of us.

I didn't think they were dead. They weren't the kind of people who died. But they were living somewhere else, someplace far away—and if the human race was lucky it was somewhere in the solar system. Maybe, even now, while I rode back to face however much time I had left, there was a mind-boggling little secret being kept by the construction teams building those habitats out near the Jovian moons; maybe some of those physicists and engineers were taking time out from a week of dangerous and backbreaking labor to spend a few hours in the company of an old man and old woman whose deepest spoken insight about the massive planet that graces their sky was how it presented one hell of a lovely view. Maybe the same thing happened when Anderson and Santiago hitched a ride on the comet that now bears their names—and maybe there's a little cottage halfway up the slope of Olympus Mons where the Mars colonists go whenever they need a little down-home hospitality. I would have been happy with all of those possibilities. I would have felt the weight of years fall from my bones in an instant, if I just knew that there was still room for them in the theme-park future we seemed to be building.

Then something, maybe chance, maybe instinct, made me look out the window.

And my poor, slowly failing heart almost stopped right then.

Because Miles, the golden retriever, was pacing us.

He ran alongside the shuttle, keeping up with the lounge

355

window, his lolling pink tongue and long floppy ears trailing behind him like banners driven by some unseen (and patently impossible) breeze. He ran if in slow motion, his feet pawing a ground that wasn't there, his muscles rippling along his side, his muzzle foaming with perspiration. His perpetually laughing expression, so typical of his breed, was not so much the look of an animal merely panting with exertion, but the genuine mirth of a creature aware that it has just pulled off a joke of truly epic proportions. As I stared at him, too dumbstruck to whoop and holler and point him out to my fellow passengers, he turned his head, met my gaze with soulful brown eyes, and did something I've never seen any other golden retriever do, before or since.

He winked.

Then he faced forward, lowered his head, and sped up, leaving us far behind.

I whirled and scanned the lounge, to see if any of my fellow passengers had seen him. The two businesswomen had stopped arguing, and were now giggling over a private joke of some kind. The kid was still intently focused on his game. But the eyes of the man with the shiny head were very large and very round. He stared at me, found in my broad smile confirmation that he hadn't been hallucinating, and tried to speak. "That," he said. And "Was." And after several attempts, "A dog."

He might have gone on from there given another hour or so of trying.

I knew exactly how he felt, of course. I had been in the same place, once, seventy years ago.

Now, for a while, I felt like I was twelve again.

I rose from my seat, crossed the lounge, and took the chair facing the man with the shiny head. He was wide-eyed, like a man who saw me, a total stranger, as the only fixed constant in his universe. That made me feel young, too.

I said, "Let me tell you a little bit about some old friends of mine."

*This one's for Jerry and Kathy Oltion,*
*the Minnie and Earl of the future.*

# Afterword

People constantly ask me why I keep writing short fiction, why I keep returning to that form when exclusive dedication to novels makes better career sense.

Well, there are any number of possible approaches to answering that. They include:

The Defensive Strategy: I've completed four media novels so far, which are individually and collectively nothing to sneeze at. Further novels in my own fictive playground remain a high priority for the future. Really. There's one that—(and I look coy, busily not describing. But just you wait.)

There's the Writerly Strategy: The shorter lengths provide such a perfect format for tales of imagination that I can't help gravitating toward those forms.

There's the Helpless Strategy: I can't do anything about it. The short story ideas keep coming.

There's the Modest Strategy: I'm still learning my craft, but I'll get back to you.

The Personal Strategy: I just got married this year. Cut me some slack.

And The Analytical Strategy: Seriously. If you look at my lifetime output, you will note that much of my early work consisted of short stories and novelettes, with an upper limit of approximately 10,000 words . . . whereas much of what I've produced in the last few years has been novella length, with an upper limit of approximately 28,000.

This does show either increased literary stamina, or increased willingness to pad. If this lengthening trend continues at its present rate, I would be completing my first non-media novels in about forty or fifty years, but I don't think anybody's gonna have to wait all that long; there are works in progress which should be poking their heads above the creative swamp quite soon now. Again. Just You Wait.

In the meantime, there's this conglomeration of Mostly Skiffy, with one Silly Horror Story inserted to provide the Habanero aftertaste. Four of the five were cover stories of the magazines where they initially appeared; four of the five made what passes for a splash in the increasingly shrinking pond known as s-f publishing. The fifth, which is a different kettle of beans entirely, does not suck.

These story notes are brief, but might provide spoilers: you should not pass this point until after you have completed the tales themselves.

The first three stories, "The Funeral March of the Marionettes," "The Tangled Strings of the Marionettes," and "Unseen Demons," all take place in the same future history. Future histories, in case you don't know, are what science fiction writers use to save wear and tear on brain cells. It's a form of intellectual recycling. It's also a helpful way to develop ideas, since fertile seeds not only grow mighty oaks but also establish sprawling forests. (Which are then cut down to make paper so the damn stories can be printed. I really shouldn't use metaphors unless I know where I'm going with them. But anyway.) The overall series, named here for the first time, is called *The AIsource Infection*, and yes, there are more installments on the way, including some which will track further developments among the Vlhani. About all you really have to know, at this earliest of stages, is that the Big

Picture is still being drawn . . . and that these three stories provide the first connected dots.

"The Funeral March of the Marionettes" was, in the words of Chico Esquela, Berry Berry Guud to Me. Reprinted in Polish, Italian, and Japanese, as well as twice in its originating language, it earned my first Hugo and Nebula nominations: realizations of childhood dreams. I report that as I wrote it, I grew more and more anguished about the fate of the doomed Isadora, and that my determination to save her mirrored that of the story's narrator. Alas: sometimes characters have to die, even if you love them. Isadora will not be resurrected, in any of the approaching sequels. Never. She is dead, dead, dead.

And not Marvel Comics dead, which is reversible whenever a new writer comes on, or even Star Trek dead, which is reversible whenever an actor signs the next contract. She is dead. Gone. Finished. Pining for the Fjords. Get over it.

I have a back-scratcher which looks just like a Vlhani. I didn't have it custom-made, but picked it up at the mall. Cool, huh?

My inept spacemen characters Vossoff and Nimmitz, who are technically citizens of the same future history, but only if you're willing to believe that even the grimmest universe has silly corners, appear unnamed at the midpoint. Find no significance in this fact. It just happened.

"The Tangled Strings of the Marionettes", which first saw print the same year as this collection, is a long-delayed sequel to "Funeral March," which raises just as many questions. I initially intended to submit it to Keith DeCandido's collection *Imaginings*, but it seemed rushed at its initial 15,000-word length, so I expanded it, dashing off another submission which Keith snatched up like the wise and discerning man he is. (Wait till you see that one. Whoa.) Nothing much to say about this one except that I hope you'll see more of Ch'tpok. I like her a hell of a lot.

You should also see more of Andrea Cort, the heroine of "Unseen Demons." I like her a hell of a lot, too, but for different reasons: I have always been fascinated with people searching for redemption, especially when they function as their own hardest critics. This particular tale, a cover story in *Analog*, is notable also for containing one of the sweetest little in-jokes, included only to score myself some personal satisfaction, that I have ever produced. By this I am not referring to Mekile Nom, the ambassador from the Bursteeni, a reference to Michael and Nomi Bursteen. It's something else.

But if you want me to say what I'm referring to, you're just plain crazy. It ain't happening. Hee hee hee.

"The Magic Bullet Theory" is the odd man out here: a horror story, though not a very serious one. It's my second comic-horror western (the last one being the as-yet unreprinted "The Good, The Bad and the Danged"). My oft-Tuckerized friend George Peterson makes one of many story appearances here, as a guy a lot less intelligent than the one he plays in "Sunday Night Yams At Minnie And Earl's." Of this tale, I say only that my love of westerns is extreme, that I imagined Sergio Morricone music playing during every scene, and that you don't want to face down levitating ammunition in general.

"Sunday Night Yams at Minnie and Earl's" is one of my all-time favorites. Folks find it sweet. They wonder how a sick bastard like myself could have written it. The answer is I dunno. But I'm certainly glad I did. The tale owes a lot to fellow *Analog* Mafia member Jerry Oltion, with whom I'd collaborated on two previous pieces; his chief contribution here lay in telling me quite forcefully that I did not need his help to finish this one, and urging me to finish it myself. That is, in fact, more significant than you can know, which is one major reason I paid tribute to Jerry and Kathy in the dedication line. The other reason is that they're good folks.

Hope you enjoyed this latest journey into Castro Country, and I hope y'all stick around for the next part of the trip.

—Adam-Troy Castro

# About the Author

Adam-Troy Castro made his first professional sale to SPY magazine in 1987. Since then, he's published more than seventy short stories in magazines including *Analog*, *Fantasy and Science Fiction*, and *Science Fiction Age*, and anthologies including *Adventures in the Twilight Zone*, *It Came from the Drive-In*, and *Skull Full of Spurs*. Among those stories are "Baby Girl Diamond" (nominated for the Bram Stoker Award) and "The Funeral March of the Marionettes" (nominated for the Hugo and Nebula Awards in 1998). "The Astronaut from Wyoming," a collaboration with Jerry Oltion, appeared in *Analog* and was nominated for the Hugo and Nebula Awards in 2000. His original short story collections include *Lost in Booth Nine* (published by Silver Salamander Press in 1993), *An Alien Darkness* and *A Desperate, Decaying Darkn*ess (published by Wildside Press in 2000). A collection of his popular Vossoff/Nimmitz stories printed in *Science Fiction Age*, *Just a Couple of Idiots Reupholstering Space and Time*, saw print in October 2002. He is also the author of the Spider-Man novels *Time's Arrow: The Present* (written in collaboration with Tom DeFalco), *The Gathering of the Sinister Six, and Spider Man: Secret of the Sinister Six*. Adam currently lives in Florida with two thoroughly psychotic cats who have been trying to kill each other since 1996.